ARLENE MCFARLANE

MURDER, CURLERS & CREAM

A Valentine Beaumont Mystery

ISBN-13: 978-0-9953076-1-2

Published by ParadiseDeer Publishing
Canada

Cover Art by Janet Holmes
Formatting by Author E.M.S.

Acknowledgments

I thought that filling the space below would be easy, but I was wrong. Once I put pen to paper, I realized a great many people had touched my life and in some ways contributed to this book, if not my career. How, then, could I express my innermost gratitude and not leave anyone out? I'm not sure if I succeeded, but please know I did my best.

First and foremost, I thank my husband for loving me unconditionally, for demonstrating the highest of integrity, for giving his whole heart to his family, and for never telling me I should give up. I couldn't have walked this road without you by my side.

Endless mushy kisses to my beautiful children, my biggest cheering squad. You've watched, learned, and appreciated the struggles I've had along this journey. I pray you are true to your passions as I mine, and that whatever you do in life, you do it with a full heart.

Huge thanks to my wonderful sister and my parents for supporting me in dozens of ways. And to my dear niece, MD: Breaking my leg to protect you from a fall was a blessing in disguise. For that, I'm eternally grateful.

Holding close my three angels ~ Marilyn, Diane, and Nicole ~ for your constant prayers and for being my soulmates. It's only when I met you ladies that I knew what true friendship was.

Detective Constable Sandra Courtney ~ You answered my every question about police work, from the silliest to the serious. You're gracious and generous with your time and always the consummate professional. Any mistakes in these pages are completely mine.

Fire Captain David Mazmanian, thank you for assisting me whenever I asked the particulars of fire safety. You're not only highly respected in your field, but also in your family.

Thanks also, Bev Katz Rosenbaum, for your initial content edit of my book. Your keen insight led me to making changes I wouldn't have otherwise seen.

Karen Dale Harris, editor extraordinaire. Not only did you love my voice, but you saw my vision clearly. Your every input was like gold, and your words, "You can do it!" spurred me on. A hundred times, thank you. Thank you for telling me I had the talent to succeed.

Noël Kristan Higgins ~ Your absolute love for my story made me feel like it was ready to soar, and your enthusiasm and generosity will forever be imprinted in my soul. The stars I see flickering are from your wand. Thank you, my fairy godmother.

My deepest gratitude and respect to you, Janet Holmes, for loving my idea and working tirelessly on my cover. You're a gem. I can't believe how lucky I was to have found you.

Thank you, Amy Atwell, for your constant graciousness whenever I had a question on formatting. And I had a lot. I treasure you more than words can say.

Butterfly kisses to my Golden Heart sisters, TRW, SOWG, Sherry, Cindy, Jen, and, oh boy, I wish I could list the rest of my gifted RWA friends. Like no one else, you people truly "get me." Sometimes a smile was all I needed to forge ahead, and you not only smiled, you brought sparkling sunshine into my life. How does one ever repay that?

Tracy Brody, your honest feedback was the icing on the cake ~ even when I thought my cake was already beautifully iced. How blessed I am to have met you and call you friend.

Liliana Hart & Scott Silverii ~ You are two of the most amazing people I've had the pleasure of knowing, and I'm overjoyed that God brought you into my life. Thank you for sharing the faith. My heart is so much fuller because of it.

To every hard-working hairstylist and aesthetician ~ Each day you make someone's life brighter and more beautiful, all because of your dedication, your hands, and your artistic talents. Keep spreading that joy. This world is a better place because of you!

Thank you to *you*, my precious reader. My aim was to tell a good story and make people laugh. It's all I've ever wanted to do. I hope I didn't fail you.

Lastly, I bow in humble thanks to God for His guidance and love, and for knowing this day would eventually come. My faith in You has made me who I am, and as always, You deserve the glory.

Philippians 4:13 *I can do all things through Christ who strengthens me.*

To my mother:

I wish you were here to share this moment with me.

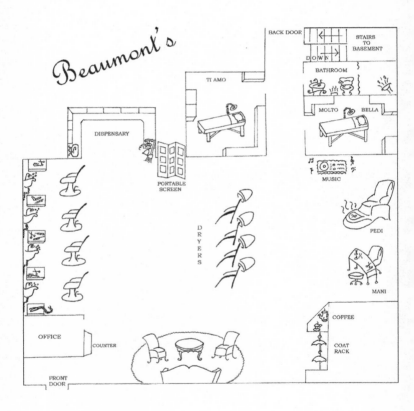

Chapter 1

"*Y*ou wound a perm rod around a man's *what?*" Detective Romero stood in the middle of my Mediterranean-styled salon, hand on his gun hip, legs spread wide. His deep voice was laced with cynicism, and his blue eyes pierced me with a look that said now he'd heard everything.

I know it sounded outrageous, but good lord. It'd been several years since "Local Beautician Valentine Beaumont Uses Perm Rod to Curl Murderer's Gonads" made front page headlines in the *Rueland News*. Was I ever going to live that down? It was an awful picture of me they'd run too, considering I was soaked in mud and covered in cuts and bruises.

Besides, there was another crisis at hand. I mean, a dead body had just been removed from the facial bed in Ti Amo—one of my treatment rooms, not thirty feet down the hall. Didn't this detective, in his faded jeans and brown plaid shirt, think *that* was a little more important?

I pulled at my tight-knit top, trying not to let him get under my skin. "For the record, that perm rod saved me from being knifed to death. Anyway, it sounds worse than it was."

"Worse than it was! Lady, that's about as worse as it can get for a man." He blew out a sigh. "I'd love to hear the full story on that one day."

I smiled sweetly. "If you're nice to me, maybe one day I'll tell it."

He glared at me, probably not certain if I was being sarcastic or sincere. Frankly, I wasn't sure about that myself.

He glanced to my right at his team tracking down the hall, then to the front of Beaumont's breezy entry where my staff and clients huddled around the ivory-colored chairs, waiting to give their statements. "And will someone shut off that music?"

An ID unit photographed and dusted for fingerprints, the shop smelled of bleach and perm solution, and in the background, Billy Joel sang "Only the Good Die Young," which was the biggest irony of all if you considered the identity of today's victim. Portia Reynolds *was* youngish, and wealthy, too, and happened to be one of my most loyal clients. But good? Some may have argued that.

Maximilian Martell, my second-in-command, rushed over to the CD player and killed the music. He gave me a wide-eyed look, which, knowing Max, could've either meant Romero was movie-star hot, or yikes, was he bossy. Without a second glance, he slipped back to the front where everyone was told to wait.

"Who's the *GQ* model?" Romero asked, moving on.

I peered back at Max. "That's Max Martell. He's the masculine component of our team and has been with me since the beginning of time." Romero was right. At thirty-one, and even on a bad day, Max resembled a cover model. If he ever tired of cutting hair, Max could make a mint in the fashion world.

I fiddled with my glittery bracelets and watched Romero scan everything from the grapevines and twinkling lights that wove across the mirrors and stucco walls to the four cutting stations behind him, each with its own sink.

He gave a head shake that I interpreted as disgust. For what, I didn't know. Being in a salon on a beautiful Thursday in June? Questioning a beautician who'd assaulted men's private parts? Maybe he wondered why he'd joined the Rueland Police Department instead of hiking another fifteen minutes south to Boston. Or maybe he just realized he needed a haircut himself. Not a minute too soon, if you asked me.

I tapped my toe on the ceramic tile. Maybe he was having a bad day. Well, guess what? Not only had I thrown up after seeing a corpse with a steamer cord around her neck, but thanks to my past fiasco, business was at an all-time low. And what about Portia? She was dead. If anyone was having a bad day, she was the one.

Romero leaned his hard-muscled body against a hair dryer and crossed his long legs at the ankle, taking his time to appraise me. Yes, Matrix 5VR accounted for the burgundy of my long hair. And my coordinating classic pants and top fit to perfection despite my less than model-like stature of my 5' 4" frame.

I curled my toes inside my favorite red rose sparkly heels to keep from delivering a swift kick to his shin for the wary look he gave me. Like he was ruling me as a possible suspect.

He shoved up his wrinkled sleeves, and an animated Iron Man watch flickered on his toned wrist.

I angled my head to take a better look at Iron Man's fiery eyes and fluorescent hands. My gaze traveled to Romero's gun and back to his striking eyes. This guy *could* be Iron Man. But a kid's watch?

"Was Portia Reynolds a regular client?" he asked, grabbing my attention.

I gulped down a swallow from his husky voice and hot stare, and okay, maybe the superhero thing. "She came in weekly," I said, regrouping, "for hair, nails, spa treatment."

He pulled out a pad and pen. "Who found the body?"

I pointed to my left at the guy with a fresh perm who sat blubbering into his hands at the end of a row of dryer chairs.

"The guy in boxers?" Romero stepped a foot back. "And slightly worn expensive-looking shoes? Isn't that Gavin Beck, the real estate tycoon?"

"That'd be him. And the expensive-looking shoes are Guccis."

He glanced down at his scuffed running shoes. "I'll remember that next time I'm looking for footwear out of my price range. Is there a reason he's half dressed?"

"He'd just had a perm and was in the treatment room kitty-corner to Portia's room, waiting for an acne treatment for his back."

"When did he enter the deceased's room?"

"I don't know. I'd started Portia's facial just after eleven. Then I left her to steam at around eleven-ten and came back here to do a quick cut. About twenty minutes later, we heard a crash. And that's when Phyllis found Gavin on the floor next to the steamer, tangled up in the cord."

Romero sighed, like he wished the day was already done. "Who's Phyllis?"

I motioned past Gavin to the front at Phyllis Murdoch. "She's my"—for lack of a better word—"employee." On top of that, she was distant family, and I was stuck with her because of a promise I'd made my grandmother on her deathbed. But that was my secret.

Phyllis reached over the sales counter and dug into a box of Friar Tuck's donuts that I'd routinely bought for work this morning. Meanwhile, a mere twenty feet away, scissors littered her station, and a mess of bottles cluttered her workspace. Not surprisingly, the thought of sweeping the floor around her chair had escaped her. Bag ladies were neater than Phyllis.

"When she saw Gavin on the floor and Portia dead," I continued, "she screamed and passed out, taking the wax pot down with her."

This was one area where I sympathized with Phyllis. I was a screamer. I shrieked at bugs and frogs. And I threw things when frightened. I couldn't blame her for dropping the wax pot.

"You heard your employee scream," Romero said, "but not the victim?"

"The salon was noisy. Music was playing. Water was running. Dryers blowing. People talking. And the pocket door to the facial room was closed, at least until Gavin went in."

"Anyone leave after the murder?"

"Only Pace Wilmont."

"Go on," he said, jotting something down.

"Pace rarely makes appointments, and since Portia's facial takes an hour and a half to complete, I was fitting him in for a quick trim. He poured himself a coffee while I started on Portia. When I left her to steam for the usual twenty minutes, I returned to my chair to give him his cut, but he wasn't there." I nodded at my neat station. "I cleaned a little and by then he wandered back in."

"How much time passed before he returned?"

I shrugged. "More than five minutes, I guess. Less than ten."

"Any idea where he went when you were in the treatment room with Ms. Reynolds?"

"No."

"Is it possible he drove away?"

"I don't think so."

Romero looked up and down the hall. The glass door at the back was being dusted for fingerprints, and my office blocked his view to the front door. "Which direction did he re-enter the room from?"

"The rear."

"So it's possible he exited the back door."

"Yes, it's possible. He parked out back and entered that door this morning."

"Is that normal practice, for customers to use the back door?"

"As a rule, it's kept locked, unless we have a delivery or a client needs assistance."

"But it was obviously unlocked this morning."

"Yes. I unlocked it when my deliveryman arrived, ten minutes before Pace showed up."

He rubbed his jaw, putting this all together.

"After I finished Pace's trim, we heard the crash. Phyllis went to the back to see what happened while I collected from Pace. Only I didn't collect, because Phyllis screamed. I ran to check on the commotion. Pace left. Without paying."

Pace was a good customer. Always a fast cut. Fine tipper, too. And definitely easy on the eyes. But the way he left out the front door while everyone else ran to the back left me bothered.

Romero tapped his pad with his pen. "Anyone use the phone?"

"Some people used their cell phones. I used the landline in the dispensary and tried my sister, Detective Dennison, in vice. But I couldn't get her, so I left my name with Dispatch."

"Not Holly Dennison."

I nodded.

"That explains a lot," he muttered, peeking over his left shoulder, past the folding screen, into the nine-by-nine dispensary.

This corner space that faced the front of the salon was like a supply room. It sat at the end of the row of four stations and had a u-shaped counter, two wheeled stools, sink, microwave, and cupboards above and below filled with beauty products and the odd kitchen staple. More importantly, it had a bird's-eye view of the main salon. It was our hub, our nook, our hangout between customers. It was where we munched on snacks, took appointments, and when the pocket door was closed—where we bandaged our wounds. For Phyllis, it was a refuge from work.

Romero looked from the French provincial phone with its curlicue cord and fancy handset to me and rolled his eyes. As if I cared. I was a modern-day girl who happened to like whimsical things. Cute phones were one of them.

"I'll want a list of deliverymen," he said, "including the one who came today."

"Easy enough. I only had one drop-off today, though Thursday is delivery day."

He gave me a grim look. "Ironically the same day Ms. Reynolds visited."

"Portia was alive and well when Albert unloaded my delivery. In fact, I signed the invoice while Portia complained about waiting, even though she was early. Then Albert went out the back. It was at least half an hour before we discovered Portia dead." I took a breath. "Anyway, Albert wouldn't hurt a flea."

"Really. You wearing a badge under that top?" He pointed to the hall and started walking. "Keys for the back door?"

Gasping at his gall, I grabbed my keys from my office—an eight-by-eight cubbyhole tucked behind the front door and the sales counter—then trailed after him.

He stopped and turned. "Did you always put Ms. Reynolds in—"

"Ti Amo," I said, in a helpful manner. "It means I love you."

"I was born in Italy, Ms. Beaumont. Was there till I was ten. I know what *ti amo* means."

I fidgeted with the sparkly *V* on my keychain. "Then to answer your question, we occasionally put Portia in Molto Bella, the other treatment room." I wasn't about to take a chance defining *that* one!

We continued on to the back door past cops taking pictures of the three-piece bathroom across from Ti Amo. Romero glanced into the bathroom, then back at me. "You have a shower in the salon? What is this? The Holiday Inn?"

"Occasionally, clients use it after specific spa treatments. I've even used it the odd time if I'm going somewhere special from work and need to freshen up."

He nodded and finished walking the hall. He had a few words with the technician who had just dusted the glass door, then dismissed the guy and creased his eyebrows like something didn't make sense. The tech took his equipment into Ti Amo, and Romero looked from the deadbolt latch on the back door to our right at a cop descending the stairs that led to the kitchen, storage, and laundry room. "Any of the team use this door before Vince dusted?" he asked the cop.

"No, sir." The cop looked up from the first landing six steps down. "Only the front door since the ID truck's out there." He turned and went down the next six steps to the basement.

Romero and I walked out into the hot sun, and I pointed to the bell on the wall beside the door. "This is the bell my deliverymen ring when they arrive." I pressed the bell with my key.

"Which you hear in front."

"Right."

"Then you come down the hall and unlock the door."

"Right."

"And you'd normally relock the door after your deliveryman leaves."

"Right."

"But you didn't relock it this morning when Albert left after his delivery."

This was where I was supposed to say right again.

"Right?"

"Maybe?"

"Is that a question?"

"No?"

He gave another exasperated eye roll. "Then care to explain why Vince had to unlock the deadbolt latch just now to dust?"

"I locked the door after we found Portia dead. Pace had already skipped out the front. I didn't want anyone else sneaking out the back."

I waited for the vein on his temple to pop.

"You do realize that from the time you unlocked this door to the moment you relocked it, someone could've entered or re-entered the building, killed the victim, and skipped out."

"Yes, I realize that." Like he was talking to a fourth grader. "Any idea who?"

"Gee, I don't know. The bogeyman? The Red Baron? Maybe Albert, for Pete's sake?"

A couple of cops scouring the alley behind the businesses glanced over at the sound of Romero's angry tone.

I moved in close and lowered my voice. "And suppose that *didn't* happen? That would bring us back to a closed circle of suspects."

A single drop of sweat rolled down the side of his face, and the smell of Arctic Spruce deodorant filled the air. I didn't know what he was thinking, but by the way he was steaming under the collar had me guessing it was in the neighborhood of *is she for real?* He looked down at my red heels, and his expression moved from disbelief to wonder.

I also looked down and realized we were toe to toe. Romero caught my gaze, and I inhaled sharply, straightened, and jumped back.

"Who has keys to the salon?" he asked.

"Just me and my staff."

"That would be Max and Phyllis."

"And my third employee, Judy Gallagher."

He scanned his pad. "Judy?"

"Yes. She went home sick first thing this morning." Lucky her.

"That's it? No one else has a key?"

"Only my father."

"Don't tell me, he does hair, too."

"No. But he does come by the odd time to oil or fix something downstairs."

"Of course. Who uses the basement—apart from your father?"

"Just the four of us. Phyllis actually went down to wash towels during all this."

"When exactly?"

"I don't know. I didn't clock her. But it was sometime after I left Portia to steam and before we found her dead."

"Big help." He gave a sigh I was already becoming too familiar with. He stuffed his pad and pen in his shirt pocket, then gestured for my keys. "Mind if I take those? We'll lock up and notify you when we're done."

"When will that be?" I detached my shop keys from the ring and handed them over.

"Sometime between later and when we're done. You do have a spare set, don't you?"

"Uh, sure." The ones it almost killed me to give Phyllis several years ago when she started working here.

"Good." He pocketed the keys, pulled out his pad and pen, and just when I thought we'd moved on, he asked me Albert's last name.

"I don't know. He works at Alluve Beauty Supply. But you're wasting your time." Maybe Albert smelled of cigarette smoke and had scraggly hair and a pockmarked face, but he was genuine and had the smile of an angel—a somewhat rotten-toothed angel. Still. That had to count for something.

Romero rubbed his forehead, struggling to remain calm. "Look, Ms.—"

"It's Valentine." I smiled innocently, hoping he'd see me as a caring, beautiful person.

He lowered his pen, and for the first time since he arrived on the scene, he actually stared into my eyes. With the sun beaming down, I wasn't sure exactly what he saw there except for the amber flecks on brown, but the hard lines on his face softened, and there was a hint of a sympathetic smile. It was short-lived, and maybe I was being naïve, yet I could've sworn I saw a smidge of compassion. Or at least curiosity.

"Look," he finally said, "everyone's a suspect."

"Even me?" I planted my hands on my hips, my key ring jingling at my side.

"Even you."

I pressed my vanilla-scented lips together, suddenly not giving a hoot what he and his hard-ass thought. "Why would I kill one of my customers? Portia spent a lot of time and money here." I wasn't going to reveal this to Romero, but without her, Beaumont's was a-goner.

"It does sound like you were the last to see her alive."

"Except for the murderer," I snapped.

I marched back into the shop and down the hallway to the front, past questioning eyes. Seeing a crowd gathered on the sidewalk outside, I jerked the blinds across the large window. If there was one thing I didn't need, it was an audience.

Romero was on my heel. "No interference," he warned. "No using perm rods to catch criminals. No sticking your nose in police business again."

"Fine." Like I was about to make the same mistake twice.

He backed up and almost tripped over Phyllis's ninety-year-old client. He looked down at the senior, excused himself, and wrinkled his nose at her hair. No shock. Her hair looked as if it'd been styled with a blowtorch. Another of Phyllis's masterpieces. Thank God I'd never been sued.

A uniformed cop wandered up from the hallway and called Romero away.

Romero waved at the cop, said a few words to Max, Phyllis, and the remaining customers about fingerprinting, then gave me the eye, and jogged toward the hall.

The minute he was out of sight, Max and Phyllis closed in on me.

"Know what that detective needs?" Phyllis licked icing off her thumb. "A good haircut."

"Too bad he'll never get one of those from you," Max said.

"Why not? I know how to cut hair."

"You also know how to dress yourself. Doesn't mean you're any good at it." Max draped an arm around Phyllis's shoulder and flicked the ends of her short red hair. "Maybe Home Depot's not the store for you."

Phyllis flinched from his embrace. "First of all, I don't shop for clothes at Home *Depot*. And secondly, why don't you ever ask that little frump Judy where she shops?"

"Because Judy's sweet and lovable?" Max moved aside for a cop rolling a cart out the front door. "Boy, Phyll, how can you even think about shopping at a time like this?"

"I—you—*errr.*" Phyllis spread her white smock wide. "If you want to know the truth, I'm done with designer stores. I enrolled in a sewing class." She pointed at her strapless dress. "And this is one of my creations. I've been told I have a unique sense of style."

Max gaped at the clumps of material layered around Phyllis, and I moved into my office, thinking now was a good time to call Judy. I wanted her to hear about Portia's death before she saw it on the news. I threw my key ring on the desk and dialed, but got no answer. Just as well. She should've been resting anyway. I'd try again later.

The afternoon pushed on. Clients were questioned. Media were kept at bay. Max and Phyllis continued bickering. I finished canceling appointments for the rest of today as well as for Friday and Saturday, when I saw Phyllis slap Max's hand away from her dress.

"Don't touch the merchandise!" she said. "At least I'm busy. Beats sitting home alone like *some* people, guzzling wine every night."

"That's a lie!" Max said. "I only guzzle wine when I have stress." He threw his hands on his hips. "Which you are contributing to greatly, thank you very much."

Finally, the police had everyone but me clear out of the salon. I got permission to throw the towels in the dryer, then came back upstairs and answered more questions. Another hour passed before Romero strode into the dispensary and excused the interrogating cop from my side. I was so relieved I almost jumped on Romero's lap.

"You'll need to come in for fingerprinting tomorrow," he said to me. "I'd like to match you and your employees' prints to the steamer." He glanced down at Iron Man. "It's past suppertime. You're free to go. Just don't go far." His stunning blue eyes were hard, the look on his face, adamant. "Until this case has closed, you'll be seeing more of me."

He meant it in a strictly professional way. Nonetheless, I blushed.

I lived in a rented Cape Cod bungalow in a family-oriented, predominantly Italian neighborhood. Tomato plants filled backyards, grapevines climbed fences, and rosaries hung from kitchen windows. I had none of that at my place. Neither did Mr. Brooks, across the street. I hung pretty scarves from my windows, and Mr. Brooks could carve a shrub into a swan with a chainsaw. It wasn't growing grapes or raising tomatoes, but we all had our talents.

The neighborhood was quiet when I got home. Minivans were parked in driveways, and kids who had spilled out of them hours ago had probably just eaten a warm supper of eggplant lasagna. I crumpled my chicken wrappers and wiped my mouth. Sure beat fast-food takeout.

I sat there glumly in my VW Bug and stared from my tiny detached garage to the watering can and wind chimes on my porch. I blew out a sigh Romero-style, then stuffed my garbage into the Lick-a-Chick bag and dragged myself inside the house.

I shut the door behind me, leaned against it, and faced the living room. What a day. Not even the sparkle from my Coco Chanel furnishings could bring me joy tonight. I switched on my jeweled Indian-style lamp and stifled a sob. How much worse could things get? A murderer killed what little business I had left? I didn't make mortgage payments on the salon building? I got kicked out of my home?

I could see it now: dumping my house keys into Mr. Jaworski's stingy, landlord-grubbing hand. Good grief. I was twenty-nine. I should've been the Vidal Sassoon of

Rueland. I should've had my *own* home. At least I owned the watering can. And the wind chimes. Sigh.

I removed my shoes and frowned at how they'd been my last big purchase in a long time. Maybe when things improved, I'd treat myself to a new pair. Yeah. Like by the next millennium.

I dropped my big beauty bag by the piano and trekked into the kitchen. I looked from my pink, heart-shaped phone to the blinking machine beside it. Three messages. I pressed Play and heard my mother's voice on all three.

I felt my neck grow hot because despite what I'd been through today, my mother would say none of it would've happened if I'd had a man to look after me. I never could quite make the connection from something as horrific as a murder to me and courtship, but there it was. My mother was Ukrainian. Her goals were to keep her husband fed, her freezer full, and her daughter aimed for marriage. My father, on the other hand, had French and Armenian blood. While he'd have liked me to marry and stop raiding their fridge, he spoke in fewer syllables.

I pitched my wrappers in the garbage. I should probably call her back, but what would I tell her? *Guess what, Mom. Your number two daughter landed in another homicide.* I didn't think that'd go over real well, especially since the perm-rod case ended badly on so many levels. Now Romero was in charge. Well, good luck. I had no intention of getting any more involved than I needed. My mother would be glad to hear that.

I was reaching for the phone when the doorbell rang. Putting off the call, I plodded across the pine floor and opened the door to my sister, Holly.

"How are you?" She raised my chin with her finger.

"Fine."

"You look like shit."

Maybe I did look rough, but I hadn't started out my day this way. My taller, stocky sister stood there in a wrinkly jacket, oil-stained pants, and mussed hair. Likely, this *was* how she started out her day. I shuddered but kept quiet. Holly had her style; I had mine. Plus, if I said anything, she might threaten me with her intimidating muscle like she did when we were kids.

"Word travels fast in Rueland," I said.

"Only when it's juicy. And you called me, remember? I was in Jersey on a case, but I heard the news when I pulled into the station tonight." She collapsed on the black beanbag chair. "So, Portia Reynolds is dead. I'd seen her around town. Cruella de Vil in the flesh." She grabbed a sequined pillow from behind her. "That peppery perfume of hers always made me gag. Isn't her husband some hotshot optometrist who travels the earth and donates glasses to Third World kids?"

"Yes. Erik was also a customer." I sat on the edge of the coffee table in front of her. "He must be devastated."

"Hmm."

"Will he be questioned?"

She tossed the pillow up in the air. "Probably already has been."

"He wouldn't be a suspect, would he?"

"Was he at the salon today?"

"No, but my deliveryman was, and he's no more capable of murder than an absentee husband."

She stopped tossing. "Back up. Deliveryman?"

"Yes. Albert could be a suspect because he made a delivery just before Portia was killed." I thought about this for a second. "I mean, that deadly look he gave her probably meant nothing."

"Hmm."

Okay, two *hmms* in less than a minute. "Holly, I know Albert. It's not possible."

"All right." Her voice was all cop. "But what do you really know about him?"

"I know he saved a client's life once. Of course, that fire never would've started if it weren't for Phyllis's carelessness. Still, how could someone save a life, then take one away?"

"It's been known to happen. What about his personal

life, his relationship to Portia? What's his last name? I can try to run a check on him."

"There's no point. He was long gone before anything happened. And there *were* others in the salon today."

"Anyone who seemed suspicious?"

I thought about Gavin in his boxers and Pace who'd left the scene. "More so than Albert."

"Fine. Have it your way. Fortunately, Michael's on the case."

"Who?"

"Detective Romero."

My toes turned up at the mention of his name. "Oh. *Him*. Your friend was so taken with my past involvement with a murderer, he could hardly concentrate on the present case."

"You've got to admit the perm-rod episode was memorable."

"I wasn't about to let two creeps get away with murdering Max's friend. And some people like to make Mount Ararat out of a molehill. I mean, did he suppose I woke up that morning, saying, 'Hmm, today I think I'll wrench off a crook's family jewels'? I'm not stupid. I weigh 118 soaking wet, for crying out loud. And if I *did* want to catch a criminal, why would I use a measly perm rod? Especially when a curling iron or razor could do twice the job."

"Ooh, sister. Seems Romero's had an effect on you." The toss with the pillow again. "It's okay. I've seen other women react the same way."

I snagged the pillow. "What other women?"

"Women he's pissed off. But all that raw magnetism draws them back. Before they know it, they're dangling their silk panties in his face."

I fingered the pillow sequins, thinking about Romero's rugged appearance, roguish conduct, and full lips—lips I wouldn't kiss even if every female on the planet thought they were sensual. "Well, he can have those women." Like I was about to sink to that level.

"Yeah," she gave a guttural laugh, "and he probably does." She grinned at the piano. "Rumor is he's got fingers like a pianist and the stamina of a bull. And if you weren't so afraid of losing your heart, you might appreciate a gorgeous piece of ass now and then."

"When did you start talking so crude?"

"When I began working with men ninety-eight percent of the time."

"Well, I've had my fill of gorgeous men. They're all the same." Privately, my biggest fear *was* giving my heart to some undeserving macho male. I didn't like arrogance in a man or harshness or indifference. I liked men who treated me with respect, who opened doors for me, who made me laugh. I scowled. Romero had none of those qualities.

"Don't be too hard on him," she said. "He wears this tough-guy image, but his reputation with the NYPD was impeccable. I gotta say, I respect him. In fact, we're lucky to have him here."

I had mixed emotions about all this. Maybe she was right about Romero's work ethic. No doubt he was a solid cop. Plus, there *was* that momentary smile. Yet my resolve was slow to melt. "Why move from New York to a town of thirty thousand?"

"Not sure. I think it was personal. Before he joined homicide, I worked with him on vice. I can tell you he's honest, hard-working, and dead serious about what he does. Not to mention damn good at his job. If I wasn't married, I'd be all over that Italian Stallion."

"Yeah, but you are. Lucky you." Depending on your point of view.

She chuckled and rolled off the beanbag. "Mind you, he doesn't like taking orders. If he gave you a hard time, I'm sure he had good reason."

She wouldn't convince me of that. Besides, I was through trying to make relationships work. I squashed down the pillow, sealing the point.

"Let Romero do his job." She opened the door. "And take a shower. You smell awful."

She was right. I did smell.

I bit my tongue, thinking about Romero while she backed out of the driveway. Tough-guy image. Impeccable reputation. Moved for personal reasons. What was that about? What made enough of an impact for him to leave his job? And home. Not that I cared one iota. I'd dated enough macho, bad boys to determine they weren't worth it. A woman was nothing more than a trophy on their arm.

I locked the door, tore off my top, and stomped into the bathroom. One thing was clear, Romero was the last person I wanted to be involved with—impeccable reputation or not.

Chapter 2

The next morning, I strolled into the kitchen, filled a bowl with Alpha-Bits, my drug of choice, and doused it with milk. I didn't want to think about the murder, or Romero, or my dying business. I just wanted to eat. I got one spoonful down when my Pooh phone rang in the living room, my hot pink high-heeled phone chimed in the bedroom, and my heart-shaped phone that once chanted a princess tune silently lit up on the kitchen counter. None of my phones had call display, but I picked up anyway.

"Why is it I have to learn about these things on the news?"

My mother. Shoot. Forgot to phone her back.

"I called you at work yesterday and Max said you'd call back later. Then your father and I had supper in front of the television when the anchorman said a socialite died at Beaumont's. Your father almost choked on his asparagus." She sighed. "Tell me you're not pretending to be one of Charlie's Angels again."

I toyed with the letters in my bowl. "I'd tell you, but you probably wouldn't believe it."

Another sigh. Next time I opened their freezer it'd be full of butter tarts. Baking was what my mother did best, and she did it in spades when she worried.

"If you had a man in your life, you wouldn't have such terrible luck."

I visualized my mother stirring her batter. I told her everything would be fine, and when my nose didn't fall off from the lie, I hung up.

I spooned the last *A*'s into my mouth when the phones rang and flashed again. Cripes. A girl couldn't even finish a bowl of cereal in peace. Figuring it was my mother again, I picked up and waited for her to continue her diatribe.

But it wasn't my mother. It was my employee, Judy. And now I was batting zero because I hadn't called her back either. First, I made sure she was okay. Then I gave her the news.

"Yes, I know," she said. "The police notified me last night."

I imagined her shaking her curly blond head, her expression more bewildered than usual.

"I keep thinking if I'd been there, maybe I could've done something." This from someone who apologized to doors when she bumped into them.

"Listen, we'll be closed today and tomorrow. Plus Monday like always. By Tuesday everything will be back to normal." Right. Even *I* wasn't buying that.

I took extra time with my makeup, then gathered my hair loosely to the side. I thought back to yesterday and the way Romero ordered me to come in for fingerprinting. *Damn*. Why did he have to have such a sexy voice? Well, just because he said *jump* didn't mean I was going to ask how high. *Tyrant*. I bet he was one hell of a commander at work. I bet he enjoyed making his subordinates tremble. I bet he kissed a woman with more than his lips. I bet his hands captured her face, his body pressed into hers. His— whoa! What was I doing? I licked my dry lips and calmed my heaving chest.

Biting down the sexual notions, I put on another coat

of lipstick—purely to moisten my lips—then slipped into a white dress splashed with candy-sized hearts. *I'll get there when I get there*, I told myself, twirling through a flowery mist of Musk perfume. I pictured Romero's smug face and gave myself another squirt.

An hour later, I pulled into the bumpy parking lot of the police station, which sat on Main Street, the opposite end of town from Beaumont's. I looked from the three-story graystone to Miss Lacy's Ballet Studio next door, and my heart warmed. I attended Miss Lacy's when I was little. After cartoons every Saturday morning, moms herded their daughters into the ballet studio as fast as possible, shielding their eyes in case a real-life crook was hauled into lockup. I ducked the shielding because this beat cartoons. I was fascinated and hoped to see what types of masks and capes real-life villains wore.

I tore my gaze away from Miss Lacy's and glared at the police station, feeling nothing but anxiousness. I took a deep breath for courage, flung my bag over my shoulder, and mounted the steps of the building. Romero wasn't going to intimidate me. He just wasn't. I probably wouldn't even see him. I was here for fingerprinting. Then I'd be on my merry way.

I entered the station and shivered from the unwelcome smell of old coffee, jail must, and stale urine. I didn't want to guess if the excretion had come from police dogs or drunks who had been arrested and leaked on themselves, but the rank odors didn't help my nerves one bit.

A cop came out of a glassed-in room, climbed two steps, and sat behind the chest-level front desk. With bifocals on the edge of his hooked nose, he held his shiny head low but raised his eyes like, *what now?* "Can I help you?" His nametag said Martoli.

"I'm Valentine Beaumont. I'm here to be fingerprinted."

He pushed his reading glasses up to his brows and studied me good and hard. "You're that hairstylist, aren't you?"

The expectant look on his face and the one-sided grin

told me he wasn't referring to yesterday's murder in my salon. "Uh, yes."

He waggled a pen in my face. "Thought so." He leaned over the creaky wooden counter and looked me up and down. "You nab criminals with nutcrackers—I mean perm rods." He chuckled. "Gives the term Boston Strangler a whole new meaning."

I made a fist. If a true-crime TV show hadn't recreated my brush with death in putting away those two maniacs, business might not be in the state it was *and* I wouldn't have to endure snide remarks like this. "Excuse me, the fingerprinting room?"

He put up his palms and laughed. "Okay, lady. No need to get *testes*."

He buzzed me through a door, and I gladly went through it. I passed a couple of uniforms and kept my eyes peeled for the fingerprinting room. I took a corner and bumped into Romero as he picked a pen off the concrete floor. He straightened to his full six feet, legs wide, arms crossed. His refreshing masculine smell just about melted me right there on the cold concrete slab.

Yep. Iron Man.

His eyes creased with tired lines, his jaw muscles tight. I recognized the look and braced myself.

"So, you here for fingerprinting?"

"No. I'm here for finger-painting." I hoped my cutesy tone would disguise the fluttering in my stomach. "Which way to the art class?"

He actually grinned, the kind that went up to the eyes, making his lashes so thick I'd swear they were lined with Maybelline. "Let me show you the room."

I looked over his shoulder, wondering who kidnapped Romero and left this guy standing here.

As we strode the hall, I glanced from my delicate dress and dainty sandals with beads dangling from the straps to Romero's faded jeans and black T-shirt—a nice change from the wrinkled one he'd worn yesterday. This one said POLICE and showed off his hard biceps.

Dwarfed by his size, all I could think was how near I was to him. A notion that I liked this guy entered my mind. *Absurd*. I came off my cloud. I was here to be fingerprinted. Nothing more. Even so, I swayed to the left. Distance was mandatory if I wanted to remain objective.

"You never told me Albert's last name."

His voice brought me out of my daze. "No...I didn't."

We arrived at a door labeled Fingerprint Room. He filled the doorframe and crossed his arms like he was in no hurry. "And *are* you going to tell me?"

"I already told you," I said, primly. "I don't know."

He nodded, intrigued. "Yet for someone who doesn't know her deliveryman real well, you seem to think he's incapable of murder. Interesting since he didn't show up for work today."

He studied me like he pictured a smoking gun in my hand, and stupid me spoke before my brain said shut up. "You think I'm hiding something? Maybe we're in this together? Some evil plot to kill my client?" Oops. Not smart.

The mood suddenly shifted. "I'll tell you what I think." He stood squarely, hands on his hips. "There's a good reason why Albert didn't go to work. Know what else I think? It's strange nobody knows where he's gone."

I didn't like where he was going with all this or his you're-walking-a-fine-line stare. Well, I was used to walking fine lines. I'd walked so many fine lines I could've been a tightrope walker. "Maybe you've got the wrong Albert. You probably confused him with someone else at Alluve."

"Ms. Beaumont, how many Alberts do you think work there?"

"I don't know." My legs were jelly under me, but I stood my ground. "Twenty?"

"Two. The other Albert is a thirty-year-old woman. Real name Alberta. Two hundred pounds, has a tattoo on her upper arm that reads *Hammer*. Now," he said in a contained voice that had me thinking he was almost at his boiling point, "does that sound like the Albert who delivers for you?"

"What kind of tattoo?"

A sigh slipped through his lips. "Has anyone ever told you you're difficult?"

"My third grade piano teacher, but that facial tic had nothing to do with me."

He scraped his hand down his face.

"Look, Detective. Albert probably had an emergency. That's the only thing that makes sense." I considered for a moment. "Why would he kill someone he doesn't even know?"

"I've seen people kill for a free ride on the Staten Island Ferry." His voice was stern. "Just so you know, Albert *Dougal* could be dangerous. Stay away from him."

He yanked the door open with such force I was afraid it'd break off its hinges. He entered the room without a solitary word. I followed to the beat of bongo drums thudding against my chest.

The room had a desk, two chairs, and the potent smell of ink. I fidgeted with my nails, trying to look anywhere but his darkening eyes pouring into mine like toner on dry skin.

He lifted a chair off the floor and shoved it in front of me. "Sit." He leaned in just enough to be sure I felt the pressure. "I'm warning you. Stay out of this and let me do my job."

Then he turned on his heel and left.

I was still fuming when a giant named Detective Saunders, sporting a hair mound like Marge Simpson, entered the room. He took my fingerprints and said I was free to go. I stomped down the hall, my gaze sweeping the station. I told myself I was *not* searching for Romero. Who did he think he was, warning me off like that? The Gestapo? I opened and closed my hands. My skin pricked with anger. Don't let him bother you. Just act civil and answer his questions from now on, no matter how much he antagonizes you. If I had my shop keys, I could at least get some cleaning done.

"Hey." Romero's voice nearly made me jump out of my skin. "The ID unit's completed the investigation at the scene." He dropped my sparkly keychain in my palm. "You're free to resume business."

Business. I blinked down at my keys and envisioned a "For Sale" sign on my shop. A moment of dread was quickly replaced by a loud *snap* in my brain. A client was murdered in my salon. Wasn't I a tiny bit responsible for finding out who was to blame? Besides, this was a matter of saving a dying business. *My* dying business. What did Romero care if I went bankrupt? Well, I wasn't going to stand by while my dreams disappeared. Maybe I wasn't a world-class detective, and maybe I did have a bad experience with a criminal, and so what if I screamed at bugs. I'd show him I wasn't a pushover. I shot back my shoulders. Head up. I had a shop to clean.

And a murder to solve.

Brimming with something between insanity and courage, I sailed through the doors of the police station. Once this case was closed, I'd never have to see Detective Michael Romero again.

The first thing I decided to do was to go back to the scene of the crime. I'd be closed today and tomorrow out of respect for Portia. Maybe not the most prudent decision, considering the state business was in, but the few booked clients seemed more than happy to comply. This meant I had time to clean and look for clues—the prospect of which was highly unlikely after the police had just spent almost twenty-four hours doing just that. But I was trying to be optimistic.

I got to the intersection of York and Darling, slammed on the brakes for a red light, and gaped at my shop. It looked the same as usual, sandwiched between Friar

Tuck's Donuts and the corner gas station, Sal's. A striped awning shaded the storefront window, flowers spilled over a window box, and a swirly sign that read BEAUMONT'S hung above the awning. Only, this morning, spectators crammed the sidewalk, people took pictures, and a TV crew was staked out front. I squinted at a woman being interviewed. I prayed she wasn't one of Phyllis's ex-clients. The murder was damaging enough. I didn't need more bad press.

I stomped on the gas for the green light and sped down the road past all the storefronts. I turned at the clip joint at the end of the street and picked up the alley that wound inconspicuously behind the businesses. Whew! No media. I snuck into the adjoining lot I shared with Friar Tuck's, passed the tall pole and its creaky arrow-pierced revolving donut, and pulled to a stop behind Beaumont's.

Mr. Feltz, my five-foot-nothing, anal-retentive bank manager from down the street, was skulking by Friar Tuck's Dumpster.

"Mr. Feltz?" I angled out of the car. "What's going on?"

He wiped his bald head in agitation. "Are you *trying* to lose this building, Valentine? Because you're behind on your mortgage payments. And you missed your bank appointment this morning. *That's* what's going on."

"*Doh!*" I slapped my palm against my forehead. "I forgot." In light of yesterday's disaster, mourning over my financial records somehow escaped me.

"It's not my job to chase down delinquent borrowers," he said. "You're just lucky I needed a coffee." He squinched his eyes at Friar Tuck's, then back at me. "You have seven business days left to make this month's installment. Otherwise—"

"Don't say it, Mr. Feltz. I'll get the money." How? I didn't have a thing to my name aside from glitzy shoes, costume jewelry, and pretty clothes. Pathetic but true.

"I'll be waiting," he said. "Well, back to the bank. My next meeting's with a man who thinks his dog should be making the mortgage payments." He shuffled down the lane. Poor guy. Grave robbers had better jobs.

My gaze turned to my VW. It was one of only two yellow Bugs in Rueland, and the only one with a hot pink daisy decal on the hood. It was just my size and the only other thing I owned. In fact, I adored my Daisy Bug. I froze, almost hearing its cheery heartbeat from under the hood. Surely I'd get a good price for it. Who wouldn't want a reliable car? No! I wouldn't think about that yet.

I stuck my shop key in the salon's back door, recalling Romero's door lock interrogation yesterday. My knuckles went white and my breath quickened. *Yeesh.* I snapped open the door. Forget about *him* too.

I stepped into the shop and sighed with relief at the quiet surrounding me. No crashes like yesterday. No screams. And most of all, no cops questioning clients or traipsing up and down the hall. At least for a while, Beaumont's had returned to its rightful owner.

I shrugged on my smock and, before I did anything else, went downstairs and folded towels that were still in the dryer from yesterday. I carted them upstairs and put them away when the buzzer summoned me to the back again.

Twix, my best friend since ballet class, stood nose pressed to the glass door, peering inside, looking like the wild woman of Borneo. At one time, Twix didn't shop anywhere but Bloomingdale's or leave home without styling her hair. Now her hair looked like freshly spun brown cotton candy, her eyes were bloodshot, and she had formula gooped on her shirt. If I hadn't known Twix or seen her van parked next to my car, I wouldn't have unlocked the door.

"I tried texting this morning after I heard about the murder." She shoved a large container in my hands. "But do you even look at your messages? And when are you going to get on Facebook? Your GPS leads you astray two or three times and suddenly you hate technology."

She was right. And it was more like seven or ten times.

Running a home and office computer was enough hassle. I wasn't going to waste my life fiddling with a finicky touch screen and pebble-sized keyboard. I had a dying business to run, damn it. "I have Facebook."

"Max posting stuff for the salon doesn't count. Anyway, most of the kids went home this morning with the flu, and I needed a donut break." She glanced out the door. "I packed the van with my two rug rats and the remaining tot, and we terrorized Friar Tuck's for a while."

Twix was a multitasking mother of a busy one-year-old and a busier three-year-old. Added to that, she operated a jam-packed daycare and babied their pot-bellied pig. Mostly she was a rational and controlled woman, but there were days she was living on the edge.

I thought about the daycare kids contracting the flu and wondered if that's what ailed Judy.

"I'm glad I found you here," she said, drawing me back to the conversation. "When I saw the crowd out front, I figured you'd be in—since I couldn't get a hold of you anywhere *else*."

"Your days are occupied." I glimpsed at the van. "And last I remember, you had a big date night planned with hubby. I didn't want to spoil it by calling about the murder."

"Fair enough." She raked her gaze over my shoulder. "So where is everybody?"

"I decided to close for the weekend out of respect for Portia. And since I just got my keys back from the police, I thought I'd sanitize the place."

She took in my attire. "Which explains the smock." Her tone was less than approving. Like she was in a position to be so condescending.

I hid behind the container. "Yes, it's starchy, white, and boring. And you know I usually wear it for messy jobs and when I clean."

"The question is why are you in here cleaning when you should be out there schmoozing with some hunky cop. You must have met a few during all this."

What was it with the women in my life?

I gave Twix the short version of the case since she'd hang me by my French-manicured toenails if she heard details from anyone else. I omitted mentioning Romero. That was one bit I didn't wish to share.

"Oh. My. Awesomeness! So? What are you going to do?"

"After I clean the shop, grab a bite to eat."

"Duh. About the case."

"Try to find a killer." I straightened bravely as this new thought took hold.

"*What?*"

We heard a happy squeal from the van. Twix dashed out the door. "Junie! Stop wiping anti-fungal cream on your brother. Listen, Val, I'd help you clean, but the kids are playing in Tony's medical bag again. If I don't get them down for naps, I'll be using their orange juice for screwdrivers."

Twix told everyone in high school she was going to marry Anthony Bonelli and that he was going to become a doctor. While not exactly a lie, Tony settled into sports medicine and became a podiatrist. He specialized in pro athletes and jocks and often smelled of toe jam and rubbing alcohol. He worked long hours in Boston that Twix didn't let him forget. When she wanted to escape the madness, she assigned him a ton of jobs at home. Then she helped me scour the salon. It wasn't a night at the opera, but it got her out of the house and gave us time to catch up. Plus, it was an opportunity to fix her unmanageable brown hair.

"Don't worry about helping here," I said. "I'm planning on making this quick."

"All right, but keep me in the loop. I could use something else to think about other than poopy diapers, Dr. Seuss, and cramped kitchen walls."

"Huh?"

"I've decided to make the kitchen more user-friendly. A harvest table, bulky cupboards, three high chairs, two playpens, and a pot-bellied pig underfoot don't exactly add up to conducive daycare surroundings. I've bugged Tony long enough about tearing things out. I'm hiring someone. Just waiting for quotes from three sexy-looking men."

"Twix!"

"What! I have food, snot, and Play-Doh stuck to me every moment of every day. Give me *something* to dream about! At least *you'll* be spending time rubbing shoulders with Rueland's finest." She nodded at the container in my hands. "By the way, thanks for the bleach. The pig's skin is much lighter. Almost got the black marker off completely."

I learned long ago the less I asked about Twix's daycare dilemmas, the better off I'd be. Not that I wasn't a tiny bit curious how six kids pinned down a pig and inked him up, but I had my own problems to think about.

She screeched out of the parking lot, and I peered at the thinning shadows of the crowd through the front blinds. Shrugging, I traipsed into the dispensary, placed the bleach on a shelf, and answered a few phone messages. Then I dove into sanitizing and looking for clues. I scrubbed sinks, mopped floors, and searched rooms. I wouldn't have stated it out loud, but I was actually getting into this job of unearthing a killer. Valentine Beaumont, sleuth extraordinaire.

I stopped cleaning and took a breath. Reluctantly, I had to admit the police were pretty thorough. I'd only found a measly cotton ball. Nothing to alert the media about.

Then I saw Portia's red sweater on the coat rack, and my stomach dropped. I wandered to the waiting area and thought back to yesterday when Portia waltzed in. She announced she had an important engagement at four o'clock. Then she flung off her sweater, knocked shampoo bottles off the sales counter, and said she could *not* be late.

I stroked the cashmere with care. The cops had been here for twenty-four hours. If they hadn't taken the sweater for evidence, then it was fair game. And it gave me a good excuse to talk to Erik.

I reached for a gold sales bag and noticed something twinkling by the leg of the glass-topped magazine table. I set everything down and crawled to the glittering object stuck in the waiting-area carpet. It was a diamond stud. A diamond! Something I knew a little bit about. At least I was familiar with the four *C*'s. I deduced this earring was a brilliant cut, nearly colorless, probably flawless, and at least one carat. But that was just a guess.

I pried it from the carpet fibers and twirled it between my fingers. How long had it been here? Could it have been lost yesterday? Was it Portia's? I was positive she hadn't worn earrings. If she had, I would've removed them before her facial like I did everyone else. Yet it looked like something she'd wear.

I opened my bag and zipped the stud in a tiny change compartment. Then I folded the sweater and placed it inside the sales bag. I'd show Erik the earring tomorrow when I returned Portia's sweater. He'd know if it belonged to her. If that turned out to be a dead end, I'd run it by my staff. Maybe they'd have an idea where it came from. I scribbled CLOSED UNTIL TUESDAY on a paper, stepped behind the blinds so I wouldn't be seen, and taped it to the front door. Then I locked up and left.

By the time I pulled onto my street, I'd finished a hero sandwich and Diet Coke I'd picked up at the 7-Eleven. The teenage Donoochi brothers who lived down the road were on the street, whacking a tennis ball back and forth. They were dressed in cut-off shorts, sneakers, and T-shirts tied around their heads, and they were giving that ball everything they had. I thought tennis was a nice change. Jake and Leo were usually whacking each other.

I slowed the car and smiled at the boys. Then I spotted it. A dusty, black, slightly banged-up pickup truck parked in front of my house. WILMONT'S CARPENTRY was painted in purple on the side, along with a website address and phone number. Leaning against the truck, flashing a smile, was Pace Wilmont, all six-foot-two of him, in a white T-shirt, jeans, and a tool belt.

I pulled into the driveway and grimaced. What was he doing here the day after disappearing from a murder scene?

Pace had a successful business, and he seemed even-keeled. But there was something about the set of his shoulders that seemed hostile. Plus, he was a womanizer. Probably why I didn't trust him and why my nose was twitching.

He took a swig from a water bottle, tossed it in the passenger side of the truck, then pushed off and crossed the lawn.

I got out of the car and my stomach muscles clenched. *Stay calm.* He's probably making sure everything's okay. Likely feels bad he didn't stick around yesterday. I took a big breath, hitched my bag over my shoulder, and met him halfway across the grass.

"I was passing by." He feathered back his wheat-blond hair. "Thought I'd stop and say hi."

"Nice of you to visit," I lied. I wasn't thrilled with customers showing up at my door. Besides, I'd never told him where I lived. Then again, since my headline days, everyone knew everything about me, right down to my shoe size—six and a half.

"Yeah, well, that's the kind of guy I am. I also forgot to pay you for my cut yesterday." He reached in his pocket and pulled out twice as much as he normally paid. "Keep the change."

What was this? Guilt money? A bribe? Throw Valentine a little extra cash to keep her quiet? And why suck up if he wasn't at fault for the murder? I wasn't about to split hairs on the amount. I needed every penny I could get with the Feltz deadline looming.

"Thanks." I folded the money in half and stuffed it in my bag when a tennis ball bounced across the driveway and landed on the grass between us. A second later, fourteen-year-old Jake Donoochi hustled over.

"Sorry, Valentine." He bent his head respectfully.

"No problem." I tossed the ball back.

"By the way," Pace said as Jake ran back to the road, "I've already had two compliments on the hair. What'd you do differently?"

"Pixie dust. I assume you heard about Portia Reynolds."

"Yeah." He widened his stance and lost the grin. "Some detective visited me last night."

I remembered I'd given Romero his name. I stared at the smudges and stains on Pace's shirt, then recalled dark stains on the one he wore yesterday. Blood stains perhaps? A scratchy feeling struck my spine, and my fingers trembled.

He looked down at himself. "What's so fascinating?"

"Uh, nothing." I slid my hand in my bag to hide the tremors. "Just thinking, you must own a lot of white T-shirts."

"See, that's strange." His eyes narrowed, his shoulders tensed. "There's been a lot of interest in my attire lately. Mainly from the cops. Know anything about that?"

"No."

"Is that so? The cops are so interested they took yesterday's shirt in for testing." He inched his fingers up his tool belt, then tapped the hammer on his hip in a slow, steady rhythm.

Unease flitted through me, and my mouth went dry. "Maybe they're curious why you took off yesterday."

"You think because I left the shop I was running from a crime?"

"I think your leaving so quickly *after* a crime doesn't look so good in the eyes of the law."

He took a step closer. "Maybe I had business to tend to. And maybe you shouldn't think so much."

I swallowed hard and looked him in the eye. "Where'd you go after you got your coffee?"

"Huh?"

"I did my routine on Portia, closed the treatment room door, and went to the front to cut your hair. Only you were nowhere around."

"I used the bathroom and went out the back to do something in my truck."

"What?"

He sighed. "I checked numbers in my notebook for a construction site. And while I was at it, I wrote up an invoice."

"And when you came back in, there was blood on your T-shirt." I was taking liberties here, but I hadn't noticed stains before he went out.

"I scraped my hand on a nail, building a gazebo at the old McCafferty place. Damn scab keeps busting open. Big deal. A little got on my shirt."

Pace had been contracted months ago by the McCaffertys, a well-known local family, to turn their Victorian home into a bed and breakfast. I scanned the rough calluses on his knuckles. I didn't know where I was going with all this, but it was unsettling that he'd taken off after we found Portia dead. It was doubly unsettling he'd used the back door like his own personal entry.

"You're worse than that cop who interviewed me. Like it's his business whether I knew the deceased."

"Did you?" I thought about the look Portia gave him and how they'd collided in the hall when he dropped in yesterday. Probably the reason she'd scowled at him before I left him waiting and led her off to the treatment room.

"Not really," he said. "I did some work for her a while back."

"What kind of work?"

He glanced over his shoulder, then zeroed in on me with a look I was familiar with: ignore her and she'll go away. Only problem was this was my property, and I wasn't going anywhere. "Do you like badgering me?" he demanded.

"You're the one who stopped by." And badgering

came easy. I'd learned it from my mother. Anyway, compared to the interrogation I'd had at the police station, this was an Armenian picnic. On top of which, I didn't like his answers. And if they didn't get any better, I was going to nag him till he wished he'd never set foot in my salon. "What kind of work did you do for her?"

"A gazebo like the one at McCafferty's, only Portie wanted a hot tub and sauna around it."

Portie, was it? "That must've taken months."

"I work fast."

I'll bet.

His eyes darkened like he'd read my thoughts. Then he eased his hammer out of his tool belt and thwacked it in his palm real slow. *Thwack...thwack.*

I breathed and stilled my quaking legs. Clearly, I was being intimidated, which, by my estimation, meant Pace was afraid of something. But what? Had something gone wrong on the work site? Was he trying to cover something up? Fortunately, God gave me gusto. And my fingers were folded around a straight razor in my bag. Who was I kidding? I had no intention of using it, but I gripped it anyway. "You have help with the job?"

"I *prefer* to work alone." He swung his hammer down so suddenly, I jumped. "You know, Valentine, you're poking your nose where you shouldn't."

First Romero. Now Pace.

I gulped and couldn't believe I was still standing. Sweat rolled down between my breasts, and I felt as if I was about to lose my hero sandwich. Anxiously, I tightened my hold on the razor, bringing his attention to my shaking arm.

"What the hell are you hiding there?" He took two strides and jerked my arm out of my bag. The impact sent the razor flying three feet in the air. It boomeranged back down, sliced Pace's arm, and wedged itself in the lawn.

Pace dropped the hammer in shock, and our eyes locked. Before the blood hit the ground, I turned and scrambled for my door.

"Oh no you don't." He tackled me from behind. "We're not done here."

We both went down with a thud, and I face-planted into the grass. The wind got knocked out of me, and I panicked. I kicked and squirmed under him. I grabbed fistfuls of grass. I struggled for air.

Roughly, he whirled me around, and my candy-heart dress twisted up over my thighs. "If you know what's good for you," he whispered in my ear, "you'll forget about all these questions." He spit on the grass. "And for your own protection, keep your razors to yourself." He dumped my bag. And that was the last thing he did because Jake, who'd sprinted over at full speed, clobbered him with his tennis racket.

Pace groaned and toppled sideways to the ground, landing on a mess of beauty products.

"You okay, Valentine?" Jake asked, helping me up.

I was still panting. "Yeah. Thanks, Jake. That's quite a backhand you've got."

"It looked like he was going to kill you."

"I think he was going more for a good scare."

He gestured down the road. "You want me to get my dad? He's off today."

Ray Donoochi worked for the Boston Police Department. He was big, soft, and cuddly, and he protected his own. If he knew Pace had jumped me, Pace would be lucky to walk away with his Adam's apple intact and his legs bending at the knee.

I wiped my lip and heaved a pensive sigh. I'd made some bold claims to Pace and slashed his arm with my razor. Who's to say I wasn't partly to blame? If I ran to the police because of a measly threat, well, I didn't need to give Romero more reasons to view me as inept. "It's okay, Jake. I'm fine."

He raised his eyebrows at me. "Are you sure?"

On the inside, I was still shaking. But I inhaled some air and gave him a firm nod.

"If you say so." He frowned down at Pace. In the heat

of emotion, he swiped the baby powder off the ground and showered Pace from head to toe until he resembled the Abominable Snowman.

Pace stirred, rubbed his head, then sneezed. He elbowed up and gaped at his talc-covered body. "What the hell?" He looked up at Jake. Then at me.

Without another word, he scrambled to his truck and squealed away.

Chapter 3

Since for once I had Saturday off, I decided to take in a morning Zumba class. What a mistake. I could barely keep up or give the enthusiastic hand clap after I did a Shakira-style loop-kick. My stomach was unsettled, my calves burned, and my nerves were raw. And it wasn't because I'd missed a few classes. My mind was still on Pace and his little performance yesterday. Truth was, I didn't want to believe he could be a murderer. But I also didn't know what to make of his aggressive behavior, or his coming and going through the back door Thursday, or his banging into Portia in the hall. At the time, I'd felt sorry for Pace, assuming Portia had no reason to growl. Now I was thinking differently. Now I imagined him with the steamer cord wrapped around his hands.

Thinking about yesterday's threat made me wince at my lack of common sense. How could I have been so stupid? Grilling Pace like I was a top-ranked detective? How did I expect him to react? With flowers and chocolate? I was lucky he didn't take my razor and slice my neck with it. I sighed. Day one of my investigation and already I'd made an enemy. I tightened my lips into a grim line. So I angered a suspect. This was all new to me. I had to give it time. I mean, Rome wasn't built in a day, right? I'd just have to get a handle on the way I posed questions.

Figuring I'd done all the damage I could do in Zumba, I skipped out early, changed clothes, and decided to put Pace out of my mind. Portia's red sweater was burning a hole in the passenger seat of my car, and if I was going to deliver it to Erik, now was the time to do it.

I drove across town to West Heights, the elegant area of Rueland. Snob West, as the locals called it. New money. Big houses. Mammoth pools. Staff, well paid. With only ten houses on the street, I didn't need a tour guide to find Portia and Erik's place. It had a long, marble-patterned driveway, possessed New England charm, and reeked of wealth. Clearly not a place I belonged.

I parked behind a gray sports car and a black four-door I recognized as Portia's. I clutched the gold sales bag, strapped my beauty bag over my shoulder, and walked to the front door. Okay, I was here. What was I going to say? *Hey, Erik, sorry about Portia. Here's her sweater. Oh, and by the way, did you have your wife killed?*

I tapped my fingers on the sales bag, beating back anxiety. Just remember to go easy. *You survived Pace's confrontation. You'll survive this.* I took a deep breath, rang the bell, and was still composing myself when Erik answered the door. He blinked wide-eyed when he saw me, like I was the last person he expected to see. I offered my condolences, and he invited me in.

Erik was late-forties and handsome in a dignified way. He had wavy, prematurely silver hair and a golfer's complexion, and he was dressed like a man of success. But as I followed him into the den, I thought he looked haggard, defeated in a way that made me realize he looked as bad as I do, especially after Zumba.

He went straight to a bar, and I opened the sales bag. "This was left...uh, behind."

He came around the bar and took the sweater. He held it to his nose, closed his eyes for a brief moment, then laid it on a wingback chair, smoothing it with his fingers. "Definitely Portia's."

I gave him time to take this in. As a beautician, I was

familiar with clients' emotional struggles. I knew how important it was to show compassion and grant a listening ear. I offered Erik a smile, then unzipped the little compartment in my bag. "There's something else." I withdrew the diamond stud and handed it to him.

He took it and twirled it in his fingers. "An earring?"

"Yes. I found it under the magazine table at work. I wondered if it was Portia's."

"Doubtful. She had earrings like this, but she misplaced them at home weeks ago." He set the earring in my palm and held it like he was reconsidering. "But if she'd found them, and this *was* hers…it's yours now."

Guilt pinched the walls of my chest. Portia died in my salon, and I did nothing to stop it. How could I keep this extravagant jewel? "I can't take it, Erik. It's too special."

"It also won't bring her back." He closed my hand around the earring as if to close the subject, then went back to the bar. "Drink?" He filled a glass with amber liquid.

I shrugged, then zipped the earring back inside the tiny closure. "Juice. Thanks."

He handed me a glass of grapefruit juice, and I asked him about Tad.

"He's home from Harvard Business School for the summer. Working at the newspaper, then returning to college for his second year. He's growing up, and I hope it means he's done with wild parties, driving misdemeanors, and arrogant behavior."

I glanced at a picture of Tad on the fireplace mantel. Realizing your kid wasn't perfect couldn't be easy. "Portia always spoke dearly of Tad."

"Yes." He smiled. "After herself, Tad was her next favorite subject."

We laughed a little and fell silent. He ushered me to the couch.

"Have the police found anything yet?" I asked, sitting.

"Apart from how to kill my business? No." He took the chair across from me. "I was at work when Portia was killed, but they questioned my clients, my secretary, and everyone else in the building." He swilled his drink, then choked up a little and wiped a lone tear from his eye.

I gave him a second to get control. "Any idea who would've wanted Portia dead?"

"Portia was a pain in the ass, excuse my French, but I never believed anyone truly harbored ill feelings toward her." He loosened his collar. "Shows what I know."

"Portia mentioned she had a special appointment that afternoon. At four o'clock."

"Yeah." He drained his drink. "I was being honored by one of her clubs. Women of the Earth Society. A fancy ceremony and tree planting, because of my work, which I do, incidentally, because I love it, not because I look for accolades."

"I heard you were in Uganda recently."

"Yes. Colombia in another week. I'll have to cancel."

He rose and fixed himself a second drink. "The kids in those countries are not only dying of starvation, but they're lacking eye care. Seeing properly may not seem all that important compared to basic nutrition, but it's what I can do to help. I donate thousands of pairs of glasses a year. I fit as many as I can personally."

"That's quite heroic."

"I don't want recognition, Valentine. That was Portia's idea. I tried talking her out of this silly ceremony, but she wouldn't hear of it. She said Rolly Bergen and Forrest Wain received trees for lesser deeds."

Just then, a small Filipino woman somewhere between fifty and ancient, dressed in a black and white uniform, padded by.

"That's Noleta," Erik said at my curious stare. "Been with us twelve years."

I sipped my juice, momentarily wondering what Noleta saw on a daily basis. Working for an eccentric woman like Portia, an upstanding guy like Erik, and a wild kid like Tad had to be eventful. My pulse quickened at the thought. I lowered my glass and gazed back at Erik. I would definitely look into that another day.

I left Erik's, thinking things had gone pretty well. I didn't insult him, hit him over the head with facts, or accuse him of murder. All in all, I'd say I was getting the hang of this investigative business.

I got in my car and pondered the things Erik had shared. He admitted Portia was a pain in the butt, but would he risk everything to have her killed? And what about his practice? Would he risk losing that? This got me thinking about losing *my* business. With Portia's murder, Phyllis's incompetence, and my unpaid mortgage, looking for new employment was inevitable. I knew I had to find a way to make more money. But how?

What if I hired another stylist? Right. What sane person would want to join the crazy circus known as Beaumont's? *Hmm.* Maybe a night job? Moonlight in another salon? There were at least a dozen salons in town; three blocks away, my main competitor, Supremo Stylists, sat at number one. I sighed. Forget that idea. For more reasons than one, I'd never work there.

I put off my money troubles and cut across town to my parents' place, thinking about a new potential problem. My mother had left a voicemail on my cell phone while I was sprawled on the floor half-dead at Zumba. Contrary to what Twix believed, I did check cell phone messages. Rarely, but still. I had a feeling something was up when my mother asked me to stop over. Her tone was pleasant, but the sudden kink in my neck told me the request was more of a direct order, and being a dutiful daughter, I would obey.

My parents lived fifteen minutes away in Burlington in a six-year-old, ranch-style house that stretched forever. Out front was a no-nonsense flower garden and a small fountain by the square porch. Out back was a vegetable garden where my father wandered around and smoked cigars.

Since the garage door was open, I slid out of my car and walked past my parents' four-door, blue sedan. I tugged a sweater off the hook on the garage wall, because the other thing their place had was central air and a thermostat that never rose above sixty-five. I choked back the smell of cigar smoke and exhaust fumes imbedded in the fabric, and stepped into the house.

My mother met me at the door in a clean dress and even cleaner apron. You wouldn't find a piece of lint on my mother's clothes, let alone an oil stain. She gave me a quick kiss on the cheek. "You look thin. Are you eating those suppers I made for you when you're working late?"

"When I get a chance." Like I was so busy I couldn't get to the meals stuffed in the freezer at work.

I followed her into the kitchen. "So what's up?" I saw a dessert pan on the counter and even noticed the house didn't feel like a meat freezer. The pull of warm syrupy sugar and cinnamon was interrupted by a burst of gunfire. I poked my head around the corner into the family room and saw my father sitting in his easy chair, the TV remote in his hand.

My father retired a year ago from the fire department. He walked five miles every morning, then tinkered around with his old black-and-white cruiser he'd bought at a police auction fifteen years ago. The rest of the day he spent aggravating my mother. If the TV wasn't blaring and his newspaper wasn't rattling, he was underfoot, asking when his next meal was.

At the moment, he was watching what looked like a bloody documentary on Napoleon. It's not that my father was big into biographies. He mostly enjoyed a good action scene and a round of gunfire.

"Oh, Nappy!" he sighed happily while Napoleon's men lay dead at his feet.

My father's aunt sat next to him, mutely facing the television. Suddenly, I realized my mother had warmed up the house for her. She wore a polyester floral dress, white sweater, baggy stockings, and knitted slippers. Likely, she wasn't absorbing much of the historical re-enactment.

"Tantig." I gave her a tender hug.

Tantig is the word Armenians call their aunt. Since all my grandparents died when I was small, my great-aunt became grandma to us. Nothing excited Tantig. Ever. When Holly and I were little, and Tantig visited, we'd tear into the living room butt-naked after our bath. Our towels trailed behind us, and we'd run around in circles, singing our song, "The Naked Merry-go-Round." Then we'd flop back on the floor, pooped. Tantig would roll her eyes to the ceiling and slowly utter in her flat tone, "Oh...my...Gaaad."

"We took Tantig to Zettle's today to pick up her dry cleaning," my mother practically shouted. "And when we came home she insisted on making your father paklava."

Tantig lived alone, and we all knew the day was coming when she'd either have to bunk with my parents or move into a home. I voted for bunking with my parents.

I fluffed Tantig's disheveled white hair, then looked point-blank at my father. "Dad!" I raised my voice above the din. "Maybe Tantig would like to watch something else."

Tantig stared at the screen. "My fa-vo-rite weath-air-man switched to Channel Seven," she said in a thickly accented monotone. "I was *so* mad. I don't watch him anymore."

There was a two-second silence while everyone processed that. Then my mother pulled me into the kitchen. "You know who else picked up her dry cleaning at Zettle's?"

Why she asked these rhetorical questions, I'll never know. "Lady Gaga?"

"Your cousin, Faren." She eyed me like I should've realized this. "You know why? She plans on wearing her dry-cleaned dress tonight at dinner when she sees *you*."

"Come again?"

"You forgot about your blind date, didn't you?"

"I can't go on a date." I palmed my kink. "I have Zumba." So I omitted to mention I already went to the morning class.

"Last time, when I fixed you up with Arnie Drup," she argued, "you had skydiving lessons. Why is it every time you have a date you're jumping out of planes or squirming around a gym floor?"

She had a point.

"Your cousin went to a lot of trouble to set up this date. And you two can catch up over dinner first." She watched me go for the paklava. "She'll be waiting at the Wee Irish Goat at six. So don't be late. You're not getting any younger."

"Thanks." I pried a piece of syrupy dessert from the pan.

"We just want you to be happy, dear."

Yes, meddling always makes me happy. I shoved a hunk of pastry in my mouth. I figured I'd lived through two murders. Surely, I'd survive another blind date.

I primped a bit extra on the slight chance my date was a wow. My hair was in long, cascading curls, and I was body-wrapped in a raspberry strapless dress with killer stilettos on my feet. All I could say was, he better be worth it.

I entered the Wee Irish Goat and was struck by the laughter, chatter, music, and smells of oregano and garlic bread. The restaurant—a little *The Godfather* and a pinch *Finian's Rainbow*—was everyone's favorite gathering place. The owners were cousins, and they'd served people for over forty years.

While I waited to be seated, I looked at the actors' pictures plastered on the walls, then glanced over at a table singing along to Frank Sinatra's version of "My Way." I opened and closed my tense fingers. *You're here. Try to enjoy the night.*

Brody O'Roarke, one of the owners, limped over, menus tucked under his arm. "Ah, there's the lass. The men will be bumping into walls when they see you tonight."

"Charmer." I smiled.

"You're okay, then?" Brody asked. "Since the death in your salon?"

"I'm fine." I was getting pretty good at saying that.

Brody gave my hands a reassuring squeeze. "You have a big date, I hear."

"So I've been told. Is Faren here? We're having dinner before she introduces me to the man of the night."

"I'll show you to her." He hobbled two steps into the main dining room, then faltered and placed his hand on my arm. "I hear you saw my lovely granddaughter Monday morning. She showed me her painted nails, so she did. It put a handsome smile on her face."

After I'd lost a childhood friend to a rare blood disease, it prompted my Monday visits to the terminal kids at Rueland Memorial. I started by taking in some lipstick, thinking a little color would make their day. Before long, I carted in my beauty bag, dumped the contents on a bed, and we'd all make each other up. I called it Mon Sac est Ton Sac, coined from my French heritage, meaning My Bag Is Your Bag. I've had false lashes glued to my brows and hair extensions taped to my chin. Basically, I walked away looking like Phyllis's disasters, but they were good disasters, and I felt happy inside. Wished I could say the same about Phyllis.

Brody's eight-year-old granddaughter Kylie, however, was a walking miracle. A stomach tumor doctors had found when she was a toddler had shrunk to three-quarters its original size. After the hospital had been home for most of her life, she was expected to go to her real home within weeks.

"She's a lucky lass to have you visit her." Brody wiped his eyes. "Praise God."

I got all choked up and forgot my anxiety. I wrapped

my arm around his shoulder while he mumbled thanks to Mary, Joseph, and a few other saints.

New guests rushed in, and I patted Brody's shoulder. "I see Faren. I'll seat myself."

"Good luck, then. And Valentine...only the best for you. Remember that."

Now why couldn't I find a man like that?

Faren and I ate dinner and caught up on family stuff while we tapped our toes to "New York, New York." She sipped a wine spritzer. I drank Diet Coke. Alcohol and I didn't mesh. I became foolish, and men who looked like Mr. Feltz magically transformed into six-foot-tall, strapping men with me trying to rip off their clothes.

"So?" Faren leaned in after we ordered dessert. "Was it as gruesome as the media said? Was she naked when you found her? Was her husband involved?"

"Yes. No. And I don't know. Now can we talk about something else? I'm looking forward to a night without any reminders of the murder."

Nina—waitress, friend of Faren, and niece to Giovanni, the other owner—brought us a huge slab of chocolate cake and two forks that would've landed on the floor if there'd been a cute guy at the table. Nina was single and perpetually shy around men. My mother could've done wonders for her in the dating department.

"Now, be honest." I dug in once Nina left. "What's this guy like?"

"He started at the dealership a month ago. Works mostly evenings. As I'm the daytime receptionist, I haven't had a chance to get to know him."

"Maybe you'd like this chance to get to know him."

She snorted. "I'm sure my lazy boyfriend would love that."

I forgot about him. "Yeah. I guess not."

We stuffed our faces. Neither one of us mentioned that Craig Stavros, my mystery man, was thirty minutes late. All of a sudden, Faren grasped my arm. "He's here!"

I looked toward the door. Oh Lord, you had to be

kidding. Shaggy sideburns. Purple ruffled shirt. Black leather pants. Was Faren blind or did she think I was that desperate?

"What the—" Faren's jaw dropped almost as low as mine. Her eyes spun back to me. "I'm sorry, Val. He doesn't dress at work like he's in *My Big Fat Greek Wedding.* Oh, my Lord."

My neck hairs bristled, and my legs went numb. "I don't think the Lord had anything to do with this." I guzzled my drink, wishing I had something stronger. Being drunk was the only way I'd get through the night.

Craig swaggered to our table, and Faren introduced us. He took my hand and fondled it, but quickly lost interest in that and slapped a passing waitress's tush. "Hey, doll, gimme Sex on the Beach." He winked at me and displayed a gold tooth. Then he sat down and cleaned his hairy ear with his car key that hung from a Porsche medallion keychain.

I stared wide-eyed. Was this punishment because of a dead client in my salon? When I couldn't stand it for another second, I excused myself, darted to the bathroom, and splashed water on my neck. I dug out my watch with the broken clasp, glowering for a moment at the unpleasant memory it evoked. Seven-bloody-forty-five. Great.

I threw the stupid thing back in my bag, which I toted everywhere. I mean, you never knew when you might do a quick cut or need a dab of nail polish. If only it'd help me now. Darn. How long could I stay in here? *Okay, Valentine.* Faren was a cousin, a favorite until now. Stop hiding in the bathroom and get out there—even if it's only to make an excuse and leave.

I peeked out the ladies' room door and shuddered. Then I took a deep breath, put on a brave face, and forged to the table. I slid my chair a safe three feet from my date.

"You all right?" Faren asked.

"Hunger pains," I said, checking the exits.

"You just ate."

Craig squinted at me, oblivious to my revulsion. "Hey, Vallie, you ever been to For Your Eyes Only?"

What was that? A James Bond movie? "I don't go to the movies." Thought I'd squelch any notion he might have of asking me out.

He flicked bits of earwax off his key. "Not the movie, sweets. For Your Eyes Only is a strip joint. You know, for us manly types." He puffed out his carpeted chest so I could admire his tire chain and three-inch gold cross that hung from his thick, hairy neck. Ugh.

I grabbed my drink and sucked on the straw.

Faren rolled her eyes. "What would Valentine be doing in a strip joint, you moron?"

Craig leered at my breasts, lip curled up. "I don't know. But she does look sorta familiar."

I snorted soda out my nose and hastily wiped my face. I leaned back in my chair to breathe something other than his reeking cologne. I sniffed over my shoulder and that's when I saw Romero. Sitting at the bar, staring right at me, masking a grin.

My heart skipped a beat, and I felt color rise in my face. What was *he* doing here? And why'd he have to look like a Roman warrior in modern-day clothes? For a moment, I almost forgot about jungle boy. Then Craig belched, and I spun forward so fast I nearly toppled out of my chair.

"Wow," Faren said. "Looks like you saw a ghost."

"I think I did." I swallowed, then snuck another peek.

Romero was in a crisp white shirt and black pants. He leaned toward a beautiful blond and whispered in her ear. Pretty cozy.

Dean Martin crooned "That's Amoré," and Craig moved in with a piece of *our* cake between his fingers. "Hey, Vallie." He smeared my mouth with cake. "They're playing our song."

I sputtered out crumbs and jerked away. "We don't have a song." We'll never have a song.

He leaped to his feet, forgetting all about me, and sang along off-key. After the last dreadful note, everyone clapped. I downed the rest of my drink. What a waste of makeup this was.

"Gotta go." I stood up. "Forgot to feed the cat."

Faren raised an eyebrow. "You have a cat?"

"A new kitty, actually. You know kittens. Eat. Pee. Eat. Pee."

Faren gestured to her cheek, but I ignored it and backed away with a wave. "Craig, it was, uh, interesting."

"Later, babe," he said, exploring the bar.

I could see that my leaving crushed him. May even take him thirty seconds to get over it.

The night wasn't a total wipeout. I managed a route to the door without passing Romero and his date. It wasn't easy. I bumped elbows, knocked chairs, and almost collided with a waiter. My focus was on the exit, and when I catapulted through it, I sighed. Big time.

I click-clacked to the parking lot out back, feeling jumpy. Crap. Where was my car? It seemed much closer when I arrived. I hugged my bag close to steady my nerves when a strong hand gripped my shoulder.

I freaked out. I had no idea what I was doing, except the screaming part. I had that down pat. I reached in my bag, whirled around, and fired a tube of tint like I was pulling a gun. Beige-colored dye splotched the heart of my attacker's white shirt. I didn't congratulate myself on good eye-hand coordination. I was too busy gasping for air. I looked from the stained shirt to his darkening eyes.

Oops. Romero.

A couple leaving the parking lot swerved over, and a busboy from the restaurant slammed open the kitchen door, tea towel slung over his shoulder. Everyone wanted to know what the screaming was about.

"It's okay," Romero shouted, badge held high. "I'm a cop."

Once the show was over, Romero gaped, arms wide, from his shirt to me. "Is there a reason you just squirted me with this goop?" He wiped a blob off his chest and put his finger to his nose.

I exhaled and waited for my heartbeat to slow down. "Uh, you probably shouldn't touch that."

"And why's that?"

"It's hair color. In about twenty minutes, your white shirt will be"—I glanced at the squished tube in my hand—"Raven Black."

"Perfect. I've always wanted a tie-dyed shirt."

"Well, now you've got one." I grabbed a tissue from my bag and waved it at him.

He wiped his finger and sent me a sour look like, if I were a male, he'd have decked me.

"Well?" My voice went seriously high. "What were you trying to do? Scare me to death?"

"If you didn't overreact with a beauty product, we could have a normal discussion."

I stuck out my bottom lip since his gaze was already steady on my mouth.

"I would've talked to you in there." He fought a smile. "Except I didn't want to interrupt you and your boyfriend from—"

"He's not my boyfriend. Ooh." I trembled, still feeling Craig's slimy hands on me. I turned and marched to my car, Romero close behind. I whipped around. "He's not even an acquaintance."

Romero tucked his badge away, his smile fading, his eyes becoming unmistakably hungry. "That's some dress."

I fumbled for my keys, rattled by his unholy stare and deep voice that could cave a thousand knees. I attempted to erase thoughts Holly had stuck in my head about Romero having the stamina of a bull and the fingers of a pianist. Then a tiny wave of jealousy hit me. A guy who looked like this never went without a woman. Maybe Holly was right about Romero's past. Maybe the blond at the bar was the reason his life changed. Whoever she was, he looked incredible for her.

The air was so still, I was afraid he'd hear my heart pounding. "Why are you out here anyway?"

He almost folded his arms. Then he slid his hands into

the pockets of his tailored trousers. "I thought you should know Portia's official cause of death is strangulation."

I unlocked the car and turned back to him. "Oh…thanks."

He came close in the soft light of the moon, and my blood sizzled a bit hotter. Dear Lord. Yesterday I was ready to choke Romero. Could this tough Iron Man be human after all? I hesitated, realizing he'd opened the door for me. Okay, so he had redeeming qualities. Still didn't mean he was my type. "Yesterday, I was maybe a little, uh—"

"Ignorant? Rude? Snotty?" He continued to take me in, humor in his eyes.

For Pete's sake, was I smudged in chocolate? "I was going to say *defensive*." I took my hand and casually swept my face, then flopped onto the seat. "Boy, it must be nice being perfect."

"It does have its drawbacks." He clicked the door shut and waited while I shot down the window. He leaned in, reeking of color chemicals, his eyes turquoise with the fading sun on his back. "A little defensive is good," he whispered in a low voice. Tint crept down his shirt and dripped to the ground. He couldn't have looked sexier.

My heart beat wildly. It'd been ages since I'd been kissed or even touched by a man, unless you counted Apeman's slimy grip. I imagined Romero's full lips on mine, his rough jaw scratching my skin. The moonlight highlighted a small scar on his cheekbone, and even that was irresistible. I edged toward him—not to feel his touch, I told myself—simply to admire the clear, starry night.

The blond poked her head out of the restaurant. "Mikey, you coming?"

Mikey?

I came to my senses and started the engine. "You better get back to your girlfriend."

"Who, Cynthia?" He pushed off from the car. "She's my sister."

"Oh?" My eyebrows went up. "You don't resemble each other."

"I know. I got all the looks."

"And all the humility."

His eyes twinkled wickedly. "She's getting married next month. There are a few details she wanted to go over since I'm the emcee."

"Nice." I brightened, and my stomach did a flip. "Better not keep her waiting."

He drew near again. "By the way, you're no longer a suspect in Portia Reynolds's murder."

"Why the sudden change?"

"Let's just say we have other leads."

"Well, hallelujah." I still wouldn't give up my investigation. Until the killer was caught, people would stay away from the shop in droves.

"Yeah, I knew you'd be relieved."

"Detective." I pressed my shaky foot on the brake. "I was never worried."

He moved in real slow, studying my lips with such intensity I thought he might kiss me. Then it struck me. I must've had cake smeared across my mouth. Darn Craig.

Romero swiped his finger across my cheek and then patted the car hood. "Don't speed."

I hit the gas and was almost airborne. Then I peeked back at Romero. He stood there smugly in his tie-dyed shirt, licking chocolate off his finger.

Chapter 4

I zoomed down the street and almost sideswiped a car. I turned right on Montgomery, jumped the curb, and slammed on the brakes before I hit a fire hydrant. I took a second to catch my breath. Then I flipped down the sun visor and checked myself in the mirror. Yep. A swirly bit of chocolate icing smeared across my lip and edged onto my cheek like a cheesy, villainous mustache. I thunked my head on the steering wheel. Terrific. I acted real suave in front of Romero too. He must've had a good laugh. Ha-ha. Foolish little hairdresser.

I nabbed a facial wipe from the glove compartment and scrubbed my cheek. Why did I feel inept when Romero was around? Because he made me uneasy? Because I was attracted to him? Maybe his good humor was a ruse—get Valentine to relax and back off. Damn, he was sneaky. Well, I wasn't falling for any stunts from any smartass cop.

I wasn't ready to go home, and with the state I was in, I needed to cool down. I drove around town and thought about Romero's comment about other leads. Had he learned something incriminating about Albert? Seemed he was intent on nailing him for this crime.

I skipped over to Darling and cruised by the shop. Happily, the press had moved on and Beaumont's was in darkness except for the three lights that funneled over the awning.

I headed down the tree-lined street and passed the drugstore and Dilly's Florist on my right. Everything was closed except for Kuruc's European Deli. I wasn't hungry, but I could use a diversion.

Kuruc's was one of the best things about Rueland. It sold everything from Italian olives and Swiss cheese to Armenian grape leaves and Hungarian goulash.

One of the worst things about Rueland was Sam Kuruc's mother—Hajna, the Hungarian witch. Habitually, I veered to whatever corner of the deli Hajna wasn't. Tonight, it was the baked goods.

I inhaled the smell of rising dough and pesto. Maybe a snack was in order. I was trying to decide on a focaccia or ciabatta bun when a threaded needle lowered in front of my nose and dropped to my stomach. The needle began to circle.

"I see a girl." Hajna pounced in front of me, one eye bulging bigger than the other. "Not one, but *two*!" She poked her fingers between my eyes so quickly, I blinked. "You have twins in your belly."

The only twins I knew were English chatterboxes Birdie and Betty Cutler—or Bitty as Birdie pronounced it. Mid-fifties, roller sets, easy pleasers. They sat under hair dryers—deaf to everything—the morning Portia was killed. Definitely not in my belly.

Everyone in the deli stopped what they were doing and cheered, as was the norm when Hajna made a prediction.

I leaned in and whispered, "I'm not pregnant, Mrs. Kuruc."

Hajna took in my dress. "Maybe you search for man to make babies. Be careful. Evil spirits crowd you."

Tell me about it.

I was paying for tabbouleh and the ciabatta bun when I heard a familiar voice behind me.

"This is a stickup. Don't move."

I spun around and almost took out the eyes of a man—

five-ten, soft-shouldered, soft-bellied, baguette in hand. "That's pretty funny." I squeezed my tabbouleh container to my chest.

"Then how come you're not laughing?" He bonked my head with the baguette.

I knew I should've known the voice, but who was this kook? "I've had my fill of laughs for one night. See ya."

"Hey, don't you know me? It's Tom, your order man from Alluve."

I sighed and felt remotely better that I knew this lunatic, even if it was only by phone.

"Sorry to hear about what happened at work," he said. "But then, you must be used to the excitement."

Moving on. "Hey, Tom, uh." What was his last name? Okay. Didn't know. That's the way it was in my business. You contacted your supplier, ordered what you needed, and bam, it arrived at your shop courtesy of a deliveryman. It was very simple. I asked Tom about Albert Dougal.

"You're the second person who's asked about Albert. The police, they don't think he had anything to do with the murder, do they?"

"They're questioning everyone who was at the salon Thursday. So how's Albert doing? Was he at work yesterday?"

"This is bizarre. Albert called yesterday morning. Said he wouldn't be in. He sounded unusual, in a hurry. There was a lot of noise in the background. Then we got cut off."

I frowned. "If you hear from him, would you call? And do you know his address?"

"Of course. Anything to help." He ripped off a napkin from the counter and jotted down Albert's address. "I hope he's not in any trouble. He's finally got his life together. It'd be a shame if he ended up back in jail."

My voice snagged. "Jail?"

"Yeah. It happened a long time ago, and he's kind of secretive about that part of his life. But if I hear from him, I'll let you know."

Great. Bad enough a client died in my shop; now I was betting my existence on an AWOL ex-con. Was it any wonder I had trouble being optimistic?

Maybe Albert looked the part. I was a good judge of character, wasn't I? Spending time locked up didn't mean he'd committed this crime. So why was I focusing on him?

That particular thought was still on my mind while I sat in the car and forked tabbouleh into my mouth. I glared at the napkin I set on the dashboard, and my thoughts wandered to Albert's connection to Portia. Was it possible he knew her? Had I overlooked something in my haste to vindicate the guy?

Portia had been educating me on hair care when I'd let Albert into the shop Thursday morning. He'd thumped the perm cartons on the counter, then given her that strange look, which I'd suspected was because she nattered on in the styling chair, drawing everyone's attention to herself. But what if I was wrong? What if something else brewed below the surface? Something I'd missed.

"You really should hire a receptionist for these petty issues," Portia had said after Albert disappeared. "And why does that hippie make deliveries when I'm here? Can't he do that at night?"

Even now, I felt collagen draining from my pores from her abrasive tone. But what if Portia was right? Suppose it wasn't just coincidence Albert delivered on the same day at the same time Portia had her weekly appointment. What if he'd purposely planned it that way? It was possible, wasn't it? He could've waited for an opportunity to strike when Portia was most vulnerable. Suppose he came in that day, dropped off the boxes, and heard us discussing her facial. He knew she'd be headed into Ti Amo shortly. Not only that, he would've walked right by the room on his way back out. What if he never did drive away?

As much as I hated to admit it, Romero had a point about someone re-entering the building. Let's say Albert hid in the bush to the left of the back door, a mere ten feet from the room where Portia was lying on a facial bed. Or better still, what if he hid in the basement? He would've been too far away in one of the rooms to detect movement upstairs, but if he waited at the bottom of the steps, he'd have easily heard me leave Ti Amo.

The biggest hole in all of this was motive. Surely Albert didn't kill Portia because he'd overheard her insult him. Yet other than that, I couldn't think of any reason he'd want her dead.

I grimaced at the address, almost seeing Albert's fingerprints on the napkin. Time to check this out for myself. *Don't do it*, a little voice sang, trying to steer me clear of a bad situation. To heck with the voice. I slapped the tabbouleh lid back on the container and cranked the ignition. It was only nine o'clock. Why waste a beautiful evening?

Traffic was relatively slow for a Saturday night. The moon played hide-and-seek with dolphin-shaped clouds, Crash Test Dummies sang about Superman, and the lead's rumbling voice sent a soft shiver down my neck. Unconsciously, my thoughts turned to Romero's deep, sexy rumble, and I trembled some more. Okay. His voice turned me on. I could have worse yearnings.

I zig-zagged through town and eased my car down Iris Street. Hard to believe I was going through with this. I was a beautician. Why was I playing CSI? Never mind. I needed to see for myself that Albert wasn't around. Who knows? Maybe he'd gone somewhere for the day and was back home. I spotted the address scribbled on the napkin, then circled around and parked a few doors down on the opposite side of the road.

With an artist's eye, I tried to find the beauty in Albert's duplex, but it was like putting makeup on a rotted corpse. The house had a small concrete porch, peeling red shutters, a gravel driveway, dried-up shrubs, and a single bulb lit over the side door. What it didn't have was one pretty flower. A two-door car with a sunroof sat in the driveway. I didn't recognize the make or model. Fashion, I knew. Cars belonged in two categories—size and color. Albert's was small and green.

Odd. If Albert had fled, why didn't he take his car? I pictured his thinning hair, jagged teeth, and lined eyes that suggested a hard life. I didn't know why he went to jail, what he spent his money on, or what he did in his off time. What any of this had to do with Portia's murder was beyond me. But since I was here, I moseyed up the driveway and peeked in the car windows. I saw a Red Sox ball cap, empty peanut bag, a cardboard cup in the cup holder, and cigarette butts in the ashtray. The latter told me Albert's car was not only small and green. It was also old.

I poked my nose over the fence into the backyard. Nothing out of the ordinary. Shed. A few worn lawn chairs. Dented garbage can.

I rang the front bell and heard a dog bark. Next door, I saw a small, shaggy mongrel perched on a sofa back, peering at me through the living room window. No answer at Albert's. I decided to check with the neighbor. Maybe Shaggy Mongrel saw something.

A stout lady with big hair and small lips came to the door, dog under her arm. "I saw Albert early yesterday, standing outside with a suitcase," she said in a high, girlish voice. "Next time I looked, he was gone."

This only confirmed what I'd already been told about Albert not being around. Though standing outside, presumably waiting for a ride when he had a car, piqued my curiosity. Had his car broken down? Did he not like driving alone? Maybe, if he flew somewhere, he didn't want to pay for airport parking. I chalked it up to peculiarity, said thank you, and walked back to my car.

I sat there, tapping the steering wheel, staring from the other duplexes on the street to Albert's. There was something else, but darned if I could bring it to light. Wait a minute. The light. Of course. Over the side door. Didn't you usually leave a light on if returning later that evening? Granted, this was night number two that Albert had been gone. Still, maybe he'd be home tonight. And when he arrived, I'd be the first to greet him. I tilted my seat back and got comfy. I could wait. I had nothing important to do.

Turned out, being on a stakeout was a lot less fun than it looked in the movies. After five minutes, I was bored stiff. I got out of the car and wiped a smudge off the windshield. Then I walked around my Bug and kicked the tires the way those tough guys did it in the movies.

I polished the pink daisy on my hood and smiled at a woman walking her golden retriever. She threw me a strange glance over her shoulder, then hustled down the street. I saw my reflection in the car window and had to agree with the strange glance. I looked like an idiot, loitering in a rundown neighborhood, alone, at night, wearing a hot dress and hotter heels.

I scrambled back into the car, kept the interior light on, and filed my nails. Wrapping that up, I cleaned out my glove compartment. Napkins. Car manual. Hand sanitizer. Wipes. Round-framed glasses? What were these doing here? My eyesight had improved since I'd last worn these. I tossed them back in the glove compartment when a taxi drove by.

I flicked off the light and slouched in my seat. The cab slowed in front of Albert's. Looked like the cabbie was checking addresses. He pulled into a driveway two doors down, and a beat later a woman came out of the duplex and jumped in the cab. *Rats*. Wait. Another car. Uh-oh. Police. I scrunched down further, waited a second, then peeked out the window.

The police car stopped in front of Albert's. A uniform got out, walked up the driveway, and glanced in the backyard. He shone a flashlight in the windows, then swept the neighboring properties and street. I slid down and held my breath while the light penetrated my windows. *Great idea this was*. I waited with that doomed feeling that

I'd been found out, already wondering what Romero would have to say about this. I rolled excuses around in my mind when the light moved on. Whew.

The cop strolled back to his cruiser, jotted something down, and drove off. What was that all about? And where the hell was Albert anyway? Funny time to take a vacation. While I thought about this, I nestled back in my seat, kicked off my heels, and curled up my legs beside me. I closed my eyes and tried to come up with a better reason why Albert disappeared. Maybe he ran off to join the circus or shaved his head and joined the navy. Or grabbed a tambourine and became a Hare Krishna. I yawned and took a deep breath, thinking of other possibilities. Next thing I knew, the clock on the dash said 2:15.

I sat up, worked out the numbness in my back, and gawked at Albert's place. Car was still there. Side light still on. No other activity. *Face it, sweetheart, Albert's not coming home tonight. Maybe he's not coming home at all.* A slight tremor slid through me at that thought, but I discounted it. He'd be home. Sooner or later Albert would be back.

Chapter 5

I got up extra early Monday morning, glad the weekend was over. Not surprising, considering the horrible week I'd had, concluding with an exasperating blind date, a waste-of-time stakeout, and Sunday passing in a mindless fog.

I looked outside and shivered. Perfect day for a funeral—miserable, cold, and threatening. Fitting, since the featured guest at *this* funeral was also noted for being miserable, cold, and threatening. Still, Portia's one o'clock service was one I didn't want to miss. I might even learn a thing or two.

I didn't want to neglect my weekly visit to the hospital or Rueland Retirement—where I made a few extra bucks doing roller sets till I was blue in the face. So I showered, ate a bowl of Frosted Flakes, then slipped on jean Capris, a lacy white tank top, a sparkly silver belt, and layered on a lightweight metallic gray jacket. The seniors were always up with the crows, so I stopped there first, fit in four sets, then pushed on to the hospital.

Rueland Memorial was a decent-sized healthcare center for a town of thirty thousand. Five large floors, dozens of doctors on staff, friendly nurses at every corner, and a new children's wing in the works. If I ever needed medical attention, this was where I wanted to be.

I was waiting for the elevator when the doors opened and my employee, Judy, stepped out in a bulky sweater, jeans, and flip-flops.

I asked if she was okay, and she said she'd just had blood work done and was on her way home to get ready for Portia's funeral.

"Aren't you going with us?" she asked. "I thought we were all riding together."

Judy had been with me for three years. She was unattached and seemed to like it that way. Though it didn't stop guys from asking her out, often when they were in her chair, having a cut.

I entered the elevator and pressed four. "I'll be ready. I'm just doing my usual routine with Kylie O'Roarke and the other kids."

"Okay." She smiled and headed to the lobby's sliding doors. "See you later then."

I got off the elevator on the fourth floor and passed busy construction workers and temporary walls of plastic sheets. Kylie was the first child I saw when I hiked through the confusion. She sat up in her bed as a nurse wheeled several children, one by one, into the ward.

Kylie held a special place in my heart. I wasn't sure if it was because she reminded me of my friend Colleen when she'd died at that age, or if it was because, despite her illness, she possessed enough spunk for ten people. She was small for eight, almost overpowered by her long red hair and freckles, and she had brown eyes that shone brightly, especially since finding out she'd soon be leaving the hospital.

Within minutes, the room had turned into a make-believe salon, the volume almost as loud. Kids whiter than hospital sheets painted each other's nails and made up one another's faces. I'd brushed my hair and left it straight down this morning. Several children, who had lost most of their hair due to chemo, braided mine and decorated the braids with ribbons, barrettes, and bows. Kylie concentrated on painting my lips with fuschia lipstick.

"When I grow up, I'm going to be just like you." She dabbed my lips meticulously.

You want to be an unlucky beautician, a doomed business owner, and a ripe old spinster? I grinned and touched the tip of her nose. "Be careful what you wish for, Kylie. It may come true."

She nodded defiantly. "I'm *counting* on it. The doctors say that when I leave here I'll only need to come in once every six months for checkups. I can hardly wait to sleep in my own bed again! Won't that be great?"

"The greatest!"

I left the hospital, breathing happily for Kylie. Once I made it through my door, I traipsed into the kitchen and saw by the microwave clock I had thirty-five minutes to get ready for the funeral. I wolfed down a peanut butter and jam sandwich, then went into the bathroom to look at myself in the mirror. Gorgeous. My hair was a spider web of braids, my face was dotted with nail stickers, and my chin was smeared with lipstick. Unfortunately, I still looked better than any of Phyllis's clients.

I let out the braids and accessories from my hair, peeled off the stickers, brushed my teeth, and retouched my makeup. Then I stripped out of my clothes and slipped on a black, Audrey Hepburn-style dress like the one she wore in *Breakfast at Tiffany's*. I swept up my hair and left bangs to frame my face. I even fastened a thick strand of pearls around my neck. No reason to go to a funeral dressed like a pauper, even if my bank account had become perilously low. Besides, I'd found the dress in one of those tucked-away, strangely cute second-hand boutiques. The dress had practically begged me to take ownership.

Thinking of my budget, I pictured my mortgage statement pierced to the bulletin board in my office at work. I was ready to go to the funeral with five minutes to spare. This was it. I had to call the bank and ask for more time to pay my mortgage. If they agreed, maybe I could figure a way out of this mess. Besides, what did I have to lose? I said a prayer, then picked up the phone.

The good news was Feltz gave me a slight extension. The bad news was I had a little over two weeks to pay up. Face it, girl. You're no further ahead. I mulled this over when I heard Max squeal to a stop in the driveway. I peered out the window and saw the dust settling under his silver four-door. It was twelve-thirty. I pushed my money problems to the back of my mind, then locked up and hurried down the steps.

Twenty minutes later, we arrived at St. Mark's Cathedral in Boston. The church was packed with high-society mourners, organ music played softly in the background, and the air smelled of lilies and wooden pews. Then we walked in. We paraded down the middle aisle behind Phyllis, searching for a place to sit.

"Did you have to wear one of your creations?" Max whispered, tugging down the right side of Phyllis's black skirt.

"You be quiet," Phyllis said. "My handiwork is one hundred percent polyester."

"Then you better visit a plumbing store. Your outfit's leaking one hundred percent fat."

I eyed a woman sniffling quietly in a pew on the left. "Shhh." I pulled Max's sleeve. "This is a funeral. Be respectful."

Phyllis shoved over the woman so we could sit down. In the process, she banged mourners with her purse and stepped on a man's foot. The man yelped and scowled at us as we sidestepped past him. Judy shrugged a sorry and quickly took a seat, followed by me and then Max.

"What's with the crowd?" Phyllis sat with such a thud she almost threw Judy in my lap. "Everyone making sure Portia's dead?"

I stifled a strangled laugh and looked around the throng to see if I recognized anyone. I didn't expect Pace to be here or anyone else from the salon that day. Then I caught a flash of sparkle from black, wide-brimmed hats several rows up. Under the hats were Betty and Birdie Cutler. They knew Portia? Interesting. They never spoke to her in the shop.

Max huddled close and whispered in my ear. "So? You didn't tell me how fingerprinting went. Did you find it as pleasurable as I did?"

"Immensely," I said as sarcastically as I could in a hushed tone.

"And did that big handsome detective who has his eye on you roll each of your delicious little fingers on that icky fingerprint form?"

"No, he did not." I nudged him away. "And I'd hardly say he has his eye on me."

Max gave me a "we'll-see" look. "At least that's done."

Phyllis leaned past Judy, who perused the program. "What's done?"

"Fingerprinting." Max slanted forward.

"If you want my opinion," Phyllis said, "that was totally unnecessary. I mean, who else's fingerprints are going to be on the equipment? Darth Vader's?"

"Darth Vader wore gloves. I swear, Phyllis, every day you get two days dumber."

"And two pounds heavier," the man who got stepped on piped.

Phyllis made a fist. "Did that guy just call me fat?"

"No, dear." Max smiled brightly. "He called you heavy. There's a difference."

Phyllis blew air out her cheeks and crossed her arms.

I didn't like to laugh when Max niggled Phyllis, but I couldn't seem to hold back. I counted to ten, made my lips tight, and attempted to stuff down the nervous giggles.

"As for fingerprinting," Max continued, "the police need to match our fingerprints to the machine so they're not on a wild goose chase. Makes sense to me."

Phyllis gawked at Judy next to her. "Did you have yours done?"

Judy looked up from her program. "What done?"

"Fin-ger-prints!" Phyllis shouted, shaking her head.

Everyone turned in their pews and gaped at us. I swallowed and tried to keep a straight face.

Judy sighed, head down. "Yes, Phyllis. I did. Not that everyone here needs to know."

I bit my lip and breathed past another chuckle. And another. Judy elbowed me, and Max gave me his you're-embarrassing-us-here stare.

The service began, but I was too busy keeping my mouth shut and biting my tongue to hear what was being said. I knew how to behave. Even if I'd never attended a funeral before, I had gone to visitations. Funny thing was I didn't know why I was laughing. There was nothing humorous about Portia's funeral. Sweat seeped down my back, and my ears were on fire. Several more minutes went by, and I still couldn't get myself under control.

"What happened to being respectful?" Max whispered, slapping a mint in my hand.

I sucked on the mint and tried to look soulful, but my jaws ached and my insides heaved. All of a sudden, the mint lodged in my throat. I panicked. I gasped for air.

"—elp!" I whacked Max on the chest.

He walloped me on the back, and the mint projected out of my mouth, flew a foot in the air, and landed on a plastic bluebird perched on a hat in front of me. The woman under *that* hat shot me a look over her shoulder.

"Insolence!" She swung her head forward so fast, the bird loosened from its roost.

I clenched my thighs and pleaded with myself to be quiet. The bird did a three-sixty on its claws and toppled ass-backward onto my lap.

Before I could process what had happened, Max snuggled close, lips to my ear. "That's what you call tits up."

I would've clobbered him. But at the moment I was in the throes of wailing laughter.

After the service, we piled into Max's car, lost in our

own thoughts, when Phyllis, sitting to my right in the backseat, broke the sound barrier.

"Did you get a load of that eulogy?" She shifted her weight toward me.

I was still catching my breath. "I guess it was a little exaggerated."

"A little?" she snorted. "If you want my opinion, that wimpy turd must've been paid to convince friends—and I use that term loosely—that Portia was a saint."

"Sort of how we'll pay a eulogist to convince your friends." Max swung off Storrow Drive, taking a shortcut to the cemetery. "At least it'll be a small gathering."

Judy shook her head in disgust, barely looking back at us. "Phyllis, you're awful."

"Oh, am I!" Phyllis pecked Judy's shoulder. "What did *you* think of all that rubbish?"

Judy shrugged, her blond curls frizzy from humidity. "It was a beautiful service. The flowers were lovely and—"

"Oh, brother," Phyllis complained. "Go put your head back in your Easy-Bake Oven."

A rusted pickup swerved toward us, and Max lurched into a left lane.

Phyllis had her head out the window. "Drive much?" She shook a fist at the driver.

I thought now would be a good time to change the subject. I shot a look at the darkening sky, overcome by a sinking feeling. "I wonder what will happen to business."

Several miles passed with no reaction. Maybe everyone wondered the same thing.

"Don't worry about us," Max finally said, veering off the exit. "We'll never desert you."

Judy nodded and clasped the dashboard. Phyllis fixed her lipstick.

Three turns later, Max careened into Rueland Cemetery. We bumped over ruts of dirt, searching for a parking spot, while a dozen people hurried to the empty grave. The priest held a Bible in one hand and clutched his robe from the wind with the other. One person I didn't expect to see was Detective Romero. Like I hadn't been through enough. He looked relaxed in a black sports jacket and pants, but I knew better. He was on a mission. When his gaze roamed in our direction, I ducked, my breath stuck in my throat.

"Will you look at that!" Phyllis snapped shut her compact. "If it isn't the good detective."

Max screeched to a stop behind a black car. "Ooh. He is a perfect ten, isn't he? Like those hunky actors. And am I the only one, or does his deep voice send shivers right down to your—"

"Enough!" I didn't want to think about Romero's stupid voice or his movie-star looks. I knew what he was up to. The sneak. Well, I'd show *him*. I wasn't taken in by sexy gestures or a smooth voice.

Phyllis settled back in her seat and smiled like she'd just been told lard was chock-full of vitamins. "How come we didn't see *him* at the funeral?"

"He was probably sitting at the back, waiting." I fiddled with my beads. "Like a stalker."

"Shall we go talk to him?" Max, always the eager beaver.

"No!" I got out of the car and hung back from the crowd, near an old oak tree, far away from the good detective. I kept my eye on him just the same.

We learned the hearse and the rest of the procession were held up in traffic, and a rumble of disquiet stirred the crowd. Meanwhile, the storm grew nearer.

"This burial is plain weird," Phyllis said. "How long are we supposed to stand here waiting for the body?" She gave a good sweep of the area. "We need a body."

"Are you volunteering?" Max leaned against the old oak.

Finally, the hearse arrived, and the casket was put in place. Nearby, two carefree children, about six or seven, chased each other through tombstones. They giggled as the skies blackened and the wind whistled. The giggling touched a deep-rooted nerve within, and my armpits itched with sweat. *Shake it off, silly. They're just kids.*

The little girl took swaying steps in my direction where I'd stepped another few feet back. "Hi," she said, happily playing with the ties on her pink dress.

"Hi," I whispered, trying not to avert my eyes from the service.

She bent her knees like me. "How come you're way back here and not up there with everybody else?"

"I prefer the view from here better."

"But you can't see anything back here." She swung her ties back and forth, unaware they were dragging in the muddy grass.

The boy closed in, took a fist out of his pocket, and a bunch of squashed dandelions fell to the ground. He sneezed, then rubbed his runny nose. "Wanna play?"

"No, I can't," I whispered. "Sorry."

Our whispers caught the attention of some mourners. I quietly took another step back when my left heel snagged on a protruding tree root, causing me to lose my balance. Waving my hands in the air, I flew ass to the ground, snagging the pearls off my neck as I went down.

I sat there, legs spread wide, feeling like a real stooge. The kids put their hands to their mouths and snickered at me. I couldn't blame them. My chic updo had toppled sideways, I was covered in dirt, pearls were sprinkled everywhere, and despite the dampness, sweat was rolling down my face. I spotted Romero in the crowd and thought he looked amused. *Ooh.*

A woman about my age disengaged herself from the mourners, grabbed the children, and tugged them back toward the front. Then she shot me a dirty look over her shoulder. Terrific.

I struggled to my feet, thankful to hear the priest say a final amen. I wiped my brow and was picking muck off my butt when a comforting warmth blocked the wind at my back. A second later, I caught the familiar scent of Arctic Spruce. I turned before I could pull my heels out of the mucky ground and tripped into Romero's arms.

He steadied me, wearing a curious expression that said *how does anyone take you seriously?* "That's quite a stain on your—"

"My what!" I fought to stand on my own two feet, begrudgingly inhaling his aroma.

He grinned at me—the wee joke—and folded his arms in front. "Nice of you to make an appearance at Ms. Reynolds's funeral."

I fumed. "It's more than just an appearance, Detective. I happen to care about my clients."

"I could tell at church how much you cared."

I tightened my lips. I wasn't going to honor that remark with a comment. And damn it, why'd he have to be so dangerously handsome and smell so...so manly?

"What are *you* doing here?" I asked. "Slumming?"

"I'm working. It's amazing who turns up at funerals during a murder investigation." He spread his jacket wide and revealed the gun on his hip.

At the sight of it, I drew in air and took a step back. I knew he was a cop and cops wore guns. But did they have to look so repellent? Maybe if guns had diamonds on the barrel or came in metallic pink. No. I'd still be flustered.

Romero surprisingly didn't give a macho-cop grin—the I've-got-a-big-ego-'cause-I-wear-a-gun grin.

My cheeks got hot. No. I was *not* turned on by this. I was *not* impressed with this self-righteous cop. I did my best to ignore the uncomfortable feelings stirring inside me. I pushed my updo back in place and focused on the emptying cemetery. "So you think your murderer's here?"

"Possibly." He scrutinized the thinning crowd. "Are you surprised they're here?"

I followed his gaze. "Birdie and Betty?"

"They belonged to the same club as Ms. Reynolds. The Women of the Earth Society." He cut me a glance. "Know it?"

"Detective, I wouldn't know Women of the Earth from Women of the Moon. My world is limited to Women of the Cut and Women of the Facial."

He nodded in their direction. "Birdie Cutler had a disagreement with Ms. Reynolds in regards to the club. I guess there was bad blood after that."

"That's fascinating. Well, I won't keep you from your sleuthing. I know how much you enjoy your work." I did a beautiful pivot and began to waltz away.

"You're nothing like your sister," he said to my back.

I whipped around and took three giant steps until I was right under his perpetual five-o'clock shadow. Stifling my fear of guns, I tipped my head back, my mouth so tense I could barely form words. "Would you care to explain that?"

He angled his head down and gave me a beguiling look that probably worked on other women. "She's tough as nails." His voice was low. "But you…" His eyes caressed my face. "You act tough, yet I'd guess it's all show."

How dare he say something so…so utterly true? Was I that transparent? Or was it the cop in him pegging me so perfectly?

He straightened. "You're puzzling, though. I'll give you that."

His amused look had quite an impact on me. I didn't know whether I wanted to kiss him or kick him in the shin. I searched for something—*anything*—to say. "Have you found Albert yet?"

"Interesting you asking me that when you were the one camped out at his place Saturday night."

My face heated. Figures he'd found out.

"Seems Albert's out of state. Not so good when you're an ex-con and cops are trying to track you." He looked at me squarely. "Which is why I told you to stay away from him. You know he has a shady past?"

Okay, it didn't surprise me he knew Albert's history. "How shady?"

"How does drug dealing sound?"

I swallowed my shock. "Sounds like you equate drug dealing with murder."

"Sounds like *you* forget there *was* a murder, and the guy had opportunity."

I had my hands on my hips. "If *you* remember, there was no apparent motive."

"You're incredible!" His eyes hardened. "Do you show this little respect for everyone?"

I jutted out my jaw. "Just those who think they're better than I am."

"Sorry to burst your bubble, Ms. Beaumont. But motive and murder aside, drug dealing is a big no-no." He raked his fingers through his dark, wild hair, probably wondering how to do away with me without being caught.

"That was long ago," I argued. "Albert's got his life together. He's delivered for me for at least five years." I bit back my words. "Or has he been dealing drugs all this time?"

He shook his head. "Suppose you tell me why you think he's incapable of murder?"

I gave a tiny shrug. "I feel sorry for him."

"What?" He rolled his eyes. "You pity the guy?"

It sounded ridiculous, but it's all I had.

"Look, there's still trace evidence that hasn't been analyzed. The last thing I need is an amateur to muddy the waters. Why don't you turn around, go back to your ideal life and cute salon. And stay away from *my* investigation!" The unwavering look said he was dead serious.

I twirled on my beloved Jimmy Choos—which I bought when times were good—and zigzag-hiked to the car. Mud sucked at my heels. Romero's gaze burned at my back. Suddenly, a loud crack of thunder shook the air. The skies opened up, and a torrential shower let loose. I stumbled to the ground again in my *Breakfast at Tiffany's* dress. Max yelled for me to hurry, but I welcomed the sting of rain and slash of wind on my skin.

"Remember!" Romero roared through the storm. "Stay out of it!"

Arrogant jerk. I staggered to my feet, blurry-eyed and not entirely sure it was from the rain. Well, no cop told Valentine Beaumont what to do. I marched to the beat of my own drum!

Chapter 6

Tuesday morning, I swung into Friar Tuck's and parked under the huge revolving donut and medieval arrow, the only sound its rusty creak, groaning tirelessly. Better than the sound of clicking photographers, I thought, searching the area for media. Whew. Nobody lurking. Could things get any better?

I strode into the bakery and marveled for the hundredth time at the inconsistency between Friar Tuck's stone-castle exterior and run-of-the-mill interior. Oh well. Didn't matter if the inside resembled Sherwood Forest, their Boston creams were as good as a donut could get.

I inhaled the sweet smells and waited in line while a pimply-faced newbie, dressed in a medieval tunic and felt crown, served coffee to a couple in front of me.

Then I ordered. "A box of Tuck's Tidbits, please."

The kid didn't seem real thrilled serving pastries dressed as one of Robin Hood's Merry Men. But I likely didn't look too ecstatic, coming to work after a homicide had been committed under my roof. "Do you want those in a box?" he asked in a croaky voice.

"Is that a trick question?"

"It's just you were pointing at the bags."

"I was?"

He shrugged, then filled a box and took my money.

I ventured out into the hazy sunshine and stepped into the back door of Beaumont's, pretty sure we wouldn't need pastries to hand out because we'd have no customers.

I sneezed at the Pine-Sol-scented air, then unloaded my things in the dispensary. The floor sparkled and the counters shone. If nothing else, I could clean. And there had to be jobs for cleaning ladies. Maybe not ones with pretty dresses and high heels, but a job was a job.

I flipped on the lights and put on the coffee. I thought Taylor Swift would lift my spirits, so I slipped in her latest CD when the phone rang. I answered it and heard a familiar smoker's cough and raspy voice that belonged to only one person. Albert.

I was so surprised to hear from him, the words wouldn't come. Didn't matter anyway. Albert did all the talking.

"I wouldn't ask this of you, Valentine, if it wasn't really important. And the truth is, I know I can rely on you. I need you to go to my place, take the envelope from the kitchen table, and mail it. There's a key under the clay duck by the side door. That will get you in." He lowered his voice. "I don't have time to explain, but you once told me you owed me for the time I smothered the fire from that client's hair. Well, I'm collecting."

Nice of you to remember, I thought grimly.

He gave me his address, which I was already well acquainted with, and hung up. I didn't get to ask where he was or why he took off so fast. And there was no call display on the French provincial phone in order to call him back. Ditto, the big number pad phone in the office. Darn. What was Albert up to? I gnawed on my bottom lip, thinking about Romero's warning yesterday. Could there be a connection between Albert's absence, his past, and the murder? I shook my head and dispelled caution signs about carrying out his wishes. My biggest concern was what if I was caught? True, there was a key, which showed I wasn't breaking in. But what if Albert *was* Portia's killer? Was this a trap? Would I be aiding and abetting a criminal?

I was thinking about this when I heard Max enter the back.

"Y-M-C-hey!" he complained, coughing. "Someone used too much ammonia when she cleaned."

He ambled unshaven into the dispensary, bringing the smell of expensive cologne and the sound of urgent news. "If I don't tell you now, you'll hear it via the beauty hotline. And I've got to get this off my chest before the others get here."

"Is this good news or bad news?"

"Depends how you look at it."

"Bad news. Go ahead, make my day."

He pursed his lips like he debated how to break it to me.

"Max! Tell me!"

He squeezed his eyes tight. "I've been offered a job at Supremo Stylists." He cracked open one eye like he expected me to punch him. And I wanted to, but my heart did one of those plummets to hell and back.

Supremo Stylists was *the* competition. They hired only the best, and their prices reflected their prestigious staff. This place was as upscale as Beverly Hills. They didn't serve coffee and donuts to their clients. They plied them with champagne and chocolate-dipped strawberries. Not only that, Supremo Stylists was owned by my least favorite person in the whole world. Candace Needlemeyer. The thorn in my side since beauty school. The one person who would love to see me fail. All I could manage was a shaky "And?"

"I'm considering it."

I didn't see this coming. "What happened to 'We'll never desert you'?"

"That was before I was offered twice the pay."

"So it's about the money."

"Not totally."

"Then what?" I gave him a brooding look as Candace and her blond hair and fake boobs blinded me from the inside out. "Where will you find another boss who loves you like I do?"

"Val-en-tine," he moaned. "That's not fair. You know I adore you, but what's-her-name is driving me to an early grave. I don't understand why you keep her on. Life could be so much simpler. I'm even running out of one-liners."

"Then here's one for you. Suck it up!"

His eyes popped out, but I couldn't stop myself. "Do you think you'll have it so easy in another shop? No conflicts? No harassments?" Like I knew what I was talking about. Ten years ago, I would've thrown myself in front of a bus for an opportunity to work at a place like Supremo Stylists. Whoa. Here was a thought—maybe I was jealous of Max. No! I loved his work and that he was adored by all the ladies. Men liked him, too. Max wasn't what you'd call a man's man, but he could hold his own. He was great for business. I just didn't want him to be great for *that* business.

The air was thick with tension, something I'd never experienced with Max before. Yet he seemed to consider my words. All I thought was I'd say anything to keep him from leaving this madhouse. Anything except the truth about Phyllis.

"Look." He avoided my eyes. "They told me to think about it. I didn't search for this, lovey, honestly. Candace phoned me."

My shoulders sank. "I believe you. Really. You *should* think about moving on. You've been here since I opened. And you're beyond talented."

What was I *saying*? My world was falling apart. Not only was I in the middle of another homicide with a condescending cop on my back, now I was in danger of losing Max, which in the end probably wouldn't matter because in two weeks I'd be out of business.

We both knew enough had been said. Max stuck his nose in the air and flapped his fingers in front of his face to keep from crying. "So tell me, are you going to heed Romero's warning about staying out of the case?"

I barely blinked. "Not if he gagged and bound me naked to Friar Tuck's donut pole."

He grinned. "He might think that has possibilities."

Phyllis stormed in wearing a green dress covered in crêpe leaves. "What has possibilities?"

"Speaking of being gagged and bound," Max muttered.

Phyllis threw her bag on the counter with a whack. Before looking at either of us, she wolfed down two jelly tidbits. "What!" She gawked at Max.

He grabbed an emery board. "Is that another of your homemade dresses?"

"As a matter of fact, it is." She paraded around the dispensary so we could get a better look.

"How long did it take you to whip that up?"

"A few weeks."

"Uh-huh." He tapped the emery board on the counter. "You look like the Green Giant."

"And you forgot to shave this morning."

"Actually, I haven't shaved since Sunday."

"What's wrong?" she cackled. "Your toy razor break?"

Max rolled his eyes. "It's called style. Something you wouldn't know about if you fell over Donna Karan herself. And before you docked in here, we were talking about that hunky cop Romero telling Valentine to stay out of the case."

"Well, he's right, even if his hair's always messy."

Judy came around the corner and hung her smock beside the others. "Morning."

"Do you think he's right?" Phyllis asked Judy.

"Who?"

"Romero!" Phyllis heaved a sigh. "For crying out loud, don't you catch anything? He ordered Valentine at the cemetery to stay out of the case."

"Val's a big girl." Judy gave Phyllis's outfit a strange glance.

"Thanks," I said to Judy. "Okay, we all know Romero's thoughts. Can we get on with the day?"

I headed to the front and opened the blinds. Then I unlocked the door and ripped off the CLOSED UNTIL TUESDAY note I'd taped up Friday. "Don't expect much business." I tossed the note in the garbage. "I'm surprised the phone hasn't been ringing with cancellations."

Max gave me a hopeful smile. "Don't be a pessimist."

"I can't help it. It's my nature." Maybe I'd been heavy-handed and laid the guilt on a bit thick, but losing my star employee was a crisis I wasn't ready for.

"That's right," Judy said. "Things always work out."

Phyllis glared at Judy as if she were an imbecile. "Well, *my* intuition tells me this place is going belly up." She crammed into her smock. "And I should know. I was born with a sixth sense."

"Sick!" Max leaped away from Phyllis. "I always knew you were seriously ill."

Phyllis jabbed her hands in the vicinity of her waist. "Sixth, you dimwit, not sick. Whenever there are weird occurrences, I get these strange ideas."

"They call that schizophrenia," Max said, "but I think you're on to something."

"You'll see. When things fold, I'll be moving on."

Maybe this was an answer to prayer. Truth was, I couldn't have cared less if Phyllis quit. She'd moved from job to job so many times, she was like those cartoon termites that ate away a house in no time flat. Two years at Beaumont's was long enough. With any luck, she'd push off soon.

As it turned out, I didn't need to worry about losing business. It was probably the busiest day in Beaumont's history. Of course, this presented a whole new set of problems. Ten minutes before opening, I felt a mixture of panic and exhilaration. The phone started ringing off the hook. New clients pushed their way in, nobody knew where to sit, cameras clicked, and appointments complained they should be at the front of the line.

Judy manned the phone. I turned off the music. Max did one of his ear-piercing whistles. Nobody paid attention. Then Phyllis whipped off her smock and twirled it in the air. Nothing.

"Is this your idea of things going belly up?" Max shouted to her over the din.

Phyllis snatched a brush and hand mirror off the counter. Then she shot up on a chair and gave the mirror a wicked bang. The mirror smashed into a thousand pieces and shattered on the floor.

"Look!" a camera guy in army fatigues said. "It's Peter Pan on steroids."

Phyllis gave a mean glare. "If you don't all shut up and sit down, we won't serve you!"

"Are you the one who found the body?" another person asked.

"And I won't answer any of your stupid homicide questions."

There was some grumbling. Then a woman raised her hand. "Where do we go if we want you to do our hair?"

Phyllis gave a that's-better nod and pointed to the left.

Everyone peered left and shuffled right.

I crouched to sweep broken glass when someone tugged my arm. I looked up at the army guy and almost got knocked in the head by his huge state-of-the-art camera.

"Can I take pictures of the crime scene?" he asked. "It's for my scrapbook."

"The only crime scene in here is that." Max pointed at Phyllis climbing down the chair, ass in the air. "But if there's an ultrawide lens on that gadget, you'll probably get a decent shot."

At six o'clock, I collected my things and hurried to the back door. Despite today's chaos, I was relieved people hadn't written off Beaumont's. I wanted to deposit the day's windfall, swing by Albert's, then drop in on the Cutlers. Max politely offered to close up shop. Things were a little cool between us since our talk, so I thought his intentions were sweet. I'd give him an extra nice Christmas bonus—if he was still around.

An hour later, I'd been to the bank and trucked by

Albert's. I pushed down the anxiety rising in my throat and told myself it'd be easy entering his house and grabbing the envelope. After all, if I was going to see this case through, I had to take charge and show some pluck.

The key was where Albert said it would be, as was the envelope. I didn't snoop around because, for one thing, it felt creepy being alone inside Albert's house, and for another, the smell of stale smoke was so repugnant, I couldn't wait to get back outside. Of course, I still did a tour with my eyes on the way out, but apart from dirty dishes in the sink, filled ashtrays, a deck of worn cards, and a bag of skinny balloons on a coffee table, there wasn't a whole lot of anything to look at.

I also reminded myself that Albert had invited me inside. If he were the killer, he wouldn't have left anything lying around that would implicate him. Like balloons? Hardly incriminating. I'd once seen him cart that bag of balloons around the kids' ward at the hospital. He'd inflate and twist the balloons into animal shapes for the children. The kids liked the creations. Of course, they liked it more when he whipped out his cards and taught them how to play blackjack.

The only thing nagging me was this brown envelope. I slid back into my car and took a good look at the scratchy handwriting on the front. It was addressed to C.D. Who was C.D.? And who did Albert know at a PO box in Bogota, Colombia?

Colombia. I rolled back the day in my mind, trying to remember if a customer had talked about being there. I'd heard it mentioned somewhere. Perhaps yesterday? At the funeral? Did a family member tell me? Wait a minute. Family. Of course. It was Erik. He told me Saturday he'd have to cancel a business trip to Colombia. *Hmm*. Strange coincidence. Or was it? I couldn't make a connection to the C.D. on the envelope and Erik. Heck, I couldn't even draw a correlation to C.D. and Albert. But a promise was a promise. I gave the envelope a shake and something rustled inside. Pictures? A letter? Baseball cards? I held it up to the light but couldn't make out details.

I hopped back onto Cambridge Street and went straight to the post office where I dropped the envelope in the mailbox out front. Albert was innocent, I told myself. I was helping a friend. Maybe he wasn't a *friend* friend. But I knew I could always count on him. I thought of the time he'd made a delivery and found a fifty-dollar bill beside a car out back. He could've pocketed the money, bought himself a case of beer and a fancy dinner, but he didn't. He brought the crumpled fifty into the shop and asked if anyone had lost it. The client who had dropped it was so grateful he'd returned it, she gave him a kiss on the cheek.

I drove out of the parking lot, took a long glance at the mailbox, and repeated to myself I'd done the right thing. But I still felt squishy inside. Could I go to jail for something as innocent as mailing an envelope? Anyway, the deed was done. Leaving that thought behind, I merged into traffic and ruminated about the Cutlers.

Were Birdie and Betty the twins Hajna saw in my future? I sighed. Had to be. But what did they have to do with the murder? Since Romero had enlightened me about the Women of the Earth feud between them and Portia, the idea of one of them killing her didn't seem so absurd.

I thought back to Thursday and suddenly couldn't be sure if the Cutlers were under the dryers the entire time Portia was in the salon. What if one of them had slipped down the hall and strangled her? They were identical in every sense, except for a beauty mark on Betty's right cheekbone. They even wore matching outfits in complementary colors. Looks aside, they were a couple of feisty ladies with enough gumption to do just about anything, short of skydiving—and probably even that, if they could find helmets that wouldn't crush their hair.

This brought me to my aim tonight. My strategy was to present the twins with coupons when I really wanted to learn more about the bad blood Romero had mentioned. I also wanted to ask about the dedication Erik had told me about, which was also Portia's four o'clock appointment.

I drummed my fingertips on the gearshift as I cruised past Snob West and entered Cutler territory. Here was a select group of stately mansions. Old money. Cars for every day of the week. Staff, upper-crust themselves. The Cutlers weren't cheap by any means, and they didn't need coupons, but they, like everyone else, appreciated a good deal when they saw one. I turned into their long, winding driveway and pulled up beside a beige Rolls Royce. I tightened my grip on the gearshift. Here's to hoping the coupons would make them smile.

I tossed my keys in my bag and fished for my perfume. I needed to freshen up and eliminate the lingering smoky odors from Albert's. I found the bottle and peeled from it several nail stickers. Not surprisingly, the stickers hadn't been put back in their rightful place after my hospital visit, and they were stuck to everything. After I gave myself a squirt of perfume, I fluffed my hair, quickly reorganized the stickers in my bag, and stepped a heel onto the driveway.

Taking a brave breath, I walked to the huge white door, rapped on the gold knocker, and shook out the jitters. A dapper servant opened the door. He wore a tailcoat and white gloves and had nostrils upturned so high it was like looking up a double-barrel curling iron. He gave me a dignified greeting, then gently peeled something from my hair.

"Yours?" He deposited a lollipop sticker in my palm.

"Thank you." I smiled sweetly and stuck the item in my bag.

A second later, Betty skipped to the door zipped in a retro, blue jumpsuit and matching hair band. Her cheeks glowed, which emphasized her beauty mark, and her brown hair was poufed up like a helium balloon. An obvious salvage from the unfinished set last week.

"Well, bugger me!" she shouted over her shoulder. "Birdie, come look who's here!"

The butler flinched from her shrill voice and gave me a slight eye roll.

Betty patted his shoulder. "Be a love, Hedley, bring us cocktails and canapés. Come, duckie." Not the least bit miffed at my dropping in unannounced, she roped me in by the arm and walked me through miles of white carpet and elegant interior. We stepped out onto a massive deck, hedged by an enchanted forest. Leading to the forest were flower paths, carved trees, fountains, waterfalls, and tall statues. I even saw two deer, a raccoon, and a woodpecker nailing a tree.

Betty smiled and displayed a slightly uneven set of teeth. "This was Daddy's love. When he passed on, we decided to never let the gardens die, here or back home at our English estate." She grimaced at the forest. "Enough, you daft woodpecker!"

Just then, Birdie, in identical lilac and matching hair band, jigged onto the deck and gave me a cheery kiss on both cheeks. While everyone was happy, I offered the coupons.

"Valentine," Betty said. "I'm gobsmacked! Free manicure with hairdo?"

Betty waved her coupon in Birdie's face. "Look, mate, when shall we treat ourselves?"

That's what I loved about the Cutlers. They weren't too rich to care about the little things.

They tittered, and I noted how identical they were. The looks. The gestures. The speech. The rubies on their ears. They were like one. "Just consider it gratitude for enduring Thursday's tragedy." I smiled and then sighed. "It'll be strange at work without Portia's visits."

"Blimey," Betty said. "You're right. How could things have turned out any better?" They hooted uproariously.

While I tried to guess the punch line, they took a deep weary breath. I shrugged and figured this was my chance to at least start with the Women of the Earth Society.

I waved toward the forest. "You sure have a talent at making our earth a better place. Have you ever considered starting a club?"

"Oh, pet." Betty sobered. "We already have a club,

which we were pioneers in establishing. It's called Women of the Earth Society. We grow the finest trees, flowers, and plants. And to put it plainly, people know it." She and Birdie did a proud nod. "When someone performs significant good works, say, builds a natural habitat for animals at the zoo or helps others less fortunate, we plant a tree to honor him or her. The person chooses the spot. It's our way of giving back to the community."

"Did Portia belong to your club?"

"Unfortunately, yes." Her back went rigid. "That cock-up."

Hedley brought out a tray of hors d'oeuvres and assorted drinks. We sat on charming wicker chairs, legs crossed, Bloody Marys in the twins' hands, tomato juice in mine. All very civilized. Then Betty dropped the bomb.

"Do you know what that beastly woman did to my dear sister just this spring?" She clutched Birdie's hand. "Birdie had this smashing idea to plant a eucalyptus tree on the fourteenth floor of Typron, in the atrium right outside Mr. Wain's office."

"Mr. Wain?" I asked.

"Forrest Wain of Typron Industries," Birdie said. "He was our last honoree."

"I quite fancied that chap," Betty sighed.

"Mr. Wain is the youngest CEO in Typron history," Birdie said. "Very deserving. He used a share of the company's profits to set up a community center for homeless kids."

"We worked on the project for months," Betty continued. "The day of the April unveiling, Portia turned up early and introduced herself to Mr. Wain as the head of the project. By the time we arrived, she had grabbed all of the credit. We were gobsmacked. It was all rubbish, but Mr. Wain applauded Portia's ingenuity, presented her to his executive staff, and treated her to a lavish dinner. It was in the newspaper and on the telly. You must've seen it."

"I missed it. So what did you do?"

"Not much we could do, pet. We told Portia to get stuffed, but the damage was already done. Mr. Wain thought Birdie and I were simple gardeners with no discerning skills of our own. Here, this whole baby belonged to Birdie."

Birdie sat as stiff as one of their statues. She twisted her pant leg into a ball, her fixed stare causing a chill to run down my spine. She finally released the material and came back to the present. "That was Portia." She gave me a forced smile. "Queen of codswallop."

I smiled carefully, thinking about last Thursday in the salon. I'd just put the Cutlers under hair dryers when Portia waltzed in. She didn't bother to notice them or anyone else because she was too annoyed at having to wait for Albert to make his delivery and leave. And sadly, her commands kept me from noticing any reaction from the twins. I thought about the reason she was in the salon: her four o'clock appointment.

"Were you taking part in the celebration for your newest honoree?"

"Erik Reynolds?" Birdie cut me a cynical look. "After the last cock-up? We weren't even sure we were going to attend."

"But you were getting your hair done just in case."

"Yes." Birdie paused and glimpsed at Betty. "Just in case."

I downed my drink, ill at ease at the shared look between the two. If the real reason they were in the salon that morning was to kill Portia, the only time one of them could've slid undetected from under the dryer and ventured down the hall was when my back was turned while I cut Pace's hair. It was risky, but possible. With all the commotion that morning, I wouldn't have even noticed if one of them had picked up a magazine or gotten a coffee. Music played. Max was busy with his two clients. What was Phyllis doing? Oh yeah. Trying to figure how to do damage on her ninety-year-old lady's hair.

But what about fingerprints? They were dressed in

polka dot dresses that morning, with matching purses, and they'd worn dainty gloves, which they seldom did. Though they'd tucked their gloves in their purses upon arrival, if one of them had gone to use the bathroom and taken her purse with her, she could've slipped on her gloves, quietly entered Ti Amo, and without leaving prints, strangled Portia. Yes, it was quite possible.

This led me to thinking about their hair. Say one of them had been absent from the dryer for even five minutes, her hair wouldn't have dried as fully as the other's. Because they'd both scrambled from under their dryers after we'd discovered Portia, and they'd left that day without me finishing their sets, I didn't get to feel the difference in their hair promptly. Darn. Observing their hair now, I thought Birdie's seemed less wavy. Or was it my imagination?

"Then there was that drama with—" Betty snapped her fingers twice. "What's that bloke's name you were on about?"

"Mr. Wilmont?" Birdie said.

A little bell went off in my head. "Pace?"

"Yes." Betty topped my glass with more tomato juice. "The dishy one in your salon with all the obscene muscles." She shook her small bosom, recalling the obscenity.

"He did some work for Portia a while back," I said.

"You could call it that." Betty grinned at Birdie. They snickered and patted milky white hands to coral lips. "Canapé, lovey?"

I took a cracker topped with cheese and smoked salmon. "Didn't he build Portia a gazebo?"

"He started," Betty said, "but Portia's brassy behavior got in the way."

"How do you mean?"

"It was just over a year ago, in May," Birdie said. "We were all at Portia and Erik's for cocktails before our yearly fund-raiser ball in Boston. It was the usual do at their house—caviar, champagne, chocolate-dipped strawberries.

The Herley Day Trio had the guests mesmerized with their jazzy music."

Caught up in the memory, Betty hummed and swayed in her chair. "Everyone who was anyone was there, and in walked this...this workman, Pace Wilmont." She batted her false lashes. "In a white T-shirt and jeans. Well, that put a spanner in the works. Once Portia caught wind Pace was there, she tore herself away from the next chap she planned to bonk and dragged Pace, or at least tried to drag him, away from the crowd." She giggled. "They had quite a row."

"What happened?" I bit into the cracker, trying not to appear too eager.

"Pace had his hand on her arm in what looked to be a tight grip. It seems Portia wasn't going to pay him in full for the gazebo. I have a suspicion the job was off the cards, so to speak. As the band finished a set, he shouted, 'No, but you didn't mind paying me in full last night.' To that, he was slapped, royally. I never saw the devil in anyone's face before, but the bloke went barmy. If he'd had the opportunity, I think he would've strangled Portia's pretty neck right there and then."

Cream cheese melted on my tongue. "What happened next?"

Birdie's eyes were sharp. "Erik, who obviously understood what was transpiring, had Pace booted off the property. Pace got into a scuffle with a hired hand, knocked over a couple chairs, and sent the chap arse over elbow. The place was a shambles, embarrassing for everyone, but Portia ignored it. 'Drink up,' she said. 'The ball awaits.' And that's the last we saw of Pace."

As I cut across town, I thought about the Cutlers. A jaunty pair, yes, but would they lie? Commit murder? It's not like they had anything to gain, spreading vicious rumors about a dead socialite. Not that Portia would've cared. Her motto was "As long as they talk, dahling, I don't care what they say."

I only knew Portia as a client, but it didn't surprise me she'd been involved with another man. Women like Portia snapped their fingers, and men groveled at their feet. Pace, however, didn't strike me as the groveling type. A bitter affair, though, did explain Portia's scowl toward Pace that morning in the salon, not to mention his vague answers to me about Portia. Had he held that slap against her all this time? He must've been humiliated in front of all those people. But was it enough to drive him to kill?

I got home, washed up, then collapsed into bed. I was nodding off when the phone rang. It was ten-fifteen, and it was my mother. I sighed and fluffed pillows. I knew why she was calling. I might as well get comfortable. I cradled the spiked heel under my ear and waited for her enquiry.

"So?" she asked. "How'd the date go?"

And there it was. "Sorry, Mom. Craig will not be the father of my children."

I heard a huge intake of air. "Are you sure, dear? You've been known to be fussy."

Ten seconds into the conversation and I was agitated. "Mom, this guy flared his nostrils every time a female walked by. I could almost see steam puffing out of his nose. In fact, he looked like a hairy bull. All that was missing was the nose ring. Instead, he wore a huge cross that dangled from a chain thick enough to tow vehicles."

"Well, maybe he's Catholic."

"Well, maybe he is, but anyone who cleans his ears with car keys, hangs out at strip joints, and calls me *babe*, is definitely not seeing *this* face again. I don't care if he's the pope himself."

"Valentine!" I bet she just reached for the aspirin.

"Honestly, I can't handle anymore losers."

"Dorothy Kalk's daughter had worse luck than you, and she found herself the nicest man."

"What, the anemic funeral home guy? With no eyelashes?"

"Terrence. I'm surprised he's not already married."

"Maybe it's because he spends his days stuffing cadavers with silly putty."

"What's wrong with that?"

"He's like the walking dead. He glares at you like he's imagining how you'd look pumped with embalming fluid. Where's the sex appeal in that?"

"It isn't only about sex appeal. If it was, I'd have left your father years ago."

Thank you for that thought.

"Rita even helps Terrence. She does hair and makeup on corpses, though she's not very good at it. I heard she tapes movie stars' pictures to the wall, then makes the dead look like them. Last week, she had ninety-seven-year-old Mrs. O'Donnell laid out, looking like Dolly Parton on her way to the Grammys." She hmm-ed thoughtfully. "Now *that's* something you could do. And you could show Rita how to apply makeup properly."

I didn't know how this conversation had deteriorated, but I hung up and thought my night on the whole hadn't been all bad. My trip to Albert's had been successful, I'd learned more about Portia, and if business kept improving, I wouldn't have to entertain thoughts of beautifying stiffs.

Chapter 7

Wednesday rolled around, almost a week since the murder. Not only was there a killer on the loose, but the clock was ticking on my mortgage payment. I was trying to be positive, hoping the increased business from yesterday was a new trend. But I reasoned this frenzy couldn't last forever. In time, things would slow down, and eventually business would come to a crashing halt. The murder aside, Max, Judy, and I couldn't completely counteract Phyllis's inept reputation. Plus, if I lost Max, then what?

I decided to give it a week. If business continued to increase, I'd have enough money to pay up and get Feltz off my back. If not, I'd go to plan B, once I figured out a plan B.

I splurged on donuts for a second day, wandered out of Friar Tuck's, and glanced toward the clip joint at the other end of the street. Why couldn't a murder have taken place in that shop or Supremo Stylists? Why was I at the front of the line when disaster struck? Added to my problems, right after opening, Judy made another last-minute phone call.

Sick again.

"Will you go see a doctor?" I asked, Max and Phyllis all ears.

"I will," Judy said, and then hung up.

Customers began to stream in, but my mind was still on Judy and how she looked the morning of the murder. Her skin had been pasty, her blond hair unruly, and she'd been perspiring despite the cool AC. Judy was not herself when she shuffled out the door, smock on, head down.

Now, a week later, she was still sick. I explained to Max and Phyllis that we'd be short-handed today. Then we got down to work.

After I finished with two clients, I went into the dispensary to check the appointment book. Max was at the sink in a trendy white shirt and Capri pants, singing "Hey Jude," Judy's favorite song, while he cleaned the high-frequency electrode with a sanitary cloth for the next facial.

"Poor Judy." He patted the foot-long electrode. "She hasn't been herself for a while."

Phyllis strutted into the room and threw her hands on her hips. "Know what your problem is?" She gave me a straight look. "You baby her."

I drummed my fingers on the counter and stared at her blankly, which she took to mean I was giving her the floor.

"You're too easy on the little frump. Poor Judy. Stay home and rest." She stuck her puffy foot in the air with zero finesse. "I stubbed my toe this morning. Boo-hoo. Maybe I should soak my foot in a hot tub all day."

"You'd have to take it out of your mouth first." Max dropped the disposable cloth in the garbage.

"Humph."

"Beautiful retort." Max could be relentless.

"Why don't you just fire the twerp?" Phyllis said. "She's off more than she's here."

Max pointed the electrode in Phyllis's face. "If Val doesn't fire you for being tactless and incompetent, she's hardly going to fire a lovable thing like Judy for being legitimately ill."

Phyllis tramped tight-lipped to a dryer and checked her client. She ripped out the lady's rollers and tapped her well-worn pumps. "Come on." She hurried the lady. "I haven't got all day."

The woman had problems dragging her oxygen tank to Phyllis's station. I wished that for once Phyllis would show some compassion. *Nope.* She rushed the woman along and gave the tank a massive tug. A hose popped off, and the lady made a strange squeaking sound.

"What the—" Phyllis gaped at the severed tube in her hand.

The senior gasped for air. She clutched her neck and pounded Phyllis's back. I was on my feet, choking back panic, mentally preparing to do CPR.

"Phyllis!" Max shouted. "*Do* something!"

"What do I look like?" she shouted back. "A nursemaid?" She plugged the tube helter-skelter into the tank, swatting the woman away with her other hand. Finally, the tube latched on.

The lady took a shaky breath and collapsed in Phyllis's chair. Max got her water, and I waited until the pink returned to her cheeks. Then Max and I slogged back to the dispensary.

"That was close," he said. "Can you see Phyllis as a nurse? Maybe that nurse in *One Flew Over the Cuckoo's Nest.*"

I listened with half an ear. Mostly I was struggling to understand why I was being punished despite my efforts to run a decent establishment.

"And where does she get off talking about Judy like that? She's about as subtle as an elephant in ballet slippers."

I was trying real hard to see the good in Phyllis. "She thinks her ideas are for the best."

"So did Hitler," Max countered.

We were still catching our breath when my next client arrived. She was Asian, east of middle-aged, and came up to my elbows. After she showed me a hairstyle in a magazine, we bowed all the way to my station where conversation was a series of smiles and nods. I pumped up the chair as high as it would go and was snipping coarse black hair, when perky coed Dana Kir bounced in, chewing a fat wad of gum.

Max ran out to greet her and air pecked each rosy cheek. "You ready to finish those highlights?" he asked.

Dana had been stuck with her hair mid-bleach the morning Portia had died, and today was the first chance Max had to tone things down. Dana popped a bubble, then gave a cunning Pollyanna-meets-Paris-Hilton smile. "Ready. But make sure the toner's not too dark and the ends aren't fried. Then I want your best conditioner and a quarter-inch trim."

While Max prepared the toner, I sized up Dana. She wore an orange tank top and her trademark short skirt, which hung well below the belly ring clenching her flat stomach. A fireworks tattoo sat on the left side of her chest, and seven or eight braided rope bracelets decorated her wrists. My gaze roamed up her arms. *Hmm*. Well-toned.

She plunked herself down in Max's chair and turned to me after he draped a cape around her shoulders. "Wasn't that incredible about Mrs. Reynolds?" she asked, freeing her arms.

Incredible was one way to put it, not the way *I* would've put it. But I wasn't a twenty-year-old with a father who sent me to Paris every year on my birthday.

Max glared at the ceiling. "Sit still, love, or Gentle Fawn #4 will be toning your eyebrows."

"Did you know Mrs. Reynolds?" I asked Dana.

"I dated Tad, her son, last summer." She swiped a stray hair from her nose. "But Mrs. Reynolds didn't approve of me. She made my life hell all summer, spying on us, lying to me, hiding Tad's cell phone so we couldn't text, things like that."

She watched me dust hairs from my client's neck. "Tad and I weren't going anywhere anyway." She shrugged. "He dated other girls, but that witch definitely sped up the process." *Snap* went the gum.

I knew the murder was getting to me, but I couldn't help wonder—could Dana have strangled Portia? I remembered Max had just piled bleach on her hair that morning when she'd asked to use the bathroom. What was *I* doing? Oh yeah. *Pace*. I'd left Portia to steam, walked to the front, and found Pace AWOL. Dana went to use the bathroom, and I cleaned around my station. She re-emerged from the back a while later, minutes before Pace.

Dana was gone long enough to snuff out Portia. Again, I thought about fingerprints. If she had killed Portia, her hands must have been covered. And of course, this would hold true for any suspect. Unless the murderer used something else. Like a towel? Maybe. But from where? The stack in Ti Amo hadn't been touched, and the bathroom had a hand dryer. The killer could've used his or her own gloves—as I thought possible with the Cutlers—or swiped a pair of latex gloves. But to find a pair meant digging through Ti Amo's cupboards.

Then there was Portia. If she'd heard anything, she would've assumed it was me preparing the next stage in her facial. Plus, she wore eye pads, steam was blowing on her face, and she was angled away from the door. She probably didn't see her murderer until it was too late.

I nodded and smiled at my customer, but I was really thinking about Dana's capabilities. She looked like an innocent girl who didn't know the difference between platforms and pumps. Yet her assertiveness said she could run a sorority house blindfolded. She seemed to have enough strength to erase Portia from this world. But why would she?

Max rolled his eyes and finally spun Dana's chair around to face me.

"In fact," Dana concluded, "she probably got what she deserved."

I had nothing against Dana personally, but her lack of compassion didn't do a whole lot for my already jaded opinion of her. "Do you still see Tad?" I asked, lowering my lady.

"Just on campus. I wouldn't know what he's up to, or if he's even in Rueland for the summer." She grinned. "But if I were him, I'd be celebrating."

Dana's indifference was overwhelming. I didn't want to be judgmental because it did sound like Portia had been unkind. But suppose this was all fabrication on Dana's part. Suppose Portia *hadn't* interfered in her son's love life. On the surface, Dana seemed like a good match for Tad. Could she have wanted Portia dead for another reason? Or if all this was true, was it enough reason to kill?

Dana left the salon an hour later, just as the Cutlers scurried in. They were dressed in matching white shirts, shorts, and running shoes.

"We were on our way to the country club," Birdie said, "for a little lawn bowling, but Betty got her knickers in a twist."

"Quite," Betty gushed. "Valentine, could we have those free manicures? We can always catch the next round of lawn bowling. But our hair and nails can't wait."

Max was about to begin a facial, so I thought I'd see if Phyllis wanted to start one of the twins, since we often pulled a tag-team on them. Just then the phone rang. And rang and rang. Wondering why Phyllis wasn't answering it, I excused myself from the twins and went into the dispensary.

Phyllis sat on one of the wheeled stools with a double-long hot dog stuffed in her mouth. I pressed my lips together and picked up the phone ringing beside her. It was a disgruntled client that belonged to guess who. Just what I needed. I promised the woman a free haircut, then hung up with a groan.

"What's wrong?" Phyllis asked, mustard smudging her chin.

"Did you not hear the phone ring?"

"It didn't sound like it was for me. Anyway, I'm eating."

I struggled to keep cool and gawked at the spread in front of her. "Slim-Fast and hot dogs?"

"They go good together."

I held in what I really wanted to say and asked if she'd start one of the twins.

She gave me a reluctant nod that meant she'd rather not lift a finger if she didn't have to. Then she washed her hands and plodded to the CD stand by the hallway. "We need music. What does everyone want to hear?"

"How about your footsteps receding in the distance?" Max paused at the hallway, high-frequency electrode in hand. "Hey, we should record that. I bet it'd be a hit."

Phyllis clocked him on the head with a Michael Bublé CD. "Maybe we could record your screams when I rip out your fingernails."

Max ogled me and mouthed, *See? Hitler!* He turned on his heel and marched down the hall.

I clenched my teeth, grabbed a CD from the pile, and slid it in the player. Within seconds, the salon filled with soothing sounds of Harry Connick Jr. Ah, peace in the valley.

I'd just finished removing Birdie's nail polish when she glanced to the other side of the room, then leaned in. "How long do you think Portia's marriage would've lasted had she lived?"

My hands went slack. "Pardon?"

"You know that tart liked to gallivant with every Tom, Dick, and…Pace." She snickered. "But the latest is, hubby's been up to hanky-panky himself."

Erik? The devoted husband? The man who didn't want recognition? Were those tears the other day real? I filed her nails and told myself this was just talk.

"Unlike Portia," she continued in a hushed voice, "we heard he's very low-key about the affair. We don't know who the pet is, but by all accounts he's very taken with her." She lowered her voice even more. "One of the members of the Women of the Earth Society called this morning. She claimed she wanted advice on what to do about Erik's tree. I believe Tess merely wanted to gossip about Portia's murder. She mentioned very casually that she bumped into Erik and a dishy brunette a couple Saturdays ago at Dino Hosta's."

Dino Hosta's was the most luxurious restaurant and

hotel in Rueland. Romantically lit circular booths. Opulent suites. It's rumored Hollywood celebrities stayed at Dino Hosta's when they visited Boston. I'd even dined there on occasion when a date tried to impress me with his financial side.

"Is she sure it was Erik?" I calculated that the date was five days before the murder.

"Tess said she was going in just as Erik and this lady were leaving. The woman had dark hair like Portia, but Tess said she definitely was not Portia."

"Maybe she was a business associate."

Birdie gave me a don't-be-silly look.

"Did Tess talk to him?"

"Erik wouldn't know Tess LaMay from this jar of cream. There are eighty-five women in our club. Though we know who's married to whom, I can't say the same for the husbands."

"How often do husbands make appearances at meetings?"

"Egad! Never. Husbands only grace us with their presence at galas or award ceremonies. They might know their wives' friends, but Erik wouldn't know all the members. And let's face it, Portia had no friends." She sighed with pleasure while I massaged each finger.

I thought back to my visit with Erik. He seemed genuine. Yet what did I really know about him? One, he came in for haircuts, and two, Portia complained he was too humble. "Do you think Portia knew Erik cheated on her?"

Birdie shrugged. "Portia could be dodgy. Blimey, she may have known all along. But I doubt she'd have broadcasted it to the world."

I snapped on the massage cream lid.

"Who knows?" she said. "Maybe Erik even wanted a divorce."

"Or Portia confronted him about the affair."

"Both are excellent motives for murder."

I agreed, not taking this lightly. If anything, I was eager

to continue in my search for Portia's killer. But my next plan was to visit Judy. I wanted to hear she'd been to the doctor. Filling in for her was no easy task, considering I was operating with a deficit—named Phyllis.

The Cutlers left, and I was deciding what to order for lunch when Phyllis's color client chuckled at something she read. I was thankful for that because the color Phyllis had slapped on earlier crept down her face like melted icing on chocolate cake. Phyllis was in the dispensary, nose-deep in carbohydrates, ignoring the running dye.

I dashed to the doorway. "Phyllis," I whispered, "the timer rang five minutes ago."

She stretched her neck past my shoulder and gave a flippant wave. "She's fine. I'll wash her off when I'm done with my pretzels."

I glared at the crinkly bag, and my blood pressure mounted. "It's past the time limit." I tried to sound calm. "Any longer and she'll freak—"

"Aaaaah!"

Too late. I spun around.

The lady was on her feet, nose pressed to the mirror, book strewn on the floor. "Why is my color so dark?" She smeared tint with her fingers. "And why is it running down my face?"

"It'll be okay." Ever the fixer-upper, I sprinted for paper towels. Come to think of it, why was it so runny? I sniffed the peroxide bottle on the counter. "Is this what you used, Phyllis?"

Max pranced past me with a dirty mixing bowl and spatula. He went straight to the sink to wash his tools, then stopped short and turned to Phyllis with an I-can't-believe-you're-so-stupid look on his face. "You didn't use that bottle, did you, Phyll?"

"Yes. Why?"

"Because it was empty. I was soaking it with water for recycling. You dimwit. You haven't got an ounce of peroxide on that poor woman's head. No wonder it's running like Niagara Falls."

"Then why is it so dark, genius?"

"Maybe because the minute dye hits air, it starts oxidizing. How on earth did you ever get through beauty school?"

"For your information, smartass, I'm certifiable."

"You mean certified." Max rolled his eyes. "But nobody's arguing with you."

Phyllis chased back a pretzel with Slim-Fast and stormed out of the room. I just stood there, rubbing my forehead, deliberating over this farce in keeping her on. I mean, how bad *would* it be, if, say, she found herself in the unemployment line? She was a fifth or sixth cousin twice removed. I was more closely related to Kim Kardashian.

Phyllis forced the hysterical woman into the chair, and the lady popped up like a jack-in-the-box. "So it's a little dark." Phyllis yanked her down again. "It's not like it won't fade in three or four weeks."

Tears streamed down the woman's cheeks, making one hell of a mess. "But I wanted my hair tawny brown," she said. "And I've always been self-conscious about the downy fuzz on my cheeks. Now it looks like I have a beard."

"Nobody's going to notice your beard," Phyllis said. "They'll be too busy staring at your nose."

Max dropped his bowl with a clunk.

"Anyway, brown's brown," Phyllis said. "I just did what you asked. Now stay put so I can wash it off."

I trudged to the office to pray and think about something other than my only-intervene-when-absolutely-necessary philosophy. Phyllis was what she was. She couldn't cut her way out of a streaking cap, but she did have a few dedicated clients. They were nearsighted and hard of hearing. Still, they never complained.

It'll all be over soon, I told myself. The case. The setbacks. The challenges. What was I talking about? Albert was missing, Pace had been under the sheets with Portia, Erik was having his own affair, Judy was ill, and the salon was turning into a sideshow for thrill seekers. And I was pretty sure we'd just lost another client. I tried to decide which was worse when Phyllis traipsed in a minute later like nothing had happened.

"You going to Kuruc's?" She counted quarters and dimes in her hand.

Max slipped in behind her and smacked a twenty-dollar bill on my desk. "What are you going to buy with that?" he asked Phyllis. "A pickled egg?"

"I can pay Val later."

"Oh, sure. Like you paid her for the pastrami sub last week. And you just ate half a pig *and* a bag of pretzels. How can you be hungry?"

"All this extra work yesterday and today has given me an appetite."

I checked my bag to see how broke I was. I found Pace's folded bills. "It's okay. I'll cover it."

Max gawked at me. "Quit enabling her. She'll never pay you back."

I heard his words, but I couldn't stop worrying about the client in the next room. "How's your lady, Phyllis?" I peeked out the door.

"She's sedated."

I shifted my gaze back to her. "What do you mean— sedated?"

"Her head bumped a little hard on the sink when I rinsed her. She's having a power nap."

Max and I bolted out of the room and stopped dead at the customer's feet. Her head was back in the sink, jaw slack, conditioner doing its job.

"Do you think we should wake her?" Max whispered.

My heart was racing, and I could barely contain my fear. "What if she has a concussion?" My voice rose. "Or worse. She's *dead*."

"Don't think like that." He leaned down. "I can hear her breathing."

I bit my lip, hoping he was right. Inside, I was freaking out. Phyllis had totally crossed the line. And the truth was with every passing day I was having a hard time justifying keeping her on. Then a little voice inside my head said this wasn't about Phyllis or her ineptness or even unhappy clients. It was about keeping a promise to a grandma I'd loved. If I didn't have that, what did I have?

Phyllis motored up behind us. "You know what we need around here? One of those toaster ovens. Then we wouldn't need to run to Kuruc's all the time. And another thing. When are you going to invest in an elevator? I'm tired of climbing up and down those wretched stairs for laundry and to use the fridge."

"Do the math, dearie," Max said. "As long as you're here, that's not likely."

The client stirred and opened an eye. "Oww, I have a headache."

"It's just color fumes," Phyllis said. "Go back to sleep."

Max swaggered into my office after closing and flung himself onto the swivel chair. "Whew!" He swung his leg over the armrest. "What a day."

"Mmm." I cleaned my desk, not daring to catch his eye. "I wonder how the competition's handling our success."

"Subtle, Val. Look, they want to see me after work Saturday. I'm only talking to them."

"So you're going through with this." The moment he set foot in Candace's salon, that'd be it.

"It's simply an introduction."

I could feel myself getting worked up, but there were too many other troubles vying for my attention. If Max left, I'd have to accept it. I couldn't take it personally. I had my own dysfunctional business to run *and* a murder to get through. "Where's Phyllis?" I asked.

"She left. Shopping for a friend's son's graduation. Did you know she had a friend?"

I shook my head. "One day she's going to dump a pot of hot wax on you."

"At least I'd get rid of these monstrosities." He grinned

and smoothed a perfectly defined eyebrow. "She does have a temper, doesn't she?"

I ceased tidying my desk, and we stared unblinking at each other.

"Are you thinking what I'm thinking?" he asked.

I swallowed hard. "What are you thinking?"

"That it's possible? Right under our noses?"

"Phyllis? A killer?"

He shrugged. "Remember when Dana used the bathroom? Phyllis practically chased her down the hall with the laundry basket when she went to do towels. Maybe she went into Portia's room first and killed her. It's possible. And she's strong enough to overtake the Hulk. Let's face it. You could plow a field with Phyllis."

It was conceivable a woman could strangle someone, wasn't it? I *had* considered Dana. And what about the Cutlers?

"Or," he said, "she could've thrown the towels in the washer, crept back up, snuck into Portia's room, and before anyone was the wiser—" He made a choking noise and yanked an imaginary rope at his neck.

"One problem with your theory. What about motive?"

This stumped him. "What's anyone's motive? Rage. Jealousy. Fear. Insanity. Greed."

I rubbed my tired eyes and yawned. "I guess Phyllis possesses most of these traits."

"It had to be someone at the salon that day," he argued. "It wasn't me, and I'm betting it wasn't you."

"Gee, thanks." I rolled my eyes. "If it *was* Phyllis, she performed an unbelievable stunt by fainting when she found Gavin and taking the wax pot down with her."

"Yeah, there is that." He shuddered as if to shake off the whole affair, then jumped out of his chair. "Be right back."

He disappeared around the corner and bounced back with a magazine in hand. "So how are you wearing your hair for Saturday's date with Jason? It'd look stunning up like this."

I took the magazine and stared at the model on the page. "Date?"

He rammed his hands on his hips. "Valentine."

I was in trouble when he used my full name.

"Don't tell me you forgot about this hot date."

"I forgot about this hot date." I handed him back the magazine.

"I arranged this a month ago. You are *not* backing out."

"Come on, Max. I just endured a disastrous evening with a guy who cleans his ears in public. If this guy's so hot, why isn't he taken?"

He leaned against the doorframe. "I don't know. But you're not getting out of this. Jason is one of my brother's best friends. He needs to get active again."

I sliced my eyes at him. "What's that supposed to mean?"

"He had a little accident, but he's fine. You'll absolutely go gaga over him."

I felt like stomping my feet—like it would do any good. "Oh, all right."

"You won't be sorry. Dino Hosta's never disappoints."

"Dino Hosta's?"

"Yeah, I know. One too many bad dates there."

"No, no." I grabbed back the magazine, my wheels already in motion. "I look forward to meeting…uh, Jason. Saturday night."

"Right." His eyes narrowed shrewdly. "Eight o'clock."

After work, I stopped and bought fish-flavored niblets at Perdu Pets for Judy's cat. Then I filled the car with gas and headed to Judy's apartment on the edge of town. I could've gone home and dreamt of my next failed blind date, and I could've spent the rest of the night tracking a killer, but I had to make sure Judy was okay.

Initially, I'd planned to grill her about skipping work half a dozen times in the past month. It's like she was taking advantage of my leniency, and the comings and goings were beginning to leave heel marks on my back. But the more I thought about it, the more I was certain Judy was not herself. Her full cheeks seemed hollow, her skin was pale, and I could've sworn she'd lost weight.

The last boyfriend took off years ago, so I didn't imagine she'd been pining over him. Then it struck me. Maybe Judy was gravely ill. She would've said if she had a virus. But what if she was terminal? My chest ached as this new thought took root. I wanted to be wrong. I'd rather hear she'd been fasting, had a tapeworm, overused laxatives. Anything was preferable to learning she was terminal. Whatever it was, I had to find out.

Judy's building was a dark brick, four-story with balconies on every level. She buzzed me into the building, and I waited for the door to lock behind me. Call it paranoia. I scouted the lobby, gave a tired glance at the stairs, then stepped into the elevator and rode to the third floor. Judy opened the door, cautioning me to be careful Princess didn't get out.

Princess was Judy's short-haired black cat. She wove around my legs, purring, looking up to see what I'd brought her. I knelt beside her, and with Judy's okay, I poured out some niblets. She blinked her pretty green eyes at me and nuzzled her nose in my hand. I smiled while she ate and turned my gaze to the living room.

Judy was neat, professionally speaking. Here, dirty clothes, empty food cartons, crumbs, and cat hair covered everything. On top of the mess, the place smelled musty. Probably because the windows were shut and it was more than a touch warm.

Judy rolled her bike aside for me to get by. "Sorry. I've been sleeping."

No wonder, in this sauna. I could probably sleep standing. I left the niblets for Princess, swung my hair off my back, and joined Judy in the living room.

"I went to the doctor," she said.

This was a good start. "What'd he say?"

"It's embarrassing. Anyway, it'll pass. Do you want a drink?"

It'll pass? Okay. I followed her into the kitchen. "Water, thanks." I wiped my sweaty brow and decided to change the subject. "Customers are asking about you."

"It's nice to be appreciated." She handed me a glass of water and poured one for herself.

I needed to pick up the conversation. I drank some water, then made my voice upbeat. "Speaking of customers, does Erik say much about Portia when he's in for cuts?"

She raked a curl behind her ear. "No. Why?"

"I returned Portia's sweater the other day and realized I barely know him."

There was a crash and hiss across the hall, startling us both.

"Darn cat." Judy shuffled to the spare room. I trailed behind. Princess was crouched on the bed, looking down at a pile of boxes, books, and a broken lamp on the floor.

"It's like she's trying to find something," Judy said, picking up glass. "Listen, Val, I'm sorry I've missed so many days. I'll be back Friday, and I'll work late if it helps."

At times, Judy seemed more like a sister than an employee, so it was doubly hard seeing her like this. "Just get well," I said, helping clean up.

She reached for Princess and cuddled her. "I will, and you'll see, I'll be the model employee."

I sighed, thinking about Phyllis's last performance. "You will be, just by showing up."

Chapter 8

We somehow managed to keep up the steady stream of clients Thursday and Friday. Except for another uneventful drive by Albert's, I hadn't investigated or questioned any more suspects. Then, Friday afternoon, Mrs. Benedetti walked in.

Mrs. Benedetti had five daughters, three Mafia-linked sons, and ten grandchildren. To erase the hands of time, she had a facial and then purchased a beauty kit regime to keep her breasts from sagging and face from wrinkling. She was thirty years too late on both counts, and plastic surgery wasn't my department. But the next best thing came to $387.10.

Mrs. Benedetti snapped her purse shut. "When I look like Gina Lollobrigida again, that no-gooda husband of mine will be sorry he took off with his bookie's wife. Stupido man." She pinched my cheek and pressed a ten in my palm. "Arrivederci, Valentina."

I rubbed some feeling in my cheek and scooted into my office to zip the tip in my bag. Then I saw the earring. I pulled it out and glared at it as if it could talk. *Tell me*, I said mentally, *did you belong to Portia?* If she lost the studs at home like Erik had said, then who did this belong to? I carted it to the dispensary where Max mixed tint and nibbled on a red pepper from a veggie platter he'd brought to work. He stopped what he was doing and gave me the eye.

"In what century do you think I'll convince Mrs. Bartok that once you hit eighty, jet-black hair isn't so becoming?"

I gave him a pat. "You'd be better off not arguing with her."

"Easy for you to say. You pawned her off on me four years ago." He shook the tint bottle and gave me a miffed look. "I'll never forgive you for that either."

I snitched a carrot stick off the platter. "You have to admit she *is* a steady customer."

He rolled his eyes. "Yeah, if only I could get her to like Phyllis."

I opened my palm under his nose.

"What is *this*?" He thumped the bottle on the counter.

"Have you seen it before?"

"No, I have not. What a beaut!"

Judy entered the dispensary and grabbed the broom. "Whew! That kid was bad. He should learn manners from those sweet kids you visit at the hospital."

I watched the pint-sized menace leave with his father. Then I showed Judy the earring.

She leaned on the broom, studying it alongside Max. "It's gorgeous. Where'd you get it?"

"I found it under the magazine table the day after the murder when I cleaned the salon. Thought one of you might know who it belonged to."

"Sorry." Judy went to sweep hair from under her styling chair.

Max tugged on latex gloves with a loud snap I suspected was meant for me. "If you don't find the owner, I'd be happy to take it off your hands."

"I'll keep that in mind."

I looked past him at Phyllis. She was leaning over a woman, doing a makeover on her. I'd ask Phyllis about the earring later.

"Oww!" the woman screeched. "You poked me in the eye with that thing."

"Well, if you'd hold still." Phyllis waved the mascara wand in the air. "Anyway, how do you expect me to lengthen your stubby eyelashes?" She shoved the wand back in its base. "You might as well forget it. Nothing's going to help you."

The woman sat up, looked at herself in the mirror, and shrieked. "I look like Alice Cooper!"

"Who's she?" Phyllis asked.

The lady shook her head, ripped the tissue from her neck, and stamped out the door.

Phyllis shrugged, then pushed past Max into the dispensary. "What were you guys debating?"

Max was leaving the room but circled back and gave Phyllis a wary eye like he'd been doing all day. "Val thinks you're dense. I think you're plain insane. You yourself said you were certifiable."

I yanked him aside and held up the earring. "Phyllis, have you seen this before?"

She barely took a peek. "Yes."

My eyes widened. "You've seen this earring before?"

"How many more times are you going to ask, because I'd like to go home by supper."

"Why?" Max said. "Was there a sale on buffalo this week?"

Phyllis flicked the mascara wand in his face.

"Okay, Phyllis." I spoke calmly. "Who does this earring belong to?"

"Anyone can see it's Portia's. Who else would wear a rock like this?"

Good point. The only other clients who might wear large gems were the Cutlers, but they stuck to their antique ruby heirlooms.

"We know it couldn't belong to you," Max said. "You only wear plastic jewelry."

I slid my index finger across my neck at Max. "When did you see it on Portia?" I asked Phyllis. "She never wore jewelry when she came in, except for that mammoth diamond ring."

Phyllis jerked her smock tighter, which made her resemble a red-haired Michelin Man. "I don't know *when* I saw it, but it's something she'd wear." She glanced out at Judy, sweeping the floor. "Like a dowdy dress is something Judy would wear."

"There's a problem with your theory," I told her. "I showed Erik the earring. He said it couldn't have been Portia's. Though she had a similar pair, she'd lost hers at home."

"Then how'd it get here, Sherlock?"

"I've been wondering the same thing."

"Don't look at me."

"We're trying not to," Max said. "But your size does make it rather difficult."

I gave Max a you're-not-helping stare. He shrugged and exited the dispensary with his applicator in hand.

Phyllis reached for the earring. "Do you want me to see if anyone knows anything?"

I pulled back. "It's all right. I'll handle it."

"Suit yourself. By the way, how long do you think it'll take me to get to the Cotton Gin by bus Sunday afternoon?"

"I don't know. Half an hour? Why don't you drive?"

"I'm having my car seat reupholstered over the weekend, so it'll be out of commission. And I need to pick up material and thread to finish my outfit for Oscar's culinary graduation."

"Oh." Phyllis drove a big beluga of a white car with rusty patches and seats with little to no stuffing. I couldn't blame her for sprucing things up.

"Of course, if someone was willing to pick me up, I wouldn't turn down the offer. I don't do so well on long bus rides."

I ignored the hint. Taking Phyllis to the Cotton Gin had about as much appeal as shaving my head bald with a dull razor. Plus, I was pretty sure I was going to be busy. "Did I say half an hour? With that new section of paved road by Clem's Bakery, you should make it there in fifteen minutes. Maybe ten."

She nodded glumly and moved on to her next customer.

I extinguished the guilt stirring inside me and cut my next client's hair. Wisps of hair floated to the ground, but my client was too busy rifling through a stack of mail to notice.

"Bills. Bills. Bills." She sighed. "Why couldn't I get a juicy love letter once in a while?"

We laughed a little over this and suddenly I thought about the letter I'd mailed for Albert. I bit my lip. Had I done the right thing? Shoot. Why was I having second thoughts?

I finished my lady's hair, took her money, then slid into my office to phone Tom, my order man from Alluve. I had to see if Albert was back.

"The answer's no," Tom said.

"No, you're not going to tell me, or no, he's not back at work?"

"Door number two. But the cops are visiting regularly."

This wasn't good.

"I did hear from him though."

"You did?" I grabbed a pen and paper. "When?"

"Just yesterday. I guess he feels guilty about taking off without notice."

Yesterday was one whole week since the murder. "So where is he? Did he leave a number?"

"Uh…no."

"Why not?"

"I guess because he's a free spirit."

"He said that?"

"Indirectly."

I had enough of this cat and mouse game. "Tom, what exactly did Albert say?"

"He's at his sister's in Colombia."

"As in South America?"

"Well, it's not as in the District of."

I visualized the envelope I'd mailed with the C.D. and Colombian address. C. Dougal perhaps? I'd mailed something to Albert's sister? But why, if Albert was with her? And why was she in Colombia? "Did he mention his sister's name?"

"Unh-uh."

"Say why he went?"

"Nope."

"When he'd be back?"

"Nada."

My frustration was building. "Does he realize there's a murder investigation back in the good old US of A and he's a prime suspect?"

"Uh, I may have tried to slip in that part."

"And?"

"And he said he'd be back when he'd be back."

Oy. Was I the only one concerned about Albert going back to jail? "Look." I calmed my voice. "If he calls again, please have him phone me."

"I will." He sobered. "Valentine, I'm sorry if I was flippant."

"It's okay." I hung up, sorry I may have been wrong about Albert. The thing was, if he'd been back at work, it might've meant he was innocent. On the other hand, it also would've meant I was no closer to catching a killer. And none of this revealed what was in the envelope, except for the fact that I may have aided a murderer by sending it. Well, I wasn't done yet. I had a blind date at Dino Hosta's that might lead to something, and I still had another person to interview.

This brought me to real estate agent Gavin Beck, the lucky guy who found Portia. Or did he? Since I didn't have any leads from that rat-fink Romero, I had to conquer my nerves, forget about my altercation with Pace, and forge ahead with the last suspect on my list.

I googled Beck & Associates and found their website. There was a picture of curly-haired Gavin on the homepage, posing like George Washington on a dollar bill. "Trust in Me" was his logo. I called the number, said hi to Gavin, then heard a loud click.

What? I gaped at the phone. Were we cut off? Or did he not wish to speak to me? Good thing I didn't deter easily. I punched the big number pad again, figuring the only way to gain his interest was to speak his language.

"I'm too busy, Valentine," he said, after I got through, "to answer more questions about the murder. So if you called about the case—"

"No. I called because I have a business proposition for you." I could tell he wasn't popping balloons with enthusiasm, but at least I had his attention.

"I'm listening. What can I do for you?"

"It's more like what I can do for you."

"I don't follow."

"I'm interested in giving you some business." I could almost hear a cha-ching in the background. "Meet me at the salon tonight after closing. I'll explain then."

It wasn't pure genius, but there was more than one way to cut hair. And I was about to clip this baby to the bone.

It was after seven, and my stomach was growling. Max and Phyllis had gone, and Judy was in Molto Bella with her last client. I trotted downstairs, pulled out my mother's spaghetti and meatloaf container from the little freezer in the fridge, and climbed back upstairs.

I walked past Molto Bella and stopped when Judy and Mrs. Sojka emerged from the room.

"That holistic treatment was wonderful, Judy." Mrs. Sojka smiled from Judy to me and then yawned. "Good night, girls. I'm going home to bed. Hank can get his own supper."

"I'm off, too," Judy said. "Everything's cleaned up in back."

"Thanks." I smiled at her efficiency. "Lock the door when you leave. I'll be here awhile."

Minutes later, I'd nuked my food and was in my office, slurping spaghetti, trying to decide what I was going to say to Gavin. My main problem was I didn't know him very well. Aside from pleasantries uttered when he was in Max's chair, conversation was at best stilted. And if I weren't so driven to unearth the real murderer, I wouldn't be speaking to him tonight. Still, there were questions that needed answering.

Like why'd he go into Ti Amo in his boxers when Portia was in the middle of her facial? Was it to chat? To show off his tiger-striped shorts? To sing a song? What was he hiding? And more importantly, could he have been the murderer? I shuddered and recalled the tension on Gavin's face when Portia entered the shop that morning. I knew it was far-fetched, but what if *he'd* had an affair with her, too? Who's to say Pace was the only other man she'd been with? Though Gavin's money and power would've held an appeal to Portia, the notion of them playing tango beneath the sheets boggled my mind.

The bell rang, shattering my deliberation. I hustled to the back door and let in Gavin.

He gave an anxious peek over my shoulder.

"We're alone," I assured him, though I didn't know why he was agitated. *I* was the one alone with a potential killer.

Gavin was short and built like a clay creation with toothpick arms and legs. He was in a shirt and tie and slightly outdated dress pants tucked under his belly. I guessed he was mid-fifties by the forming jowls and strong nose-to-mouth folds. "Great." He pecked his head back and forth like at any minute he was going to lay an egg.

His jumpiness made this whole idea a giant red flag in my head. But I stuffed down my reservations, put one foot in front of the other, and led him down the hall. Once we were in the main salon, he leaned over a dryer chair and propped open his briefcase.

"Okay." He straightened. "What can I do for you?"

I roamed the salon and touched the dryers with fondness. "Business has slowed since, well, you know." I laid it on thick. "I thought it's time I considered selling the building."

"You *are* in a good zone," he said, buying my act. "Since I deal mostly in commercial real estate, you came to the right place."

"Good. Then what do you think for an asking price?"

He smoothed his tie. "First, I'd have Barry come in and do a routine appraisal."

"Who's Barry? I called *you*."

"I could give you a number, but what if I cheated you out of a bigger piece of the pie?"

"Then I'd eat cake."

He puffed out his cheeks, his freshly permed brown curls doing little for his bulging red face. "Okay, Valentine. Let's see what you've got."

I gave him the grand tour. He commented on lights and mirrors and stated what stayed if the building sold. I hurried him through the kitchen, storage, and laundry room in the basement. Then we arrived at the top of the stairs, a few feet from Ti Amo's doorway. Instinct told me this could be a dicey move, but I ushered him into the room anyway. I wouldn't learn anything talking real estate all night.

I waited while he did a few shoulder jerks. Then I asked the big question. "Why did you come in here when Portia had her facial?"

"That was between her and me." The twitch in his cheek told me he was back at the murder scene. "We needed to straighten something out."

"In your boxer shorts?"

He sighed heavily. "She tried to ruin me, okay? Didn't matter anyway. When I got here, she was already dead. I was so startled I tripped on that screwy machine."

"Sounds like you and Portia had a history."

He shook his head. "I only met her when I sold Erik his office building years ago. Then she came to me in April, wanting to buy the Zudora mansion north of Boston."

I listened and noticed the wax pot hadn't been shut off. I flipped the switch, then sat on the facial stool.

"I usually stick to commercial real estate like I told you. But this was a three-million-dollar deal. I couldn't let the commission go. So like any good agent, I presented her offer to the seller."

"And?"

"The seller refused it. Not at first. But another offer came in the same afternoon. It was a cash deal for another ninety thousand. Mr. Zudora accepted it. He wasn't interested in a bidding war." He mopped his oily brow with a hanky, then stuffed it in his pocket. "When I told Portia the news, she said she'd sue me, the seller, and the other agent." He threw his hands up in the air. "Sue the world! She called me unprofessional, ill-prepared. Accused me of being incompetent. I wanted to set her straight. If she'd been in my shoes, there's nothing she could've done differently."

I wouldn't have underestimated Portia's capabilities, but this was his moment.

He moved from the fading sunlight seeping through the glass-tiled window. "She spread vicious lies everywhere. Soon I was blackballed. I lost my Boston condo, my golf membership, even my BMW." His face fell. "Now I'm driving a Ford Focus, for crying out loud." He swiped his mouth with the back of his hand, the misery in his eyes morphing into the look of a madman.

I edged off the stool, having the distinct feeling things were about to get worse.

He slashed his fingers through his hair, snarling at me like he was seeing Portia in the flesh. "I had every right to kill you. You bitch. You made my life hell." He tore the high-frequency electrode off the counter, thrust the heavy tool in the air, and thundered for me, calling her name. "I'll never forgive you! *Nev-errr!*"

Fear ripped through me, and I was petrified he was going to play whack-a-mole, with me as the mole. With no time to think, I dipped the wax stick in the pot, twirled it like a baton majorette, and threw it at Gavin.

"What the—" He clapped a hand to his head, and the electrode hit the floor with a solid thunk. "My hair! I'm on fire! Aaaaah!"

"Calm down!" I shouted. "You're not on fire. It's just hair wax."

"*Just!*" With his hand stuck to his head, he ran around in circles as fast as his spindly legs would carry him. "Aaaaah!"

Yep. This was way better than a chance at helping Rita apply makeup at the funeral home. I slid closer and struggled with him while he screamed. I didn't know what to do. The guy tried to harm me, and here I was trying to be compassionate. At the moment, that wasn't working. So I slapped him upside the head, then yanked his hand off the wax that was still stuck to his scalp.

"Huh?" He stopped with a jolt and gawked from his freed palm to me like he was seeing Valentine Beaumont again.

I gave him a moment to get control. Then I took my hand and ripped the wax off his scalp.

"Aaaaah!" he screamed bloody murder, holding his head, bending up and down at the waist. He grabbed my wrist, eyes popping at the hairy piece of wax in my hand. Then he inched his fingers up his scalp. "My head feels like my ass!"

He either meant soft or bumpy. Either way I didn't want to know.

"It's not that bad," I said. What *was* bad, I sounded like Phyllis. I dragged him down the hall to my station and held up a mirror. "See?"

He looked as if a speeding treadmill had been snatched from under him. "I look like Moe from the Three Stooges."

I really hated to do this, but I was a stickler for detail. "Actually, it's Larry you look like."

His bottom lip trembled, and I thought I better make things right. "So there's a little bald path down the center. Let me cut the rest to match."

"What?" he shrieked. "Don't touch me!"

"Come on. Nobody wears their hair in an Afro anymore. I'll cut off the waxy bits."

"You stay away from me!" He backed up, grabbed his briefcase, and darted for the door. "And when you're ready to sell, *don't* call!"

I wasted no time locking up and heading home. The whole Gavin thing gave me the creeps. In fact, the past week made me feel like Alice in Wonderland, only my rabbit hole was the salon and the peculiar characters were my clients. But I wasn't Alice. I was a grown woman, physically anyway. That aside, it struck me that everyone except Albert had a reason for wanting Portia eliminated from this world. Of course, I wasn't sure about Albert anymore either.

I turned into my driveway, shut off the engine, and stared at my pretty yellow house. It wasn't big, it wasn't fancy, and technically it wasn't mine. But I loved my little rental and my diverse neighborhood all the same. This got me thinking about Portia and her big fancy house—a house many could only dream of owning. Why was she so desperate to move? Wasn't she happy in Snob West? Was buying a mansion an attempt to save her marriage? Or did her lavish spending just give Erik one more reason to see her dead?

I mounted the porch steps and stopped dead in my tracks. Sitting in front of the door was a blank envelope. Strange place to leave mail, considering there was a perfectly good mailbox nailed to the wall three feet away. I took a cautious look over my shoulder and scooped up the envelope, trying to curb the uneasy feeling creeping over me.

Then the phone rang. I jumped for the setting sun and almost flew back down the steps. Sighing at my jitteriness, I steadied my legs, let myself inside, and flicked on the light. I picked up the cordless handset off the Pooh phone and took a quick look around.

It was Romero, and he didn't sound happy. "What do you think you're doing?"

I swallowed, relieved it was him, even if he did sound as grouchy as he'd been when I last saw him at the funeral. "Thought I'd put on a *Seinfeld* DVD. I could use a good laugh."

"So could I. Especially after I learn you not only deliver Portia's sweater to Erik, but you visit the Cutlers and keep driving by Albert's."

I kicked off my shoes and waited for him to say someone saw me enter Albert's house, but he didn't. And I didn't volunteer it. I'd probably be in big doo-doo if he knew I'd mailed something for a prime suspect, especially to a location where said suspect was likely stationed. I collapsed on the couch and fiddled with the envelope.

"Is there anything else you plan on doing that I should know about?"

I huffed. "What makes you think I delivered a sweater?"

"I'm a cop, remember?"

"Is returning someone's belongings a crime?"

"The crime here is that you're not listening very well."

"You're right. I'm not listening." I hung up with a self-satisfied smirk. I'd had a rough night. I didn't need a sermon from Father Romero.

I took a moment to calm down, then focused on the envelope. I held it up to the light. I gave it a shake. Whatever it was, it was weightless. I ripped it open when the phone rang again.

I shot back, half expecting Romero's arm to reach out through Pooh's honey pot and throttle me. Best to let the machine take it. When I heard Holly's voice, I sighed with relief and picked up. She started in with the same lecture, but after hearing it from Romero I was in no mood.

"Let me ask *you* something," I said. "Why am I being followed?"

"You're not being followed, per se," Holly said. "But because of your past, uh, police involvement, they want to keep an eye on you."

I slapped the envelope on the coffee table. "Is my phone being tapped, too?"

"Look, cops will use any method to find a killer, even if it means teaming up with you."

I grimaced at the backhanded compliment. "Well, I don't like being watched."

"Romero's only interested in your safety."

"Ha!" I could be childish and stubborn given the right circumstances.

"I'm not joking. The station's halls are reverberating with his dark mood. I have a feeling it's because a particular exotic beauty's had an impact on him."

"Really?" That slipped out too eagerly. "You couldn't be more wrong. He's only acted professionally toward me."

"Yeah, makes you want to rip off his clothes, doesn't it?"

Secretly, it did, but he'd boiled my blood one too many times. No. Thank. You. Any romantic thoughts I had of Romero would remain buried. "Why is he here in Rueland anyway? Why doesn't he just go back to New York?"

"I don't think that will happen anytime soon."

"Why's that?"

I heard her do a slow sigh, and a troubled feeling worked its way into my gut.

"There was an incident in New York about five years ago," she said. "Just before he came here."

"What kind of incident? And why didn't you tell me this before?"

"I don't know what it was about, but it shook the department. And I didn't tell you because when this whole thing started he didn't seem that important to you."

"He's not," I said quickly. "I...I was just curious."

"Right." The edge in her voice told me she knew better. "Anyway, part of the police surveillance is because I asked Romero to keep an eye on you. I don't want you to get hurt."

Holly was born Christmas Day, three years before I came on Valentine's Day. She always protected me as a kid. Even took out Jamie Santor's front teeth because he'd teased me about our parents' knack for timing in having us. I admired and respected my sister, even feared her at times.

"Stay with us for a while," she said. "The kids would love it. And it'd be a break from their regular routine."

If Holly taught me anything, it was to stand up for myself. "No thank you. Last time I stayed and gave your kids a break from their regular routine, I woke up to find snails in my boots and bubblegum in my hair." Once again, I felt like the baby sister. I'd just have to go about my business and entertain the Rueland police force along the way.

I hung up, stared at the envelope for a second, then freed the note. It was typed and said:

> You're very nice, you're liked a lot.
> As for Portia, she deserved what she got.
> You know you don't need to get in deep,
> Better not continue, or you'll permanently sleep.

Heat rose to my face, and nausea swirled around in my stomach. I forced myself to breathe, but air was caught in my throat. *Don't panic.* It's just a note. Okay. Then why am I shaking? I set the paper on the table. Who could have delivered it? Dana? Pace? The Cutlers? Phyllis?

I cracked my knuckles. I debated calling Holly back but didn't feel like her I-told-you-so speech. Suddenly, watching *Seinfeld* had lost its appeal.

I shoved the note back in the envelope and slid it under the Cinnamon Bun candle. I sat there, knees tucked under my chin, staring at the faint scar on my left hand, courtesy of the perm-rod nutso who tried to kill me. Then I thought about Gavin and the way he attacked me. I really had to think of a better way to protect myself. I couldn't hurl wax at people whenever I felt like it. Or razors. Or dye. I pictured Romero's splotched shirt. Okay, *enough*. I wasn't going down that road again. I was just overreacting. I needed to set my mind on something else.

I flicked on the TV for a distraction. I surfed through a horror movie, a homicide show, and a reality makeover. Sigh. When makeovers didn't appeal, something was wrong. I clicked off the remote and tossed it on the coffee table.

I glanced at the piano. Maybe playing out my frustrations was what I needed. I jumped off the couch and dashed to the piano bench. Heck, I still played a mean sonata. Perhaps it really was time to sell the shop. I could brush up on my technique, try the classical route, or go back to playing in clubs, which I did for extra cash when I first opened the business.

I pulled out some jazz and hammered away, but my timing was off and my fingers were stiff. I traipsed into the kitchen, ran hot water on my hands, and came back to the living room with nimble fingers. I hit the keyboard again, but nothing sounded right and I couldn't concentrate. I slammed down the lid and dragged out a groan.

Damn. What was happening to me? I didn't even recognize myself anymore. Tossing razors? Hurling wax? Who was that person? That wasn't me. That was Twix. Twix! She wanted to be kept in the loop. Well, welcome to it. She'd put things into perspective.

"She's not here," Tony said when I called. "She and the kids are having a sleepover at her parents'. They should be home tomorrow night."

I flopped back on the couch. "Tomorrow, huh?"

"Yeah. She had a list of things to do before the renos, and I'm in and out a lot this weekend. So she left the kids with her mom, then started at the hardware store to look at paint chips."

I sat up. "Wait a minute. Renos?"

"Yeah. She's going ahead with them, and you know

Twix. To save a few bucks, she's going to work alongside the contractor. The guy said he prefers to work alone, but she's pretty convincing."

"Prefers to work alone?" I didn't like the sound of that. "Who'd she hire?"

"His card's here somewhere." I heard him shuffle around the kitchen, then *crash*!

"Shit!"

"What happened?"

"That damn pig. Knocked over the water cooler. I gotta go, Val."

Terrific. I hung up, then tried Twix's cell. It was only nine-thirty. She'd still be up. True, but her cell wasn't on. One time I needed to talk and her phone was off. Fantastic. I couldn't unload to Twix. Worse, I wanted confirmation about who she hired. Like I didn't have enough to worry about. I'd give Tony time to wipe up the mess, then call him back.

I went into the bedroom, stripped out of my clothes, and came back into the living room in my pink Pooh nightshirt and shorts. I curled my feet under me again and stared at the note beneath the candle. After a minute of that, I decided sitting with my feet up wasn't going to solve anything. I lived in a neighborhood full of people. Someone must've seen something.

I marched back into the bedroom, stuffed myself into a pair of yoga pants, wiggled on my flip-flops, and flew out the door. I smelled smoke and instinctively looked to the right. Perfect. Mrs. Calvino was out on her porch, obliterating her lungs. Night had fallen, and she was sitting under her porch light, talking on the phone, moths darting around her head. She waved from her lawn chair, feet up on the railing, cigarette parked in the valley of two fingers. She plastered her hand to her face, inhaled hard, then laughed into the phone while smoke seeped out her mouth and nose. I'd come back to her later.

Except for Mrs. Calvino's laughter and a couple of teens skateboarding down the street, the neighborhood was quiet. I crossed the street under the dimly lit streetlights and went to Mrs. Lombardi's house. At seventy-one, Mrs. Lombardi was as good a Catholic as the pope, maybe even better. Her son was a priest, Chester the poodle was her dearest friend, and her binoculars were the size of a space telescope. If anyone on the street ever needed one of the five *W*'s answered, Mrs. Lombardi was the woman to see. Though she could be surly. It was rumored Mrs. Lombardi liked to dip into the sacramental wine.

I passed the three-foot-high statue on her lawn of the Virgin Mary, then rang her doorbell. Chester yapped from inside and scratched his nails on the door. Mrs. Lombardi answered a moment later in a summer housecoat, a dour look on her face. Her steel-gray hair was disheveled, like she had just run a rake through it, or else I'd woken her.

"Yes? What is it?" She stepped onto the porch, keeping Chester between her wishbone-shaped legs.

"Hi, Mrs. Lombardi. I live across the street."

"I know who you are. You're the one who has a thing for men's genitals." Her face showed no change of expression as her eyes slid up and down my nightshirt.

Chester gave a short, fierce bark.

Right. "I wondered if you saw someone drop an envelope on my porch today."

"Who do you think I am? Agatha Christie? Watching everyone's doorstep, waiting to see who comes and goes?"

"Yes…I mean no."

"Why don't you just open it and find out?" She narrowed her eyes like she was trying to catch me in a lie.

"Good idea." I turned to leave. "Thanks for your help."

"Don't mention it."

Well, that was enlightening. If Mrs. Lombardi didn't see anything, there wasn't much hope anyone else did. But I tried Mr. Brooks since I was passing by. He was in his garage, wiping his lawnmower with a white cloth. Grass and gasoline smells tickled my nose.

"Sorry," he said. "I was in back all day, filling my fishpond. Didn't see a thing."

I tried a few more neighbors, but they weren't much help either, and Mrs. Calvino would be cackling into the phone till Marlboro rolled her next pack of cigarettes.

I plodded home, crestfallen. Honestly, sometimes I felt invisible. How could someone show up, leave a note, and nobody see anything? Well, that's the way it was. Get over it.

I stumbled up the front steps and found the door slightly ajar. I was sure I'd pulled it shut in my haste to run around the neighborhood. Pretty sure.

I looked at Mrs. Calvino. She'd swung her back to me and almost choked on her laugh.

Wonderful. What now? My bag of tools was inside. Not much good to me from there. I forced down the queasiness and told myself I was safe. Too bad my stomach didn't pay attention. It always seemed to know when I was most frightened more than my head did.

I put my ear to the door and listened for sounds. I didn't know what I expected to hear. Someone vacuuming? I watched Mr. Brooks close his garage door, then shut off his porch light. I glanced at Mrs. Lombardi's house. A millisecond later, her lights switched off, too. A door clicked, and a puff of smoke evaporated where Mrs. Calvino had been. Beautiful. All alone, except for my wind chimes tinkling in the breeze. Darn. Now what?

I looked down at the watering can. My only defense. Mentally repeating *you're safe, you're safe*, I gripped the can in two hands, nozzle out, like a gun. I whacked open the door just as a crash came from my bedroom. Charged by adrenaline, I sprinted down the hall, burst into the bedroom, and shrilled *hiyah* like I was Jackie Chan. Chester the poodle pounced off the dresser, knocked the watering can out of my hands, and landed on my chest.

I screamed like a maniac and fell to the floor, sudden tears spilling hotly into my hairline. Damn dog. He must've scooted between Mrs. Lombardi's legs, escaping all her love and attention to make my night even more perfect. Knowing this was the logical explanation didn't help one iota. I sniveled and mumbled like a crazy person. My alarm clock hung from its cord upside down, and my bras were scattered across the room.

"Why me?" Why the note? Had I put a killer on edge?

I wrapped my arms tightly around myself. I hated being scared like this. I had to do something. Take a self-defense class. Or get a dog. I looked around the room. Maybe not a dog. I sniffed. A big strong man for comfort would be nice. Like a teddy bear, only less stuffing.

I wiped my eyes and gulped back a shaky swallow. Romero was like a bear—more a grizzly than a teddy—yet at times I could see myself taking comfort in his arms. Then again, trusting my heart to a man was ten times scarier than being alone *or* unprotected. Shoot. I was pitiful. What would Romero want with someone like me anyway?

I smeared my hand across my runny nose, scraped up the watering can, and staggered to the door where Chester sat, wagging his tail. Lovely. If I wasn't so ticked off, I'd admit the white fuzz ball was kind of cute. I plucked him off the floor, crammed him under my arm like a football, dropped the can on the porch, and stalked across the street.

Mrs. Lombardi was waiting for me. She snatched Chester from my outstretched arms, then slammed the door in my face.

"You're welcome," I said. Loudly.

I padded back across the street, let myself in, and went straight to the kitchen for a shot of, a shot of…right, I didn't drink. I didn't even have a bloody bottle of liquor in the house because I couldn't handle my booze. Well, all I needed was a sip. I banged cupboards. I had to have *something*. Where was that bottle of wine that Twix had brought over for supper that time? Oh, yeah. She'd polished that off single-handedly. Wait. I'd once used Irish Cream in a cake recipe. What'd I do with that bottle?

I dug through the last cupboard, past the toaster and plastic bowls. *Aha.* My little brown jug. I poured out a shot and sucked back some Irish Cream. The caramel taste lingered on my tongue, and a numbness rose from my fingers to my cheeks. I took a deep relaxing breath, put the cap back on, and drifted to the bedroom. After I cleaned up, I floated into bed and fell right to sleep.

Chapter 9

I was amazingly rested the next morning, and it only took two minutes to get the starch back in my legs. I showered, dressed, and was backcombing my crown when it hit me I'd forgotten to call Tony back. I pulled the top part of my hair into a clip and then lunged for the phone. It was only seven-thirty and Tony was home alone, probably catching up on sleep. Unfortunately, I didn't have the luxury to wait. I had to find out who Twix hired for the renos. By surprise, Twix answered.

"I thought you were at your parents'," I said.

"Left the kids there for another night and came back early. I wanted to finish getting this place ready for Monday. We're tearing down the wall between the kitchen and dining room. It's going to look so much bigger."

I wanted to be positive, but I couldn't shake the chill settling on me. "Who did you hire?"

"You'd go absolutely gaga over this guy, Val. He does *incredible* work. He's tall, dreamy, and has these *incredible* muscles."

Fear gripped me. "Twix. His name?"

"Even that's dreamy. Pace Wilmont."

A bitter taste settled in my throat. "You can't hire him."

"What? Why not? He has these large hands, beautiful blond hair, and—"

"I don't care if he has hair like Rapunzel. He's a customer and a suspect in Portia's murder. I don't trust him."

"Oh." I could feel her bubble deflating in her cramped kitchen. "What do you mean, you don't trust him?"

"He had a thing with Portia, and he has a temper." It didn't mean he was a killer, but he was unpredictable all the same. I didn't want to tell Twix he'd attacked me for fear she'd hunt him down and drive a spike through his head. I felt horrible but hoped she'd trust me on this. "Can you find someone else to do the work?"

She let out a loud sigh. "You think hunky renovators grow on trees?"

"It couldn't hurt to look. And you may find someone better."

"Sure. And if I start now, maybe I'll find someone before the kids go to college."

I'd gotten through the day without any last-minute walk-ins and was home getting ready for my big date. To pump my nerves, I had *Scooby-Doo* on the TV in the living room and Sam Smith on ear-splitting beside it. I was gloved into a black halter dress with a slinky rhinestone chain that scalloped the high neckline. It wasn't hot—it was *roarrrr*!

Despite the fact I was all dressed up, I would've preferred to stay home tonight. But if I told Max I bailed on Jason, that would put a bigger strain on our friendship. I knew he meant well and wanted to see me happy, but he didn't realize how vulnerable I was. I didn't want to fall for a guy, then discover he was cheating. I was afraid to have my heart trampled on and cry myself to sleep at nights because I'd been hurt. If I wanted a date, I'd find one on my own. Like shoe shopping. I just needed a good fit. And some sparkle.

At least this date was at Dino Hosta's. I might actually learn something about Erik and the mystery lady Birdie and Betty's friend saw him with.

I took Max's advice and clasped my hair up, leaving a few wisps around my face. Maybe I did dread blind dates, and maybe my heart wasn't into it, and maybe my mind was still on that note, but dressing down was *not* in my vocabulary.

Looking ahead, I danced in and out of the bathroom and gave myself a final spritz of Musk, twirling through the fragrant mist. I pirouetted into the living room and sang sweetly while I slid my feet into black satin, ankle-bowed heels. I zipped up the backs and cranked down the music when three curt knocks hit the door.

I yelped and flung my back to the door. *Relax.* Who could it be? The note sender?

Three more raps. Heavier this time. I tried to rewind to a few minutes ago when I was singing and dancing, but the angst wouldn't let go. I wiped my sweaty hands down my dress and peeked out the window.

Romero stood on the porch in jeans, a black Pearl Jam T-shirt, and an unbuttoned red flannel shirt. Whew. I hadn't seen his face since the funeral. What was he doing here? More interrogating? I shook the nervousness out of my hands and opened the door.

"Ms. Beau—" The rest of my name died on his lips as his gaze worked its way up my legs, slowed at my waist, and stopped at my eyes, which, in all modesty, looked dazzling.

For the first time since we'd met, he was speechless. Not something I would've figured Romero capable of. He went to speak, then swallowed instead.

Instantly, self-confidence came over me. I squared my shoulders, raised my chin, and gave him and his rock shirt a self-assured smile. "You're drooling on my mat, Detective."

The corners of his mouth slid into a carnivorous grin, and by the look in his eyes I knew I'd just been completely undressed. *Ooh!*

He did a quick surveillance of the place, glancing from the TV back to me. "On your way out?"

"As a matter of fact, I am," I said, trying to regain control. "Can we talk?"

"I guess. Come in."

He closed the door behind him. "Nice place." He studied the room over my head. "Not what I expected."

"What did you expect?"

"Modern. Chrome. Sectionals. Carpet. Definitely not overstuffed furniture, pine floors, and—" He looked to his right. "Is that Winnie the Pooh?"

I glanced at my phone. "Yes."

He stepped over, picked the handset off Pooh's tree trunk, and shook his head.

I tapped my fingers on my thigh and waited while he returned the handset. Then he gazed across the sea of sparkly pillows and back to me.

"The glitter isn't surprising. I knew there'd be lots of that." He leaned down and breathed so close, it tickled my neck. "And I'm beginning to expect the floral fragrance. It's your signature."

The room suddenly seemed small, and my thoughts ran rampant with visions of him pulling me in and kissing me madly. Of course, at the moment, I wasn't even sure what day it was. Determined to look poised, I centered my gaze on the scar on his cheekbone. I inwardly caught my breath at the sexy way it lined his cheek.

"Would you like a drink?" I tamped down the attraction I felt for him. I had an eight-o'clock date, damn it. Why didn't I rush him out the door so I could meet Jason at Dino Hosta's? Okay, maybe I knew the answer to that. I gazed back up into his piercing blue eyes, enjoying the warmth I felt from the way he stared at me. "I have orange juice, apple, strawberry, peach."

He shook his head no, then backed me into the living room. "I have news on Albert." He stopped to smile at the beanbag chair, then grasped a white, beaded, silk pillow from the couch.

"You do?"

Wordlessly, he tucked the pillow back in place while Sam Smith sang about staying with him. We locked eyes, and my face flushed. The sexual tension was so thick a machete couldn't cut through it.

I rushed over and shut off the music once and for all. Fiddling with the ring on my index finger, I blurted, "Is this about Albert being in Colombia?"

Romero assumed the cop stance. *Uh-oh*. When Romero flattened both feet, a shouting match was pending. "Do you mind telling me how you know that?"

"Um, I have my sources?" I wrung my hands, doing my don't-pee-my-pants stance.

He crossed his arms, revealing his Iron Man watch. "You going to answer all my questions with another question?"

I gave a teensy shrug. "Maybe?"

He sighed tight-lipped. "Do you also know Albert's staying with his sister?"

"Yes, but that's all I know."

"Uh-huh. We've uncovered something that's starting to tie this whole thing together. His sister, Caroline, once dated Erik. And get this. In less than a week, Erik's going to Colombia."

Caroline, who had to be C.D., dated Erik? I didn't figure on this. Was Erik going to Colombia to see her? Albert was there. It didn't make sense. "It's probably coincidental. Unrelated."

"Maybe. Then again, it might be totally related, and we're looking at premeditated murder. Caroline has an eye practice in Colombia."

"So why share this? So you can gloat over Albert maybe being involved?" I knew I should've confessed I'd mailed Albert's envelope, but what would that prove? The envelope was gone. Albert was with Caroline. And no one knew when he'd be back.

He shoved his hands on his hips. "I'm telling you because this isn't a game of Clue. Murderers are dangerous, manipulative, and psychotic."

I dismissed the warning. "I'm sure Albert is just off on a nice visit with his sister. I've heard Colombia is lovely this time of year."

"Or maybe Albert's hiding out. Could be he's taking the fall for Erik. We've got our eye on him, just the same."

"You're following him?"

"Informally. One of the guys was owed vacation time. He always wanted to visit Colombia. We also talked to Albert's mother, who runs the Cotton Gin. She wasn't saying much."

Mother? The Cotton Gin?

I had to talk to this woman. See what I could learn. Maybe she'd open up to me, another female, Albert's friend, a colleague of sorts. But how would I approach her? I needed a dummy. A decoy. *Phyllis.* Wasn't she going there tomorrow? I'd offer her a ride. If I didn't, and I ran into her there, well, it could get ugly. So much for a peaceful Sunday afternoon. "What about Erik? Are you detaining him?"

"Not at this point."

I fiddled with my earring, planning my next question. "Do you think it's possible Erik could've killed Portia because she wanted to buy a mansion in Boston? Maybe it was more than they could afford? More than he wanted?"

He gave me a shrewd look. "Buying a mansion? Who've you been talking to?"

"Gavin." I added, "It just came up."

"When you were grilling him about the murder?"

"Well, it wasn't when I was waxing his hair." I rolled my eyes, recalling that fiasco.

"Waxing his—forget it. I don't want to know."

"So? What about this theory?"

Romero took a measured breath. "According to Erik, Portia had a thing about upgrades. She liked to remodel the house. Tour estate sales. Contact agents. He didn't think she'd ever find something she truly wanted."

"Maybe this time she did, and he didn't like it."

He considered this. "Maybe."

"But wouldn't an affair complicate things?"

"Affair?"

"Yes. Erik and Portia both had affairs. You must've known about them."

"Portia, yes. Erik, no. Who's the lady he was seeing?"

"I don't know her name. And I'm not sure we're talking past tense."

He grimaced. "Do I ask how you obtained this information?"

I knew that tone. What possible information could a simple beautician have? "It's hearsay."

"You mean gossip. I suppose you'll make it your civic duty to find out the truth."

I was getting tired of him second-guessing me. I scrunched my hands into fists, took a step in his direction, and met his stare, bold as brass. "How about *I* find out so *you* can find out."

"You lost me."

"Then let me translate." I had my hands on my hips. "You've had me followed so you can find out what I learn." There. I'd show him I wasn't such a space cadet. I knew plenty about what was going on.

He remained silent.

I glared at him and ground my teeth. "Are you going to say anything?"

"No. I'm kind of enjoying the moment."

Ooh! Dealing with Romero was a head against heart tug-of-war. How could I be going on a blind date? I was fighting an insane desire for him, even if he did make me want to scream.

"All right," he said. "Maybe we are keeping close tabs on you. It's also my job to protect."

"Really!"

"Yes, really." He narrowed the gap between us, took his fingertip, and tucked a curl behind my ear.

I'm almost certain I was still standing because I felt the floor under my feet and my back was erect. But part of me was sure I'd just keeled over. I swallowed and tried to ignore the electricity. "Then this might be a good time to show you something." I walked on shaky legs to the coffee table, sank on the couch, and handed him the note.

"What's this?" He sat next to me, holding the paper by its edge.

"I'm not sure, but I don't think it's a party invitation."

He scanned the poem, his look turning serious. "When did you get this?"

"Last night."

"Last night!" He released the paper and gave me his hard stare that made me think he was about to blow. "And you didn't report it?"

"I thought about calling," I said as ladylike as possible.

"And?"

"I decided against it."

"That's just swell! While you were at it, you got fingerprints all over this note."

"Well, I didn't have to show you, you know. If I mishandled a piece of evidence, I'm *sorry*." My frustration was compounding, and when I got upset like this, I cried. But I wouldn't allow it. "Did you think you'd find the culprit's name and address on the back? Everyone knows if you're going to write a threatening letter, it should be untraceable."

He was on his feet, arms waving. "You're something else! Do you get all your information from detective shows? Or just *Scooby-Doo*?"

I had my head down, avoiding his eyes at all costs.

"Look at me, damn it!" He dragged me to my feet. "You know your safety's important to me?"

I stared into his livid eyes, wondering what triggered this intense emotion. What happened in his past to make him so passionate? So barbaric.

He let me go and raked the note off the table. "I'm taking this in for examination."

"Fine!"

"Fine! And I'm giving you my number. That's for you to call if you're in trouble."

"Fine!"

He gave me a sharp look, then pulled out a notebook and pen from his shirt pocket. He scratched on a paper, ripped it off, and smacked it in my palm. "My address is there, too." His voice simmered, but I could feel his anger brewing. "I can be here in eight minutes if you need me."

"What if you're not on duty?"

"I'm always on duty." He took in my dress again. I could see he wanted to know more, but at this point I wouldn't make it easy. What was his problem anyway? I was just another face in the crowd, or more precisely, witness in the salon. Deep down, I wanted to believe I meant more, but I didn't dare wish for the impossible.

He stuffed the notebook and pen in his pocket and looked into my eyes like it was useless trying to figure me out. "Call me," he said, and then left.

"I will." I whipped a lime green pillow at the door. "When hell freezes over."

By the time I arrived at Dino Hosta's, I was relatively calm. The sun glowed pinkish orange, lights around the patio swung in the warm breeze, and my watch with the broken clasp said I was ten minutes late. Not bad, considering.

I put on my perma-smile, left the car, and strolled toward the patio where I listened for a moment to a pianist playing a Norah Jones tune. I wondered if the musician would consider switching places with me. He could meet Jason, and I could play Norah Jones. Somehow I didn't think he'd go for it.

I entered the busy restaurant and thanked the maître d' for showing me to Jason's table, a circular booth occupied by Jason—who looked familiar—and another man. They both half rose, and I slid into the booth with a guarded smile. What was going on?

Jason was dark-haired, stocky, late thirties. Good-looking, as Max said. Crutches leaned by his side. The man between us was thinner with blond hair and blue eyes. All-American boy.

Jason smiled at me. "You probably don't remember we met at the visitation for Freddie."

"Of course." The perm-rod case. Which still didn't explain the other guy.

"I'm Andonios," All-American said. "Call me Andy." He elbowed Jason. "We played basketball together until this guy broke his legs in a motorcycle accident." He tilted his head toward the bar. "I start work over there in five minutes. I was bugging Jason till you arrived."

I said I was sorry about the accident. Jason suggested we order drinks. Andy asked who Freddie was.

"Freddie was a friend of my employee Max. He was stalked and murdered by two men."

"Valentine owns Beaumont's over on Darling," Jason explained to Andy. "She single-handedly caught those two guys. How long has it been?" he asked me.

I gave a mild smile. "Upwards of I try not to think about it?"

Jason nodded as if he understood. "That long, huh? So, you looking into that Reynolds woman's death?"

"Well, yes."

Andy swallowed, and his eyes grew big and round. "I knew I recognized you. Portia Reynolds died in your salon. Oh man. Do you think the husband did it?"

I shrugged. "I don't know."

"I saw his picture in the paper. The husband's always guilty. Either has a hot little tart on the side, or his wife is racking up some hefty bills and hubby can't stay afloat. Happens all the time."

He had a point. Which brought me back to wondering how Erik viewed Portia's spending and desire to buy a new home. And did he know about her affair?

"Was Erik Reynolds a regular client?" I asked Andy, thinking he might have seen something.

He bit his lip. "No, but I think he was here, maybe a few weeks ago with her."

"With Portia? You sure?"

"Yes. No." He scratched his jaw. "Maybe not. I was behind the bar, and it was dimly lit as usual and pretty busy. Now that you mention it, there was something about the woman that didn't seem right. I don't know what, though. But there was definitely something."

Great. I already knew about Pace and Portia, but I was curious whether they'd flaunted their affair here. "What about Portia? Did she ever come in?"

"Yeah, on occasion."

"With anyone in particular?"

"It's been eight or nine months, but there was a guy who'd come in wearing a white T-shirt like those guys in the aftershave commercials. Taller than me, huskier too, like he works out."

Jason smiled, displaying a chipped tooth. "I thought you had a dress code."

"We do. The guy didn't appreciate the collared shirt we offered for emergencies. Didn't matter, though, what he wore. Portia was all over him. Name was Chase or Trace."

"What about Pace?" I asked, after the waitress brought our drinks.

He snapped his fingers. "That's it." He looked at his watch. "I gotta get to work."

Shoot. Already? I sipped my Shirley Temple to hide my disappointment.

Jason began to slide out of the booth to let Andy pass.

"Let me." I set down my drink and slipped out as elegantly as I could in my tight dress.

Andy followed, then stopped suddenly. "You know? It just hit me why that woman with Erik wasn't Portia. Did you ever notice how loud and showy Portia was? Like she wanted the whole world to adore her? The woman Erik brought in was nothing like that. She looked like Portia." His gaze slid down my frame. "But she was more…refined."

I thought about Albert's sister Caroline and wondered if she could've been the woman Erik was seeing. I didn't know what she looked like or how she acted. And I couldn't guess if she resembled Albert, or if she were more polished. Plus, wasn't she supposed to be in Colombia?

After Andy trotted off, Jason and I had dinner. He told me about a friend who was helping him get around, and there was a slight but unmistakable twinkle in his eyes. "The truth is, Valentine, you're as beautiful as ever. Heck, the men couldn't take their eyes off you as you walked across that floor." He chuckled. "The green-eyed wives couldn't either."

Two women in the next booth looked over, whispered to each other, and giggled like the joke was only something they would get. I tried not to wince from their laughter or revisit sad childhood memories. My mind was too busy computing where Jason's speech was headed.

"But my friend, Natasha, has been so good to me. And really, she's more my speed." He put up his palms. "I'm sorry, Valentine. Especially when Max was so insistent about setting us up. Can I say it was great seeing you again?"

I was actually happy for Jason and Natasha. All the same, this was another reason why blind dates were a rotten way to spend an evening.

I climbed into bed, thinking about Jason, and strangest of all, the giggling women in the next booth. They reminded me of the popular girls in grade school and the cruel pranks they'd pulled on me. Like how they scattered my clothes throughout sixth-grade camp and flushed my hair bands down the toilet. Because I looked different. Because I wasn't like them.

Then one day, Twix's mother gave me a take-no-shit lecture. "God made you stand out," she'd said. "Won't matter what those eejits do, they'll never have your lovely bones or your kind heart." At the time, I didn't have a clue what she meant. Now, years later, I choked down a swallow, thinking if that was so true, why couldn't I find someone to love me for me?

Jason was polite, funny, and outgoing. But he had Natasha. My thoughts turned to Romero who didn't even know the meaning of polite. And he was about as funny as a captain on a sinking ship. So why did I ache for him?

I tossed to one side, punched the pillow, and tore my thoughts away from Romero. I had a murder to solve. I needed to focus on Portia.

I tucked the pillow under my ear and envisioned her and her long legs, strutting into my salon the very first time, years ago. I was creating an updo with no less than six bobby pins stuck in my mouth. I nodded at Portia, then at the waiting room chairs. But Portia wasn't going to sit, and she wasn't thrilled to speak to the help. And she certainly wasn't pleased with the appointment Judy had tried to set. "Tuesday!" she shrieked. "That will never do. It's got to be this Saturday, no later than one o'clock. I absolutely *have* to be fit in."

She paraded over to me, her black hair almost blue from shine. "You come so highly recommended. I just *had* to try you." She peeked over her shoulder, then leaned in. "They're planning a surprise fortieth birthday party for me. The fools. Like I don't know. But I'll do my part to look shocked."

My jaw dropped at her crass tone, and several bobby pins pinged on the floor.

"You won't be sorry. If I like what you do, I'll spread the word like wildfire."

And she did. I obtained a respectable following, even if clients came in under duress.

I rolled onto my other side and gave a loud yawn. It was true, Portia was bossy and she made enemies easily. But it stumped me why someone felt she should die.

Chapter 10

I woke up the next morning, feeling exhausted and out of sorts without a clue why. Okay, maybe I did know why. And it wasn't Romero. It had more to do with enduring a failed date I didn't even want. At least that's what I kept telling myself.

I showered, ate breakfast, then yanked on a dress, riding out the pity theme. My clothes didn't shout loser, so why did I feel like one? I was a good person, wasn't I? I kept on a useless employee when sharp business sense told me otherwise. I went out of my way to style hair at the retirement homes. I visited the hospital kids frequently. What kind of loser did those things?

I bent my head forward and brushed my hair, still counting deeds. I called my parents often. I believed in God. I gave to the homeless. I even fed stray animals.

I flung my hair back and let the waves go where they pleased. I wasn't in the mood to coax curls. I stroked on an extra coat of mascara and made a decision. I was officially done with blind dates. *Finito!* All I had to do was sell my mother on the idea. Today.

I stared at myself in the mirror. Good enough. I hadn't been to church since the perm-rod case. I was due for a major tuning.

I phoned Phyllis and told her I'd be there by one to

take her to the Cotton Gin. It wasn't a major modification, but it was a good start.

I cruised to St. Luke's Anglican Church and had a few private words with God during the service about my present situation. I didn't want to seem ungrateful for anything, so I gave thanks for my meddling family, my zany staff, my pathetic life, and for healing Brody's granddaughter Kylie.

After the service, I walked down the front steps into the sunshine. I should've felt at peace after leaving church, but I didn't. I felt jumpy, and something niggled at me. A square-peg-in-a-round-hole feeling. Something didn't belong. And then I saw it—Pace's truck parked at the curb ahead of three other cars.

I tensed and revulsion snaked through me. What was he doing here? He certainly wasn't in church. All right. It was a free world. He could've been here for any number of reasons. Visiting a friend. Putting up a roof. I didn't hear any hammering, and that jittery feeling persisted. Just as I was deciding what to do about it, the truck pulled away from the curb and sped away.

I slowly drove through town on my way to my parents'. Sunday traffic was light, and you could count the cars on the street. Nevertheless, I kept looking over my shoulder like someone was following me. I was being paranoid, but I couldn't help myself.

I stopped for a red light and glanced to my left at shops lining the downtown core. My gaze stopped at Karate King. The narrow storefront had SELF-DEFENSE CLASSES and a phone number written in black ink on the window. Inside the building I could see people in white uniforms moving around.

My heart picked up a beat. I stared at the red light, then back at Karate King, deciding what to do. I didn't want to put off talking to my mother, and God forbid I kept

Phyllis waiting. Impulsively, I dug out my phone, called the number, and signed up for the two-for-one program. That was it. Tuesday night I'd take control of my destiny. Valentine Beaumont, karate queen of Rueland. Of course, Max might not be so thrilled about being my partner, but I wasn't going to fret over that right now. This was a major step in conquering my fears. Excited about my decision, I waited for the light to turn green, then stepped on the gas and pushed on to my parents'.

My mother wasn't in her usual sanctuary when I entered the house, with an apron tied around her waist or utensils glued to her hands. Mumbling and banging came from one of the rooms down the hall.

I took off my heels and stumbled past an old hat box by the door. "Mom? Where are you?"

"In here," my mother called.

I rubbed my arms from the cold house, thinking my great-aunt obviously wasn't around. I bent over the counter for a whiff of apple pie, then meandered down the hall, raising the thermostat to sixty-eight along the way. I poked my head in every immaculate room. At last I found my mother in their ensuite bathroom. Her apron was in place, her head was stuck in the gurgling toilet, and a roll of tinfoil sat on the floor.

"Are you expecting?" I asked, and she threw me a dirty look. "Well, it's not every day I see my mother hunched over the toilet bowl." I watched for a moment while she fiddled. "What's with the tinfoil?"

"This silly toilet's running again. The plumber told me to wrap tinfoil around this thing-a-ma-jig, but I'm not having any luck. And your father's out buying Metamucil." She tossed the bit of tinfoil in the garbage. "I give up."

After Holly and I moved out, my empty-nest parents went from a one-bathroom house for four to a three-bathroom house for two. I guess progress had its pitfalls.

"Why don't you use one of the other bathrooms?" I slid onto the sink countertop. "You have enough of them."

"We like using this one if we get up in the middle of the night." She rose to her feet. "Lord only knows when that man will be home. He's probably humoring all the old ladies at the grocery store before he helps them home with their bags. It's like that movie—*Four Widows and a Chauffeur*."

My parents weren't overly social people, but given an audience, my father loved the opportunity to crack jokes while my mother silently shook her head at his dry wit.

"The movie was called *Four Weddings and a Funeral* because someone dies."

She grimaced at her wedding ring. I knew what she was thinking, and it wasn't pretty. "I didn't even get to church. I was so busy worrying about this toilet."

"Then it's good you didn't go. God doesn't have time for problems or miracles."

She ignored my sarcasm and washed her hands. "When did you get a cat?"

"Cat?"

"I talked to Lorna last night, and she said you had a cat."

Lorna was Faren's mother, my mother's first cousin. I knew her question stemmed from my brilliant lie about having a kitten in order to get out of my date with Craig, but I wasn't sure she'd see it that way.

I straightened perfume bottles on the counter and shamefully lied some more. "I was actually cat-sitting for a friend."

"She also told me Faren's colleague wants to see you again."

I hiccupped my response and almost laughed in her face. "Sorry. That will never happen."

"Was he that bad, dear?"

"Bad. Awful. And repulsive." I smacked a Cachet bottle down for emphasis. "Which brings me to why I'm here. No more blind dates...at least until Portia's murder has been solved."

She didn't even blink. "If that's the way you want it."

"It is." I wasn't fooled by her nonchalance. I followed her into the kitchen where she put the pot on the stove.

"I'm taking a cup of tea outside while I pull weeds. Want one?"

"It's ninety degrees outside."

"That doesn't seem to bother you when you're chasing crooks."

Huh? "You lost me somewhere between pulling weeds and chasing crooks."

She pursed her lips. "Why do I get the feeling you're not letting the police handle this case? Ernie Sluk told your father he saw a picture of you on the news. How are you going to find a man if you're always in the news?"

Of course we couldn't let the dating thing rest. "So what if Ernie Sluk saw me on the news?"

"So! I'll tell you so! You're a moving target. How do you know this Portia woman was the intended victim? Maybe someone's really after you."

"Nobody's after me." James Bond here echoed my exact fears. Maybe I'd forget telling her about the death threat.

The pot boiled over, and I said I had to go.

"What?" My mother flicked off the stove. "Aren't you staying for supper? There's apple pie."

My mother's pies were possibly the best in the universe. Saying no to apple pie was...well, actually never happened. But eating it without wanting to rip out my hair wasn't likely to occur.

"Can't. I have to take Phyllis to the Cotton Gin."

"On a Sunday? Why can't she drive herself?"

"Her car's tied up for the weekend."

She sighed, then wrapped up some pie for me. "Can't you take her another day?"

"Afraid not." I slipped on my shoes and tapped the hat box with my toe. "What's up?"

She pulled back a graying piece of brown hair from her still-soft skin. "This old box is just taking up space in the closet. I'm getting rid of it."

I suddenly had a vision of climbing a chair when I was little, then pulling a wig out of this box and playing with it. I bent over and popped off the lid. "It's empty. Where's that dark wig you used to wear?"

"That old thing? I gave it to Holly a while ago."

I was lost in thought. "What'd Holly want it for?"

"For a woman whose husband ripped out her hair." She shuddered. "There's another one who loves working with danger."

"Holly's good at her job."

"You both like playing with fire. You get that from your father." She fanned herself despite the air hovering around frigid. "Do you want me to see if I can get the wig back? The lady's hair's probably grown back in."

"No, it's fine." I frowned, not sure that statement was true. I kissed her cheek, gratefully accepted the pie, and headed for the car, the wig still on my mind. I hadn't thought about that old thing in years. Why now? I guess I couldn't shake Birdie's news that Tess LaMay had bumped into Erik and a Portia look-alike, or Andy's theory from last night that Erik's date resembled Portia. Was it possible Portia had a twin? Was this merely coincidence? Or had the woman at Dino Hosta's disguised herself as Portia by wearing a wig? If this was the case, who would've been brazen enough to pull that off? And why?

Phyllis was waiting for me by the shrubs at the front entrance of her rundown, three-story apartment building. I was a few minutes late because I'd stopped on my way to her place and bought peanut brittle. If I had to face Phyllis on my day off, I needed lots of sugar.

She hustled to the car, wearing a brown dress identical to one I'd worn a few weeks ago, with small colorful circles overlapping each other. Only, on Phyllis the circles looked like big beach balls. I popped a piece of peanut brittle in my mouth and crunched hard.

She yanked open the door and dropped on the seat. She was in a mood, but I didn't ask any questions. I waited for her to shut the door, then I burned rubber. I hoped this outing wouldn't take long.

"I know what you're thinking." Phyllis heaved the seatbelt around her. "And why can't I wear the same dress as you, anyway?"

I tightened my grip on the steering wheel. My tongue worked a bit of candy stuck to my back tooth, thankfully keeping me silent.

"You think you're the only one with a figure small enough to wear pretty dresses."

"Phyllis, it's *fine*. You look fine. Everything's fine." Though it really wasn't. Having my corpulent, pain-in-the-butt cousin mimic me in the wardrobe department was beyond annoying. I'd never wear my dress again. I crammed in more peanut brittle.

"Good. Because when you told me where you got it, I went straight to the store and bought the last one on the rack. Then I sewed this neat insert up the back." She leaned forward and showed off a frightful piece of brown spandex that unevenly pulled two sides together.

I coughed on a peanut.

"We're related," she reminded me, helping herself to some peanut brittle. "It's no wonder we have the same tastes."

Phyllis was *nothing* like me. She operated in clutter. Her work was sloppy. She had no sense of style. And she drank Slim-Fast with hot dogs. How could we be related? We were damage and repair, destruct and construct. We were as similar as oil and water. I did a quick prayer we wouldn't run into anyone I knew. I hoped to see Albert's mother. Period.

The Cotton Gin was an aged, gold-brick fabric warehouse in a forgotten part of Rueland. I dropped Phyllis off at the door and parked on a side street beside ancient railway tracks, long ago covered in weeds. I walked up the steps to the main entrance when I spotted a red

Corvette in the parking lot. I didn't have to look at the license plate to know it said HOT BAE and belonged to my nemesis Candace Needlemeyer. I seethed. What was she doing here? Buying string to make a thong?

I stepped lightly across the rickety floorboards into the dusty, mothball-scented store. I was trying to keep a low profile when Candace bustled out of an aisle and bumped into me, fake boobs first.

Candace was tall, blond, and full of phony enthusiasm. But she never fooled me.

"Well, well," she said, through her collagen-enhanced lips. "If it isn't Rueland's famous ball-buster." She placed her hands on her curvy hips.

Just smile, I told myself through clenched teeth. "Candace. Shopping for material?"

"Actually, I'm getting ideas for a new look in the salon. I'd like to personalize my capes."

"Witches' capes?" I tried to hold back a grin, but I wasn't successful.

"I don't know what you have to smile about, Valentine. An unsteady business. Unhappy employees." She spread her arms wide. "At least when you go bankrupt, they'll have a home at Supremo Stylists."

I could feel sweat behind my knees and tension in my fingers. If Max chose to work with this woman, I'd have to accept it. But I sure as hell wouldn't let her see my disappointment. "I'm glad you said that. Phyllis is over there. I'll let her know you're looking for help."

Candace glanced over her shoulder at Phyllis in the thread section. Familiar with Phyllis's reputation, Candace gave me a huff and pushed past me to the exit.

I smiled at her back and caught up to Phyllis. She had her head down, eyeing a spool of thread from a five-dollar bin, and another from a one-dollar bin. She picked up both spools and held them up to a sour-looking woman, four feet away, measuring fabric. "What's the difference between these here threads?"

The woman, about sixty, probably would've thanked us

if we turned around and left. She had diehard smoker written all over her, from her greasy, yellow-gray hair and stained fingers to the puffy bags under her eyes. Her nametag read Joy. No joke.

Joy lifted her eyes off the row of fabric. "One's quilter's thread," she rasped out in her smoker's voice. "The other's machine thread."

Phyllis gaped at her. "I can see that. But this one looks shinier, and this other one says all-purpose."

Joy put her head back down, I imagine wishing she could have a cigarette break instead of helping the likes of us.

Phyllis took her finger and did the universal cuckoo sign around her temple. I shook my head, hoping to discourage her from saying the wrong thing. I just hoped Joy wasn't Albert's mother.

Phyllis continued examining threads. She grunted. "This one over here says fifty cents. Why is it fifty cents?"

Joy slapped down the bundle of material with a loud thwack. "My guess is because it's cheap. Just what is it you're looking for?"

Phyllis had six spools in her hand. "Black thread. And I need lots of it."

"Phyllis." I had my eyes peeled for Albert's mother. "Just pick one."

She dropped the spools in a heap. "Boy. Sure can't find good help these days." She grabbed a thread for a dollar and gave a mean look to the woman. "Thanks for the help."

"You're welcome," the lady said with an instant well-trained smile.

"I'm going to look for material." Phyllis clomped off to the wooden stairs.

I turned my back and spotted a woman with eyes that resembled Albert's. She was cutting a bolt of blue material for a middle-aged man. The woman's shoulders looked stooped from worry, the hollows under her eyes obviously from strain. She pointed to the checkout, gave the customer a slight nod, then cleaned fabric scraps off a long table.

I stared at her for a bit. I wanted to be sure I wasn't about to make a fool of myself with the wrong person. Worst thing that could happen, she'd be as courteous as Joy. I drew in a breath of air, moseyed over, and introduced myself. Then I started with Albert's delivery the day of the murder.

"Did Albert see the murderer, then?" Mrs. Dougal asked in a helpful manner.

"That's what the police are trying to establish. Did Albert say anything to you about that morning? Maybe he didn't go back to work or was acting differently?"

"No. His dad and I don't see him as often as we'd like."

I pushed on. "Did you know Portia Reynolds?"

"Only that she was that socialite who stole our Erik from Caroline."

Our? "Was Erik close to the family?"

"He *was* family. He and Caroline went to optometry school together and traveled the summers. They worked in Colombia one year." Her eyes remembered other days. "We loved him like a son. Albert had even picked names for nieces and nephews." She tucked a pair of scissors away. "Albert loves kids, though I doubt he'll ever have any of his own. He's had his problems, but he's worked hard at turning his life around."

But had he? Doubt scrambled to the surface. "What happened to Caroline and Erik?"

"After Portia walked into Erik's examination room, Caroline was out in the cold." She pulled a picture out from under the table and passed it to me. In it, a redheaded girl stood by a young-looking Albert. "This is my favorite picture of my kids. It was taken the year Caroline met Erik. After he left her, Caroline lost so much weight I thought Albert would kill Erik for what she went through. She never got over him. When she moved away, Albert blamed Portia."

"Do you know where your son is?"

Her eyes were sad. "Bogota. He said he and Caroline were fine and not to worry. But I do worry. Caroline's in trouble. She won't tell me with what, but a mother senses these things."

I had to agree with Mrs. Dougal. My senses told me something about this was very, very wrong.

Chapter 11

I planned to do hair early Monday morning at Rueland Retirement and pop in at the hospital. After that, I intended to spend the rest of the day doing a little investigating and some much needed bookkeeping at work. Last week's marathon had to amount to something.

I decided to start my snooping at the old McCafferty place, where Pace said he was working. Probably a bad idea, considering our last encounter. But I wasn't going to give in to fear. I was just going to have to play it smart if I didn't want a repeat episode with a razor. I'd signed up for self-defense class, after all. I could handle this. Plus, I had to find out why Pace lied about his relationship with Portia, and why his truck was at St. Luke's yesterday.

I slathered syrup over my waffle, deciding I'd be the model interrogator. Miss Tact. Miss Diplomacy. Seeing his truck at church yesterday didn't intimidate me. No siree.

Before I went anywhere, I sat at the computer and did a search on Caroline Dougal. I thought about her mother's concerns and wondered if Caroline's troubles were linked to Portia's murder. I couldn't imagine how if she was in Colombia.

Her eye-care website popped up along with a headshot. I printed off her picture and stared at the woman Erik once loved.

Caroline's hair was still red, her face serene. But there was a cynical line to her mouth and a coldness in her eyes that was absent from the photo Mrs. Dougal had shown me. Or was I looking for something that wasn't there? I wondered if Andy the bartender would recognize her as the woman with Erik. I tucked the photo in my bag. Since Dino Hosta's was closed Mondays, I'd run it by some others today. I'd show Andy tomorrow.

The sun sat low and heavy in the morning sky. It promised to be a cool day with no humidity. I dressed in a cap-sleeved white turtleneck and jeans with silver laces down the seams. I gathered my hair high into a sleek ponytail, and because it was always about the accessories, I slipped on rhinestone-hooped earrings, a spangled bracelet, and chunky silver rings. I slid on blue sandals from a knockoff store at the Cape, and with more balls than a juggler, I strutted out the door.

School was done for another year, and kids were all over the streets. A cruiser rolled down the road, Mr. Brooks geared up the chainsaw in Paul Bunyan mode, and Mrs. Calvino was smoking on her porch, hooting into the phone.

I was in and out of the retirement home by ten-thirty. When I got to the hospital, a traveling magician had the kids mesmerized with his top hat and bunny. That was okay with me. My volunteer time wasn't written in stone, and I was happy to see others cheer up the kids.

Seeing as how I'd mapped out the day, I headed over to see Pace. The McCaffertys lived on Cherry Street, a whole five minutes from the hospital. I pulled up in front of the house and stopped behind Pace's truck parked at the curb.

Now that I was here, I stifled a panicky bubble. I thought about Pace lurking around the church yesterday. At least I assumed he was there. After all, who else would be driving his truck? His mother? I visualized his rough hands and thought about his story about the blood. Okay, he was used to scrapes and cuts. Evidently, the guy never wore work gloves. But even if the blood on his shirt was his own, and he hadn't worn gloves, it still didn't mean he couldn't have wrung Portia's neck. How he covered his hands was another question. I was so anxious to hear the truth I wanted to squeeze it out of him.

Pace was dressed in the usual white T-shirt and tight jeans. He was deep in concentration, banging under the roof of the gazebo, drowning out the birds and the traffic. I tiptoed across the lawn and stood safely behind him, my bag at my side. I'd just collected my thoughts when he suddenly turned and almost fell off his ladder.

"Do you always sneak up on people like that?" He stomped down the rungs.

"Do you always lie to people like that?" So much for tact. But if I was being totally honest, it wasn't just the blood on his shirt or yesterday's sighting that troubled me. I'd been edgy since I'd received that note. If Pace hadn't already threatened me outside my door, I probably wouldn't have suspected him as the sender. But he had. And that, on top of the other things, didn't put him in a very positive light at the moment.

He flung his hammer to the ground, his eyes looking bloodshot, like he was having trouble sleeping at night. "What are you talking about?"

"You lied about your relationship with Portia."

"I didn't lie." He smirked, showing the real Pace. "You asked if I knew her. I said, 'Not really.' Sure, I knew what she liked in bed."

I let an embarrassing hot flash from that pass. I twisted my rings, trying not to stare at the recent scab on his arm, thanks to yours truly.

"But she was one confusing dame. She'd like something one minute, then blow her stack a second later. Like these railings." He backed up and pointed to the gazebo. "She insisted on square ones like these. Plain and simple. When they came—on a rush order, by the way—I installed them. Then she stormed out of the house, screaming I'd ordered the wrong style." He shook his head. "I couldn't keep straight what she wanted. It's like she had chronic PMS."

I moved on. "Why'd you crash Portia's party?"

"What party?" He swiped his hammer off the ground.

"A year ago in May. Portia was entertaining, black tie, jazz band, caviar, you know, the whole bit, and in you walked with a giant chip on your shoulder."

"That giant chip was because Ms. Reynolds refused to pay for work rendered." He rubbed his neck and rested his hand on his collarbone. "We had an agreement she'd pay halfway through the job for half the work. She was racking up quite a bill and becoming a pain in the ass. I wanted to make sure I got what was owed me. Can you blame me?"

Portia could be difficult. Ask Gavin. "What happened?"

"What, after I made a scene?" Pace ushered me to a bench in the gazebo. "That's the funny part. We'd been sleeping together a couple of months by then. That night, late after her party, she came knocking. I plodded to the door butt-naked and there she was in her red sparkling gown. I asked what the hell she wanted, and she acted as if nothing had happened. 'You're not still mad at me,' she taunted. I was plenty mad and told her to buzz off in so many words. I went back to bed, thinking she'd leave. A few minutes later, she crawled in next to me, naked as a jailbird." He grinned. "You can imagine what happened next."

Yep. Crystal clear.

"After that night, I told her to find someone else to finish the project. I had other jobs lined up. I didn't need her harassment."

"Weren't you afraid she'd ruin you?"

He nodded. "She tried to hurt business, but after a while she gave up. I guess she was more interested in keeping the romance alive."

"How long did you see her?"

"Till this past Christmas. I got tired of it all. The lies. Her showing up at my job site wearing a fur coat and nothing underneath."

"Yeah, I can see how that would tire you."

He raised the corner of his mouth. "I had a reputation to uphold. I couldn't take off in the middle of the day or whenever Portie wanted action." He stood. "I got my money and told her to go home and concentrate on her marriage."

"Breaking up *and* giving advice. I bet she was really pleased with you."

He shrugged. "She told me Erik was twice the man I was. It kind of stung. But I was through with her games. There wasn't much she could say that would hurt." He jumped off the gazebo. "That day in your shop was the first I'd seen her since it ended. Looked like she was still angry."

I stepped down from the gazebo. "Do the police know any of this?"

He tilted his head from side to side. "A simplified version of it, yes."

"So what were you doing at St. Luke's yesterday?"

He squinted at me. "I had a quote to give some folks across the street. Why? Were you there?"

"Maybe."

"Well, don't flatter yourself. While you were in church talking to God, I was being sermonized on the proper way to build a shed. I really gotta stop working Sundays."

I stopped at the shop, as I often did Mondays, and sat in my office, studying bank statements. I was deep in thought, comparing data on the computer, when I heard something crash through the front window. I shrieked and vaulted around the corner to see what it was.

Hot flames scorched the waiting-area carpet and curled up the leg of the magazine table. Under the table was a hairspray bottle tied to a hefty rock. The bottle hissed out noxious fumes.

I lurched for air and almost doubled over from chemicals burning my throat. Coughing madly, I breathed into my shoulder, telling myself not to panic. I grabbed the fire extinguisher from under the counter and twisted the plastic yellow tie securing the pin. It wouldn't give, so I nabbed a pair of scissors and snipped the tie. Then I pulled the pin and squeezed the handle. The sudden pressure backfired, and a cold blast of white foam shot up like a volcano, knocking the wind out of me.

I yelped and staggered back, spraying foam all over the ceiling and walls. I gave my head a shake and breathed into my arm. Finally, I got control and aimed the nozzle over the flames. A second later, the fire extinguisher spit out the last drops of foam, and then died.

My heart was beating so fast I was sure it was going to give out on me. I dropped the fire extinguisher, wiped the powdery foam from my face, and searched for something else to tackle the flame. I darted to the dirty towel bin. Empty. *Of course.* I never left dirty wet towels in the salon over the weekend. Damn my efficiency. I raced into the dispensary and noticed a sheet soaking in the sink. I wasn't sure why it was there, but it was good and wet, so I hauled it to the front and threw it over everything.

Instead of dousing the blaze, it exploded into a huge fireball. Heat struck my face, and glass table fragments shattered into the air, knocking me blurry-eyed to the ground. I blinked to clear my head, then hastily scrambled to my feet and called 911.

Within minutes, sirens pealed down the street. A fire engine, EMS truck, and a couple of cruisers squealed their brakes in front of the salon. Firemen battled the inferno, which, after the initial explosion, ended up being nothing more than a campfire. Of course, my speeding heart didn't believe that. I sat on the sidewalk and gulped air between sniveling and shaking uncontrollably. I tried to answer the fire chief's questions while paramedics fed me oxygen, checked my pulse, and cleaned my scrapes.

Traffic had come to a standstill. An ID unit had pulled up, and cops held back the crowd. Pastry employees stood gaping in their felt crowns, a camera crew filmed the circus in the street, and there was window glass and large puddles everywhere.

"You Bruce's daughter?" the chief asked while the crime scene tape went up.

I sniffed and nodded.

"Thought so. There's a resemblance."

I didn't know what he meant by that. But just then, to make my day even more pleasant, Romero squealed to a stop thirty feet from the scene, in a silver pickup with wheels that looked like they belonged on a tractor. He leaped out of the truck, his hair wild, his manner unbending. He was in jeans and a faded green T-shirt that accentuated the muscular planes across his chest. The man was so virile, my breath caught at the sight of him.

A few uniforms hustled toward him as he jogged toward the scene, but his eyes were dark and fastened on me. Lucky for them they knew when to back off.

I ducked behind a paramedic, hoping Romero would get detained. I didn't want him seeing me like this, and I wasn't up to another screaming match. No good. He pushed his way through the crowd, spoke to the fire chief, then knelt at my side, his thigh muscles pressed into my back. I didn't actually die from his touch, but I swear a bright light came toward me.

He took me in with a quick sweep. "She okay?" he asked the paramedic.

The medic finished blinding me with the arc of his flashlight, then slid it in his shirt pocket. "Her blood pressure was a bit high, and she's got minor abrasions from the explosion." He bestowed a reassuring smile on me. "But she'll live."

Romero gave me a grim look. "Really."

I tightened my cracked lips at that.

He patted the medic's shoulder and stood, his Iron Man watch staring me in the face. That's it? No hollering? No shouting? He got called away, and I swallowed heavily.

An officer carted over my bag and keys. "Thought you might want your things," he said. "And I think your bag is ringing." He opened it wide, and I reached inside for my cell phone.

"Hello?"

"Hee-hee-hee!" *Click.*

I felt color drain from my face. This time I actually thought I was going to pass out.

"Everything okay?" the officer asked.

"Uh, yeah." I scanned the crowd and saw Gavin Beck's newly shaved head duck past onlookers. He zipped into his car and peeled an inch of rubber escaping the scene. My mouth went dry, and my sense of unease doubled. I choked back a sob and locked my terrified gaze on Romero.

He was deep in conversation with a fireman, but when he saw my face, he raised his hand to stop the discussion. Knowing something was seriously wrong, he walked over and pulled me to my feet. "What is it?" His voice was tense with emotion, his touch strong but warm. Despite that, I was shivering.

"I-I don't know. I got a call. I think it was the person who did this, a hysterical laugh, then nothing. And I saw Gavin Beck take off."

"Slow down. Did you check the readout on your phone?"

"No?"

He gestured with his hand for more. "Because?"

"I don't know! I just didn't." Without explaining my aversion for cell phones, I swiped my keys from the officer's hand. "I need my car," I said, making a bold dash to follow Gavin.

"Oh, no you don't." Romero circled his arm around my waist, hiked me three inches off the ground, and carried me to his pickup. He deposited me in the backseat, tossed a blanket over my lap, and posted the cop on guard. "If she moves, shoot her." He left the uniform and trucked over to another cop.

Of all the nerve. I stuck out my bottom lip—like he'd see it—then peered down at my phone. My hands were still trembling. Okay, maybe I wasn't in any condition to run after Gavin. Romero wasn't the boss of me.

I huffed out a sigh, snatched my bag from the cop, and tossed my keys inside. Then I looked up in the rearview mirror. *Agghh!* My face was red, my nose runny, and bits of foam and debris decorated my hair. I looked like a sunburned Albert Einstein. Ugh. I leaned over the front seat and slapped away the mirror.

Could things get any worse? Bad enough I had an unstable business and inferior dating life. Now my salon had been torched, and I couldn't even protect myself. I had no special powers. I was a failure. I wasn't even all that pretty without the makeup and fancy clothes. It was all smoke and mirrors. I was a joke. The worst part was I was afraid I was falling for someone decidedly not right for me.

I spied the ugly gun on the cop guarding me. Then I looked at Romero. His gun was fixed at his side, and I didn't doubt he had another hidden discreetly. Oh boy. We were worlds apart. Romero was tough. I was froufrou. He drove a mean truck. I drove a Bug with daisy-shaped brake lights. Romero wouldn't think twice about shooting a crook. If I ever handled a gun, I'd probably shoot myself right through my beauty bag and send a product into orbit. Still, I needed something that would protect me. I remembered my upcoming self-defense class when my cell buzzed again.

I froze, my gaze set on Romero who was too far away to hear the ring.

The officer cranked his head around with an arched eyebrow, probably wondering why I wasn't answering it. I clutched the blanket, swallowed, and this time peeked at the call display. It was my mother. I exhaled and pressed talk.

"I put on the television and saw your face staring back at me. Are you okay?"

I turned away from the cameras, held back a sniffle, and told her I was fine. What I really wanted to do was run home into her arms with carefree abandon. To be out of harm's way, to feel loved and protected. I disconnected and took a deep breath, telling myself I was okay. I was alive, wasn't I?

I decided to get out of the truck and find out what was going on, but just then, Romero caught my eye. I settled back in my seat and waited like a kid in detention, when the cop Romero was talking to walked over and asked for my cell phone.

"We need to trace that earlier call, ma'am."

I handed over my phone. "Fine. Take it. Dumb thing is a nuisance anyway."

About an hour later, the crowd dissipated, the EMS trucks sped away, and the police cars left one by one. The fire chief and ID unit stayed back to gather evidence since Beaumont's was a crime scene for the second time.

Romero hustled over and slammed the door to the backseat of his truck, with me still inside. Ducking behind the wheel, he sped around to the back of the shop, pulled into a parking spot, and turned off the ignition. He angled out of the truck, took a deep breath in what looked like an effort to calm himself, then walked around to the passenger side and climbed in back next to me.

"So?" He stared straight ahead like he didn't trust himself to look at me in case he blew his top.

"So…" I was not going to cry. I was not going to cry.

"Let's have it. What happened?"

I fluttered my eyelashes toward the window, trying to dry my eyes. "You probably heard it enough times already."

"Nooooo. I live to hear it again. *From you.*" He took his finger and pulled my chin around.

I sighed but wouldn't look at him. "I was in my office when something crashed through the front window."

"What kind of something?"

"A bottle of hairspray."

"From your salon?"

"No, a drugstore variety, and it caused the fire. I tried to put it out, but my fire extinguisher malfunctioned."

He raised one eyebrow. "How does a fire extinguisher malfunction? You pull the pin and aim."

"I don't know *how*," I scowled. "But it did. And when I went to kill the flames with a wet sheet, the bottle kind of…exploded."

"Do you know why?"

"I think so."

"Then please share."

I glanced sideways at him, not liking his sarcasm one bit. I folded my arms in front of me, praying tears wouldn't roll down my cheeks.

He sighed gently. "Let's back up. Do you know where the sheet came from?"

"Mmm-hmm."

"Do you know why it was wet?"

I nodded, not trusting myself to speak.

"Do you want to tell me in people talk? That would make things move a lot quicker."

I snapped my eyelids at him. "The sheet was from one of the facial rooms. We cover clients with a sheet before spa treatments."

"Now we're getting somewhere. How did it get so wet?"

"It had been soaking."

"Do you know what it had been soaking in?"

"Mmm-hmm."

He waited a beat. "Care to tell me?"

"It was bleach." If ever there was a moment I wanted to be comforted and held safe, it was now. But he didn't offer, and I didn't beg.

"Is that it?"

"Mixed with hairspray. I remember Phyllis had poured hairspray all over a sheet when I left work Saturday because she'd accidentally dumped pasta sauce on it."

"Pasta sauce."

I shrugged. "Hairspray takes out stains. If that doesn't work, we try bleach."

I caught him rolling his eyes. "You know hairspray is highly flammable?"

"Look, if I'd detected anything odd, I wouldn't have used it to put out the fire. But the initial fumes from the blaze were so overpowering, I couldn't smell anything else. And I was in a bit of a hurry." I gnawed on my dry lips. "I think I smelled another chemical burning, but I can't put my finger on it."

"We'll look into it. You better phone your insurance company. They love this sort of stuff."

We entered the shop through the back door, and I called my insurance man from the phone in the dispensary. After going a few rounds on claims and deductibles, he slipped in a word of warning on arson and insurance fraud—just in case I was guilty of setting the fire and hoping to make an illegal gain. Boy, did everyone know I had money problems? I hung up and tried to look at the bright side. The shop didn't burn down, I didn't start the fire, and I wasn't seriously hurt. And if I tamed the Albert Einstein out of my hair, I'd almost look human again. I fiddled with my bangs, then realized I hadn't contacted my staff about the explosion.

Since Romero was at the front, talking to the ID unit, I picked up the phone again and one by one called my employees. I left a message at Phyllis's and gave Max and Judy each a short explanation. After I confirmed for the last time that we'd be open for business the next day, I hung up and went to work on my hair.

Romero wandered into the dispensary. "I've assigned a couple of guys the legwork on this. So how about lunch? I haven't eaten more than apples and donuts in two days."

I gave up fixing my ponytail in exasperation. "Lunch?"

"Yeah." He stepped closer and dusted foam residue off my shoulder. "You *do* eat?"

"Is this lunch being provided free of lectures and I-told-you-so's?"

"I won't make any promises."

I moved on to sponging sooty spots off my chest. "I'm a big girl, Romero, in case you didn't notice."

"Oh, I noticed." He studied me, full-on sex appeal. "Every time you fall ass-backward, I notice."

My breasts began to tingle. Not the reaction I needed at the moment. I set down the cloth and tried not to stare longingly at his hard body and tight jeans. Romero wasn't big into fashion, yet it wouldn't have mattered if I was swaddled in satin and he was sheathed in a loincloth. What mattered was how I was feeling. And could I trust this growing emotion?

"How about pasta?" he asked.

"Look at me." I hesitated. "I'm not exactly presentable."

He grinned. "You look adorable. And I noticed a similar top hanging in your office."

I blushed at the adorable comment. "That's for emergencies."

"Sweetheart, the national guard would deem this an emergency."

I put up my chin and sniffed. "Fine. Let me take a quick shower."

I grabbed the top from my office, and while I was at it, I detached my shop keys from my key ring. For a second time, I left them with the police. "My insurance guy is coming in ten minutes," I said, heading for the hall. Hopefully, he wouldn't be followed by Feltz, who would have something to say over this catastrophe.

"Where's his office? Around the corner?"

"Three doors down. When he heard the sirens, he pulled my file."

I felt reasonably normal after I showered, changed my top, and redid my hair. I didn't really care where we ate, but I was surprised when Romero cut west across town and parked in front of the Wee Irish Goat. I had to give myself a second to consider how I felt coming here again. In a way, it was like home, and I knew the food was fantastic. But I was a little uncomfortable.

We grabbed some menus and seated ourselves by the front window. After we decided on tetrazzini, Romero leveled his gaze on me. "I didn't know if you'd want to come here after you had your heart broken at that table over there."

Okay. So he was going to throw the Craig date in my face. I looked at the table, occupied by a family. A week ago, I hated every minute of my date, picturing Craig's head on a platter instead of two inches from my breasts. Now I was anticipating every moment.

"Funny thing about hearts," I said, my insides like Mexican jumping beans. "They mend rapidly."

"Really." The smile left his eyes, and I wondered what was going on inside his head. What did he really think of me? What took place in his past? Being the impetuous person I was, I blurted out the first thing that came to mind.

"How long have you been in Rueland? I mean, I didn't see you when I was involved in the uh, perm-rod case." Stupid. Stupid. Stupid.

"I was on vice for four years. So unless you assaulted criminals involved in narcotics, prostitution, pornography, or gambling, chances are you wouldn't have run into me. And fortunately or unfortunately, I didn't run into you."

I wasn't sure if that was an insult, but I held my head up like I wasn't bothered by his words.

He studied my face. "And speaking of running into you, who do you think did this?"

"The fire?" Since it was still so fresh, thoughts of Gavin clamored around my brain. Then Pace's face obliterated Gavin's. Could he have followed me from McCafferty's? Made sure I was holed up somewhere before he smashed my window? Payback for slicing his arm? For making him look like a fool in front of my neighbor?

"You do know whoever's behind this wants you to back off. The note. The phone call. The fire."

"I recognize that."

"Then you'll agree when I say you should stay with family till this is all over."

"I'm not going anywhere till I find Portia's killer." Guess I wasn't so agreeable.

Before steam whistled out Romero's ears, Brody hobbled over, took our order, and left us with bread. Then Romero left the table to take a call. I ate some bread and watched him talk on his cell phone, the whole time thinking he didn't realize how far I'd go to establish the truth. My reputation was at stake, not to mention my business that, with the exception of this past week, was dying its own murderous death. The salon was more my baby than if I'd given it an eighteen-hour birth. The blood, sweat, and tears I'd spilled were my greatest sacrifice. I wasn't about to let my dreams end because a killer couldn't be found.

"They pulled Gavin over," Romero said, returning to the table.

"And?"

"They're detaining him. He said he had an appointment on Duchess Street. He stopped when he saw the commotion. They're checking his story." He took some bread. "By the way, you may notice a cruiser patrolling your street."

"That's not necessary, Romero. I can look after myself." Who was I kidding? I screeched when a grasshopper leaped in my path.

"I'm not taking any chances."

Okay. So he was chivalrous.

"And since we're breaking bread, maybe it's time you called me Michael."

"You mean you're not going to holler at me for wanting to see this thing through?"

"Would it do any good?"

"No."

It looked like he was fighting a smile, and my heart swelled. Oh no. I'd stick to calling him Romero. It wasn't as personal, and for the time being, seemed safer.

"So, what about Albert?" I asked. "I mean, he wasn't even in the country to set the fire *or* to deliver the note."

"The note. Yeah. No fingerprints, other than yours. As for Albert's whereabouts, he goes to his sister's clinic daily."

"That's pretty incriminating."

"Okay, Ms. Beaumont. Time will tell."

"What happened to breaking bread and first names?"

"That was before you became a smartass."

I struggled to keep my smile from being smug.

"Don't forget," he said, "Albert was here for the murder. And this could be a team effort. Which brings me to Erik Reynolds who's leaving today for Colombia."

So he didn't cancel his trip. "Are you saying he set the fire?"

"I don't know, but he had opportunity. I've got a couple of guys questioning him before he takes off."

Did I have Erik all wrong? Was that performance he put on for me at his place real? Could he have also delivered the note? I thought about the envelope I'd mailed, and once again thought about Erik dating Caroline. "Did you question Erik about the woman he's been seeing?"

"Even asked about Caroline. He said they were over long ago, and he's not having an affair."

"He's lying."

"About which part?"

"Maybe both."

We paused for a moment while Nina brought our food. She set our meals down and gazed starry-eyed at Romero. I understood Nina's reaction. Romero brought out a sexual awareness that made women hot on the inside and flustered on the outside. He smiled at Nina, and she sighed. Naturally. A smile like his could bring a nun out of celibacy.

"I didn't know you had a fan club," I said, after Nina floated away.

"She must have a thing for Italian men."

"Really."

"It's a guess."

"Why is it for an Italian, you have blue eyes?"

"Mixed breeding."

I grinned at that and brought my mind back to Portia's murder. "I don't get it," I said. "Why suspect Albert or even Erik when Gavin was in the room with the dead body?" The twins flashed to mind. "Heck, the Cutlers wore gloves into the shop that morning. Maybe one of them slid down the hall, slipped on her gloves, and strangled Portia." I held up my hand before he could speak. "I know what you're going to ask, and no, I didn't keep track of them the whole time."

He shook his head at me, tight-lipped.

"Well? It's possible, isn't it?"

"No one's been ruled out." He stabbed a mushroom on his plate. "Regarding Gavin, I'll tell you something unofficially. It's unlikely he killed Portia."

"Huh? Are you not aware of their history?"

"Yes. It would seem Gavin had his own motive for murder."

"A very strong motive."

He set the mushroom back down. "Where was Gavin when you walked in the room?"

"On the floor, entwined in the steamer cord."

"Let's say he did kill Portia. He would've had to use gloves to handle the cord as his fingerprints were nowhere near Portia's head or on the cord that was wrapped around her neck. And the twisted way he fell, it's unlikely he would've disposed of gloves. Plus, you didn't mention him wearing any. He could've used a towel. But the only other towels that weren't in a stack were tucked neatly into Portia's chest area and around her head."

I was intrigued, yet at that moment I had an eerie feeling. Like someone was watching me. I looked casually over Romero's shoulder and even looked over mine. Lots of happy diners. Busy staff. Nothing out of the ordinary.

"According to you," Romero said, "nothing was

disturbed on her body. Gavin could've taken the part of the cord attached to the steamer, rather than the plug end, and strangled Portia with it. But when he fell and took the steamer with him, there's a good chance, actually a ninety-nine-point-nine percent chance he would've taken Portia down with him."

"I don't follow."

"Portia's lying on the table. In walks Gavin in his boxers. He takes part of the cord hooked into the top of the steamer and wraps it around her neck. After he chokes the life out of her, he trips on the legs, gets caught in the cord, and falls back. Since the steamer goes with him, and the cord nearest the steamer is wrapped around Portia's neck, down she goes off the table."

"But Portia was on the table in the same position I left her," I said, "and the *end* of the cord was still around her neck. So you don't think Gavin could've killed her."

"Not in that fashion. From skin samples on the cord and rope burn on her neck, the plug end was used to strangle her. Gavin's fingerprints were only on the floor where he landed."

Considering Romero had made some valid points where Gavin was concerned, I decided to let it digest and move on. The thought of Erik and Albert as a team still bothered me, but I'd ask Romero later what he learned on that. In the meantime, I had other trouble to get into.

We drove back to the salon and found the ID unit packed up. The glass people had installed a new window, commercial cleaners had washed the interior, and industrial fans were switched on for the night.

Romero had a quick debriefing with one of his men, then handed me back my keys and cell phone. "That call earlier was made from a pay phone downtown a few blocks away. Sorry it's not better news." He said he had to run and told me to be careful.

I watched him leave, then reattached my keys to my key ring, hoping this would be for the last time. After everyone left, I locked up and made a fast trip to the grocery store. I figured the best time to buy food was on a full stomach. Plus, if I didn't stock up on carbs and proteins, my mother would take to delivering food to my house. And while receiving things like apple pie wasn't a bad idea, my mother was crafty and before long she'd be delivering other things to the house. Like the opposite sex.

I unloaded groceries when I got home and threw my soiled top in the wash. Then I reassessed my day. I still needed to talk to Tad Reynolds and Noleta, Portia and Erik's maid. True, I was a bit disheveled from my ordeal, but I wasn't about to let a setback like the explosion stop me.

In case Erik hadn't left yet for Colombia, I decided to stop at the newspaper first to see Tad. I wasn't sure what I'd say when I saw him because in all honesty I felt guilty about questioning him. He was working his way through college and had two cheating parents, one recently deceased. That had to be tough. Of course, maybe he didn't know about their affairs. Well, I wasn't going to hit him over the head with it. I'd just see what he knew.

I debated walking into the *Rueland News* as myself and almost choked on the idea. Since the perm-rod incident, every local reporter had an eye peeled for Valentine Beaumont and the next calamity. I'd been poked at, teased, even once compared to Lucille Ball in a local "Who's Famous Around Town" magazine article, with a big heart-shaped caption that read I Love Valentine instead of I Love Lucy. Cheeky reporters. Well, I wasn't about to give them any more ammo, especially after the day I'd had.

I charged into the bathroom and rummaged through my makeup bag. I concealed the marks on my skin, smoothed my lightly charred eyebrows, and dabbed foundation on my lips. I wanted to look clear-skinned and naïve, not like I'd barely survived the trials of *Lost*'s island. I groped through my closet for my Oliver Twist hat, then remembered it was in the backseat of my car. Perfect. I'd finish my disguise once I got to the newspaper.

The *Rueland News* was situated in a two-story glass building two miles north of downtown and several miles east of Beaumont's. It was a decent paper that had been there as long as I could remember. I didn't subscribe to the paper, but I often caught headlines on sports heroes, crazed murderers, and occasionally daring beauticians.

I pulled into the visitor parking, my stomach rumbling at what I was about to do, my forehead beading sweat. I inhaled deeply, thought positive thoughts, then glanced at myself in the rearview mirror. *My hat.* I reached into the backseat and tossed aside my sunhat, a ball cap, and a bandana that I kept for bad hair days. I grabbed the Oliver Twist hat, tucked my hair up inside, and slid on those handy glasses from the glove compartment. I hardly recognized my slightly blurred self in the mirror. "More soup, sir," I said in a childlike voice. I rolled my eyes at my silliness and took another deep breath. *Okay, Valentine. Here goes nothing.* I locked the car and marched through the front door.

The marble foyer was empty except for a receptionist perched behind a desk. I pushed up my glasses, clicked along the polished floor, and stopped in front of her. "Excuse me." I smiled warmly, a little intimidated by her tight bun and pointed expression. "Is Tad Reynolds in?"

"Who, may I ask, are you?" Like she wasn't buying the Oliver Twist routine.

Nervousness peaked inside of me, and suddenly, in the midst of this harebrained scheme, I acquired a cockney accent. "I'm Tad's sister, uh, Holly." Sorry, sis. "Just arrived from England. Was at flight attendant school there." I took my hand and swept it up in the air, imitating a plane taking off. "Whoosh."

Inside, I was sweating bullets. Tad's mother had just been murdered, and this was a newspaper. They'd know about Tad's immediate family and likely be suspicious of anyone asking questions. Who even knew if Tad would be here? His mother was buried a week ago. At best, this would be his first day back at work. Why didn't I think of all this before?

I loosened my collar and smiled while the receptionist turned and muttered into her headset.

A moment later, she told me to go through the doors on her left and enter the office on the right at the end of the hall.

Not believing my luck, I said thanks, chucked the accent, and walked through the doors into a huge room where people chatted over a maze of partitions. Phones rang, machines buzzed, and the air danced with the aroma of fresh paper, coffee, and ink. Amidst all the excitement, I turned left and stumbled into an office where a burly, bald-headed man with bushy eyebrows yelled at a young man with knocking knees and quaking fingers. Poor guy reminded me of Ichabod Crane.

"Yeah?" the bald man barked at me. "What do you want?"

"I'm here to see Tad Reynolds." I was determined to keep from shaking in my boots, or heels as it were.

"Across the hall!" he shouted.

The younger man clenched his teeth in an attempt to smile at me or maybe to stop them from chattering. Either way, he wasn't very successful. He dropped his head in shame.

"Sorry." I banged into the door, whipped around, and shut it behind me. Whew! I leaned against it, sure my beating heart was still inside the room.

I crossed the hall and observed the door plaque over my glasses. H. Jackson, Senior Editor. *Hmm.* Maybe Tad was inside. I knocked. No response. I peeked in, but the room was empty. May as well wait since this had to be the right office. I sat in the chair opposite the huge, wooden desk, stifling the urge to rearrange the messy workspace.

"Do you always walk into people's offices without knocking?" a familiar voice boomed.

I shot out of my chair, almost lost my hat, and turned

toward the man who'd reamed out the other guy. "I'm sorry. I did knock."

He moved behind the desk and sat down. "Well, park yourself since you're already here."

"Thank you."

He grunted. "What do you want to know about Tad?"

"Is he here?"

"No, he's not. This is *my* office."

"But the receptionist said—"

"I know what the receptionist said. Look, Miss—"

"Reynolds. I'm Tad's sister, Holly."

He slammed his beefy arms on the desk. "No. You're. Not."

My nervous insides shouted *don't argue.*

"Look," he said. "I'm having an extremely bad day. And you coming in here, trying that line on me, well, let's just say I have a temper. Let's start again, shall we? Who are you *really*, and why are you asking about Tad?"

"My name is Valentine Beaumont."

He leaned back and folded his arms. "Now we're getting somewhere. And take off those silly glasses. They make you look cross-eyed."

I bent my head and slid off the glasses.

"Uh-huh." He wagged a chubby finger at me. "We did a story on you a while back. You're that sadistic broad who wrenched off a guy's scrotum with a perm rod."

"He was about to get away with murder. And I didn't *wrench* it. I merely…twisted it a bit."

"Did you have to make him a soprano?" He shook his head like he wondered what was wrong with the world today. "So! You own that salon where Tad's mother was killed. One of my freelancers just came back from there with a piece on an explosion." He sifted through a pile of loose papers. "Know anything about that?"

I pulled my scraped arms closer to my sides. "Yes and no."

"Good answer." He propped his elbows on the desk

and folded his hands together. "Now, why all the interest in Tad?"

"I have some questions for him."

"Uh-huh. I should have you thrown out, coming in here, nosying around about my employees." He squinted at me. "But I like you. You got spunk." He nodded. "Let me tell you about Tad. Kid came to work for about a week after I hired him. Then he hardly showed up."

"Why not?"

"I don't know. I didn't set up an interview to find out. But I have a feeling it had to do with a curvy blond. She showed up every night when Tad finished work. And every morning he'd come into work a little bit later. By the end of the first week, he was over an hour late. I could tell he wasn't going to amount to much. Lots of those snot-nosed college kids come here expecting to be spoon-fed."

Tad was an only child, and his mother had just died. Where was this guy's compassion?

He chugged from a mug labeled BOSS, then banged it down and wiped his lips like he was thinking things through. "I only gave him the job because his father asked for a favor. I've known Erik for years, done several articles on him. Now *he's* outstanding."

"Maybe Tad's finding it hard to live up to his father's reputation."

"I'm not interested in any psycho-babble, Ms. Beaumont." He turned up his sleeves. "If the kid has issues with his father, and who doesn't, then he needs to deal with them. This is a big mean world. Nobody's going to hold wee Johnny's hand when he's all growed up."

Since I knew how he felt about the Reynolds men, I plunged on. "Did you know Portia?"

"Enough. Can't see what Erik saw in her. Seemed like a gold-digger to me, always in the picture when the camera clicked."

He stood to his full height of about five-nine, walked around the side of his desk, and helped me out of my chair. He carefully avoided the scrapes on my arms. "Look, you must have more fun things to do with your time than chasing criminals. Why don't you put a little ointment on those boo-boos and take my advice. Leave the investigation to the police."

I rolled out of the parking lot and ditched the hat, glasses, and annoyed attitude. H. Jackson wasn't going to deter me. I was just getting warmed up.

Luckily, I had a plan in place for my talk with Noleta. It involved asking if she could recommend a cleaning lady for my mother. The fact that my mother could clean circles around Noleta—or anyone else—was beside the point.

Erik's car wasn't in the driveway when I pulled up to the house, and I was fairly certain by now he'd left for Colombia, but it couldn't hurt to ask.

"The police were here earlier, asking the same question," Noleta said, letting me in, "but they missed him."

I nodded and wondered again if Erik had anything to do with the explosion. Noleta glanced at my scrapes with big round eyes but didn't ask questions. Thankful for that, I focused on what I came for and inquired about cleaning ladies.

"Maybe I could be your mother's maid." Noleta wrung her hands. "I might need a job now that Mrs. Reynolds is gone."

Huh? "Wouldn't you rather stay here? I'm sure Dr. Reynolds wouldn't want you to leave."

She shrugged. "I suppose. But I took my orders from Mrs. Reynolds."

"Do you think that bothered Dr. Reynolds?"

"No. He travels a lot, and Mrs. Reynolds liked to make the decisions."

To say the least. "Did those decisions include entertaining while Dr. Reynolds was at work or away?"

"Yes." She hesitated. "Sometimes friends came over to use the pool or for drinks."

"Anyone, perhaps, more than a friend? Or more often than usual?"

"There was one man." She looked down. "Building a gazebo. He never did finish." She met my gaze. "Mrs. Reynolds was always angry at him. But even after he quit, he came by."

"Why?"

She went red. "They were having relations," she whispered. "One day, Dr. Reynolds came home and almost caught them. But Mr. Wilmont snuck out the back as Dr. Reynolds came in the front door." She looked behind her cautiously. "I think Dr. Reynolds knew. The smell of sweat and sawdust was everywhere." Her eyes widened in horror. "You don't think Dr. Reynolds killed his wife because of the other man, do you?"

I didn't know what I thought. I pulled out Caroline's photo. "Do you recognize this lady?"

She frowned at the picture. "No. Should I?"

"Not necessarily. Did Dr. Reynolds ever bring anyone home?"

"The odd male friend. They'd use the hot tub." She shook her head. "I shouldn't think out loud, but the son is more like his mother. Dr. Reynolds takes Tad golfing once in a while, but mostly he keeps at him about school and parties and not spending enough time finding a job."

I slid the photo back in my bag. "But Tad has a job, right?"

"I don't think Tad has much desire to work. At least at the newspaper."

His boss would agree with that. "Can you tell me where, in Colombia, Dr. Reynolds is staying?"

"Cartagena. The Caribe."

From what I remembered of South American geography, Cartagena wasn't exactly next door to Bogota. That's not to say Erik couldn't jump on a plane and fly, in a short time, to be with Caroline and Albert. I guess the biggest question was, would he? And if so, had that meant they'd conspired to kill Portia?

"Do you want to see Tad?" she asked.

"He's here?"

"Arrived shortly after the police left." She guided me out to a two-tiered pool and then left.

The late afternoon air had cooled, yet Tad was in a bathing suit looking tanned and trimmed, cuddling Dana in a lounge chair next to him. Deep down, I wasn't surprised to see them together. Hadn't Dana said they *used* to date?

"Hi, guys." I gave a little wave to Tad, then turned my fixed smile to Dana.

Her hair was in a ponytail and her private parts were covered by material no wider than an elastic band. She fingered her fireworks tattoo on her chest and gave me a Barbie-doll smile.

"Wow. What happened to you?" Tad sauntered over and gawked from my face to my arms.

"Got too close to exploding objects." I looked for signs of remorse on his face because at this point, everyone looked guilty. All I got was a curled lip.

"Must've been some explosion."

Right. I wasn't sure how much mileage I had left on my coupons, but they were my only in. "I was driving by." I pulled out the coupons. "Thought I'd treat you to a few haircuts."

"Hey, that's pretty nice." In kind, he reached for a bowl of cherries on the patio table. "Want some?"

I appreciated the offer, but I was busy glaring at gum-snapping Dana. She stood and drew circles on the patio with her feet. Maybe she could draw me the reason she lied about their relationship. "So how did you two bump into each other?"

"Huh?" Tad looked confused. "We've been dating for a year."

"Oh?" I looked at Dana. "You didn't mention this when you had your hair done."

"We had to hide it." She chomped back her gum. "His mom hated me."

Tad went over, grasped Dana's hand, and worked his fingers through hers. "Now that she's gone, we don't need to hide our love anymore."

"Congratulations. Where were you when your mother died?"

His eyes narrowed at me. "School."

"Haven't you been home since school finished?"

He crossed his arms over his hairless chest, his choice of body language not getting by these observant eyes. "Why should I answer your questions, Valentine?"

"Your mother died in my salon, Tad. I feel I owe it to her to find the killer." Plus, I wanted to clear my shop's name. "Anything you may remember or feel is important would be helpful."

He uncrossed his arms, looking less defensive. "I've been back and forth a lot from school."

"I understand. Who relayed the news about your mother?"

He cut a sideways glance at Dana. "She did."

I tried to imagine what Dana had said. *It's done? She's dead? We can be together?* Or was my imagination running away from me? "Any idea who could've killed your mother, Tad?"

His mouth thinned. "I've been gone so much I couldn't tell you who my mother made enemies with lately."

Oh boy. This kid had good looks, wavy hair like his father, a confident swagger like his mother. The grieving son he wasn't, which made me wonder whether he'd planned the murder even if he hadn't executed it. I pulled out the picture. "Have you seen this woman before?"

Tad studied the photo. "Nope. Who is she?"

"Just someone your parents might've known."

Dana glanced at the picture, then wandered to the patio table, pulled up a chair, and helped herself to a cherry. Bored, I suspected.

"Was there anyone special in your mother or father's life?" I asked Tad.

He gave a strange look from the photo to me. "What do you mean? Like a therapist?"

"No." How did I say this? "Something more."

He sneered. "How the hell am I supposed to know who my parents are fooling around with? Up until now, I never thought about it." But now that he had, he squinted at me. "Are you telling me a skank killed my mother? Is that woman in the photo involved in this?"

I shoved the picture back in my bag. "I'm not sure. I'm just trying to find a murderer."

I left the coupons, said goodbye, and was almost at the car when I heard, "Valentine, wait!" I turned around and saw Dana tug a teensy shirt over her head while skipping across the lawn.

"About a month ago," she said, stopping in front of me, "one Sunday after final exams, I rode my bike past Dr. Reynolds's office when I saw Mrs. Reynolds go into his building. I was about to call her name, thinking I could talk to her, get her to like me. But something stopped me."

"What?"

"I don't know. There was something different about her, something weird. Instead of calling her, I hopped off my bike and hid behind a tree."

"Spying."

"Kinda. About five minutes went by, then she and Dr. Reynolds came out of the building. After a better look, I realized the woman wasn't Mrs. Reynolds. She was sort of the same build, but it was the hair that was different. It was bulky and wiglike with that fake sheen. Nowhere near as sleek as Mrs. Reynolds's hair."

"How far away were you to be so sure?"

"Far enough not to be detected, but close enough to guess it was fake." She paused, then gave me a patronizing grin. "Before I got into Harvard, I played with the idea of being a famous hairstylist. You know, the kind who makes a ton of money and works on the stars."

"Yes, I know the kind. Did you recognize this woman?"

"Yes and no. She reminded me of someone, but I can't think who. It might've been the woman in the photo. She wore large-framed sunglasses, so I couldn't make out the face. But it seemed like they were really close, as if they'd known each other their whole lives."

"Did you see where they went?"

"They walked along Mariner Street and disappeared down one of the side streets. By then, I'd lost interest. I jumped on my bike and pedaled back the way I came." *Snap.* "I didn't want Tad upset by any of this. Mrs. Reynolds was a witch, and Dr. Reynolds probably deserved an outlet. Tad still doesn't need to know. His father is all he has left."

This was kind of Dana, considering she was a suspect, too. Which had me wondering why she was being so cooperative. Could it be she was eager to put the blame elsewhere? Clear her name? There was no love lost for Portia, so I knew she wasn't doing it for memory's sake.

I pulled the earring from my bag. "Have you seen this before?"

She blew a bubble the size of my fist, then sucked it in. "Whose is it?"

"Portia's."

"Really. Huh."

"Dr. Reynolds said it disappeared at home a while ago. I found it at the salon the day after the murder."

"And you think I took it and dropped it in your shop."

She was quick. "I'm only asking since that's where it was found."

"It's the first time I've seen it. Anyway, Valentine, diamonds aren't for me. I like the trendy stuff."

This was true. Rope bracelets decorated her wrists like always.

"By the way"—she swung her ponytail in my face—"with all these highlights, do you think I'm too blond?"

"Too blond?"

"Yeah, you're right. Ridiculous." She flipped her hair back and skipped up the lawn.

I groaned and slid behind the steering wheel of my car. I was confused about a lot of things. Topping the list was the obvious question. Had Caroline been in Rueland? And was she the woman Dana had seen? But wouldn't Mrs. Dougal have said if her daughter had come back? If she'd known? Maybe not. After all, this would make her daughter a suspect, and what mother wouldn't try to protect her child?

I couldn't pinpoint what it was, but something felt off.

Chapter 12

Before everything closed for the day, I drove around town like a madwoman and bought a new magazine table, picked out new carpet for the waiting area, and purchased a few other necessities for work. Satisfied I hadn't forgotten anything, I dropped off the goods at the shop, pulled into my driveway fifteen minutes later, and let myself into the house.

I had one message. It was from Brody. And he didn't sound like himself. He'd only called once before from the restaurant to tell me a blind date that I was meeting there had flown the coop. Of course, this was after my date had learned about my past mishap. "Don't worry yourself," Brody had said. "The lad had a face like a monkey and the manners of a boar. He did you a favor in leaving."

This message wasn't over a blind date.

"I have something, Valentine," Brody said into the machine, "in regards to the murder. Don't concern yourself. I'll go to the police station straightaway."

Saying not to concern myself was like suspending shimmering diamonds at eye level and telling me not to touch. I glanced at the clock. Six-thirty. Dinnertime at the Wee Irish Goat. I'd wait two hours, then call and find out what Brody was talking about. Heaven knows, I could use a clue.

I decided on French toast while I waited. I beat an egg, added milk, then doused two pieces of bread in the mixture. I browned one side of the slices when the suspense got to me. I just saw Brody a few hours ago. What could he want? I picked up the phone and dialed the restaurant. No answer. Not even a machine taking messages. Odd. I hung up, deciding who to call next when the phone flickered. It was my cousin.

"You won't believe it," Faren wailed. "And you just saw him on your date a week ago."

"My date?" I turned my back on the frying pan and envisioned Craig. Though I winced at the thought of him, I didn't wish anything terrible to happen to him. At least nothing big and terrible. Something small and terrible like crashing his Porsche would be horrible enough. By the anguish in Faren's voice, this had to be of astronomical proportions.

"It's Brody," she said. "He had a massive heart attack."

"What?"

"Nina called, said she couldn't make our glass-blowing class. She's a real mess. Val, Brody died on the way to the hospital."

"*No.*" A spear shot through my heart. My back slammed against the counter. I couldn't believe it. I just saw him a few hours ago. I hung up and stood motionless, staring at the cupboards in a daze until a sizzling sound alerted me.

I spun around to the smell of burnt toast filling the room. I switched off the burner and fanned the kitchen with a tea towel. Then I threw my smoldering supper in the garbage. I stumbled to the answering machine and listened to Brody's message again. I couldn't make sense of his words, and the sound of his voice made me weak. I sucked in bravely, and then it all came out in a jerky rush. I pressed the tea towel to my eyes and sobbed like a baby. I cried for Brody, and I cried for Portia. I cried for the hospital kids and the Third World kids needing glasses. I wept until I was spent. I was a mess. And when I finally made it to the bathroom, I blubbered in the mirror at my blotchy-eyed, chattering-lipped face.

I unraveled a mile of toilet paper and blew my nose. Then I scuffed into the living room and slouched on the sofa. The phone rang, but I ignored it. My mother's voice came on the machine, and there was sorrow in her tone. Undoubtedly, she'd heard about Brody, but I didn't feel strong enough to talk. I just wanted to be alone.

The night wore on. I dozed and sobbed and blew my nose, which was raw from blowing, so I smeared Vaseline around it, making it more red and shiny. I wasn't aware of time, but thankfully, I fell unconscious and woke the next morning to the sound of some deliriously happy, barking dog.

I peeled my eyes apart, hauled myself off the couch, and glared soberly outside. It was the last day of June, almost two weeks since the murder. Neighbors were stringing up flags for the Fourth of July this weekend, and my spirit was sinking into oblivion. Thoughts of cookouts and fireworks didn't bring me any joy. I turned from the window and almost missed a cruiser roll down the street, same as yesterday. At least Romero's gesture warmed me.

I stood under a pelting shower, then numbly wrapped a towel around me when the carpet people called. They'd be at the salon by eight to install the new carpet in the waiting area. Great. Life went on. I packed a sandwich, brushed my hair miserably, and moved into overdrive so I could let them in.

By nine o'clock, the last staple had been shot. The industrial fans were removed, the workers pulled out, and my staff trickled in, everyone talking about the fire.

"This is too much." Phyllis waved her water bottle around. "Murder. Missing deliveryman. Lost earring. Crazy paparazzi. Unexplained explosion. And don't get me started on the shop suddenly being as popular as a Beverly Hills spa."

"It's interesting meeting so many new people," Judy said.

"Who cares what you think?" Phyllis cranked over to massage her foot. "And why don't you get real. My feet are so swollen by the end of a day, I can hardly stand." She peered in her bottle. "I wonder if there's something foul in the water."

"There's something foul in here," Max said, "but it ain't in the water."

"Everything's back to normal," I said. "The window's fixed, the rug's perfect, and there's no permanent damage. I even got in a little shopping yesterday and found this cute antique-bronze magazine table with the curlicue legs. Plus, I picked up a new stack of hair books and even bought a new hand mirror." I held back from giving Phyllis a lethal look for smashing the other one to smithereens. "I also purchased a new fire extinguisher. This one is idiot-proof."

"That means even you can use it, Phyllis," Max said.

Phyllis stuck out her tongue at Max.

"If things are back to normal," Max said to me, "why don't you look normal? And I don't mean the scratches on your arms."

No one had to tell me I looked like hell. My hair had a wild Steven Tyler thing going on, my shoulders were heavy, my eyes puffy, my nose chapped. Everyone stared at me so expectantly I had to stifle the lump in my throat. "Brody, from the Wee Irish Goat, died yesterday."

"What?" they chorused.

"I love that place!" Max said.

"Me too," Judy echoed.

"They make the best veal Parmesan," Phyllis said.

There were a few more sad comments, and then everyone got to work. I took a second in my office to fix my face. The only answer to red-rimmed, swollen eyes and uneven skin tone was more makeup. I smudged on green eye pencil to neutralize the red. Then I powdered my nose and tamed my hair. After I looked semihuman, I decided to call Romero at work since I'd left his cell number at home. He'd probably heard about Brody. But I also wanted his take on Tad. Was the boy simply irresponsible or was he well acquainted with the police? And what about

Dana? Was she as conniving as she seemed? Maybe I was way off. At least he could tell me if they caught up with Erik.

"Detective Romero left for New York this morning," the sergeant on Dispatch said.

"New York? When will he be back?"

"Couldn't tell you."

What did that mean? He didn't mention anything about this yesterday, although he said he had to run after he brought me back from lunch. Was this related to the case? His past? I fumed. Of all the times to take off. Well, if he wanted me to know what was up, he'd tell me. Right now, I was mourning the loss of a friend and no closer to finding Portia's murderer.

I hung up and plodded past Max and Phyllis. Max was in the middle of a spiral perm. Phyllis was at a hair dryer, seeing if her lady in rollers was dry. I entered the dispensary and pulled out hair extension trays for my next client. Judy gathered tools by my side to assist me.

"I may have to pop down to Eddie's Garage Friday afternoon and pick up my car." She closed a cupboard and placed a crochet hook in the tray.

I eyed Phyllis, then Judy. "Tell me you're not having your seats reupholstered, too."

She opened her mouth to answer when we heard a cracking sound at the hair dryers. We looked out at Phyllis hoisting the dryer hood off her lady's head for the second time. The lady rubbed her head and rolled her eyes around like the marble in a pinball machine.

"If you'd been sitting properly," Phyllis said to her, "you wouldn't have gotten conked. Now sit still. You need another minute to dry."

The woman sat like a statue, holding her breath, and Judy smiled at me. "No, my problems are more serious. My car's been backfiring. Eddie thinks it might need new spark plugs. He said to bring it in Thursday in case he gets to it earlier."

"That's fine," I said. "Go when you have a break."

The morning slid by, and around noon I had a moment alone in the dispensary where I stole a bite of lunch. I had my sandwich in my hand when Max paraded in with a towel full of spiral perm rods. He dumped the rods in the sink and got to work washing them.

The explosion had been on my mind all morning, and the news of Brody's death left a painful gnaw in my stomach. But I picked away at my sandwich, currently worrying about other things. "Are you going to tell me how Saturday's interview went?"

Max looked over his shoulder at me. "I'm here, aren't I?"

"What does that mean?"

He turned and leaned his back against the counter. "It means I turned down the job."

I examined my sandwich to hide the relief washing over me. "You're not staying because of all the madness here, are you?"

"We're still in one piece, right?"

"Barely."

"Well, it turns out you were right."

"I was?"

"Maybe they do have champagne treats, caviar dishes, Godiva chocolates—"

"Max! What was I right about?"

"The part about being loved. You're my partner, my friend, and I'll always treasure your love and support. There wasn't much love at Supremo Stylists. And aside from that, every last one of them was as phony as a three-dollar bill. I wouldn't have lasted there a day." He grinned. "Phyllis and I may have a love-hate relationship, but at least it's real. So?" He tossed the washed perm rods onto a clean towel and jiggled it lightly. "How was *your* weekend?"

"Fine." To be truthful, I wasn't up to admitting another failed blind date. I took a bite of my sandwich and swallowed.

"Fine?" He did his hand on hip thing. "There are a hundred ways I could interpret *fine.*" He threw the rods in a tray, grabbed a stool, and rolled up to me like he was in for a treat. "*Now.*" He rubbed his hands together. "What really happened?"

That's what I liked about Max. He lived for details. "You're right. Jason is funny, handsome, and interesting."

"Then I don't get it." He frowned. "What were you doing yesterday with the good detective?"

"Who told you I was with Romero?"

"Nobody." He rolled the stool back a foot. "I wasn't sure until now."

"Am I missing something?"

"Jason saw you and Tall, Dark, and Handsome enter the Wee Irish Goat yesterday."

My throat ached at the mention of Brody's place. "We went for lunch to talk about the case, if you must know."

"Yeah? So how is a disabled person like Jason supposed to compete with Mr. Long Arm of the Law?"

"Max, Jason won't be on crutches forever. And he's not interested in me."

He slapped his chin to his chest, eyes bugged out. "So he's blind and deaf, too?"

I smiled at Max, my greatest cheerleader. "You're a little behind on his love life. He's found his own romance."

He sighed a sigh when love's gone wrong. "Then the date was all for nothing."

I peeked out the dispensary, then back at Max. "It was actually a very enlightening evening." I took a big breath. "Also, I've signed up for self-defense class." Not exactly where I intended for this conversation to go, but saying it aloud made it feel real.

"*What?*" He looked out at the others cutting hair, then lowered his voice. "When did you do that?"

"After the murder and before today."

"Why, for heaven's sake?"

I told him about my threatening conversation with Pace, my fear over Twix hiring Pace, what I'd learned from Andy, my incident with Gavin, the phone call, and the note. "Not to mention the explosion. I feel creeped out, like someone's watching me. And I'm beginning to attack people."

"You threw hot wax on Gavin's head? Why do I miss all the fun?"

"The pot was turned off, and it wasn't burning. Plus, he went nuts."

"You're just on edge. Heck, I had to crack open a bottle of Zinfandel the other night. Of course, my edginess is because I'm still having nightmares after seeing Phyllis's tuchus."

I peered out at Phyllis licking her hand, then smoothing her client's hair.

Max got up and pulled the pocket door halfway across. "What you need is a handsome, virile man to watch over you like Kevin Costner protected Whitney Houston in *The Bodyguard*."

I sized him up. "Right."

"Don't talk to me like that. I'm not volunteering to be your Kevin Costner. My body's a temple." This from a guy who guzzled Sangrias like Kool-Aid. "I don't much like the idea of dodging bullets for anyone. Though I could be like Costner if I wanted to. We have the same build, but he's getting paunchy."

I shook my head. "That's okay. I don't know how protected I'd feel by someone with a degree in hairdressing."

He crossed his arms. "If you don't want my help, just say so. No need to get offensive."

Why me? "I'm probably just extra nervous because Romero's in New York."

"New York? What for?"

"I don't know. But I'm not sitting around like a damsel in distress."

He slapped his hand on the counter. "Good for you."

"I'm glad you feel that way because I signed you up, too."

"What?" He plopped back on the stool and wheeled away from me. "No. No. No."

I yanked him closer by the shirt. "I can't walk in there alone. I need you to be my partner."

"Partner! What about Twix? She's your bosom buddy. Take her."

"She's too busy throttling kids and tearing down walls. It has to be you."

He squealed. "Where is this place?"

"Downtown, six blocks south."

He put up his palms. "I don't do downtown. It leaves a bad taste in my mouth."

"Then gargle when you get home."

He did some deep breathing, most likely buying time. "Okay. Let's look at this rationally. You want to protect yourself because you're scared."

I bit my bottom lip, waiting for the Max logic to kick in.

"I can appreciate that, but a self-defense class?"

"Karate actually."

He looked like he'd swallowed jagged glass. "This is ridiculous. Buy a German shepherd. An alarm. Better still, get an electric fence. You can zap anyone suspicious who comes calling."

"I'm not getting any of those things. It's got to be karate. You should be thanking me."

"For what?"

"For taking the necessary steps to help you protect yourself."

"Hey, those who live by the sword die by the sword."

"There won't be any swords. The only weapon you'll have is you."

"I don't want to be a weapon. And you already carry an arsenal in your bag. It's who you are. I mean, who else walks the streets of Rueland with a straight razor, scissors"—he held up his fingers, counting off items—"hairspray—"

"Okay, I get it."

"Flat iron."

"Max!"

"This isn't Boston, you know. When you caught Freddie's murderers, you damn near killed the one brute, puncturing him with your metal tail comb. By the time you finished, he had more spouts than the Trevi Fountain."

He was right. I could be tough when I was frightened into it.

"And you castrated the other guy, winding that perm rod around his family jewels a gazillion times."

"Oh, yeah. I almost forgot *since I haven't been reminded since yesterday!* Anyway, I did him a favor. He's lead vocalist in the penitentiary choir. And I let him keep the perm rod as a remembrance of who to thank."

"See? You need karate about as much as I need lip moisturizer. Although, my cherry flavor is getting down. Come to think of it, I could use some hydrating cream."

My life was in shambles, and Max was jabbering about cosmetics. "Another few weeks of this and you can have my supply because *I'll be dead!*"

He shuddered.

"Karate. Tonight. Seven-thirty. I'll pick you up."

Max wasn't a quitter. "What about Zumba?"

"They won't miss me for one week. If I like karate, I'll go to Thursday Zumba class."

I slid open the door, looking him squarely in the eye. "Seven-thirty. Be ready."

Chapter 13

For the first time in like, ever, Mrs. Horowitz had made an appointment. Mrs. Horowitz was rich and had nothing better to do with her time except visit beauty salons. On any given day, she'd ramble in at five minutes to closing, push past clients who actually went to the trouble of making appointments, and ask me to manicure her horny nails or color her brittle hair.

I'd handled Mrs. Horowitz in several ways, ranging from sympathy to honesty. But she was wily and heard what she chose. What's more, if we didn't fit her in, she'd wander down the street and pull the same stunt in the next shop. But within a few months, she'd be back after tiring the competition. Despite all that, I liked Mrs. Horowitz. She added a unique flavor to the salon.

Today, she wanted her eyebrows raised and wrinkles removed. The wonderful thing about Mrs. Horowitz was her absolute faith in me. I led her down the hall, contemplating how I could make a silk purse out of a sow's ear. "I'll do my best, Mrs. Horowitz." Not that I'd imply Mrs. Horowitz was a sow. I could at least decrease her frown lines and bring to light a fresh layer of skin. The rest was up to the good Lord. And in the end, she'd still be the same watery-eyed, close talker. God love her.

The phone rang, and a moment later Phyllis yelled for me like I was in a deep dark mine.

I ushered Mrs. Horowitz into Ti Amo, a.k.a. the murder room, and waited for her to get settled. That was the other nice thing about Mrs. Horowitz. She'd be happy in Siberia as long as there was someone there to pamper her.

I got to the phone and heard Tom's voice. My heart surged, expecting news on Albert.

"I don't want any tears," my order man from Alluve said.

Tears? I sucked in air, afraid something had happened to Albert.

"Your nail polish is on backorder."

"Oh." I exhaled. "Thanks."

"I have other news."

I knew Tom's sense of humor. "What, nail files are on sale?"

"No. Albert's back."

"What? When?"

"Yesterday. He reported back to work this morning."

Was it my imagination or was it odd Albert had arrived back the same day Erik had left for Colombia? "Can I speak to him?"

"He's out on deliveries, but I can have him call you."

I wasn't ready to condemn Albert, but I wasn't entirely certain of his innocence since I'd learned of his past. "Have you talked to him?"

"No. He was in back, loading trucks by the time I came in. Our paths rarely cross."

I wound the phone cord around my finger while a dozen questions ran through my mind. Despite growing evidence, deep down I still didn't believe Albert had killed Portia. But what if I was wrong? What if this was some grand scheme that had taken years to plot and had finally unfolded in my shop? Albert obviously knew Portia because of Erik's relationship with Caroline. And he did give Portia that queer look before he left that day. That's *if* he left.

More puzzling was that two decades had gone by since Erik had dated Caroline. Still, it was a possibility they were involved again. It happened all the time. I'd once dated a guy for a year, broke up, then dated him eight years later. He was still a loser, and God only knew what I saw in him the first time. But the fact was we'd reconnected.

I wondered if Erik had planned this trip to Colombia to begin a new life with Caroline. Had he exterminated Portia without getting his hands dirty? If so, a guy with a convicted past was the obvious choice to do the job. But would Albert help a man who'd once broken his sister's heart? Things just didn't add up. Hard as I tried, I couldn't see Albert planning something so evil. Then again, what was the envelope I'd mailed all about? *Stop already*. No more speculating. At least not until I'd spoken to him.

Judy stomped into the dispensary after I hung up. She went straight to the cupboard and pulled out colors and peroxide, banging everything onto the counter. "Every time that weirdo Sean Buckley comes in," she said, "he asks me out."

I put aside my thoughts on Albert and shrugged at Judy. "So, go out." Listen to me. Dating expert.

She screwed up her nose. "Have you lost your senses? Look at him."

I peered at Sean squeezed in her chair. He had a face like an unshelled peanut, red hair that resembled rooster feathers, and he was dressed in a green velour jogging suit. I didn't waver. "Guys are always asking you out. How long has it been since you've dated?"

"Not long enough to consider dating this screwball." She mixed products in a bowl. "You know what he does when I work on him?" She closed in on me. "He stares. Not like most people who watch in the mirror. No, this guy stares right into my eyes the whole time. Even when I'm at his side, he squirms in his chair so he can see my pupils. It's so not normal."

The only other time I'd seen Judy so put out was when Portia called her Orphan Annie. Judy sprinkled salt in

Portia's tea, then served it with a smile. "So he likes you. He's lovable, in a stray-dog-covered-in-fleas sort of way."

"Yuck." She pulled back a curl from her forehead. "I'm going to give him purple hair and a Mohawk."

I watched Sean make googly eyes at Judy, and out of the blue I saw Craig in his purple ruffled shirt, leering at my breasts. "You're right." I turned back to her. "Go nuts."

I glanced at the clock. Mrs. Horowitz! I rushed down the hall and found her patiently sitting on the facial bed, swinging her legs, inspecting her yellowed, horny nails. Huge sigh.

"Do you have time for a manicure, too, Valentine?" Her voice was demure, but I knew better.

The days were getting crazier, a murderer still hadn't been found, and Mrs. Horowitz was a constant reminder my world would never be perfect. Yet I wasn't losing sight of my goal. Albert was home, and I needed to ramp up my search.

I lowered Mrs. Horowitz back on the table. "I'll definitely try to make time."

Except for Zumba and mountain biking, I wasn't particularly into sweating, smelling foul, gasping for air, or shaping my body into a pretzel. I was a self-declared prima ballerina at age seven. That was the extent of my fitness life. I didn't do shorts, T-shirts, or running shoes with check marks on the sides. And I didn't wear red, white, and blue stripes. Those were for flags and race cars. Not Valentine Beaumont! Nevertheless, I dressed in a white spandex top and black leggings, doing my best to appear athletic.

Since I was ready in good time, I wanted to make three quick stops before I picked up Max.

First, I had to drop by the hospital and see Kylie. My eyes misted, thinking about Brody's passing and how hard this would be for her. Maybe a surprise visit would bring a smile.

The mood in the hospital was somber, like everyone knew a legend had died. In a way, Brody had been a legend. Without a doubt, he'd touched many lives.

I reached Kylie's room and found her surrounded by her parents and siblings. They were talking about the upcoming funeral and visitation. I didn't want to intrude, so I made my condolences brief, gave Kylie a big hug, and left her a tube of her favorite vanilla-scented lipstick. Her eyes brightened at that, and this soothed my heart. Kylie had survived cancer. She'd pull through this, too.

Next, I drove to Albert's. I had so many questions for him, I almost tattooed a list to my arm. If Albert worked a full day today, he'd probably be home unpacking from his trip. Then again, from the messy state of his place, unpacking likely wouldn't be top priority. When I got to his duplex, there was no one home, and his car was gone. Beautiful.

I may have struck out at Albert's, but I also wanted to show Andy Caroline's picture. Luckily, I caught him in Dino Hosta's parking lot on his way into work. I gave him a toot and pulled up beside him. I showed him Caroline's picture and asked if she was the woman he saw with Erik.

"Could be." He tucked his white shirt into his trousers and grabbed the photo. "Like I said, it was dark and busy. And the red hair's throwing me. Can I say she's a definite maybe?"

I thanked Andy and zoomed away less than satisfied. Seemed nobody could positively identify Caroline. If she wasn't the mystery woman, then who was? I wrestled with that thought until I picked up Max at seven-thirty at his condo in Waltham.

He jogged to the car and slipped inside looking like tennis champion Roger Federer.

"Where do you think we're going?" I asked. "Wimbledon?"

"I didn't know what to expect."

"You can expect being tossed by a karate expert with a white robe and black belt. Now take off the head and wristbands."

He yanked off the sweatbands and put on a pout. "By the way, you're late."

I followed his eyes to the clock. It read 7:38. "I'm not late." I whipped out my watch with the broken clasp. "See? Seven-thirty."

Max tugged the watch out of my hand. "You still carting around this old piece of junk? When are you going to move on? It can't even keep time." He threw it back in my bag.

Okay, so it was a little off. Maybe I wasn't ready to get rid of it. Anyway, it was none of Max's business. I didn't tell him what to eliminate in his personal life.

We drove on in silence and pulled up to Karate King twenty minutes later. The business was crammed between a pawn shop and a sub joint. Both places were open. Neither was busy.

Max pointed across the street. "A coffee shop! Why don't I treat you to a cappuccino?"

"I don't drink that stuff, remember?"

"I was hoping you'd start."

I parked at the curb and caught the stench of onions from the sub shop. I dragged Max inside Karate King, a second later, wishing for onion stench over the rank, sweaty gym smell.

Twenty or so people in white outfits were partnered up, tossing each other onto thick padded mats. There was a lot of grunting and thwumping. The smell was so offensive I slid my perfume out of my bag and sprayed a mist over myself. *Ahh.*

A tiny Asian man, with black hair jutting out three inches in every direction, abandoned his partner and approached us. He bowed.

Max and I looked at each other and bowed back.

"You new people."

"Yes," I said.

"You call me Sensei." He clapped his hands, and from the back of the room a three-hundred-pound man—give or take an ounce—with a tiny ponytail spiked on top of his head, lumbered over. He gave a toothy smile and rubbed his humongous hands together.

Max looked up at the giant and back down at Sensei. "What's that?"

"Dojo. His name mean 'place of training.' Good for big man in karate shop. He your partner."

It looked like the lights went out on Max. Dojo took a step forward, and Max jackknifed his knees high and sprinted around the room, screeching like a fifth grader.

"Dojo is pussycat." Sensei smiled at me. "Good for beginner."

Max zipped out the door we'd just entered, Dojo on his heels.

"You, *my* partner." Sensei waddled to a changing room and handed me a white outfit.

Moments later, I pulled the curtain aside, my hair in a no-nonsense bun, my body swathed in a white jacket and pants that were ten inches too short. I plodded barefoot into the gym, ready to aerate someone's back with my toes.

I met Sensei on one of the mats, eager to begin class. He gave five simple instructions, then without warning emitted an earth-shattering cry, yanked my arm, and threw me four feet in the air. I fell hard, my head missing the mat a good three inches. Stubbornly, I rubbed my scalp, then scrambled to my feet. I wasn't going to be discouraged by a little guy wrapped in Kleenex.

Sensei looked pleased. "Good reflexes. First lesson in how to scare off bad guy." Then he gave me another artistic fling.

I screamed bloody murder and landed spread-eagle with a *wump*. For a second, I couldn't see a thing, maybe because my eyeballs were rolling around in my head. I gasped for air and clutched my chest. This was it. I was having a heart attack. I wheezed for oxygen and turned to the exit. Where the hell was Max while I was dying here?

After a few more rounds being hurled everywhere but the mat, I finally had my chance. I memorized everything Sensei had told me. Then I huffed and puffed and gave him a mean toss to the ground. I screeched in pain and broke three nails in the process, but it felt empowering flinging the little sadomasochist.

"Not bad." He rubbed his hip. "You fast learner. Next time we work on karate kicks."

I staggered out the door fifty minutes later and saw Max sitting beside Dojo on a bench outside the coffee shop. I ripped out what was left of my bun and limped to the car, dropping my bag inside.

"Yoo-hoo!" Max skipped over. "Uh-oh. What happened to you?"

"I fell."

"How many times?"

I gave him a murderous glare. "Where'd you go, hero?"

"For a latté with Dojo." We watched Dojo clump back into Karate King. "He's actually pretty sweet."

I could barely turn my head. Even my hair hurt. "I'm glad you had a tender moment."

He kneaded my shoulders and sighed. "Now I'm going to relax in a friend's hot tub."

"Hot tub! You didn't *do* anything."

"The thought of all that thumping made me sore. So? When are we coming back?"

"How's never?"

"I tried telling you." He helped me into the car. "The ammunition in your bag is more powerful than all the karate champs in the world. Now do you believe me?"

I blinked stupidly, wallowing in self-pity. I was a petite female with shiny hair, good skin, and nice teeth. At the moment I didn't know if I'd live to see tomorrow. I couldn't have cared less whether I had enough ammo to blow up the Great Wall of China.

Wait a minute. I possessed a certain amount of toughness, didn't I? I kept bouncing back when I could've given up. If I admitted defeat now, I may as well kiss my future goodbye.

I imagined my shop for sale, my landlord blockading my house, and me moving back in with my parents. When I saw me slicing my neck with my razor, I poked up my head with new resolve. "Let's go."

"Where to?" Max buckled up.

"Tomorrow."

I tossed and turned and finally slept on a side that didn't need bandaging. Then a knocking sound woke me. I fought the pain in my shoulders and sat up. Eleven o'clock. *Oof.* I collapsed back on the bed and heard it again. Ugh. Sounded like the door. Groggily, I rolled out of bed, traipsed to the front door, and flung it open.

Romero stood one hand on his hip, the other resting on the doorframe. He was dressed in black jeans and a cream mock-neck top, and he looked extremely handsome.

My heart thumped at the sight of him. "You're back."

"Back?"

In the reflection of the streetlight, I noticed more closely he looked worn, his hair seemed wilder, and he smelled of sharp cologne, a reminder of the big city.

"From New York." I slid up the dimmer switch on the wall, wondering, despite his apparent fatigue, if he'd missed me.

He gazed below my neck, and I thought I had my answer. If nothing else, the heat in his eyes almost dissolved my sore spots. I glanced down where he was staring and suddenly realized I was half naked. *Yikes.* I backed up toward the bedroom, my finger high. "Stay right there."

"Need any help?" If he hadn't looked so serious, it might've been funny.

"No!" I threw a robe over my sheer baby-dolls, slipped on my puffy slippers with cupcakes on top, and gaped in the mirror. *Eek*. My hair was teased up into a cone, my face—still tender from the explosion—reflected my aches, and I hadn't bothered fixing my hacked-off nails. Plus, I was moving like Quasimodo. It didn't get any uglier than this.

I grabbed a brush in one hand, lipstick in the other. How long would it take to whip up a decent image? Whoa. What was I doing? What did I care what Romero thought? I stopped short and really looked at myself. Valentine in the raw. Had the childhood mocking gone so deep that the real me felt this inadequate? Slowly, it dawned on me. If I planned to move forward with my life and *any* relationship, I had to first accept myself for who I was, warts and all. Okay, not warts. If I had warts, they'd be removed. But blemishes and all. I dropped the brush and lipstick, tightened my robe, and mustered some self-confidence as I walked back into the living room.

"I woke you," Romero said.

I scraped a ripped fingernail through my hair. "It's okay. I'm wide-awake."

His eyes looked drawn, his shoulders tense.

"What's wrong?" I asked, forgetting about myself.

He rubbed his unshaved jaw. "Are those scarves hanging on your windows? I didn't notice them last time."

"Yes, they're scarves, and they're not new."

His gaze roamed down to my feet. "Cupcakes, huh? I think I like the sexy red shoes better."

I blushed at Romero recalling the shoes I'd worn the first time we'd met. But these were stall tactics. Romero didn't stall. "Is this why you came over at eleven o'clock at night, to discuss my style of decorating? And talk about footwear?"

His gaze settled on my eyes, his lips tight. "Dana Kir is dead."

"What?" I reached for the wall, steadying myself while the news sank in. Tears blurred my eyes, and I began to shake. "Why didn't you just tell me instead of talking about window fashions and shoes and *staring* at me like that?"

He raised his palms like he couldn't believe my hysteria. "You came to the door with nothing on."

"I was *sleeping!*" Every sore muscle, every traumatic event in the past twelve days, swam to the forefront. I swiped my eyes and clomped back and forth, trying to keep a lid on. But it was no good. Two clients were dead, and all my efforts to find a killer hadn't helped a bit.

Romero spun me around and dragged me to his chest. The look in his eyes said he wouldn't apologize for being a man, so get over it.

My heart throbbed fiercely, my gasps for air uneven. I backed out of his embrace and got a hold of myself. "How? When?"

"Tonight," he said. "She was waiting at the Reynolds's for Tad to return from counseling. The maid was off. Dana had a key. Someone came into the house and shot her."

"Robbery?"

"Nothing was touched, according to Tad. Likely, the murderer was there for another reason. Dana got in the way."

I sat on the couch to relieve my wobbly legs and think about all this. Tad seemed pretty devoted to Dana, but what if I was mistaken? "You think Tad's telling the truth?"

"Anything's possible," Romero said, bringing me a glass of water. "We checked them both out after Portia's death. Tad's had priors. Speeding tickets, driving under the influence, minor assault a few years ago."

"He didn't strike me as having a violent streak."

"Typical Bay State bullshit. Rich kid plus lots of money and pent-up energy equals trouble."

"What about school?"

"Flunked half his classes."

No sense bringing up the employment argument. "What about Dana?"

"Clean."

"Do you think the murders are connected?"

"Probably."

"But you just said the murderer was there for another reason and Dana got in the way."

"There's still a link."

I frowned and chewed on a jagged nail.

"I'm afraid to ask." He sat beside me. "But what are you thinking?"

I sipped my water, ignoring the jab. "When we discovered Portia, Dana acted like she'd spotted Katy Perry. Didn't even bat an eye over the dead body. In fact, you'd have thought she'd just received a lifetime supply of bubblegum." I thought about this some more. "Say she was involved in Portia's murder, why would someone turn around and kill her?"

"Maybe she pissed off her accomplice."

"But who else could she have been involved with?" I sighed. "Does Erik know?"

"He's flying back tomorrow. And just when we cleared him of any involvement in the fire."

"So he didn't set it?"

"He was nowhere near the salon. He'd been at his office before driving to the airport."

I nodded and went to the answering machine. "This came from Brody." I clicked play.

Romero looked grim. "I guess you heard. He had a coronary when he got to the station. They found him slumped over the steering wheel in the parking lot."

A gnawing ache pressed in the pit of my stomach. "What do you think the message meant?"

"Not sure. We're interviewing everyone at the restaurant." He paused. "There's something else. Albert's back."

I hung my head. "I know. I found out this afternoon."

"What the hell, Val. You protecting the guy? Why didn't you tell me?"

The first time he used my given name, it had to be in anger. "I have a business to run, if you remember. And I was working on customers. Hardly an opportune time to call."

"You think hair and nails are more important than finding a killer?" He got off the sofa and chucked a pillow upside down.

"Maybe when I tried calling, you were off gallivanting in New York." No need to admit I called *before* I learned of Albert's return. "And leave my pillows alone."

"Maybe some things are none of your business." He gave an extra *grrr* for the pillow comment.

I bit the insides of my cheeks, holding in the sting from his words.

"Your friend flies home Monday, and this girl's murdered the next day. If Albert did it, he didn't waste any time."

I had to agree. "You're not going to arrest him, are you?"

"Not yet. But you can be damned sure he'll be interrogated thoroughly." His hot gaze slid down my robe, which had come loose. Strange thing was I didn't care. I would've stood there bare-breasted, and it was all Romero's doing. Coming here late at night, all overworked and barbaric, smelling so manly. It was crazy to think of anything but the horrifying news he'd just delivered, but in that instant, I hungered for his mouth on mine, his beard chafing my skin. I almost reached up to satisfy my yearning when reality struck. He was a cop here on business. *And you're a fool to think otherwise.*

"By the way," he said, not averting his eyes like any decent gentleman would, "Gavin's story checked out. Appointment on Duchess Street was legit."

A second later, he was gone.

I seethed. Yay for Gavin. I blew out a sigh and yanked my belt tight. *Ooh.* One minute I wanted to inhale Romero, the next I wanted to shave every last hair spilling over his collar. So I knew about Albert's return. Did Romero think I worked for the police? Ha! Not bloody likely! I had a business to run, too. *And* he didn't mention New York. What was that? More secrets?

I locked the door, smacked off the lights, stamped back

to the bedroom, ripped off my robe, and flopped on the bed. I breathed deeply and attempted to eradicate Romero from my mind. No good. After ten seconds, I pummeled the mattress in a mini temper tantrum. Mad as I was, I couldn't stop thinking about his hot stare or my stupid eagerness.

My heart raced, and blood coursed through my groin. I looked down. Great. And my nipples were raised. *Errr!* I wanted to hit something. I wanted to wrestle a lion. I wanted to scream.

I stumbled out of bed and did the only reasonable thing in this state. I sucked on an ice cube and took a cold shower. Then I plodded back to bed. I was swaddled in my robe, shivering, but at least my mind was off Romero.

I was wrapping my head around what I'd just learned when the shoe phone clanged. By reflex, I lunged for it. No one spoke. Just a gurgled sound that shifted to heavy breathing, and then a bloodcurdling scream. I shook my arm, dropping the high heel like it was a leech sucking my blood. I ripped the cord from the wall and dove under the covers.

My whole body trembled, and I ached all over. I should've called the police, or at least Holly, but I didn't want to face anyone right now. I didn't want to think about Portia, Erik, Dana, or Tad. I didn't want to worry about scary notes, fire bombs, or chilling calls. I especially didn't want to think about Romero. I was tired, and I just wanted sleep. I closed my eyes tight, curled into a ball, and prayed morning would come soon.

Chapter 14

I woke the next morning to the peaceful rhythm of a neighbor watering his lawn. I laid there a minute and listened to the steady sound, when a dream I had last night came to mind. I couldn't remember details, but I had a huge ghostbuster of a can of pepper spray in my hands, and I sprayed everyone and everything that came at me within a six-foot radius. It was a little overkill, but in view of what I'd been through, equipping me with pepper spray didn't seem all that ridiculous.

At least my emotions were in order today, and I felt more in control. To heck with Romero and his policing. I was as kickass as Lara Croft: Tomb Raider—or I would be once I could feel my toes.

I rolled out of bed and sucked in a painful breath. Not only were my toes numb, I felt like I'd been piñata-ed to death. I shuffled in a Frankenstein walk to the shower, where I stood under hot water until I could move without cracking. Once I felt almost flexible, I fixed my nails and ate while I did my makeup. Then I slipped into a lightweight-but-clingy pink dress and clasped on my Austrian crystal bracelet and matching earrings. My theory was if I looked good, I'd feel good.

I flicked on the TV and cranked up the volume on Dan

the Weatherman. Then I hobbled back to the bedroom and plugged in the phone.

"Batten down the hatches," Dan said in his chipper-yet-grave tone. "Sunny today, but a storm's heading up the eastern coast."

I stuck my head around the corner in time to see his Colgate smile. Then I trotted to the front door and peeked outside. My wind chimes were doing a strange little dance in the turbulent breeze while Dan went on about a hurricane taking out the Florida Keys.

After I nearly put out my back brushing my teeth, I sat on the tub's edge, frosted my lips, and sized up my day. It had been a week since I'd made an oath to reassess the direction work was taking. Apart from the temporary setback from the explosion, business was thriving and money was rolling in. If this continued, I could pay up on my mortgage. I strapped on my heels. Maybe even buy a new pair of shoes. At least I wouldn't have to moonlight in another salon or hire someone who could bring in more clients. Gee, would my luck ever run out?

With my bag in hand, I clicked off the weather and grasped the doorknob. It turned the other direction. Someone was trying to get in, and I couldn't lock the door mid-turn. What if it was the heavy breather...and the heavy breather was the murderer?

Panic pumped through my veins, and my throat went tight. I fought to hold a firm grip, but my palms were sweating and my arms ached. I tried to remember kickass Lara Croft. Hastily, I reached in my bag and fingered a cluster of perm rods. *Rats.* The door burst open, and in a tizzy, I scooped up the cluster and flung hard.

"What the hell?" Holly scowled from under a blue halo of rods that clung to her like bugs to flypaper.

"Whoops." I plucked a rod that drooped over her eyebrow.

"If the TV was below deafening, you'd have heard me knock." She knelt beside me in her wrinkled pants and worn penny loafers, and shoveled perm rods off the floor. "You sure are up to your eyeballs in shit these days."

I looked her in the eye. "You should be a writer. You really have a way with words."

She grunted. "Any word on the fire?"

"No."

"Any idea who did it?"

I shook my head and got up.

"Now another murder." She looked me up and down. "How are you?"

"A little jumpy. I got a friendly phone call last night. The message was short on words, but they had the breathing nailed." I dumped the rods back in my bag. "If I'd had a microdermabrasion machine here, I probably would've hurled that at you, too."

She pursed her lips. "You want to tell me about the marks?"

I peered down, unsure which marks were from the explosion and which were from karate. "No. Did Dana at least die instantly?"

"Can't get more instant than a gunshot wound to the heart. They brought in your deliveryman for questioning."

"I figured as much."

"Look, Nancy Drew, the guy's got a record. He could be a murderer."

I shook my head no. "I don't believe he did it."

"A Molotov cocktail sails through your storefront after he arrives back in the States. Then there's another murder." She followed me into the living room. "Doesn't that ring any bells?"

"Something's not right."

We sat on the couch. Her eyes narrowed. "What's going on? What aren't you telling me?"

My stomach was in knots from this continual feeling of insecurity. Karate had been a bad idea, and I was getting desperate. "I'm thinking of buying pepper spray." Well, it had been a thought of sorts.

"Ha. Mom's going to love this."

"Mom's not going to find out. And she should be used to this. You're a cop. You carry a gun."

She raised her chin. "Why the spray?"

I thought I'd spare her the details of the note. The scary call was enough to trust her with. "I'll feel safer. So how do I get some? The hardware store?"

She laughed. "This is Massachusetts, honey. You'll have to go to the police station, show two types of ID, fill out a form, and pay upfront."

"That's it? They'll give me a can?" I thought about walking into the police station and asking for pepper-spray forms. Martoli, at the front desk, would crack another joke. And the cop with the hair mound would likely pass on the news to Romero. Then everyone would have a good laugh. Tee-hee-hee. Wee helpless hairdresser needs protection from a can of pepper spray.

Holly bit her lip as if she wondered what to make of all this. "It'll come in the mail a few weeks later."

"A few weeks! I could be dead by then." I took a firm breath. I wasn't going to cave yet. Max was right. I had my own arsenal. As long as I carried a few tools of the trade, I'd be okey-dokey.

I scraped myself off the sofa. "I've got to get to work. Phyllis will have a conniption if I'm late. Then you may have another murder."

Holly stepped onto the porch. "Why don't you just fire Phyllis?"

I studied her penny loafers, wondering where she found such vintage shoes. She was waiting for an answer, but the penny loafers seemed more interesting than past promises about Phyllis.

"Well?"

I met her stare. "Look, this honoring the dead business isn't easy. But until I figure out what to do about the situation, I'll carry on the magician's act. Phyllis will continue to make customers disappear. And Max, Judy, and I will do cartwheels to make them reappear."

She shrugged and walked down the steps. "It's your

business. By the way, the murderer was inside the house when Dana arrived. Knew exactly where to disarm the alarm. No vehicle parked nearby. Only Dana's."

She slid into her unmarked car. "Few things to consider. Did Albert have access to the house? And would he know about the alarm?"

"Sounds doubtful," I said from the porch. "I guess Romero will find out for sure."

She revved the engine and grinned. "I'm sure he will."

I shut the door on her smug look, a second later realizing I forgot to pack a lunch. I pulled a bottle of Clamato juice out of the fridge and loaded up on crackers, smoked Gouda, and celery sticks. I tossed everything into my bag, then opened the front door.

"Mr. Jaworski!" I clapped a hand to my chest and gaped down at my seventy-year-old landlord.

"I saw your sister drive away." He eyed me warily. "She's the fuzz, isn't she?"

Mr. Jaworski had beady eyes, spidery eyebrows, and bony arms and legs. He also had an overly suspicious mind.

Oh Lord. Keep me sweet and keep me sane. "She was just visiting."

"This early? Cops only knock on doors this early if there's trouble. I don't want no trouble."

"There's no trouble, Mr. Jaworski."

"Where's my rent? Were you trying to get away without paying this month's rent?"

Mr. Jaworski appeared the first of every month, rain or shine, to collect his rent check because, among other things, he didn't trust the mail. Plus, he liked to verify I wasn't doing anything illicit, being the wild and crazy girl I was. Once upon a time, rent was never an issue. Lately, seeing Mr. Jaworski was like welcoming the Grim Reaper.

"I've seen you on the news. You and your salon." He spied my bruised arms. "I told you I don't rent to anyone who's in trouble with the law. I made that clear from the start. I said, 'I want no trouble in my house.'"

"Don't worry, Mr. Jaworski. I'm in no trouble."

"I'm not worried about *you*." He stretched to look inside. "I'm worried about my house."

Some things never changed. I ripped off the check, pressed it in his palm, and hoisted my bag over my shoulder. "Well, don't fret. I've got the house surrounded by mothballs."

"Mothballs! What in the hell are you doing with mothballs?"

"They keep predators away." I slammed the door after me and left him slack-jawed on the porch.

Max was first to strut into my office. "What is it with the crazies on the road this morning?" He shoved his keys in his pocket. "Does everyone already have the holiday weekend on the brain? It's only Wednesday, and I almost got sideswiped three times."

Max drove to work on rocket fuel every morning. It was only by the grace of God he arrived in one piece.

"Maybe you should try driving just under the speed of light." I opened the box of donuts I'd just bought.

He looked pointedly at me. "Are you saying I can't drive?"

"Gee, no. Where'd you get that idea?" I rolled my eyes. "Anyway, you should be relaxed after soaking in a hot tub last night."

"Didn't go. My friend wasn't home."

"Oh." I frowned at that, momentarily sidetracked. Then I told him about Dana.

He undid a button on his Pierre Cardin shirt and plopped on a chair. "She had her whole life ahead of her." He grimaced. "Though she could be exasperating."

"I'm sure she had redeeming qualities, if one looked deep enough."

"How deep are we talking?"

He took a powdered donut, and I glanced at the clock.

Where were the others?

"Anyone home?" Judy called from the hallway a moment later, then poked her head into the office. "What are you doing? Having a powwow?" She flicked a strand of hair off her pants and reached for a maple dip.

"There's been another murder," I said.

"What?" She lowered her donut. "Who?"

"Dana Kir. She was shot last night at the Reynolds's home."

"That's terrible." She set the donut back in the box.

"Poor Tad." Max dusted off his hands. "First his mother—such as she was—now his girlfriend."

We all had our heads down in silent respect when Phyllis bustled in. She was dressed in orange from head to toe and had her hands on her hips. "What's going on in here?"

"Yikes!" Max slapped a hand over his face. "What's that on your hips, I mean lips?"

Phyllis puckered up. "It's called Tangerine Twist. It matches my new creation. I thought I'd dress monochromatic today." She smoothed her hands down her shiny pencil skirt.

"I thought it was Halloween," Max said, "and you were pretending to be a jar of Cheez Whiz."

Phyllis made a fist. "I'll Cheez Whiz you."

"When?" Max wanted to know. "Before or after you finish the jar."

"Blockhead."

"Cow."

I shook my head. "Are we about done with the insults?"

"I'm done," Phyllis said. "He's not rankling me today. I watched Dr. Phil this morning."

"I was beginning to wonder why everyone was late."

"Well, I had good reason," she said. "Dr. Phil talked about channeling your energy into something positive, ignoring the negative."

"Hooray for Dr. Phil." Max clasped his hands in excitement. "What does he say about overeating?"

"You see? It's working already. I don't even hear him."

"Too bad, because your button's undone."

Phyllis wrenched her head down, and Max gave a satisfied smile.

"Phyllis," I said. "We were talking about the murder."

"Not again." She rolled her eyes. "I'm at the end of my rope with all this cloak and dagger. Isn't there anything we can talk about other than Portia's murder?"

"We can talk about yours," Max said. "But first we'd have to plan it."

"Hardy-har-har," Phyllis replied.

Why me? All I wanted was a successful business. Was that asking too much? "We weren't talking about Portia, Phyllis. There's been another murder. The victim was Dana Kir."

"*Who?*"

Max sighed. "Get your head out of the refrigerator and pay attention. Dana Kir. You know, tall, blond, young, pretty. All the things you're not."

Phyllis narrowed her eyes at Max and grunted. "So there's one less debutante in the world."

"Phyllis!" Judy was red-faced. "You should be ashamed of yourself. Dana was a young girl. She didn't need to die." She shook her head and tramped to her station.

"Nobody *needs* to die," Phyllis said to Judy's back. "It's God's plan for us."

"When's God planning your death?" Max piped. "I might be able to sell tickets."

The first appointments weren't for another fifteen minutes. Judy and I strung up red, white, and blue scalloped ribbons on the front window while Max and Phyllis sprinkled the sales counter with patriotic-colored sparkles. Then I reviewed a new facial with everyone. I scribbled a special in neon ink on a black sandwich board and propped it outside on the sidewalk.

The others got to work, and I slid into my office to finish what I'd started the day of the explosion. Files checked. Entries compared. *Huh.* June was a record-breaking month. I should've been celebrating, but the truth was I didn't feel so hot profiting from something so horrible, even if it would be a relief handing over the money to Mr. Feltz.

I'd just put the computer to sleep when the phone rang. I picked up and was greeted with a shaky exhale in my ear. It sounded like the beginning of another disturbing call. I swallowed thickly and forced out a greeting. More heavy breathing. This could be the person who wrote the threatening note or threw the fire bomb.

Who was I kidding? Whoever did those things knew who I was *and* where I worked.

"Valentine?"

"Tad?" I was good with voices, at least when they were used.

"I saw your card on my mother's dresser, and well, I just wanted to say I'm glad you're trying to find her killer." A sob escaped his throat. "I hope you find Dana's, too."

I was hoping the same thing.

"The Fourth of July was her favorite holiday." He steadied his voice. "She collected anything with fireworks on them. Cups. Pens. Stickers. I was going to propose to her at the fireworks in the park Saturday night."

I visualized Dana's colorful tattoo. "I'm sure she would've loved that." I didn't know what to say, but I wanted him to feel better. "Can you tell me what happened?"

"Yeah. I had a counseling appointment. When I got home, Dana was dead. Don't worry. The cops have checked out my story." He sighed. "I know Dana was sorta direct, and she may have offended people, and…gee, it just occurred to me, she was a lot like my mother. Funny Mom didn't care for her. Still, why would anyone kill her?"

"I'm really sorry, Tad."

His voice was soft. "Her parents have decided to have a private funeral. Family only."

"I can understand that. What about your family? Have you spoken to your father?"

"Last night. It's me and him now. I wanna be someone he'll be proud of. All I've ever done is disappoint him."

It did sound like Tad had been one giant pain in the butt, but I wasn't here to judge.

We said goodbye, and a moment later Birdie Cutler walked in ahead of two new clients. Max and Judy led the new customers down the hall for facials. Birdie chirped about the latest murder and the fire.

"It's been all over the telly." She sniffed the ammonia-filled air, looking around expectantly. "Well, bugger me! Where's all the fire damage?"

"New magazine table," I said. "New window, new carpet."

She looked deflated at the news. There was nothing juicy about staples or pile.

"Don't worry." I led her to my station. "With my record, there'll be another calamity by tomorrow." I stopped to watch Phyllis douse her lady with perm solution. "Or sooner."

"Blimey," Birdie said over my shoulder. "That woman looks beastly."

The woman was writhing in agony. Purple perm rods were twisted erratically on her head, sprigs of hair stuck out from the rods, and reeking solution dripped down her face. "Yee-*ouch!*" She pressed her eyes tightly. "Don't you have anything that doesn't sting?"

"Yeah, water," Phyllis said. "But you won't get much curl from that."

I pulled Phyllis aside. "Why didn't you wrap cotton around her hairline?"

"Because I used it up on pillow stuffing for Oscar's graduation present."

"When did you do that?"

"When you weren't looking."

The only thing hotter than my temperature at the moment was my curling iron. "A *whole* box of cotton? That's over five hundred feet."

"It was a big pillow."

This was what I had to put up with. I grabbed two

towels and planted them in the woman's hands. Then I deducted ten percent off her perm.

"You already promised me that when I made this appointment because last time dimwit almost sliced my jugular with a straight razor."

"Right." I dabbed a stream trickling down her temple. "Make it twenty percent."

"Thirty," she said, "and I won't slam your salon to my friends."

I felt like kicking a wall since I couldn't boot Phyllis. I took a deep breath and reminded myself I'd just had a good month businesswise. I agreed to the discount, shook out the tension, and brushed the backcombing out of Birdie's hair.

"Wasn't that poor girl here the day of Portia's murder?" Birdie asked.

"Girl?" Seems the tension wouldn't leave me.

"The girl that was killed. She was here that day."

"Oh, yes. Dana. She dated Portia's son."

"I didn't see her at the funeral."

"They kept their relationship quiet."

"Because of Portia, no doubt." Birdie shivered. "Now everywhere you turn, there's murder. You know Rueland Hardware has a table out front full of alarm systems? I wanted to buy one, but Betty said we already have top-shelf security."

I lowered her to the sink. "Where is Betty?"

"Right knackered. We went to our Women of the Earth meeting last night after tennis. Betty got rat-arsed on too much sherry and got dicky in the car. Do you know what removes red stain from carpet?"

"Try hairspray." It wasn't meant to be a joke, but she giggled and then moaned contentedly as a rush of strawberry-scented shampoo filled the air.

An hour later, I removed Birdie's rollers and ushered her back to my chair. She gave a loud yawn and said, "I almost forgot to tell you, I spoke to Tess LaMay last night."

I brushed her curls and thought about Tess bumping into Erik and the unidentified woman. Say the woman was Caroline, and she'd killed Portia. Why Dana? It didn't make sense.

"Tess visited Rueland Travel on Saturday," Birdie continued. "Then left there and saw the same woman leave your salon that she saw with Erik."

"What?" I thumped the brush in the roller tray. "Is she certain? What time was it?"

"I'm not sure. She picked up a plane ticket, then did a little window shopping this way. That's when she saw the woman come out of your shop. Do you recall a client who resembled Portia?"

"Not really, but we've had lots of walk-ins since the murder." Damn. I'd also left early Saturday for my big date.

"You should check last Saturday's appointments and see if it jogs an idea. And don't rule out the male species. In the right getup, even a man with a beautiful face and slim build like Max could pass for a woman."

Say what? Max posing as a woman? I ignored the silly remark. After all, that would mean Erik was *really* leading a double life. Not to mention Max, my right-hand man, my friend, my sounding board.

I dampened down the metallic taste quickly climbing my throat. Just because I'd left early Saturday and didn't see Max leave, well, it was too absurd to think about. Why would Max get dressed up like a woman at the salon where he works and then traipse down the street? I imagined other scenarios, wondering if I would have spotted a transvestite in the salon. I felt sidetracked yet again but couldn't put my finger on the cause.

I picked up the metal comb. I wasn't going to focus on the most ludicrous idea. There was no reason to think Tess saw anyone except a woman who happened to resemble Portia. Whoever it was, it was eerie this person could've passed in and out of the shop, and I hadn't paid any attention. "Do you think I could speak to Tess?"

"Oh, duckie, you're too late. She's off to the Bahamas for her second facelift. It'll be weeks till her lips are flapping again."

I scarcely heard Birdie's last words. I grabbed a chunk of hair and stretched it high. I teased. I sprayed. I coated. I coughed. Who was this mystery woman? I could smell her involvement. But how could I get in touch with Tess? If I phoned her, I'd need to call before she went under the knife. Not only that, I'd need to find out where she was staying. *Hmm.* Another problem.

After Birdie and everyone else left for the day, I hauled in the sandwich board. Then I pored over the appointments and made some phone calls. No matter how I tried to rationalize things, how much cellulite or wrinkles I tried to erase, I came up with a big fat zero. Nobody fit the bill. Nobody had Portia's million-dollar look. Whoa! Hold everything. Here I was tearing out Birdie's hair, when the answer was staring at me from down the street.

Chapter 15

I locked up, eased into my car, and seconds later swung into the angled parking in front of Rueland Travel and Town Taxi. A couple of cabbies played checkers on the sidewalk, waiting for mid-week fares as I dashed by. At least in my mind I was dashing. By the cabbies' strange expressions, most likely I was lumbering awkwardly.

I left them to their game, went into Rueland Travel, and tripped on a fishing pole blocking the front entrance. Before I fell flat on my face, I picked up the pole and propped it against other poles leaning over a small pond.

Rueland Travel once specialized in selling airline tickets and vacation packages. Today it relied heavily on outfitting campers, hikers, anglers, cyclists, and sports fanatics.

I skirted past the fishing poles, wove around bikes and pop-up tents, and landed at the back where Karen Jett, the owner, was sitting under a fake palm tree, talking on the phone at her computer. Shoot. Oh well. I could wait. I meandered around and listened to the tinny Caribbean music. Like a kid, I squeezed a stuffed parrot. It cawed. I yelped. Typical.

Karen rolled her eyes like I was a naughty four-year-old. I thought I better make myself busy, so I sank into a kiddie chair and worked on a half-completed puzzle of the Eiffel Tower. Minutes later, Karen strolled over, flinging back her Pippi Longstocking braids. "About time you paid me a visit." She grinned. "How have you been?"

"How much time have you got?"

"Uh-oh." She took a closer look at me, scrapes and all. "What do you need?"

"Last Saturday, a woman named Tess LaMay came in to pick up a ticket to the Bahamas…"

Karen sat at her desk and punched the computer keyboard. "What do you want to know?"

"Where is she staying, and can you give me the number?"

She gave me a stern look. "I'd like to help, Valentine, but this is privileged information."

"I know."

"Then give me one good reason why I should hand it over to you."

"I can give you two. Portia Reynolds and Dana Kir. Two clients killed right here in Rueland within two weeks of each other. I don't know about you, but I'm not sleeping all that well with a murderer running loose."

Karen's mouth dropped open. "Me either." She scribbled on a piece of paper and flattened it in my palm. "If you tell anyone I gave this to you, I'll make your life miserable."

I folded my hand around the paper. "Get in line."

I left Rueland Travel, feeling more hopeful than I'd felt in days. I was feeling so optimistic I decided to let Romero in on the news. Okay, I wanted to gloat. I hadn't solved the crime of the century. I had a phone number for someone named Tess who saw Erik and another woman together. I had no idea if Tess could identify this woman or if the woman had anything to do with the murder. Despite all that, for me, this was epic.

I dug out my cell phone. The sooner I got hold of Tess before her surgery the better. Plus, maybe I'd have some new information to share with Romero. I knew I'd promised myself to stay clear of him, but this feeling was too good to pass up.

I fiddled with my phone and found it was dead. Damn thing. I must not have turned it off last time I used it. And who knew when I'd previously charged it. With my cord at home, I'd just go to Romero's first and call Tess later from my place.

I shoved the phone back in my bag and stood on the curb, thinking about my latest theory. Suppose this woman wasn't Caroline. Who else could Erik have been seeing who may have moved in the same circles as Portia? Wait a minute. What about one of the cultivated ladies from the Women of the Earth Society? How many did Birdie say belonged? Eighty-five? But surely Tess would've recognized her. And would Erik be so reckless as to date someone that close to home? I couldn't see it. Of course, I couldn't see how he'd married a woman like Portia.

My dilemma now was, how did I show up at Romero's door unannounced? Every time we saw each other we ended up in a shouting match. But that was because he was arrogant and pig-headed. I stowed my prized clue in my bag and put my chin up. Well, maybe he'd see I wasn't just some mindless beautician.

Before I confronted Romero, I ran across the street to the drugstore and bought myself a pack of gum and a sympathy card for Dana's family. Then I went next door to Dilly's Florist and ordered the family a fireworks-type spray of flowers. I knew cards and condolences wouldn't bring back their daughter, but I hoped this small gesture would carry a slight measure of comfort.

After the flowers were taken care of, I got in my car and popped a cinnamon burst on my tongue. Taking a deep, spicy breath for courage, I started the engine and shifted into gear. This next stop was for the good of the case.

Chewing madly, I hopped onto Route 128 and merged into speeding traffic. I passed my exit at eight o'clock, and it was at that moment my courage started to wane. I began this brazen plan, feeling real smart. Me, queen sleuth of Rueland, toting a genuine lead.

Ha. My stomach was in a thousand knots and my legs were doing the jumpy twitch. This was a dumb idea. What was I thinking? I vowed I'd never show up at Romero's door. I didn't even know if he'd be home. I had my own problems and my own responsibilities. Yeah, my life was what it was, but at least it was real.

Nothing seemed real since I'd met Romero. The murders, Brody's death, Max's job offer, Phyllis's royal screw-ups—which were always there but seemed more disastrous lately. And most especially, my deepening feelings for a guy with a gun and a mysterious past. Even my romantic fears seemed like they were out of a thriller. Drat. What was I doing? *Turn back.*

Then again, didn't Romero say to call if I learned anything? Didn't he give me his address? It was practically an invitation with a pretty pink bow on top. Unless the killer was caught, I'd live in fear the rest of my life. In addition, people would forever think of Beaumont's as a middle-of-the-road salon with an oddball staff and a permanent scent of death.

I inhaled deeply and told myself this was no time to chicken out. I had a lead. The killer would be caught, order will be restored, and the salon will be a sensation. Well, two out of three wasn't bad.

I pulled my Daisy Bug to the curb on Clove Road and idled in front of a stone two-story with a maroon door and shutters, and a lantern over the porch. A mishmash of rambling flowers and the sweet smell of lilac gave the property an English countryside feel. All very homey. Not the cold concrete fortress I'd expected.

Okay, Valentine. Get on with it. You're not buying real estate.

The car clock said 8:08, and my inhibitions slid away. I sat there, smiling like an idiot. All because Romero had said he could drive from his place to mine in eight minutes. Timing the ride seemed sexy and made me feel hot inside. So now what? His truck was in the driveway, and I was glued to my seat, working up my nerve to knock on his door.

My smile faded. What if he was still brooding because I'd known about Albert's return? What if he slammed the door in my face? Well, he could be a real horse's patoot. He wasn't the only one with pride. *I* had pride. Maybe this *was* his investigation. I still knew a thing or two about solving a murder. Okay, not so much. At least I had persistence. And I could be tough. Despite what Romero thought! I had the wounds to prove it. I shut off the engine. I was here. I'd at least see if he was home.

I checked my makeup and sprayed on a mist of perfume. Then I brushed my hair and adjusted my lacy bra. I took a deep breath, slung my bag over my shoulder, and stepped my strappy heels onto the driveway. The wind instantly flicked up the edge of my dress. I slapped my hand at my thigh and tugged the hem down. Then I sashayed to the house.

I rang the doorbell and shook out my sweaty palms. An elderly woman at the house to my right swept grass off her driveway. She smiled. I smiled back and rang the bell again. Figured, Romero would make me wait. Probably watching from a window, laughing at my chutzpah.

"Well, well," he said a second later, leaning a muscular forearm against the side of the house, work gloves covering his strong hands. "If it isn't Rueland's most resourceful beautician."

Clearly, I would've had something to say over that comment if my throat hadn't thickened at the sight of him. This was agonizing. A yellow tank top hung loosely from his sweaty, tanned shoulders, his hair was damp and wavy, and he was covered in grass flecks right down to his work boots. Filthy. And entirely mouth-watering. My gum went down in a hard clump.

"I was on my way home from work," I said, hating how breathy I sounded. "Thought I'd stop by."

Romero took his time analyzing me, then raised an

eyebrow. "You would've had to pass your exit and three others to get here."

My face warmed. "I took the long way." What was I saying?

I tried to retrieve those tough emotions I held moments ago, but I couldn't even conjure up a harsh word. I glanced down at my pink dress, spangled bracelet, and high heels and realized I didn't look tough at all. I looked like Brunette Barbie. *Dumb, Valentine!* Could you not have worn such a hot little number today? It shouted *va-voom*. Romero would see it as a come-on.

I took awkward strides toward him. "I didn't actually expect you to be here."

He grinned, his sultry gaze holding mine. "Oh? And why's that?" He was evidently enjoying the moment. Damn self-confident, sexy...cop.

"Because you're in the middle of a double-homicide investigation. Shouldn't you be on a stakeout somewhere?"

"Is that how they do it on *Scooby-Doo*?" He winked at me, almost leaving me breathless. "I *am* allowed to come home once in a while," he said. "And since my grass was a foot high, I mowed the lawn. But don't worry. I'll be back to fighting crime tomorrow bright and early." He looked over his shoulder. "That's all for tonight, Mrs. Stevens. We'll trim hedges next week."

I melted a bit, seeing Romero treat his elderly neighbor with such gentleness, and my respect for him just climbed a notch. I'd suspected he had a compassionate side, but boy, did he do an excellent job hiding it.

Mrs. Stevens lifted her hand off the broom and waved. "You're too good to me, young man. Go have yourself some fun."

He stripped off his gloves, bent forward, and slipped his warm strong hand in mine, natural as breathing New England air. Well, it wasn't natural for me. I tried not to show it, but I found it difficult to breathe. Every nerve ending shot to my hand that was attached to his. This was our first romantic touch—except for the finger on the

hairline thing—the one new lovers experienced, the one
that sent pulses soaring. Everything else was a blur as he
guided me around the back of the house.

"You eat steak?" he asked.

"Sure," I said hoarsely, liking the smell of sweat and
fresh-cut grass, this feeling of being in his world.

He tossed his gloves in the shed, then led me through
the back door where he chucked his boots beside a half-
filled case of empty beer bottles. I tried not to stare when
he pulled his tank top over his head. Or when he threw it
in the laundry tub. Or when he wiped grass flecks off his
abs. Gulp. This guy was hard right down to his hipbones. I
gaped open-mouthed, wondering if the shorts were next.
He unsnapped the button, and our eyes met.

He leaned in real slow, his lips just beneath my ear.
"Now who's drooling?"

I clamped my mouth shut, certain that I was blushing.
Naturally, he'd be the elephant who never forgets. I was
trying to collect myself when he stepped closer and
reached...reached...oh Lord, he's going to kiss me. I
closed my eyes, feeling the heat from his body, the
hardness of his core. Chin up, lips slightly apart, I waited.
And waited. I cracked one eyelid open and saw him back
up with a towel, a devilish smile on his face.

"I'm taking a shower." He turned toward the hallway.
"Make yourself at home. There's stuff for a salad or nuke
some potatoes. I'll finish them on the grill."

I did a full body quiver and willed myself to breathe.
*Okay, Valentine. Get your head screwed on. Remember why you're
here.*

Once I calmed myself, I toured down the hall
and found the kitchen. This room didn't have Martha
Stewart-flair, but it was functional. Toaster. Coffeemaker.
Fridge displaying takeout menus. Round table. Four chairs.
Empty shoulder holster slung on the back of a chair.

A huge steak, enough for an army, marinated on a
warped metal tray on the counter beside an open jar of dill
pickles. Next to the jar was a bag of potatoes along with

Romero's keys, Iron Man watch, an iPad, and loose change. No pretty platters. No delicate china. No female touches. I smiled at how all-male the place was.

I heard the shower start, then darted outside and snipped an orange rose from the garden. I couldn't find a vase, so I poured water into an empty beer bottle and sank the rose inside. I tried to forget that Romero was in the other room, soaping his toned, wet, naked body. But it wasn't easy. My hands were shaking, and my heart was thumping inside my chest.

I took a deep breath and concentrated on setting the table. Plates. Forks. Knives. Napkins. I slammed cupboard doors. *No napkins?* I ripped off two paper towels, sculpted them into tulips, and placed them by each plate. I pulled lettuce, tomato, and cucumber from the fridge. *Pop* went the cucumber out of my hand.

Holy smokes, Valentine. Get a grip.

I sighed and cleared my head. I could do this. I was a highly organized individual. I just needed to focus. I finished the salad and placed the bowl on the table beside mismatched salt and pepper shakers.

I angled my head at the shakers and felt a tender pang in my chest for Romero. Here was a cop who worked around the clock, trudged through fatalities, and had a determined beautician on his heels. It was pretty obvious he didn't have time to shop at T.J. Maxx. Oddly, the mismatched shakers left a warm impression in my heart.

Once I was done with the table, I wandered over to the counter and picked up Romero's watch. *Hmm.* Heavier than I expected. Masculine. I examined the armored man's blazing white eyes and glow-in-the-dark hands. Maybe a niece or nephew gave Romero the watch, or maybe he had a thing for superheroes. I was thinking of other possibilities when I smelled the tangy scent of dill. I put the watch down, pierced a pickle with a fork, and crunched on it, trying to keep the smile off my face. Only problem was I couldn't unstick my grin.

So I was in a cop's kitchen, and he wore an Iron Man

watch and ate dill pickles. Big deal. I was here to share what I knew about the case. I tried to remember that while I nuked some potatoes.

Suddenly, his iPad dinged. Down the hall, the shower was still running. I edged closer to the iPad, telling myself I had no business reading Romero's messages. I wasn't interested in his private life.

I did an about-face and checked on the potatoes. I opened the microwave, seized a potato, and flung the piping hot spud so fast I didn't see where it went. I shook my hand and scurried to the floor, searching for the stupid thing before Romero came out and saw me on my hands and knees. It wasn't on the floor, so I checked behind the fridge, but it wasn't there either. I got to my feet and threw my hands on my hips. At a complete loss, I stared at the counter. Staring back at me right beside the iPad and the message appearing on the screen was the potato. Mocking me.

I snatched the spud, keeping my eyes off the iPad. I had willpower. I wouldn't look at the message. But what if it was urgent? A family emergency? I'd be doing Romero a service in reading it. I bounced the potato in my hand. Up…and down. And up. And down. Oh, what the hell. I leaned forward and scanned the email. *You left so soon. I didn't feel we really said goodbye. Call me back. Please.* It was signed, *Ingrid.*

My heart pumped violently, and my ears burned. Who was Ingrid? And why did I read the message? It was obviously private. Now I had this to contend with. Well, what did I expect? No signs of a woman in the house didn't mean he wasn't involved with one. Or many.

I went back to the microwave and tossed the potato on a plate with the others.

The shower stopped, and a few minutes later, Romero swaggered barefoot into the kitchen. His wet hair was slicked back, his stubble prominent, his shocking blue eyes more dazzling than sapphires in the sun. He looked from me to the prettily made up table. "Nice."

He took a beer from the fridge, leaned over the counter, and checked the iPad.

I stood there in silence, playing with my bracelet, trying not to look interested.

He read the message, flipped the cover over the iPad, and knocked back a quarter of his beer.

That's it? No reaction? No eye roll? No "this woman's just a pain-in-the-ass colleague" or "she's just an ex-girlfriend"? I gave an inner head shake. Fine.

Forgetting Ingrid for a moment, I centered on his Yankees T-shirt and jeans. "You'll want to be careful where you sport that T-shirt. You're in Sox territory now, friend."

He wiped his mouth. "Once a Yankee, always a Yankee."

Sex appeal dripped from his voice. It almost made me want to leap into his arms. But I wasn't Ingrid or any of those other women. I'd never dangle silk panties in a man's face, and I wasn't going to start chasing this one. I was here on business. Period. While I congratulated myself on being pure and saintly, he strolled over, intimidatingly close, beer in hand.

"Want one?"

"Thanks. I don't drink beer."

"No." He smiled. "I didn't think so."

The smell of fresh soap and beer surrounded me, and all of a sudden, the kitchen seemed half its size.

"So." He lightly dragged the cold wet bottle across my bare arm. "Want to tell me why you're here, dressed in a killer outfit like that?"

A shiver rushed through me that had nothing to do with the icy bottle. "I, uh—"

"A dress like that in the wrong neighborhood could get you in a lot of trouble."

He was right. Damn glamour ingrained in my pores. I even "dressed" to go to Market Basket. I hoped my legs wouldn't give out. Luckily, his cell phone rang before I hit the floor. Probably Ingrid calling, ticked she couldn't reach him two seconds ago.

He thumped his beer down and pulled out his cell phone from his jeans pocket. "Yeah," he said, rounding the corner from the kitchen into the living room.

Holy Moly. Holly was right. What was it about Romero that made women cave?

I turned to the counter and steadied my breath, trying to understand the attraction and desire running through my veins. Or was it just fascination? I wet a paper towel and dabbed my neck, arguing against the likelihood of a cop and me making it work. Even if something did happen in the near future, what about after the case? Would that be the end of Romero? He didn't appear to need anyone in his life, least of all a troublesome aesthetician. Even so, my spirit sank at the thought of not seeing him again.

"That was work." He returned to the kitchen and dropped the phone on the table. "I just got dumped with another case...which I've got to pull duty on in a few hours." He poured the rest of his beer down the drain, then gripped the meat platter and a fork. "Grab the potatoes and come with me."

I sat on a white stackable lawn chair while Romero fiddled with a weather-beaten grill. It finally lit, and a smoky charcoal smell filled the air. I was about to press Romero about the case when he disappeared back in the house. Fine, we'd play it his way.

Moments later, he returned with two drinks. He handed me a glass. "To match your dress."

Mmm. Pink lemonade. I took a sip, then coughed and sputtered. "What...is this?"

"Hard lemonade."

I coughed some more, and a warm trail blazed to my toes. "How do you drink this stuff?"

"I'm not. Mine's straight lemonade on account I have to work later."

"Oh, so you're trying to get *me* drunk."

"From that?" He arched a brow. "It's more sugar than alcohol."

"Right." I didn't always make the best decisions—as if

that were news—but past experience told me if I drank much more of this, I'd be sloshed on the patio stones, promising sex up the yin-yang. Still, Romero didn't need to know *all* my weaknesses.

He scraped the grill with a long, metal spatula, eyes focused on the job. I took a pretend sip of my drink, savoring the way he both calmed and excited me. Mixed with the warm setting sun, I was glowing. Yep. Best not to pour *any* liquor down my throat.

"I should tell you why I'm here." I opted not to bring up the heavy breather on the phone. Maybe I was being foolish, but not contacting Romero again wouldn't go over real well. Plus, what would it prove?

"You mean it's not for my handsome looks and witty personality?"

Oh boy. If he only knew.

He slapped the steak on the grill, tucked in the potatoes, grabbed his drink, and sat beside me. As the steak sizzled, I explained about Birdie's friend and my thoughts on the wig.

"So you think if you can find out from this Tess LaMay who the woman was leaving your salon, you may have the same woman Erik has been having an affair with. And she may have something to do with the murder."

"It's a theory."

"A good motive to eliminate Portia if Erik was involved. Though he was squeaky clean while he was in Colombia. Went down there with thousands of glasses, did his charity work, and rushed back home after he heard the news about Dana."

I thought about this, not ready to put Erik on a pedestal. "I wonder if the person he's seeing could be a member of the Women of the Earth Society."

"Any new clients mention being a member since the murder?"

"No, but with so many new customers, I haven't kept track of everyone. What about you? Have you looked into this avenue?"

"We've talked to most of the members. Still need to interview a few who are away."

"Any leads?"

"Not really. Most of the ladies weren't fond of Portia." He poked the steak with his fork. "Anyone else come to mind who fits Portia's description?"

"I've ruled out everyone I can think of for one reason or another." And I ruled out Max out of loyalty and because it was too bizarre to think otherwise.

"You sure? There are ways of masking one's identity."

"True. My client, who's four-eleven, could've worn stilts under her dress. And a two-hundred-pound woman could've crammed herself into a corset, and—"

"Has anyone ever told you you're difficult?"

"Yes. You."

"Besides me."

"No, because I'm practically perfect in every way!"

He gave me a look that would melt paraffin wax, then slid the steak on the platter. "Let's eat."

During supper, he told me about his sister's upcoming wedding. "Do you like weddings?" He stabbed a piece of meat. "Or do you laugh at those, too?"

"No. I actually cry at weddings."

"Figures." He forked steak into his mouth, studying me while he chewed. "I may be sorry for asking, but do you want to go with me?"

"What? I can't go. I don't even know your sister."

"What do you need to know? We have the same parents, and she was always a pain in the ass. You've probably never been to a Scottish-Italian wedding on a yacht before."

"It'd be a first."

His eyes darkened. "I like firsts."

I nabbed my paper towel and fanned myself.

I wanted to believe Romero cared for me, even a tiny bit. But I'd been down this giddy road before. The outcome was always the same. I gave an internal smack upside the head, telling myself not to be taken in by his ruggedly handsome face or low, sexy voice. Even if my insides were bubbling with excitement.

"I need to go." I slapped the paper towel down. "I want to call Tess before her surgery."

He scraped back his chair, gripped the phone, and plunked it in front of me. "Let's call now."

All right. Let's. I dug out the paper Karen had given me, dialed the hotel, and dealt with a finicky front-desk manager and endless static. "Bad connection," I whispered to Romero.

He leaned arms on the table and watched me with a steady grin while I practically begged the manager to connect me with Tess. Thinking I'd actually succeeded, I gave a big fat smirk to Romero. Then I got disconnected. "Huh? It's dead."

"Maybe she didn't want to speak to you." He grasped the phone, dialed, and used his cop voice. Then he handed the phone over with a look that said this is how it's done.

I stuck out my tongue and whirled away, picking up the conversation with Tess.

"Portia's murder was a terrible shock." She cut in and out.

"Yes, it was. Tess, I understand you saw Erik Reynolds at Dino Hosta's." *Crackle.* "Hello?"

"A hurricane's brewing off the coast," she slurred. "I had to take something for my nerves."

"I'll make this brief. Was Erik with another woman?" I pressed speakerphone so Romero could listen in.

"Yes. And late this past Saturday afternoon, I saw the same woman leave your salon."

"Can you tell me what she looked like?"

"Walked right by me." She faded. "Recognized her from the night I bumped into them, except she wasn't really—" *Crack.*

"Hello? Wasn't really what?"

"Black...not...blond...was sure..." Her words were disjointed, and then *buzz*.

The line went dead.

I tried three more times. "I can't get through."

Romero took the phone and shook his head. "Does this amount of determination run in your family?"

I paid no attention to that and tapped the table. "She must've been talking about the woman's disguise. More specifically, the wig."

"Maybe she wasn't referring to the wig at all."

"Black, not blond? If she wasn't referring to the wig, then what?"

He put up his hands defensively. "Take some advice. Sleep on it. The answer will probably come to you in the shower tomorrow morning. It usually does for me."

My gaze slipped to his well-defined chest, and one thing was clear. Next time I showered, I wouldn't be thinking about a black, blond, pink, or blue wig.

I rifled around my bag before I said something stupid. I grabbed my watch with the broken clasp, putting Max's words about getting rid of it to the back of my mind. "Look at the time." I stood. "Gotta go."

He grasped my arm and reeled me in, staring intently into my eyes. There was a moment of raw need in his face, heated to the point of torment. I knew he wanted to kiss me, and if all those rumors were true, he wouldn't wait for permission. His brows creased—a look I'd seen before, like he wanted to unload but didn't completely trust me. He let go, then said goodnight.

I drove home, utterly confused, trying to ignore the Romero-induced tingles coursing through my body. I was putty in his hands, for Pete's sake. What held him back? Doubt? Concern? And when had this startling transformation happened in me? When had I gone from wanting to slap him silly to craving his mouth on mine, to feeling his hands on my willing body? Wasn't I still betting he'd be a jerk like the past losers? That if we got close, he'd get what he wanted and take off, leaving me with a broken heart?

I bit my bottom lip. I wasn't sure of the exact moment, but something inside me had definitely changed.

Thankfully, I had a message from Twix to distract me when I got home.

"Another client was killed? Junie! Get your hands out of the toilet. Val! Call me!" *Click.*

I plugged in my cell phone to recharge overnight, then called Twix back. I filled her in on the case, omitting Romero's name. Bad enough I had Max pumping me. Twix would be all over me like antiseptic on clogged pores.

"I'm not taking toddlers to the park," she said, "until all this is over. I've even found another guy to do the renos. His name is Tony. You'd like him." I could hear mischief in her voice.

"I thought you were tired of waiting for him."

"He's taking two weeks off from the foot practice. It'll get done. On the other hand, Tony's pretty hot in a muscle shirt. Might take three weeks."

I said goodbye and looked at the clock. Quarter past ten. Almost too late to call Albert, but I was feeling reckless. Plus, I had to speak to him. In truth, the more time that passed without connecting with him, the more I doubted his innocence. I dialed his number and waited, but his phone was turned off. Probably getting lots of unwanted calls these days.

I hung up, undressed, and went to bed. I tossed and turned well past midnight. Thoughts of Albert flooded my brain, and because they weren't happy thoughts, I did my best to keep them from interfering with logic. There was still a murderer out there, but I was getting warm. I went back to thinking about Tess's words and what she was trying to tell me. Darn, if I didn't check every client who'd been in that day. But what did I miss?

Chapter 16

The howling wind woke me the next morning. I tripped out of bed, stumbled to the rain-streaked window, and saw a tree uprooted on Mr. Brooks's lawn. A king among optimists, Mr. Brooks would be out later, sawing the trunk into birdhouses, the adoring neighborhood animals sniffing at his feet. I shut out the storm and my clanging chimes, then flicked on the radio.

"It's here!" the announcer said, like he was advertising a shoe sale. "Don't bother with umbrellas. Stay inside."

I switched off the knob and ambled into the shower, my soul heavier than a wet sponge. I couldn't stop thinking about Tess's words. *Black. Not. Blond.* What had I overlooked? A black wig was a black wig.

Wait a minute. What if Tess was really trying to tell me the woman wasn't in the black wig when she left the shop? Maybe she was now a blond. I thought back to work last Saturday. There were probably a dozen blonds there that day. Light blonds. Dark blonds. Wavy blonds. Straight blonds. The only problem with this was the fact that I wasn't in the shop late Saturday afternoon to see anyone leave. And walk-ins weren't habitually recorded in the appointment book. So that left me nowhere.

I stepped out of the shower and went light on the powder and perfume. For makeup, I brushed on mascara and swiped on lip gloss. I didn't know why I bothered with cosmetics at all. My eyes didn't sparkle, my skin lacked radiance, and my lips looked pouty.

After staring mindlessly in the closet, I finally pulled on a black cotton dress printed with large pink and red roses. It was already kinky-hair muggy, so I swept mine high, twisted it into a knot, and pierced the whole damn thing with two decorative metal chopsticks given to me by Mrs. Horowitz after her trip to China.

I put my red rose sparkly heels in my bag, feeling a shiver slide down my spine at the thought of Romero's reaction to them. Regardless of how much he liked my shoes, or how much I liked that he liked them, I still felt lousy. However, there was no reason to subject my favorite, hard-earned heels to the nasty weather.

Following a fruitless search for my umbrella, I tossed my charged cell phone in my bag and sprinted head down to the car. By the time I threw everything inside and fell onto the seat, a bucket of rain had poured in, all but drenching me. I looked in the mirror and squeezed a wet ringlet drooping over my nose. Swell. Just the look I wanted. Drowned rat. I wiped myself dry and jerked my umbrella out from under the passenger seat. Yep. Good to have.

Once I reached work, the morning streamed by with several cancellations, the tone in the salon as dismal as the weather. Max looked ominous, dressed in black. He gave me the odd acute stare, probably trying to figure out what was on my mind. I kept busy, avoiding direct eye contact, attempting not to picture him in a woman's getup. If there's one thing I didn't need, it was Max playing Hercule Poirot...or Miss Marple.

Adding to the bleakness of the day, the power flickered half a dozen times. Finally, it conked out at 4:10. All went still, except for Phyllis, who was flicking her clippers on and off behind her lady's head.

"What's wrong with these things?" She whacked them on her station's chair, and the clippers jumped to life along with the lights. They mowed three inches up her customer's head and died when another bolt of lightning killed the lights for a second time.

I was looking for a place to hide from the inevitable when Max and Judy ran in from the hallway and darted to the front window.

"Wow!" Judy said. "It's frightening out there."

"It's almost as scary as Phyllis's Tangerine Twist." Max gasped. "Holy Doodles! There goes someone's umbrella down the street." He stretched his neck to the right. "And there goes the poor soul, chasing after it." He paused with deliberation and turned to Phyllis who was trying to cover the clippers hanging from her client's hair. "Dearie, what are you hiding?"

Phyllis edged closer to her lady's head. "Nothing. Mind your own business."

Max strode over and tried bear-hugging Phyllis out of the way, but with Phyllis's feet planted firmly, it was like hauling a moose uphill. He danced to the side and clapped a hand to his face. "Phyllis! You just carved a hole the size of Maine in this poor woman's head."

The lady straightened stiff as a lightning rod, and I had a bad feeling sparks were about to fly.

"Do I look stupid?" Phyllis barked, a piece of hair dangling from her chin. "It's not a hole. It's a new look. I got just as much talent as you."

"Well, I don't send clients home with hardware in their hair."

The lady's mirrored gaze ricocheted from Max to Phyllis. I could see she was getting ready to have a meltdown. And I couldn't blame her. I felt the pulsing of a panic attack myself. Slowly, in the dim lighting, her hand crept up her scalp.

Phyllis slapped it away. "Well, I don't like everybody picking on me all the time!"

The woman slid her hand up again, but Phyllis was off and running. "And I don't like—"

"Aaaaah!" The lady leaped to her feet, clippers swinging

at the back of her head. "Get this thing off me, you, you butcher!" She ripped off her cape and struggled to free the gizmo. "You're standing there arguing, and look at me! What kind of hairdresser are you?"

"Unfortunately, not a very good one." Max stepped aside.

"Well, if you'd sit still!" Phyllis yanked her down, reached for the scissors, and snipped around the tool like she was cutting metal. "There!" She held up the hairy clippers. "You'll never know the difference."

"Never know the *difference*! How is that possible when there's a crater on my head?" The woman was on her feet, hurling anything she could get her hands on.

I hated with a passion interfering in Phyllis's flops, but I didn't like where this was going. "Look." I dodged a gel tube. "We'll give you a free cut next time you're in."

"*Next* time! I'd rather have my eyelashes waxed off by a blind drunk than come in here again." She lunged for the blue shampoo for gray/blond hair, took aim, and squirted hard.

Phyllis ducked, and a big blue blob spurted on my face and down my dress. I blinked and sputtered, clearing my head. Then I scrambled after the woman. But she was too quick.

She seized a water bottle off the counter, pointed it at Phyllis, and backed up. "You're a disgrace to the profession! You're...you're *talentless!*"

"And you have bad breath," Phyllis said, "but I wasn't going to tell *you* that."

Max's jaw dropped and he slid the lady another bottle. She grabbed it and fired double barrels at Phyllis.

"So you wanna rumble?" Phyllis squinched up her eyes. "Well, rumble this." She jerked the hose from the sink and wrenched up the tap. The sudden pressure knocked the hose out of her hand and fanned water all over the place.

The lady shrieked, and the bottles slipped to the floor with a flump. She ran out the door, chunks of curls chasing after her.

Phyllis struggled with the flailing hose. She finally grabbed the nozzle and took aim. "Huh?" She hammered down the tap. "Where'd she go?"

I gaped from Phyllis to the huge mess. Blue puddles soaked the floor, water dripped from the sink, and busted products were everywhere.

"Talk about ungrateful." Phyllis swooped up the cape. "Like it's my fault the power went out."

Max tap-danced through puddles and set out candles, like this was an everyday occurrence. I just stood there, gawking at myself in the mirror. With my hair up in a bun and my face shiny blue, I resembled one of the Blue Man Group. Only I looked crazier because steam was piping out my ears. I swiped a glop of shampoo from my face, feeling the tremors of a Hulk eruption, when the front door blew open.

A man in a gray trench coat stumbled in, shaking off the rain. "You open for business?" He ogled my blueness and swallowed hard. Apart from the time bomb ticking inside me, everything went silent. "Um," he hesitated, taking in the million glowing candles. "You folks celebrating something?"

I was whirling into one of those maniacs in the movies who was about to jump off a bridge or set fire to their hair, and I couldn't seem to stop it. "Yes!" I smacked a blue hand on a dryer hood, my voice dangerously unstable. "Independence Day Celebrations!"

I wasn't far off. Judy, who'd started mopping puddles, went white from my outburst. Max turned deep red. And ha! I was already royal blue.

"Uhhh…" The guy backed up slowly. "I guess I'll leave you to it." He spun around.

"Wait!" I hollered, tripping over myself.

He yelped and halted like there was a gun on his back. "Honestly," he said, hands high, "my hair's not that bad. My wife can take her grandpa's clippers to me."

"Maybe she can teach Phyllis how to use them," Max said.

"Oh, ha," Phyllis chirped. "Mr. Funny Man."

The guy slid a foot toward the door.

I yanked him by the collar and dragged him to a chair. "Sit!"

He slunk into the seat, his bottom lip trembling. If I wasn't so crazed at the moment, I would've let the poor guy go. But I was unstoppable.

"Judy," I barked. "Cut!"

Judy dropped the mop and got to work cutting.

I took a deep, shaky breath, attempting to get hold of myself. But calmness wasn't what I wanted. I was afraid if I put words to what I really wanted, I'd live to regret it. Gritting my teeth, I snatched a towel and scrubbed my face until I looked less like Smurfette. Then I wiped goop off the walls. As long as I was busy, I wouldn't say what I'd wanted to say for a very long time.

After the clipper guy left, Phyllis started in again. "If you want my opinion—"

"We don't," Max, Judy, and I chorused.

"Well, I don't think there's any sense hanging around if there's no work to do. Oscar's graduation is next weekend. I could be putting the finishing touches on my blazer."

"Maybe I should go, too." Judy picked up the dispensary phone. "My car's at Eddie's Garage. If their power's down, they won't be able to see what they're doing."

"How'd you get here then?" Phyllis grabbed a sprinkled donut left from yesterday.

"I walked from the garage," Judy said, dialing.

"You do know about walking," Max said to Phyllis. "Same idea as eating, only the mouth rests and the feet work."

"How'd you like me to work my fist?" Colored sprinkles fell from Phyllis's lips.

"We won't cancel anyone," I said. "The hot water should last until closing." On the brink of insanity, but always the entrepreneur. I glanced at Judy. "Anyone answering?"

"No." She hung up. "They must be gone. I'll get a cab home."

"Don't worry about it. I'll take you." Would this day ever end?

She smiled her thanks, then gazed serenely at the candles. "We should work by candlelight every evening. It'd be pretty."

Phyllis threw her arms across her chest. "You imbecile. What planet are you from? You think everything's vanilla pudding. Well, I'm a realist." She glared at me. "If you expect me to go blind, working in bad lighting, then you're even stupider than I thought."

Excuse me?

Aghast, everyone looked from Phyllis to me, and like a shot, a detonator lit inside me. I promised myself I'd never get to this point, but I was at my limit. I'd had it with Phyllis's ignorant rants, eternal screw-ups, and belittling of Judy. Now she was insulting me. If that wasn't bad enough, my feet felt icky in my red rose shoes. I glanced down. *My Slimy. Ruined. Shoes.*

I balled my hands into fists, my throbbing eyes narrowed at Phyllis. It took months to save for these beauties. Shoes Romero loved. Destroyed. All because of *Phyllis.* I tried telling myself I was just agitated because of the events of the past two weeks, but my mind was having none of that. The honest truth was I felt like pulverizing my incompetent, inconsiderate, incomprehensible cousin. A loud *ping* went off in my head, and before I could stop myself, I shouted, "Phyllis! You're *fired!*"

Three sets of eyes popped out at me. Max could barely pick his mouth up off the floor. Judy shot her gaze from face to face, and Phyllis gibbered, "Well, I never!" and "Of all the…"

As far as I was concerned, there wasn't much else to say. I stamped into my office, kicked off my heels, and collapsed on the floor, exhaling the boiling rage from my chest. There'd be hell to pay once word bled to busybody Aunt Lorna and the rest of the family. But I wasn't going to worry about that now. The noose had just loosened from my neck.

I sat on my rear—the only thing not smudged in blue—and wiped away tears while I ransacked my stash of standby shoes under the desk. I tossed sandals and clogs left and right, not really seeing anything except tears blurring my eyes. I finally slid on black shoes, then took a deep breath, and swiped my nose.

All my efforts to run a decent salon, to be a good boss, to catch a killer. Whatever made me think I could be a success or solve Portia's murder? I was so clueless I made Inspector Clouseau look brilliant.

The phone rang, and I jumped, hitting my head on the underside of the desk. *Ouch. Ouch. Ouch!* I bet Lara Croft never had days like this. I rubbed my head where one of my pointy chopsticks dug into my scalp, then answered the phone.

"I'd love to take you out for a real supper," Romero said after the hellos, "but I won't be around much till this case is wrapped up."

I relaxed a bit just from the sound of his voice. "It's okay. I'm here until seven. Then I'm driving Judy home. Her car's in the shop."

"You still have power there?"

"We're working by candlelight and the little light from the front window."

"That window's one of the reasons I called. I got the crime report on the explosion. Acetone was the other chemical you smelled. You know what acetone is found in?"

I straightened. "Nail polish remover."

"Bingo. Mixed with bleach and hairspray, it was likely hard to detect." He sighed. "The person who broke your window knows the beauty industry or they're playing with you. *Or* we've missed something."

There was a pulling at my consciousness, but I couldn't grasp it.

"So why stay until seven?" he asked.

"My last customer is a manicure. I can do that blindfolded *and* without power."

"Lucky you. I'm on my way to the hospital. And since you'll learn about it anyway, the new case I'm on is a hospital kidnapping."

"What?"

"Original, isn't it. After you left last night, I spent the rest of the evening in the kids' ward."

"This is insane."

"You're right. What's even crazier is this particular kid's already been dealt a handful lately."

"A child's been abducted?" My chest tightened. "Who is it? I see those kids almost every week when we play Mon Sac est Ton Sac."

"You play what?"

"My Bag Is Your Bag, a game I created. I drag in my supplies, and we make each other up. Kids love it."

"Do you do stags and birthday parties?"

I wasn't going to be put off. "Romero, who's been kidnapped?"

No answer. And his silence was made worse by the alarming stab in my gut.

"Tell me, or I'll never speak to you again." Two-second pause. "*Well?*"

"I'm thinking about that."

"Okay. Have it your way. I'll find out on my own. I'll—"

"All right. I'll tell you, but this is off limits. Understand? No barreling into the hospital like a gun half-cocked in your spiked shoes, sexy dresses, and bag full of goodies. Got it?"

I crossed my fingers and my eyelashes, too. "Promise."

"Yeah, right. Why waste my breath? It's Kylie O'Roarke."

"Brody's granddaughter? Can't be! She was supposed to check out of the hospital any day. Why would someone kidnap her?" I pictured Kylie in her hospital bed when an image of Albert came to mind with his long, scraggly hair, blowing up balloons next to her.

"Oh no. No. No. No." I started hyperventilating and suddenly I couldn't see.

"What is it?"

"I've made a terrible mistake. Albert. He——" I blinked but couldn't focus on anything.

"He what?"

"I saw him at the hospital, making poodles and giraffes with those balloons."

"What balloons? When?"

"Those skinny balloons. He had a bag of them in his house, and I saw him at the hospital about a month ago. He was with Kylie and the others." I couldn't keep the anguish out of my voice. After all I did to convince everyone he was innocent. "I haven't been able to reach him either. What if he's the one? What if he hurts Kylie? You said whoever broke the window knows the industry. Albert knows the industry."

"Slow down. Did he make a delivery today?"

"No. I didn't have an order. Maybe he wasn't even at work today. Maybe he's——" I couldn't think it, let alone say it.

I breathed in and out, focusing, trying to keep from screaming. But my insides burned, and I couldn't keep still. "I have to call Alluve." I was on my feet, pacing the office. "This is all a misunderstanding. Has to be. Albert's innocent." Oh God, what was I saying? "You've got to find Kylie," I rushed on. "All she's been through, the cancer, and with Brody just dying——"

"We'll find her, but you've got to stay out of it."

"After Portia's murder? And then Dana's? What if she's killed? What if——"

"Calm down. We'll find her."

Calm down. Right. I hung up, my insides rattling. I wanted to clout something. I wanted to shriek. I wasn't any good at remaining calm when there was a volcano erupting inside. I picked up the phone again and dialed Alluve. Tom told me Albert was out on deliveries, but that didn't reassure me one bit. He was out on deliveries when Portia was killed.

Somehow I made it to seven o'clock. The shop had cleared out, Phyllis included.

Max poked his head in the office, sucking on a piece of chocolate. "Everything's locked up." He slid a small chocolate pyramid across my desk. "I'm off to celebrate you finally sacking that poor excuse for an employee."

I pushed the chocolate away from me. The last thing I felt like was a celebration. "Where's Judy?"

"In the dispensary, cleaning out Phyllis's food cupboard." He flopped on the chair beside me. "Do you know Phyll hid a whole case of Toblerone? Never even offered us a tiny slab."

I stared at the chocolate in the dim light. "She'll be back for it. Don't eat anymore."

He moved closer and searched my eyes. "What's up, Kemosabe? You've been on edge all day. Firing Phyllis proves it. Something else bothering you?"

Max wasn't a Harvard grad or a scholar among men. But he was intuitive and knew me like a book. I smiled even though the world was crumbling at my feet.

"It's nothing." I really wanted to talk to him. But I couldn't. Not now.

⚱

A blur of red taillights swam in front of me. I wiped the foggy windshield with my palm, concentrating on a truck's bumper ahead of me. At the same time, I played twenty questions with Judy. She wasn't gabby at the best of times, and her quietness was unnerving.

"How does Princess react during storms?" I asked.

"Oh. You know Princess. A little storm wouldn't daunt her."

She looked out the window, ending the small talk. Actually, that was fine. As soon as I dropped her off, I planned on heading to the hospital, see if I could learn anything about Kylie's disappearance. I glanced down at myself. Even if I did look like a madwoman. I flicked caked shampoo off my lap, then cranked the wheel onto Judy's street.

"There's an entrance by my spot," she said. "It's up the ramp on the other side of the building."

Normally, I would've parked on the road, but to make it easier for her, I turned into her lot, passed the Dumpster, and went up the ramp.

"You're still blue," Judy said with a shy smile. "I've got some miracle soap that will get your dress clean if you want to come up for it. Plus, I'd appreciate the company, at least till I get inside my apartment. I'm a little nervous going into a dark building with a murderer loose."

Who did she think *I* was? Miss Braveheart?

I looked at the car clock. It was already past seven-thirty. I didn't want to waste another minute, but when I saw Judy's timid face I thought, safety in numbers. "Okay. Let's go up. And the soap will be wonderful. Thanks."

I parked in her spot, and we traipsed to the third floor, our footsteps the only sound in the hushed building. I held Judy's things while she unlocked the door. Then she tripped into the dark and muggy apartment.

"Princess!" She regained her footing and scouted around for the cat.

I squinted at the shadows around me, but other than the tea towel Judy had stumbled over and a makeup bag on the bench in the entry, I didn't see Princess anywhere. "Maybe she *was* scared." I picked up the tea towel, dumped our stuff on the bench, and knocked over the makeup bag. Lipsticks and nail polish bottles tumbled out. Shoot. I stuffed the cosmetics back in the bag while Judy instinctively switched on the light. Nothing.

"That cat is always into something." She lit a candle in the living room, then headed down the hall to her bedroom. "Give me a few minutes to look for that soap. For some reason, I think it's in a travel bag under my bed."

"Okay." I looked at her in the barely flickering light. "May I use the bathroom?"

"Yes," she said over her shoulder. "Just stay clear of

the bedroom. Princess hacked up a hairball this morning. I haven't had a chance to clean it up."

Good enough for me. I'd seen enough unpleasant messes for one day. No need to add cat vomit to the list. Not that I'd see anything in this darkness.

Judy shut her bedroom door, and I stepped in the other direction and found Princess sitting tall at my feet. Her green eyes glowed as big as fluorescent marbles. She gripped a dark, thick-looking scarf between her teeth, displaying it as if she were presenting me with a trophy mouse.

"Whatcha doing, Princess?" I whispered, crouching.

She dropped the scarf in my hand and sat back proudly. I was fingering the silky-stranded texture, trying to identify the feel, when simultaneously the power clicked on. Carbon monoxide detectors beeped throughout the building, and the light Judy had switched on earlier shone brightly.

"It's about time!" Judy called out. "Darn. Where is that soap?"

I stood and took a moment to absorb the clarity around me. Then I saw red spots on the floor five feet away. They were in front of the closed door to the spare room. I blinked, thinking my eyes hadn't adjusted to the light. But the spots were real, and I couldn't ignore the unease pouring through me. I told myself not to look up at the door, but I couldn't restrain the urge. I peeked up, and all at once the air went out of me. Bleeding down the wood in reds, pinks, and purples was a large drawing of fireworks. Just like the fireworks tattooed on Dana's chest.

I slapped my hand across my mouth to keep from screaming and peered over at the makeup bag holding the lipsticks and nail polish. Then I stared back at the door, recognition setting in.

I felt like I was being smothered. Blood spiraled to my toes, and my hands shook uncontrollably. I looked down and noticed I'd dropped the scarf. But it wasn't a scarf at all. I'd been holding a black wig. *Yikes.*

Suddenly Hajna's warning came to mind. *Be careful. Evil spirits crowd you.* I didn't want the old witch to be right. *I* didn't want to be right. But I couldn't stop seeing huge puzzle pieces flying together. Acetone. Explosion. Blond hair. Black wig.

I gasped for air. Judy was the woman Tess saw leaving the shop. Which meant she was the woman on Erik's arm. Which meant…no. *No.* I gaped at the lipstick drawing. She couldn't be the one responsible for two murders, could she?

I glanced down the hall, recalling Romero wanting to match our fingerprints to the steamer. Wait a minute. Judy never used Ti Amo or that steamer. Ever. Why hadn't I thought of this before? She preferred Molto Bella because it was darker and had no windows. And I never objected. If Judy's fingerprints were on the steamer, it would've been from the day of the murder.

Hot panic surged through my body. How should I proceed? How did I tell someone I cared about the jig was up? I didn't have a stellar record when it came to catching criminals. I had an incident with a perm rod and a metal tail comb. I wasn't that female sleuth on *Murder, She Wrote.* Heck, I wasn't even Lara Croft. Like I had to be told *that.*

I heard a muffled cry in the spare room. By now, I was breaking out in a sweat, and my chest felt buried under wet sand. I knew I didn't have much time to act. Bracing myself, I pushed the door open and saw Kylie curled up in a tense ball at the head of the bed. Her hands were tied to one side of the frame, mouth gagged, eyes scared but heavy, like she was coming out of a drug-induced state. Her shoulders relaxed when she saw me, and her eyes calmed with recognition. My blueness was obviously no contest for the wild creations she'd seen on me before.

I swallowed. Thank God she was alive. Then anger gripped my core. Was Judy's car problem a ploy? Hedging her bets I'd offer her a ride home? And why would she ask me up to her apartment where I could find Kylie and the painted door? The answer seemed pretty simple. I wasn't meant to leave. Was her plan to drug me, too? Keep us both prisoners? Or kill us? Not if I had anything to do with it. I had just enough crazy left in me from the day to face this head on. I put a finger to my lips, and Kylie nodded, her brown eyes full of trust.

I'd just closed the door when Judy reeled out of her bedroom, her right arm tucked behind her back. "I couldn't find the soap." She froze and looked at the floor in front of me. "What's that?"

I picked up the hair. "A wig?"

"So it is." She looked around for Princess. "Darn cat must've found it after all." She brought her arm around and pointed a gun at me. "I think you know what this is."

I leaped back. "Yeah." I tried to steady myself, but my legs felt wobbly, and the bottom dropped out of my stomach. Judy seemed oblivious to my fear. Or she'd already spiraled so far down a black hole she'd lost touch with reality.

She waved me into the living room, snatched the wig, and flung it on the end of the sofa. The gun didn't leave her hand.

"You couldn't stop snooping, could you?" She spit out the words, slashing back curls from her clammy face.

I wasn't sure what she expected me to say, but I had to ask, "Why'd you do it, Judy?"

"I *love* him." A tear ran down her cheek and splashed on the gun. "I wanted that baby."

Baby? My pulse pounded, keeping beat with raindrops pinging on the window. "What happened?"

She squirmed uncomfortably. "That day you came here, I was recovering from a miscarriage. I bled late the night before, and the bleeding wouldn't stop." She choked on her words. "I had to go to the hospital...I loved that baby...it was part of Erik." Tears streamed down her cheeks, and I would've comforted her if a gun hadn't been pointing in my face.

In all likelihood, I was going to be the next victim. And Kylie was petrified for her life in the next room. My eyes wandered to my bag by the door. I was going to die, and my tools wouldn't do me a lick of good. Some hero I was.

Judy wiped her eyes and blew her nose. Then she plunked down on the couch. The best idea was to keep her talking. Maybe I'd think of a way out of this mess.

"Did Erik know you were pregnant?" I asked, cautiously sitting across from her.

"No." She squeezed her eyes tight, then opened them wide. "He wanted to leave Portia, but she never would've let him go. Yet she ran around. If it wasn't Pace, it was someone else."

"You knew about Pace."

"Ha. Everyone knew. It was a joke. Poor Erik, putting up with that slut."

She bunched her tissue in a ball and pitched it on the floor. "That's when he'd had enough. One night, months after that bogus cocktail party where Pace made a scene, I stayed late to cut Erik's hair. He started talking. Ended up we went out for coffee." She shrugged. "Things grew. Neither one of us expected to care so much."

A frown crossed her face. "Then I saw the studs at his place one night, and I stole them. I thought by taking something of Portia's, maybe she'd feel my pain." She swiped her frizzy hair. "I didn't want anything of hers. I carried them around in my purse as a reminder that Erik was mine, too. Then I lost one of them."

How invested was Erik in all this? "Was he involved in Portia's murder?"

"No. He may have wanted out of a bad marriage, but he never talked about killing her. He was always gentle. He used to sing 'Hey Jude' to me to make me smile." She slumped into a broken doll. "Don't you see? It's all gone bad." She closed her eyes for a second, then looked up at me. "I don't want to kill another person, but at least my secret will die with you."

I didn't want to die. I had too much to live for. My mother's meddling, more horrendous blind dates, a bungled business. I had to keep her talking for Kylie's sake, if not for my own.

"That morning, you went home sick."

She nodded, glowering at the gun. "I was getting my daily dose of morning sickness. Then I saw Portia's name in the appointment book. I almost threw up on the spot." She glared at me. "How could I work when she was coming in to get dolled up for that stupid ceremony for Erik? *She* was going to be there, honoring him, while I had to live in the shadows, wearing disguises just to be with him in public. If I was ever going to have Erik, this woman had to go."

She scrubbed her temple, her eyes feverish. "I was so mixed up. I had to get out of there. I drove to Kuruc's and sat in the back corner of the deli, forcing down a muffin. Thinking. Sam hovered nearby, and Hajna made me crazy with her needle and thread. Thankfully, they got busy and forgot all about me. I left the car there, walked back to the shop, and saw Portia's Mercedes in the lot. Ten minutes before eleven. No surprise. She was always early. Then I saw Albert hop in his truck at Friar Tuck's and drive away."

She blinked down at the gun, then back at me. "I knew you had the Cutlers booked and wouldn't be able to start Portia's facial until eleven. This was my chance to enter the back door and hide. And when I tried the door, it was unlocked. I had my key, but this was a sign."

Now she was into omens.

"I waited behind that heavy shower curtain, thinking I was safe. I didn't figure on hearing the back door open and catching Pace walk past the bathroom. Then I heard a scuffle in the hall and recognized Portia's voice. I guessed she was on her way into Ti Amo. But she didn't sound happy." She sniffed laboriously. "It seemed like forever until Portia was alone and everyone was done traipsing up and down the hall. Then I finally slid into Ti Amo and saw her lying there, quiet for once. I told myself to just leave, but I couldn't. I kept seeing Erik's face. I closed the door, unplugged the steamer, and wrapped the cord around her neck. She didn't even know it was there until I popped off her eye pads. Then I tightened the cord."

A vision of Portia's inert body rushed to mind, suffocating me from the inside out. How could I have worked alongside Judy and not seen any signs of instability?

"Judy," I said, my voice croaky. "Why'd you remove Portia's eye pads?"

She glared at me like it was perfectly clear. "So she could see her murderer."

Chapter 17

My stomach was about at its limit. But I had to hear more. "What about Dana?"

"Troublemaker." She spied the wig and then gazed down the hall at the painted door. "You like my drawing? It's in honor of her."

I gulped back a swallow, not trusting myself to respond.

"I wanted to go places with Erik," Judy said, "but we couldn't risk being seen. The wig made people think I was Portia. Then Dana confronted me about it. Said she knew it was me all along."

"People would've eventually figured it out, Judy. One of Portia's society sisters bumped into you and Erik outside Dino Hosta's. But you had dark hair. Then she saw you leave the shop Saturday. Same face. No wig. Some people have a knack for that sort of thing. But why'd you leave by the front door Saturday?"

She looked dumbfounded. "It was nice out. I walked to the drugstore for my prescription."

She reached for the black wig. "I've had this old thing since high school. I wore it in a school play." She threw her head forward and yanked on the wig, humming to herself.

"Judy? How did you kill Dana?"

She lifted her head, smiling right through me. Black

strands drooped over her blond curls, and in that moment, I knew I'd lost her. I choked back the ache in my throat and watched helplessly as she ripped off the wig and hurled it at the wall. She narrowly missed Princess, who had been sitting tall, taking everything in.

The cat dusted her nose to the ground and marked cautious steps to the wig. She pawed it, dropped on top of it, and then washed it with her tongue.

Judy dragged her eyes away from Princess. "I'd left my Beatles CD at Erik's. It was special because he'd given it to me with a personal message inside the flap. I didn't want it traced to me, so I went to get it." She rose from the sofa and backed toward the balcony. "I parked two blocks away, then used the key Erik had given me, ready with some lame condolences if Noleta was there. I turned off the alarm, went to the den, and searched for the CD. It wasn't where I'd left it. I looked everywhere and almost gave up when I found the gun in the desk drawer. Who even knew they had a gun? Then Dana slinked into the room, waving the CD at me." Tears slid down her cheeks, and she paled to a ghostly white. "She was going to tell Erik I killed Portia."

"Did you admit that to her?"

"Of course not." She slashed away tears. "She kept throwing insults in my face, saying Erik wouldn't want a nobody like me for long. The whole time, my hand was on the gun. When she said she was going to the police, I said I'd kill her first."

She lifted the gun and aimed it at my head.

I croaked on my next word, praying I wouldn't faint. "And?"

"She laughed. Said I wouldn't dare shoot. But she was wrong."

I cringed, desperately trying to hold it together. Softly, my cell phone chimed from somewhere in the depths of my bag. At the same time, thunder and lightning struck outside. It caught Judy's attention. Thank you, God. I inched toward the ringing, and Princess gave a short meow.

Judy whirled around, confused by the noise. She pointed the gun at me, then at my bag, then at the wig, forgetting, or not seeing through the tears, that Princess was curled on top. "I don't want to kill you, Val." She waved the gun back at me. "I tried to warn you. *Stop moving!* Or I'll shoot you right now!"

The phone quit jingling, and any ideas I had of acting brave died with the fading ring. The only sound came from soft purring.

"A lot of good that old mop did," Judy cried, her makeup streaked with tears. "It didn't make anything better."

Another crack of thunder pierced the air. And she fired the gun.

Princess jumped, and there was a lot of screaming. Judy cocked the gun and aimed for the black mass again.

"*Nooo!*" I screamed and dove to stop her. I felt a sharp sting in my arm from the shot, and the room began to spin. I collapsed to the floor, fighting for consciousness.

Judy hovered over me, but I couldn't make out what she was saying. I blinked heavily from my searing arm to the sight of all the blood, to the cat I was trying to protect. I cleared my eyes through the bleary fog, but I didn't see Princess anywhere.

A bleak sob escaped my throat, and guilt encompassed me. I hadn't acted soon enough, and now I feared the worst for Princess. Tears flooded my eyes, and Judy just kept talking. She didn't seem aware of the blood or that Princess was missing. Meanwhile, I couldn't stop crying. I inhaled short raspy breaths, forcing my mind to get it together. I couldn't save Princess, but Kylie was depending on me.

"I'd overhear you talking about the murder at work," Judy said, the gun trembling in her hand. "I thought subtle hints would get you to stop. The phone call. The note. The fire bomb." She tightened her lips. "Remember that time Phyllis had spilled nail polish remover over that Christmas candle, and then poured hairspray over it to put out the flames?" She groaned, recalling the incident. "It reminded me how combustible our products could be."

I blinked, attempting to stay with her. "So you decided to put that knowledge to good use and stir up an explosive cocktail."

"I thought the note would be enough to get your attention. I even paid a kid twenty bucks to deliver it to your door. Told him it was a surprise and it was important he wasn't seen. He succeeded too. Waited until the smoker next door went inside for a fresh pack of cigarettes, then he dropped off the envelope and scrammed."

I closed my eyes then willed them open. I had to get up. I had to do something.

"When the note didn't work, I thought a fire would scare you off. I even disguised myself with the wig in case anyone saw me." She scratched her forehead so hard it left a mark. "Why did you have to keep digging? *Why?*" she screamed.

I leaned up on one elbow, my throat blocked with emotion. "Believe me, Judy, I didn't want it to be you."

She shook her head, not wanting to hear more. She marched into the spare room and came back out, hauling Kylie by the hair.

I stared at the delicate redhead and tried to fill my lungs with air, clenching my teeth from the burning pain in my arm.

Judy threw Kylie to the ground, the gun pointed at her head. Kylie glared from the blood on my arm, to Judy, to the weapon. Her eyebrows creased in horror, her chest heaved.

"After I saw you at the hospital that day," Judy told me, "and it became obvious you wouldn't quit prying, I got the idea to kidnap one of your precious kids. Maybe you'd have something else to focus on and forget about finding Portia's murderer. Now I'll have to kill her as well."

My mind was hazy, but didn't Judy realize that looking for Kylie's kidnapper would have led to her, too?

Kylie moaned behind the tape, and her freckled face reddened. Small and powerless as she was, she wasn't going to give up. On the flip side, I was barely hanging on. My arm was on fire, blood was smeared everywhere, and I thought I might throw up. But I couldn't let her see me beat. I had to pull myself together. Just then, I spied Princess's tail move from under the couch. My heart jumped in my throat that she'd be okay after all.

Determined to save Kylie, I decided to tackle Judy for the gun, astonished that I was actually going to fight for the cold metal thing. I took a mouthful of air and staggered to my feet. Judy aimed the gun at me, but it didn't stop me. I bit back the sting in my arm, cried "hide" to Kylie, then lunged for the weapon.

Kylie fled the room, and Judy shoved the butt of the gun into my stomach, giving me a fierce push. I grabbed her arm, and we tumbled to the floor. The gun shifted between us, and a shot fired into the air. With one hand, she gripped my bun and hammered my head on the floor. I tried not to shriek, but my metal chopsticks dug into my scalp, stabbing me in pain.

I flashed back to what Sensei had taught me in karate. Telling myself I could do this, I mustered enough strength and gave Judy a karate chop across her gun hand. Then I kicked her off me. The gun dropped to the ground with a clunk. I yanked the chopsticks from my hair and stabbed at her as if I was popping balloons. One chopstick lodged itself into her collarbone, and she gave a horrific scream.

My mind raced, and my heart boomed in my ears. Mostly all I could think was, seize the weapon. I reached for the gun, panting like I'd never breathe again.

I convinced myself everything was going to be okay, when I heard footsteps thundering up the stairs.

The door flew open and Romero barreled in, his hair damp, his shirt wet, his body language, *don't fuck with me*. He relieved me of the gun and crouched to restrain Judy. Then he reassured Kylie who'd edged back into the room. I was weak and exhausted, and I felt his eyes doing a double take of my face and arm. If he had something to say, he thankfully kept it to himself.

Blood trickled from Judy's neck, and she moaned in pain and rocked helplessly. I started unsteadily toward her. Romero pushed me back. Just as well. I wasn't sure if I was going to throw up or faint, but I didn't feel so good.

He checked Judy's neck and looked up at me. "Get me a towel."

Holding my throbbing arm, I stumbled to the bathroom, grabbed a towel, and stuffed it in his hand. Then I completely freed Kylie's hands and untaped her mouth. I hugged her to my side and watched Romero apply pressure to Judy's neck and call for backup and an ambulance.

He glanced from the fancy chopstick poking out of Judy's collarbone to the one on the floor. He raised an eyebrow at me. "Yours?"

I nodded, my nose buried in Kylie's hair.

"Why doesn't that surprise me?"

All the blood had made me dizzy, and my eyes began to roll. I liked red all right, when it was mixed in tint, or in lipstick, or on a splashy dress. The gushy wet kind, pouring out of body cavities was less appealing. My voice was almost gone, too. I couldn't hear words I was sure I was saying. But I hung on. I wanted Judy to be all right.

"She's going to be fine." Romero echoed my thoughts. "You missed the artery."

Relief hit me, and the lights went out around me. Next thing I knew I was in Romero's arms while medics tended to Kylie and Judy. He wiped my smudged face and held up a blue finger. Shampoo I must've missed.

"There was a little shampoo episode at work," I mumbled.

He smoothed back my hair. "Honey, with you there's always going to be an episode."

"You're a hero," Max said to me in the laundry room the following Tuesday.

"I don't feel like a hero." I folded a towel and dropped it in the laundry basket.

"In my eyes, you are. Putting your life on the line for that kid? Lovey, that took courage. And you saved that poor kitty from losing one of its nine lives."

The thought of Princess almost dying still touched a tender spot deep down. "Judy didn't hurt Princess in the end. She wasn't thinking straight when she fired the shots."

"She killed two people. She could've killed you, too, you know." He gave me a gentle squeeze, carefully avoiding my bandaged arm.

"I'm okay. It's only a flesh wound. The bandage comes off Friday."

"So what happens to the cat?"

"I'm keeping it. I could use a roommate." Truth was, I'd become protective about the furry creature. I figured Princess needed me as much as I needed her.

"You're a sweetheart." He wiped lint out of the dryer, then slammed the door. "All this Valentine sleuthing proves my point again."

"And that would be?"

"Simply that your tools of the trade and this whole beauty industry are the very things that make up wonderful you."

I warmed at his words with a humbled thought that maybe he was right. It's certain that life for me would be desolate without those things. Nonetheless, it was going to take a while to get over this. At least I still had Max. The thought of losing him had made our relationship tighter, and for that I was grateful. Even the dark aura that swam over the salon the past few weeks had lifted.

The pain of Judy's betrayal, however, would probably never go away. "You know what I learned from all this? People aren't what they seem."

He rolled his eyes and flicked the lint into the garbage. "Don't get deep on me. Judy had big problems. She just hid them well."

"I should have realized. I looked in all the wrong places. I even had a moment where I thought you were the Portia look-alike."

"*What?* Bite your tongue."

"It's just that you matched Portia in height, and with makeup and a wig, you'd put any woman to shame. Plus, Noleta said Erik had the odd male friend over to use their hot tub. Then you mentioned using a friend's hot tub. And when your friend wasn't home and Erik wasn't home—"

"You put two and two together and got five."

"Something like that. I'm sorry, Max."

He offered a forgiving smile, then kissed my cheek. "The suspects did all have their quirks."

"Yet the murderer was the sweetest girl in Rueland. Hard to believe."

"If it were Phyllis, I'd believe it. Talk about jerks, I mean quirks."

"Judy's sweet personality drew people to her. That's probably why Erik got involved with her."

"Unlike Phyllis, who repels people. Which is why nobody gets involved with her."

"You've made your point."

"I'm glad she won't be darkening these doors anymore. Her haircutting was bad enough. I don't think I could've taken one more of her do-it-yourself outfits."

This would've been a good time to confess my family secret and share the guilt I now felt over firing Phyllis, but I was a coward. Besides, I was looking to the future. Maybe I'd find someone with talent and skill, someone who had a well-established clientele. "It's just going to be you and me until I hire another stylist."

"Am I complaining?" Max picked up the laundry basket. "I liked the business we raked in this past month. It reminded me of the good ol' days, before Lady No Talent arrived."

"It'll mean less time off this summer."

"You know I don't take summer holidays. I daren't let the sun assault my epidermis." He dusted a piece of lint off his Dolce & Gabbana striped shirt. "What'd Mr. Feltz say when you made the payment?"

"He wiped his bald head and gave one of his skittish smiles. It wasn't earth-shattering." I shut off the light and closed the door, thinking about one last thing I had to do as we climbed the stairs.

I left Max to stuff towels in the cupboards while I went to the office and searched my bag. Seconds later, I trekked back to him, my hands in fists. "I've got two surprises."

He brightened. "I love surprises! What is it? What is it?"

I opened my left palm, and Max's face fell. "What's so surprising about that gold-plated piece of junk? Except that you're still clinging on to it."

I dangled my watch by the broken clasp over the garbage pail. Max was right. It was time to let go of bad memories. The watch had been a gift from my first love, a poisonous relationship from day one. The only thing the guy had given me, other than heartache, was this piece of jewelry. When he'd hurt me for the last time, I should've thrown the stupid thing away. Instead, I'd kept it and hung onto the theory all men were untrustworthy beasts. Not anymore.

Wordlessly, I dropped the watch into the pail with a clink.

Max clapped his hands. "Yay, lovey. The best thing that jackass ever did for you was to set you free." He narrowed in on my other fist. "What's the second surprise?"

I placed the diamond earring in his palm.

He was breathless. "For *moi?*"

"Erik doesn't want it, and I won't wear it. So yes, it's yours."

He dashed to the mirror and slipped it in his ear. He posed this way and that. "It's really me, isn't it?"

"And then some."

"Thank you." His smile quickly faded. "About Erik—"

"Romero called this morning. Erik's already paid Judy a visit. I think he really cares for her."

"I'm glad. Hard as I try, I can't hate Judy. Do you think she just wanted to be loved?"

"It's a good possibility. Isn't that something we all want?"

Chapter 18

Saturday, almost two weeks later, I stood beside Romero on a yacht. Stars twinkled above us like diamonds in the ebony sky. Water glistened navy blue below, and thousands of tiny white lights illuminated the deck. Nearby, a classic Barry White song played, sending tingles up my spine. It's this thing I had for deep, sexy voices.

Romero moved in behind me. He swept my loosely curled hair over one shoulder while his lips did suggestive things to the back of my ear. I drifted in a romantic cloud and inhaled the white roses in my hand. I wanted to soak up every bit of the evening. Magnificently set tables, women in long gowns, huge white bouquets, milk chocolate fountain—which I wasn't going anywhere near—and Romero in black formal wear.

I playfully swung around to face him. "It's rather hard resisting a man in a tux."

He lightly squished the bouquet between us. "I can take it off if you like."

I didn't need to see him naked to know he was perfect. Even so, I choked at the thought.

Romero pressed his nose into my hair. His strong hands circled my waist. "God, you smell good." He glanced down at my dress—a green that was so dark it was almost black, and daringly gathered over one shoulder. "And in case you didn't know by the stares, you're stunning."

Women giggled nearby, but my stomach didn't drop. I didn't feel shame, and I didn't feel haunted by my hurtful past. If anything, I felt elated. Freed.

I gave Romero a contented smile. Maybe I'd finally found someone who appreciated me for who I was.

His gun pressed into my hip, and instead of jumping, I remained on two feet. He studied my eyes, perhaps a little surprised by that. "Did anyone ever tell you—"

"That I'm difficult?"

His look intensified. "I was going to say that your eyes are an autumn color. Not really brown, more like a burnt amber."

"Some would say they're my best feature," I said, trying to be cute.

His gaze lowered a few inches, then another few inches. "At least one of them."

I blushed. "I didn't think you noticed my eyes. You never really looked into them without hollering."

"Honey, I noticed your eyes the first minute I saw you." He leaned back with a naughty grin. "And when I wasn't looking at you, I was thinking about you. You know you can turn me on with that smile? So damn much I've been having a hell of a time concentrating at work."

I warmed, touched by his confession.

"One day, your sister put me in a headlock in front of the chief. Said I better not pull any badass shit on you or I'd have *her* to contend with."

I was sure Romero was only put in a headlock if he wished to be put in a headlock. But I smiled anyway.

I took a moment to admire him and breathe in his masculinity. Not only was he appealing in a deeply sexy way, but standing close, sharing easy banter, I felt safe and secure. He was a man I could trust. And that thought brought out the softer side in me.

He slid his fingers along my waist. "So will you tell me what happened with that other case?"

"You mean, how did I manage to wind a perm rod around a man's—"

"That's the one."

I shrugged. "If you really want to hear it."

"You have no idea how much."

By the tone of his voice, I knew he was playing with me. I put up my chin. "I thought you would've read the police reports."

"Official reports don't explain everything. Like what you were doing at the dump that day."

"Oh. That." I fingered the rose petals in my hand. "I'd just done a major cleaning at the salon and had a bunch of bags ready for garbage. Only the Dumpster was already overflowing with Friar Tuck's waste, and it wouldn't be emptied for another week." I brought the roses up to my nose and breathed them in. "Do you know how bad cotton smells after it's been saturated with perm solution and sitting a week in the hot weather?"

He made a sour face.

"Exactly. So, trying to be a good neighbor, I took the bags to the dump."

"Very considerate of you."

I ignored his sarcasm. "I was tossing my bags when I saw this truck parked way back by the backhoe, and two guys climbing the trash pile, hurling black garbage bags into the middle. It just felt off. I mean, why not toss your trash at the edge? It's not like you need to hide trash. Right?"

"So you got suspicious."

"Enough to watch them. I noticed the smaller guy limping and having a hard time maneuvering around the rubble, and then I recognized the bald guy."

"You knew them?"

"Not exactly. But a month or so earlier, I saw them jump in a truck and take off when Max and I stopped at Freddie's Top Dog Groomers to donate some old towels from the salon for the kennel. Freddie was all shook up after they ransacked his place and threatened him because he told the scumbags he was going to expose them for running a puppy mill. A week later, Freddie was found dead with a dog leash around his neck.

"When I realized the guys at the dump were the same ones we saw leaving Freddie's shop that night, I pulled out my phone and moved closer to take a video clip."

Romero raised a palm. "Why didn't you just leave and call the police?"

"I needed evidence. After Freddie was killed, Max and I told the police about the men threatening him. But I'm not sure they took us seriously."

He feigned disbelief. "I can't imagine why not."

I sliced him a narrow-eyed look. "Do you want to hear my story or not?" Because if he delivered one more sarcastic remark, I was going to shove my bouquet up his nose.

"Of course I do. Go on." He gave me one of his thick-lashed sexy winks like that's all it would take to melt me. He was right.

"Like I said, I wanted to give the police a video, but I couldn't figure out how to film from my new phone." *Damn thing.* "And then the thugs saw me. I was so scared I thought my heart was going to leap out of my skin. They started yelling at me, and I ran to my car."

"Were you wearing the red heels?"

"What? No. You honestly think I'd wear sparkly heels to the dump?"

"It wouldn't surprise me."

"Well, you would be wrong." A pang swept through me at the thought of my ruined shoes now being trash in a landfill. "On top of which, it had poured rain the night before, and there was mud everywhere. I'd hardly wear fancy heels in those conditions."

He nodded. "So what happened?"

"The bald guy tackled me. Next thing I knew, he was on top of me, his hands around my neck. I just knew I was going to die like Freddie, and in a panic, I whipped out my tail comb and jabbed him in the stomach. When he saw the blood on his belly, he passed out. By now, I was so high on adrenaline, I stumbled to my feet, full of daring. I managed to take down one guy. How hard could it be to catch a guy with a limp?"

I waited for another smartass response. Nothing.

"When I spotted him trying to escape over that huge pile of rubbish, I chased him."

"Is this where you offered to perm his hair?"

"No, it's where I whacked him with my bag. Then the garbage and mud under us gave way, causing a mudslide. Everything came rushing at me, including the killer waving a knife in my face. I lost contact with my bag, but not before grabbing something to fend him off. Unfortunately, it was only a perm rod."

I raised my left hand and displayed the one-inch jagged scar. "The guy sliced me, promising to do more if I didn't back off."

Romero smoothed the scar. "You really have a way of getting under a person's skin."

"Am I telling this, or are you?" I grimaced. "These guys killed Max's friend. In addition, they were mistreating animals. There was no way I was giving up. We were covered in mud, grasping at anything we could get a hold of. I grabbed onto his baggy shorts. The shorts slid off, the guy was, uh, commando, and...the rest is history."

"I bet he'll never go without boxers again." Romero grinned.

"I also got a few more cuts, and by then, one of the workers at the far end of the landfill rushed over to help. But the creep got the worst of it in the end."

"Yeah, I think we covered that."

"Anyway, the police found a bunch of Freddie's tools and merchandise in the trash bags, the guys confessed, and the puppy mill was shut down. They were convicted of Freddie's murder and are now sitting with their striped boxers behind bars."

Romero crossed his arms, put his finger to his lips, and gave me a concentrated stare. "So tell me, is this any indication of what you'll be like in a relationship?"

"Relationship?"

"Yeah. Like if I kissed you right here, right now, would you have an urge to rearrange my body parts?"

Gulp. I wasn't sure how to answer that. Would he really pursue a relationship with me? Was I too unusual for him? Were we in different leagues?

My past dates usually soured by now. Funny thing, I can honestly say I never cared, but I cared now. I wanted that exhilarating feeling, being turned upside down by a man like Romero.

I smiled innocently and looked past the five-o'clock shadow up into his gorgeous eyes that, tonight, had lost a bit of the hard edge. I was so taken in by his character and strength. Blind passion rushed through me, and all at once truth struck. I craved the same thing those ladies with the dangling panties desired. I wanted Romero.

He gave my nose a light flick, abruptly ending my ardent thoughts. "Cynthia likes you. I have a feeling she'll be on you like flies on a horse."

"Thanks for the comparison."

He tucked a flower behind my ear. "She threw you the bouquet. She must see something."

"How do you see me?"

There wasn't a moment's hesitation. "Impulsive. Creative." His voice deepened. "Sexy."

Oh boy. I clutched a passing waiter's arm and swooped a glass off his tray. Romero watched, entertained, as I dumped everything but the ice overboard. That, I sucked on, hard.

The song ended, and Romero led me back to the crowd. He stopped a few feet from the bar and gave me a sideways glance. "By the way, is there any chance you might sign up for the police academy?"

"Ha! As it is, I can't run into one of your colleagues without being dealt perm-rod or chopstick jokes."

"That would change. They'd know who they'd be answering to."

I had a feeling I was blushing. In all honesty, I wasn't

sure what my future held. I knew the beauty industry inside out. Sleuthing? That had come at a price. Nevertheless, it had been an education. And if nothing else, I had a newfound respect for our men in blue.

He pulled me up to the bar. "As much as it pains me to admit this, I admire your perseverance in seeing this case through."

"Excuse me?" I blinked cutesy-eyed, hoping he'd repeat himself.

"Most of all, I admire your loyalty to a friend." He moved in close, and a grin crept up his face. "No. Most of all, I like those red shoes you wore the first day I laid eyes on you." He pressed his hard thigh into mine, smoothed his hand down my leg, and lifted my dress an inch off the deck. "Though I gotta say these heels might just top them."

Good, my heart pumped crazily. Because the red ones were history. I lowered my dress out of his grasp and returned the smile. "I'm glad it all worked out for Albert."

"Yes, it did. Though if he hadn't have taken off so fast after the murder, this whole case may have taken a different direction. You know where he went after he left your shop that day? To print off his ticket and do a few other errands for his trip. On company time. Employers get a bit sticky about that sort of thing."

"Why didn't you tell me any of this?"

"Because I couldn't. Time was slipping by, I'd been waiting for lab reports to come in, plus, the chief was breathing down my neck. He wanted a confession before there was another murder and the commissioner fired *his* ass."

Stupid me had thought we were playing show-me-yours and I'll show-you-mine. Like I had any sort of credentials. But Romero didn't play by my rules. He'd had the political game-book in his pocket. One more confirmation, I'd been way out of my league.

"Where was Albert when Dana was killed?" I asked, getting over myself.

He avoided my eyes. "Volunteer lawn bowling with underprivileged teens."

"Come again?" I feigned shock at such horrible news.

"See?" He let a grin slip out. "I told you, you don't know much about the guy."

"I guess not. Don't they hang people for that?"

He gave me a wry look. "It's nice to know the system works. He'd put in his hours at the community center for homeless kids when he was released on parole. I guess he's a natural with kids. What's more, the Cutlers belong to the country club that hosts lawn bowling. Seems now that Albert's a regular, they've taken it upon themselves to keep him on the straight and narrow."

I smiled at that. Albert shared similar news in a lunch date a week ago. He'd also thanked me for mailing Caroline the money. Said she did homecare when she wasn't in the office. Her receptionist-slash-assistant had quit, and Caroline couldn't be on the road and keep the office open with no support. She almost gave up at finding help, and expenses were mounting. Albert merely came to the rescue. His car was on the fritz, and he was in such a hurry to cab it to the airport he'd left the envelope behind by mistake.

Romero's look turned serious. "There was so much hysteria that Wednesday at the hospital because of the abduction, it took till the next day to get the story straight. We finally narrowed it to a dark-haired female abductor and brought in a sketch artist. When the artist finished his portrait, Judy's face stared out at me. I went cold. I knew you were walking into a trap."

I felt warmth spread through me from his concern. "How did Judy take Kylie from the hospital?"

"She told Kylie she worked with you, and that you wanted her to bring Kylie to your salon for a big party involving that game you play—Mon Bag is No Bag."

I rolled my eyes. "It's Mon Sac est Ton Sac, for your information."

He poured me a soda, a teasing spark in his eye. "Kylie

jumped at the chance. Since security cameras were down because of the expansion, she easily followed Judy unnoticed out of the hospital. Judy took Kylie to her apartment, drugged her, and tied her up. By the time we figured it out, you were already on your way there. And I couldn't reach you on your cell. Don't you ever answer that thing?"

I smiled sheepishly.

"Nice touch, by the way, parking in Judy's spot."

"Believe me, it wasn't my idea."

He grabbed a beer, then gave me a concerned glare. "How's the arm?"

"Good as new."

Silence.

Sensing a lecture, I buried my nose in the fragrant roses I held.

He took his finger and lifted my chin. "You should've told me your suspicions. That badge I wear isn't for decoration."

I let that comment go, figuring the outcome was all the same. At my stillness, he raised an eyebrow. "I went to Brody's funeral. Funny, I didn't hear you there."

"Ha…ha. I'll have you know I went to see the family."

"In your case, that's probably best."

I left that alone. "What do you think led him to make that call?"

"Nina saw him talking to our Portia look-alike after we left the restaurant that day. Seems Judy was keeping close tabs on you."

That creepy feeling that we'd been watched came back to me, and I held back a shiver.

"Nina heard her introduce herself as Portia Reynolds. Kind of strange when Portia was dead. Just shows how unstable Judy was." He shook his head. "Brody likely wanted to share all this. I guess we'll never know what caused the heart attack."

I sighed. I wanted to feel alive and enjoy the beauty around us. I looked up at the midnight sky. A helicopter hovered in the distance, the propeller softly whirring. It added to the romance of the evening. And I was about to ruin it. "What about New York?"

His back stiffened. "New York?"

I wished I could take back the question, but it was out there. Blunt and naked. "Yes. You'd just returned when you came to tell me about Dana."

"What do you want to know?"

Okay. This wasn't going well. If it was related to the case, he'd tell me. If not, and he wanted to keep it private, then so be it. I wasn't going to grovel. "Nothing. Let's change the subject."

"No. You brought it up."

"And now I'm ending it." I slid back his sleeve and smiled at Iron Man. "Where'd you get the unique watch?"

He stared at his beer bottle, probably debating whether he could trust me with some hard truths. Then our eyes met. I sensed the ache under his tough exterior, and I did my best trust-me smile, but the muscles only tightened on his face. "I'll say it once, then I want to move on."

Now I really didn't want to know. It sounded serious, and I didn't want to be crushed. I wanted to plug my ears and run away, shouting la-la-la-la-la. I gulped my soda and waited anxiously.

"I'd been dating someone for a few years, and I finally popped the question. Day after she said yes, she was killed by a cop I'd fingered in a drug ring. It ripped a hole in my gut. I was afraid I'd track the son-of-a-bitch and kill him. She had three brothers. One died in Afghanistan, so this devastated the family."

The fine lines around his eyes deepened as he drew in air. "She was an artist and a horse nut. We planned on buying a ranch in Vermont, but after the shooting I was reckless and insensitive to everything and everyone. I buried myself in my work." He took a slug of beer and set it on the bar. "After busting my ass for another year, my boss thought I needed new scenery, away from the big city. I even got promoted. Go figure. The job was in a town north of Boston. Rueland." He paused. "Know it?"

I gave a small smile.

"Ingrid, her mother, still calls periodically, asking me to visit. But it hasn't felt healthy. The parents are just trying to keep her alive, but I was getting buried in all that sorrow."

From what I'd seen, Romero didn't easily give into tender emotions. The shouting and toughness was all part of the job. But he'd suffered and carried this burden deep.

He bent his wrist. "The watch was a parting gift from the guys at the station. Made of platinum and micro ball bearings. It can do everything but sing and dance. Iron Man was a reminder to hang tough." He smiled, taking his thumbs to wipe tears washing down my cheeks.

Damn emotions. I had no control.

"Recently," he said, studying my eyes, "I've been able to put the past in the past. I went to New York that day to let her parents know I wouldn't be back. Ingrid took it hard and emailed the next day. It'll take time, but they understand I have to get on with my life."

His words touched me.

The disc jockey called the newlyweds onto the dance floor. Romero gave a faint smile. How hard was it for him when he sensed I was in danger? It must've dredged up his horrible past.

We took our drinks and sat down. My thoughts drifted back to the case. "I thought once the murderer was found I'd be thrilled. But I'm not, at all."

"That's the downside of police work. It's not always a happy ending."

His words rang true. How did I erase Judy from my life after working side by side for three years? Such an unassuming person deserved a better ending than this. "What happens to Judy?"

"She'll go through the process. Mental assessment. Trial."

I listened with a heavy heart, and my thoughts shifted to the past weeks, to the setbacks and fears. Even at my lowest, I hadn't crumbled, and I hadn't given up. Maybe I was even a bit stronger.

I stared into Romero's eyes. He was so handsome. Why was he here with me? And why wasn't I making a fool of myself, tripping, or wearing food? Was it luck? A phase? Or was I becoming the self-confident woman I strove to be?

The music livened, and I took a grateful breath and snuggled closer to Romero. I soaked in his presence and admired his strength and integrity. It was a nice feeling, just like the warmth of his leg brushing mine.

He gave me one of his captivating looks, then leaned in so close I could feel the stubble on his jaw. "For the record," he said in a low voice, his masculine aroma swimming around me, "I don't think you're difficult."

I could barely swallow. "Well, you said it enough times."

"I've reconsidered." His lips lingered by my cheek. "You're more...challenging."

I backed up, and we locked eyes. "Oh, that's so much better."

"And when I'm with you, it's like breathing fresh air."

I grinned. "I like that."

He cupped my face softly, his mouth breathtakingly close. "You'll like this even more."

What's Next in
The Valentine Beaumont Mysteries

MURDER, CURLERS, AND CANES

Valentine Beaumont is back in her second hair-raising mystery, this time trying to find out who had it in for an old nun. Only trouble is there are others standing in her way: hot but tough Detective Romero, sexy new stylist Jock de Marco, and some zany locals who all have a theory on the nun's death.

Making things worse: the dead nun's secret that haunts Valentine, another murder, car chases, death threats, mysterious clues, an interfering mother, and a crazy staff.

Between brushing off Jock's advances and splitting hairs with handsome Detective Romero, Valentine struggles to comb through the crime, utilizing her tools of the trade in some outrageous situations. Question is, will she succeed?

Murder, Curlers, and Cruises

In her third fast-paced mystery, Valentine Beaumont leaves Massachusetts's autumn winds behind to board a Caribbean "Beauty" cruise. What could be a fabulous voyage turns desperate when she's joined by her well-meaning family and madcap staff, including hunky stylist Jock de Marco. If things aren't bad enough, Valentine learns dark and sexy Detective Romero is away on a case with his new partner who happens to be a female.

Once the ship sets sail, a feisty passenger is murdered, a drug smuggling operation is afoot, an employee becomes seasick, a family member is kidnapped, events of a hair contest wreak havoc, Jock is irresistible and mysterious, Romero and his partner get too close for comfort, death threats mount, and Valentine is in the middle of it all.

Will this impulsive beautician save the day, or will this cruise turn into another fatal Titanic?

Book Club Discussion Questions

Share these questions with your book club. Enjoy the banter!

1. Was there a business that you frequented that ever had to shut down or close temporarily due to an accident or disaster?

2. Who did you feel were the biggest suspects? Did you anticipate who the murderer was? If so, what clues led you to believe this?

3. Do you think Valentine was justified in keeping Phyllis on for so long? If you were in charge, would you have struggled to keep the same type of promise that Valentine made?

4. If MURDER, CURLERS, AND CREAM were optioned for a movie, who do you see portraying the main characters?

5. Based on Valentine's personality, do you think Romero is a good match for her? Why or why not? What type of man would be best suited for her?

6. Valentine volunteers her time and talents at Rueland Memorial Hospital. What type of volunteer work do you view as important?

7. Every business has its competition. For Valentine, it's Supremo Stylists. Have you ever worked in an establishment where there has been fierce competition with another company? Competition within the same establishment? Explain.

8. Valentine has had her share of disastrous dates. What is the worst date you've ever been on?

9. When Valentine finds herself in a threatening situation, she relies on her work tools to protect herself. If you had to defend yourself, what items do you carry that would keep you safe? Go ahead. Check your bag. Or would you rely on something or someone else?

10. What was your favorite scene? Favorite character? Why?

Note to Readers

Thank you for taking the time to read MURDER, CURLERS, AND CREAM. If you enjoyed Valentine's story, please consider telling your friends or posting a short review. Word of mouth is an author's best friend and much appreciated. Thank you!

Social Media Links

Website: www.arlenemcfarlane.com

Facebook: facebook.com/ArleneMcFarlaneAuthor/
Newsletter Sign-up can be found on Arlene's Facebook page.

Twitter: @mcfa_arlene

Pinterest: pinterest.com/amcfarlane0990

Arlene McFarlane is the author of the *Murder, Curlers* series. Previously an aesthetician, hairstylist, and owner of a full-service salon, Arlene now writes full time. When she's not making up stories or being a wife, mother, daughter, sister, friend, cat-mom, or makeover artist, you'll find her making music on the piano.

Arlene is a member of Romance Writers of America, Sisters in Crime, Toronto Romance Writers, SOWG, and the Golden Network. She's won and placed in over 30 contests, including twice in the Golden Heart and twice in the Daphne du Maurier.

Arlene lives with her family in Canada.

www.arlenemcfarlane.com

Made in the USA
Coppell, TX
15 August 2021

60547129R00173